Susan Beale's first novel, *The Good Guy*, was shortlisted for the Costa First Novel Award in 2016. A graduate of the Bath Spa MA in Creative Writing, she lived in Brussels for over sixteen years and currently resides in Amsterdam.

Praise for *Misplaced Persons*

'Susan Beale's writing is alive with subtlety and flair. Her stories unspool with a confident voice, a relish for detail and deft shifts in perspective'
Tessa Hadley

'Timely but has great warmth and readability, too'
Good Housekeeping

'How skilfully Beale negotiates a minefield in this lucid account of colliding realities' *Saga*

'Thought provoking and powerful . . . Superbly written, this is a significant and poignant story that will resonate with many people at different stages of their lives' *Buzz*

Also by Susan Beale

The Good Guy

Misplaced Persons

SUSAN BEALE

JOHN MURRAY

First published in Great Britain in 2021 by John Murray (Publishers)
An Hachette UK company

This paperback edition published in 2022

1

A CIP catalogue record for this title is available from the British Library

Paperback ISBN 9781473630406
eBook ISBN 9781473630390

Typeset in Sabon MT by Palimpsest Book Production Ltd, Falkirk, Stirlingshire

Printed and bound in Great Britain by Clays Ltd, Elcograf S.p.A.

John Murray policy is to use papers that are natural, renewable and
recyclable products and made from wood grown in sustainable forests.
The logging and manufacturing processes are expected to conform to
the environmental regulations of the country of origin.

John Murray (Publishers)
Carmelite House
50 Victoria Embankment
London EC4Y 0DZ

www.johnmurraypress.co.uk

To my mother, Cam, who taught me how
to be heard, and in memory of my father,
Barry, who taught me how to listen

Neil

Chloé passed the conference room's glass wall in the direction of the elevator banks, umbrella in hand, a defence against the mid-October drizzle of Brussels. Neil watched out of the corner of one eye. It was the third time she'd passed in half an hour; they were meant to be eating a romantic lunch, at an out-of-the-way bistro. His meeting should have been over an hour ago and would have been, had any of his colleagues stayed on topic. Since the previous pass, Chloé's stride had changed, becoming purposeful and maybe, just possibly, a bit fed up. Neil risked a furtive glance her way, hoping to convey his shared frustration. Their eyes met. Her lips flattened with displeasure as she walked on by. Just like that, the moment he was most looking forward to, shrimp croquettes, Waterzooi, and holding hands under the table, crumbled to dust. The meeting droned on for another hour. Neil left the conference room with twice as many things to do and roughly half the time in which to do them. Furthermore, he needed to figure out what Chloé had meant when she answered his apologetic text, tapped out beneath the table, with a squid emoji. However, neither work nor Chloé topped his to-do list.

'Marcy call?' he asked his assistant.

'Afraid not,' Ingrid replied. 'Plenty of other callers, however. You're quite popular today.'

Neil ran a hand through his hair – a nervous habit left over from the days when thick, wavy, auburn locks had flopped down over his forehead in what he liked to think was a Hugh Grant-ish sort of way. Now his fingers slipped along skin before meeting the first follicle somewhere level with his ears. 'Anyone I want to speak to?'

'You must be the judge of that: Harrison, Morris, two agency guys, looking for business, I think, and the office of Monsieur G.'

Neil felt the muscles in his shoulders tighten upon hearing the European president's name. 'You saved the best for last, Ingrid,' he said. 'To what do I owe the honour?'

'The regional directors meeting on the Innovation Plan has been pushed back to the twelfth.'

'The day I'm supposed to be . . .'

'In Munich for the Vision 360 presentation.'

'Ah,' he said.

'Monsieur G says that if you cannot make it, Marco should go in your place.'

Fucking Marco, he thought.

Vision 360 was a sophisticated, multi-layered software system to integrate forecasting into the existing enterprise resource planning. It had the potential to transform the business. The Innovation Plan was the American CEO Benny Marsh's latest vanity project. He couldn't resist tossing a million or two at every management craze McKinsey peddled to him over lunch. Two years ago, Neil would have gone to Munich without a second thought, believing tangible achievements mattered more than political manoeuvrings and self-promotion.

'I can make it,' he said. 'See if we can reschedule Munich. If not, have Morris run it.'

'I'll look into it after lunch, yeah?' she said. 'You're headed out, I assume?'

Neil shook his head. 'The meeting ate my lunch.'

'In that case, shall I bring something back for you?'

Neil was surprised, and a little distressed, by the degree to which this simple act of kindness moved him. Good old Ingrid: efficient, practical, unsentimental and as dependable as she was sturdy.

'A tuna sandwich would be lovely, Ingrid. Thanks.'

He shut his office door and, in the small space around his desk, rolled his head in circles to release the tension in his neck and shoulders, before picking up the phone to dial his ex-wife.

Estranged wife, actually. They were mere weeks into a separation that needed to run six months before he could petition for divorce, and that was only if Marcy consented to all the terms. A big 'if'.

'Hello, Neil.'

Her voice jogged loose a memory from earlier that morning when, in a hypnopompic stupor, he'd reached across the bed in full expectation of finding her familiar curves, only to recoil in shock when he instead met the sharp edge of Chloé's hip. It took no more than a fraction of a second for his brain to sort out the situation, but the unsettled feelings it stirred up lingered on.

'Where have you been, Marcy?' he asked. 'I called three times this morning. Didn't you see my messages?'

'Sorry, no.'

A few seconds of dead air passed before Neil understood that nothing further would be offered.

'We need to talk.'

'Do we?'

Marcy's speech had taken on an airy, sing-songy quality of late, that grated on Neil's nerves. It was, nevertheless, vastly preferable to the fevered fulminations of a few weeks ago, which, in turn, had been an improvement on her unexpected mental and physical collapse the night he left. The trend was positive. That said, the preternatural calm made him anxious, suggesting an emotional detachment not at all in character. He wondered whether she was taking sedatives, or possibly losing her marbles.

'Are you actually planning to give the television to a homeless shelter?'

He felt awkward asking. It wasn't his business anymore. He wouldn't interfere if not for the children.

'No,' she replied. 'I am not planning to give the television to a homeless shelter.'

'Thank God,' he said, exhaling loudly.

'I already gave it to a refugee centre.'

'I'm sorry, what?'

'I gave the television to a refugee centre,' she said and then giggled like an adolescent. 'You know, Neil, it was wonderful the way their faces lit up.'

'But the kids, Marcy.'

'That's what I'm saying. The television they had was so small. They had to scrunch together on the floor whereas now—'

'I meant *our* kids, Marcy,' he said. 'Sasha called. I didn't get the impression that she loved the idea.'

'But she hardly watches TV,' Marcy replied.

4

'She watches it sometimes,' he said, 'and she appreciates knowing it's there when she wants it. That is not unreasonable.'

The line went quiet. As Neil listened and waited, he fiddled and tugged on his wedding ring. His fingers had swelled over two decades. It wouldn't budge over the knuckle, not even with the help of soap or butter.

'We're too attached to things, these days,' Marcy said, finally, giving the word 'things' the sort of sinister inflection commonly reserved for rapists and drug lords. 'Sasha will come around. It will be freeing.'

'And will Alec feel the same without his PlayStation?'

Another giggle. 'What's the point of a PlayStation, Neil, when there's no TV? Besides, those games are so violent.'

'All the kids play them. Alec knows fantasy from reality.'

'Well, not under my roof. Not any more.'

'He could have brought them to mine.'

Another pause and then: 'Buy a console, then, for when he visits.'

This might have been a dig, though the serenity with which it was uttered made that impossible to say with any certainty. Sixteen-year-old Alec would not answer Neil's calls, or reply to his text messages. Their elder son was an inconsistent correspondent at the best of times, but Neil did not delude himself in thinking this was normal or unintentional. Alec was angry. Neil accepted that and, though the lack of contact pained him, he had vowed to be patient and allow Alec to come around in his own time.

'The television was too big, anyway,' Marcy continued. 'I doubt there'll be room for it when we move. Houses are smaller on that side of the city.'

Neil's neck tingled with irritation. 'Not this again,

5

Marcy,' he said. 'You aren't seriously considering moving the kids to Molenbeek?'

'I need to learn to live with my means, Neil.'

And just like that, he snapped.

'Your means, Marcy? Come off it! You know darn well that your little job—' He paused. The word 'little' was a mistake, obviously. Patronising. He recognised this immediately and as he did, his brain stalled on the word 'job', stretching it as if for ironic emphasis. He took a breath. 'What I mean to say,' he said, searching for the sweet spot in which he controlled his rising frustration without sounding condescending, 'is that teaching English part-time is not your only source of income, as you are well aware.'

'Am I, though?' she asked.

He clenched his teeth. Let the record show he was trying to keep the conversation respectful, but the implication that he would worm out of his responsibilities to her or the children was deeply offensive to him. He told her:

'I find what you're suggesting deeply offensive.'

'When was the last time you looked at the current account balance?'

He flinched. There was no denying that these past months had brought more than their share of exceptional expenses: the three-month security deposit for his new apartment, which had also needed to be furnished. Crazy hours at work led to his eating out more than he'd like. In shame, he lowered his gaze, bringing into view his new Burberry suit, medium blue plaid with accents in darker blue and yellow. Perhaps it had been unwise to make such a purchase when . . .

But his brain would not permit him to finish the thought. This was exactly the mindset he was trying to break, the knee-jerk guilt and self-denial that kicked in whenever he so much as considered indulging in something for himself, something he truly wanted: a classic suit that made him feel good; made him feel competent. And that, though significantly more than any suit he'd previously owned, was a steal at forty per cent off, would last forever and therefore prove a net saving, in the long run.

'Cash flow,' he said. 'Everything will be fine once the house sells.'

The family home, he meant, a five-storey *maison brux-elloise* on a narrow triangle of land between three boulevards – a large and crowded traffic island, really – near an abbey and several embassies. It was their only real asset, aside from his pension, which was untouchable for another sixteen years. Neil intended to take just enough from its sale for the minimum twenty-per-cent deposit on a new place, plus the seventeen per cent he'd need to cover fees, of course (damn Belgians charged a fortune). With what remained she could get a nice apartment, in a modern building, with parking underground, something the current house lacked. There was no need to play the martyr, dragging the kids off to one of the city's poorest communes.

'I will not have my children living in that neighbourhood,' he declared, wishing he didn't have to put his foot down, but she would push him so. 'Jake's only seven, Marcy. Think of his safety.'

'Thousands of people live their whole lives in Molenbeek,' she replied, with a laugh full of embarrassment . . . for him.

'Until they go to prison or some terrorist-training camp.'

The words shocked him. Marcy could do that: exasperate him until he said things he didn't mean.

'Our children are so pampered, Neil. We aren't doing them any favours, you know? They need to be challenged. They're more resilient than we think.'

The height of hypocrisy, delivered in that maddeningly placid tone. If their children were pampered, it was Marcy who'd done the pampering. He was the one trying to instil the importance of discipline, the need for constant self-improvement, while, behind his back, she rolled her eyes and told them they were special.

'Who allowed Alec to quit football after a single game?' he cried.

'What's the point if he's not having fun?'

'And complained to the school over homework?'

'Two hours a night for Jake is ridiculous.'

'You know what's ridiculous? You running up thousands in dental bills from grinding your teeth at night worrying about his end-of-year exams.'

'His teacher doesn't like children. You should see her when she brings them down at the end of the day. They all line up to give her a *bisou* and she twists her face away in—'

'It was *première primaire*, Marcy,' he yelled. 'Not a bloody doctoral viva. Jake is seven.'

'That was my point!' she said.

He needed to take a step back. Her craziness was making him crazy. It was a major impediment in their divorce. He was willing to bend over backwards – within reason – to reach an equitable settlement. Naturally, he expected her to ask for too much, at first; that he would counter with an offer somewhat lower than what he was ultimately prepared to give, and that they or their lawyers would go back and forth a few times before arriving at an agreement.

Wasn't that how negotiation worked? But he could not play his part until she started playing hers, which, for reasons that baffled, she refused to do. He didn't dare float a proposal for fear she would accept his initial, low-ball offer and he would come away looking like a bully and a bellend.

. This was not the Marcy he had known for a quarter century, who, on their first holiday together, to Rome, had grabbed a young girl by the hair. To be fair, the girl, a shoeless street urchin, had been trying to pick their pockets. Neil had been too enchanted with Rome and Marcy to notice, but Marcy's street smarts were sharpened from living in New York in the early nineties, when it was still gritty. One moment they were strolling, arm in arm, around the Trevi Fountain, full of pizza and cheap wine, the next, Marcy was up to her forearms in the girl's stringy dark locks, hissing like an angry swan.

That was the Marcy he had expected to sit across from at the negotiating table. He thought she'd come at him hard, demanding not only a disproportionate chunk of their savings and assets but also, he feared, the right to take the kids back to America. That's what Gerry Fisk's wife had done a few years back, after Gerry left her for a younger associate. But Gerry was head of a region, with a salary robust enough to support households on two continents. Even Marcy must recognise the difference in their situations and, if she didn't, the law certainly would. But having the law on his side was only marginally re-assuring. The cost of such a battle, financial, yes, but more particularly emotional, was daunting.

'I can't talk anymore, Neil. I've got a lesson.'

'Please, Marcy,' he said, because pleading was the only

option left, 'promise me you won't decide anything, won't give anything more away, until we talk. Would you do that for me?'

'So long, Neil. Thank you for calling.'

'It is a trick,' Chloé said, over after-work drinks. 'She wants the house.'

Chloé had forgiven him for their ruined lunch date, though, as usual, not before a bit of coaxing and a small token offering in the form of a tube of lipstick from her preferred designer, picked up on his way home from work. It was a game they played – she, the offended party, withheld affection, while he, the persistent suitor, won her back. Neil adored the chase, adored the moment she relented, when her mouth, which was what had first attracted him, turned from a pout into a smile.

'I thought the same, at first, or maybe it was a punishment.' He swirled his gin and tonic and took a thoughtful sip.

'Exactly.' She fiddled with the skewer of fresh peach slices that had come with her drink – something to make it appear worth the outrageous price of fifteen euros. 'If you say to her, "Okay, you move to Molenbeek", watch how quickly she backs off.'

'What if she doesn't, though?' he asked. 'Stubbornness runs in her family, craziness too. Her sister is convinced she can speak in tongues; her mother thinks *The Da Vinci Code* is a documentary.'

Chloé shifted her position and pursed her lips to express scepticism, or maybe impatience. Time alone was a precious commodity; she did not like wasting it discussing Marcy, let alone Marcy's family.

They were in their preferred booth of their favourite

resto-bar, around the corner from Neil's apartment in an unglamorous but perfectly respectable part of the community of Saint-Gilles.

It had the same cobbled streets, the same tree-lined squares as in the tonier neighbourhoods of Ixelles and Uccle, but the buildings were a bit narrower, the ceilings a touch lower. Why didn't Marcy consider moving some place like here, Neil wondered. Why the fixation with Molenbeek, the go-to first stop in every terror investigation? It was as if she was trying to punish him.

'Perhaps this craziness was something you ought to have considered before moving out?' said Chloé, adding a one-shoulder shrug.

'Darling, please don't,' Neil pleaded. 'I've already admitted it was rash.'

He had thought she would be overjoyed when he left Marcy; instead, it triggered their first tiff. He saw now that it had been wrong of him to sign the lease and move out before consulting her.

'Barely a week after Jérôme moved out,' she added.

He was as determined as she was to keep their relationship a secret until after Vision 360 wrapped; however, he suspected her fears were somewhat overblown.

'You think people won't put one and one together?' she cried, lit up with that short temper of hers.

'Two and two,' he corrected her.

'You are one,' she insisted, holding up the index finger of her left hand. 'And I am one.' She raised the index on her right hand, and then snapped them together in front of his face, triumphant. Her befuddlement at English idioms was utterly charming and he smiled, which irritated her further still, and charmed him all the more.

'It's all a joke to you,' she said. 'Whenever affairs are discovered at work, it is always the woman who is forced to leave, to protect the man, who is senior.'

'Darling,' he replied, struggling to keep a straight face, 'I'm as concerned as you are about keeping this between us until we're ready.'

'You should be,' she said, eyes narrowing. 'If he knew, Jérôme would *kill* you.'

'So you've told me.'

'He believes the blame for our rupture is his.'

'And I assure you, I am only too happy for him to continue thinking so.' Jérôme was Chloé's jealous, police inspector of an estranged husband. Not only was he armed and, Chloé assured him, capable of bench-pressing more than Neil's body weight, he also had access to the national database, including Neil's address. 'You were on holiday with your parents,' Neil reminded her. 'I had to make a snap decision. I didn't want to lose the apartment.'

'There are tens of thousands of apartments in Brussels.'

'But not in this building.'

'What does it matter?'

'It matters to me.' He took her hand in both of his. 'You know why.'

A friend of Chloé's had an apartment in the same building, two floors down. They had used it a few times for early evening, after-work trysts. The apartment he'd rented had an identical floor plan, and he had arranged the furniture similarly.

'It is so small,' she said, but she was softening.

'It's temporary,' he soothed. 'Once the house sells, we'll get a place in Châtelain, or a loft apartment out by the canal.'

Extracting themselves from their respective marriages was like a minuet: various steps needed to be performed, with grace and at the correct time, for the sake of their careers, yes, but, more importantly, for their future blended family. It was absolutely vital that Chloé get off on the right foot with his children, the two older ones, in particular.

Chloé didn't see what the big deal was.

'It is not their business,' she said. 'They will adapt.'

She could not be expected to understand. Her daughter Aurélie was only three, and of course francophones were far more evolved than Anglo-Saxons when it came to matters of the heart. Neil would never lie to his children. Of course he wouldn't. However, provided enough time was allowed to pass between his moving out of the house and Chloé's introduction, he hoped to sidestep the more pointed questions, the answers to which would only cause pain and delay the healing and coming together of their blended family. A few months, at the very minimum, were required, and there was no time to lose. He wanted Chloé to join them at his parents' this Christmas. More to the point, he wanted to take her to bed. Ten minutes ago. He rattled the ice in his glass and swallowed watered-down dregs.

Chloé puckered her mouth again.

Her glass was still half full. She raised the fruit skewer, slowly opened her glossy red lips, bit off a corner of a peach and rolled it suggestively around with her tongue, teasing him. She needed to be at her mother-in-law's within the hour to collect Aurélie, and then drive to her mother's house for an uncle's birthday party. That left little time to go back to his building, climb the four floors to his apartment, and make love. He suspected she enjoyed running down the clock, stoking his desire, so that they would have to rush, fumbling about, partially dressed, on the couch, a chair, or the floor. It was rare, in fact, that they made it all the way to the bed. Thanks to her, his libido was a raging furnace. He felt twenty years younger, which, Chloé noted, made him five years younger than her. Second youth brought a pressure to innovate. Neil was on a constant search for new positions – his own personal Innovation Plan – in a chair, on the dining table, atop the bathroom sink. On the night in question, he had her up against the wall, an approach that demanded a different technique entirely. They had had six minutes to spare when they began, and there had been a couple, let's say three, false starts, and they had only settled into something that might be described as a rhythm when the phone rang. He was determined to ignore it. After five rings the old answering machine the previous tenant left behind kicked in, and, against the sound of his and Chloé's urgent moans, came his recorded message in bumbling French followed by the passion-chilling sound of his mother's ever-cheerful, West Country chirp.

'Hello, darling,' Denise 'Denny' Yardley said, as her son stood, trousers and boxer shorts puddled at his ankles, giving it to his mistress. 'We tried to reach you on your mobile, but you didn't pick up.' (Polite Pause) 'Thought we might catch you here.'

In the silence that followed, Neil focused on the task at hand, blocking out the thought of his mother on the other end of the line, waiting, and the urge, or one might say *compulsion*, to pick up.

'Give us a call when you have the chance,' she said.

'Nothing to worry about,' his father chimed in. 'Just want to know how you're getting on.'

'Hope you're not working too hard,' his mother added.

'Ooh, he is definitely working hard,' Chloé groaned.

Before Chloé, Neil would have shrivelled like a raisin at half so suggestive a remark, but some of her frankness about desire had rubbed off on him. He was liberated, uninhibited. He wasn't twenty years younger, but thirty – the rebel seventeen-year-old, having sex under his mother's nose.

'So hard,' he repeated, between thrusts. 'So hard. So hard. So hard.'

After Chloé left and he'd had a quick shower, he phoned his parents back.

'You were at the gym, I bet,' his mother said.

'I was working out,' Neil replied, wishing Chloé was there to share the joke.

Since the separation from Marcy, Neil's parents had been checking in more often, short calls in which they asked the same questions:

'How are the children?'

'Are you eating well?'

'Are you still coming for Christmas?'

Never about Marcy or the divorce, and yet those unspoken questions filled every awkward pause. He and Marcy had been together so long, two decades. They breezed through the seven-year itch that had tripped up Chloé and Jérôme. At a certain point, he guessed, people assumed a couple has 'made it', that the risk of divorce has been effectively side-stepped, too much water under the bridge. He had believed this himself. Now he pitied such folk, condemned to lives of quiet desperation. His parents would adore Chloé once they met her. How could they not?

He popped a ready meal of roasted chicken in the microwave and poured himself a glass of wine. Had Chloé stayed, he would have cooked, fussing about the kitchen, putting together something tasty while she perched on a stool, glass of Chardonnay in her hand, and told him again how Jérôme could barely boil water. Neil enjoyed cooking for other people, but when it was just himself, it hardly seemed worth the bother. There always seemed to be some key ingredient, tool, or appliance he lacked. The kitchen in his apartment was a curious blend of excesses and deprivations: an abundance of stock cubes but no cinnamon; seven speciality beer mugs but a single undersized mixing bowl; a smart set of chef knives, but no cheese grater. The knives were Japanese. Stunning pieces of engineering, they sat on the uncluttered counter next to the hob, in a stylish block of oak. He turned to admire it as the microwave pinged.

Neil sat down with his plate in front of the television, and scanned through the channels with the remote until his eyes spied the soothing green of a football pitch, a league game, by the looks of it, or perhaps an early round of one of the lesser European tournaments. He didn't recognise the kit of either team, one yellow, the other black, nor was he clear about the broadcast language – vaguely Germanic, to his ears, but what did he know? The cable packages in Brussels featured channels from the weirdest places.

The football commentators' constant chatter was distracting. Neil tried hitting the mute button but that was worse. The apartment was too quiet.

He missed his children terribly, missed being connected to their daily lives. Once Vision 360 was delivered and he filed for divorce, he would push for fifty-fifty custody. For the boys, of course, because Sasha would be eighteen soon. If she stayed in Brussels for university, next year – as Neil hoped she would – they could meet for dinners or coffees around her lectures. He'd buy tickets for exhibitions, concerts and talks. Their relationship would enter a new, delightful phase.

By then, Alec was bound to have come around. They could watch football matches together, proper football, Champions League, as they had last season on the television that now entertained residents of a homeless shelter.

No, it was a refugee centre.

Neil regretted not having been more helpful on that score. He wondered if Marcy's behaviour alarmed the children as much as it did him. He was afraid to ask, lest he add to any anxiety they might be feeling. The situation had to be pretty dire for Sasha to involve him. And if she was struggling, you could bet the boys had it ten times worse. The PlayStation had been Alec's Christmas gift. It really was outrageous for Marcy to give it away. Poor Alec. Neil took out his phone and texted:

U OK, Bud?

He was breaking his own rules, he knew, but it was just a short, friendly text to let his son know he was thinking of him and, more importantly, was *on his side*. It didn't matter if Alec replied or not. Neil put the phone down and returned to the game, but he couldn't concentrate. He was straining to hear the ping that signalled a response. One minute; two minutes, three. He picked up the phone to see if he'd muted it by accident (he hadn't) and then typed.

Wtching ftbll; thnking of u

Neil texted like it was 1999, when his ability to communicate in vowel-less, consonant-plus-number abbreviations won him praise from younger colleagues. The tone he was trying to strike was light-hearted; in fact, his son's silence weighed on him. Neil had known his children wouldn't exactly cheer his moving out – at least, he had *hoped* they wouldn't. It was a disruption, for sure, one he regretted; however, divorce was hardly a rarity these days, and, thankfully, there was no longer any stigma attached. He had assumed Jake, being the littlest, would have the hardest time, but the old chap had slid into the new arrangement without fuss. Sasha had registered her disappointment; Alec's reaction surprised him. He wasn't normally the type to carry grudges or hold on to anger. Neil had to hand it to him. He'd shown remarkable resolve, though he did think it curious – and by curious he meant unfair – that he wasn't holding his mother to the same standard. Neil picked up the phone and texted:

Srry abt the tv & ply stn

He ought to have stopped there, but the silence gnawed at him. People talked about parents having favourite children, but no one talked about children having a favourite parent. Neil wrote:

I jst wnt 4 us 2 be frnds agn.

No answer. In despair, he wrote to Sasha:

U alrght?

She replied in seconds, his wonderful daughter.

Dad, there is no character limit for texts.

Never mind that it amounted to a scold, he was ecstatic:
a connection! He wrote:

I'm old school. Everything all right at home?

She replied:

All good

He typed:

Any more craziness from your mother?

And then deleted it. He had vowed not to talk Marcy
down to the kids. In its place, he wrote:

Alec surviving without PlayStation?

Dots rolled across the screen, the animated ellipse that
signified typing. They rolled and stopped, rolled and
stopped, rolled and stopped.

He's fine she replied, finally. More animated dots and
then: studying

He wrote:

You took a long time to write a little

But was afraid he sounded critical, so he erased it and wrote:

Whoa!

And then added:

lol

No answer. Apparently, she didn't think it required a response. Five minutes later, he typed:

Kiss to Jake

She replied:

He's in bed

Of course, Neil thought, feeling stupid for forgetting his son's bedtime.

Miss you he wrote.
Miss you, too
Need to go; test tomorrow

The semi-colon made him smile. He pictured her seated at the dining table, notebooks piled in front of her, pens lined up in a neat row.

Of course
Good luck tomorrow
I'm sure you will do well

Don't stay up too late
Love you

He stared for an overly long time at the heart emoji she used to sign off.

The match was nil-nil at the interval. Neil took his plate to the kitchen and placed it in the dishwasher. A whiff of fetid air escaped as he opened the door. That was one of the problems of living on his own. It took most of a week to dirty enough dishes to run a cycle, by which time fuzzy mould had sprouted on plates and the dried granola and yoghurt stuck to the sides of cereal bowls like cement. At home, they ran a load every day and still had things leftover to do by hand. Alec and Sasha had helped him clean the kitchen after dinner, while Marcy took Jake up for his bath. Neil thought of his young son returning for those goodnight kisses and cuddles, his damp hair smelling of citrus.

On nights like these, alone in this small apartment that felt like a regression, temporary though it was, it was clear how easy it would have been to stay in his marriage for the kids' sake. He and Marcy had bumped along with minimal friction. Their marriage had withered rather than exploded, shrinking into a stale division of labour. She didn't like it any better than he did. He sympathised with her career frustration, but the universe didn't owe her a dream job in graphic design. His own job was often shitty and unlike *some* people, he didn't have the luxury of walking away from it. God forbid, he complained. 'Your shitty job is the only reason we're here,' she'd say. Or *had* said. Once.

The cloud of disappointment had been hanging over them for months; years. When he announced he was leaving, right up to the moment she dropped to the ground, he had expected her to be well, not glad, exactly, but *relieved* that he'd taken the first step they both knew needed to be taken. Moving out had been the right thing to do. The *only* thing he could do. Had he stayed he would have become a bitter, bitter man. Chloé had saved him, offering a second chance, the opportunity to start over, to do things right, this time. How ironic, then, that his first thought, upon hearing she would join him on Vision 360, had been to try to swap her out for someone else.

'Nobody, and I mean nobody, in this place has organisational skills like yours,' the big boss, Monsieur G, told him. 'No one comes close.'

It was a nice way of saying, 'You're our very best bean counter, Neil!', which would have been demoralising enough had it not also been utter bollocks. The project had THANKLESS TASK written all over it. The timelines were too short, the budget too small and the promises of future savings and efficiencies were wildly optimistic. He considered Chloé's inclusion on the team proof that other departments weren't taking it seriously. Helen, her boss in coms, had been trying to offload her on to another department for months.

Neil caught that little shit, Marco Santolli, smirking. Marco, ten years younger and handsomer in his slim-fit Brioni suits and skinny ties, with his better, thicker hair. Marco, intoxicated by the sound of his own voice, always first in line when there was a picture to be taken or a client to be entertained; conspicuously absent the moment actual work needed to be done. His one talent, so far as Neil had observed, was an uncanny ability to conjure an *appearance* of strategic thought. Amazing no one had taken a pop at the guy. The only reason Neil hesitated was the dreadful and yet persistent suspicion that one day, and sooner rather than later, Marco would be his boss.

Neil made himself a tea and returned to the sofa. The second half was already underway. There had been a goal, for the yellow team, he thought, though he couldn't be sure.

He probably should have taken the Hong Kong job. Well, hindsight was twenty-twenty. The timing had been bad, coming weeks after his mother was diagnosed with MS. Six years on, she was doing great, but back then the doctors said things could go either way. He had no regrets. Also, good though the offer had been, it wasn't as good as the one he'd turned down a few years earlier: to head up the Baltics region. That would have involved moving the family to Tallinn. He and Marcy had only just bought the Brussels house; they hadn't even moved in. He assumed there would be other offers. Lately, though, he'd started to wonder if he'd been shelved. Leadership's attempt to dress up Vision 360 as an opportunity smelled like pity or worse. Was someone setting him up to fail?

It required weekly meetings in Nijmegen, the only city in the Netherlands lacking convenient rail access to Brussels. Neil had to make the three-hour trip by car, and he had to take Chloé with him.

How stilted conversation had been on that first trip last September. An uncomfortable silence descended before they cleared Brussels' city limits. He remembered staring at the road, picturing this scene as it was repeated every week for the next year and thinking *Shoot. Me. Now.* It was only on the way home, when he popped a CD of the Traveling Wilburys into the player, that the ice between them began to thaw. He wasn't surprised she hadn't heard of the band, but he couldn't believe that she didn't know any of the singers – Jeff Lynn or Tom Petty he could perhaps understand but, seriously, Roy Orbison? Bob Dylan? George Harrison, for God's sake! He had to remind himself that she was francophone and barely thirty, a thought that made him weary.

Educating her in seventies and eighties music was an easy way to fill the drive time. He focused on his personal preferences, an eclectic mix of American Southern Fried Rock, British Synthpop and New Wave. She listened thoughtfully to the playlists he composed: Depeche Mode, ZZ Top, Squeeze, Elvis Costello and Lynyrd Skynyrd.

'Who is this?' she asked the first time she heard 'Free Bird', face wearing an expression of pure wonder.

She brought him snacks for the journey: croissants, finely sliced apple tarts and homemade almond biscuits that were buttery, and crumbled in his mouth. They griped about their frustrations with Vision 360. After a particularly difficult meeting, Neil confided his fears that it was all going to go pear-shaped and take with it what remained of his career. It was such a relief to say it aloud to an empathetic listener.

'Marcy just can't understand,' he confessed.

'That must be difficult,' she replied.

'Does Jérôme?' he asked.

She let out a little snort.

'One cannot expect sympathy about work frustration from *un flic*,' she said. 'You come home, you say, "Uh, I had the worst day!" He asks, "Did anyone shoot at you?" There is no comparison.'

'Being married to *un flic* sounds a bit like being married to an American during the Olympics,' Neil said. 'Imagine that your country – the host nation, I might add – pulls off its most successful Olympics in living memory, a real blinder, and you think you've got something to cheer about, right? Sixty-five medals for team GB. Sixty-five! Twenty-nine of them gold. Meanwhile, on the other side of the sofa, my wife is grousing because her country "only" has a hundred and four.'

Chloé's laugh was light as a bell's.

'You'd think when they get to eighty or ninety, they might relax a bit, kick back and say, "Well, that's a fine number: well done us." Fat chance! They've got to win gold in basketball, in beach volleyball, got to win gold in bloody women's water polo, and still she frowns at losing the men's four-by-one-hundred relay.'

Chloé was an excellent sounding board about issues with Vision 360, which was proving to be every bit as difficult as he envisaged. From there it was easy to segue to other frustrations, such as parenting challenges, and the shortcomings of their respective spouses.

One day, he asked her to drive to Nijmegen. He was too tired. Chloé tossed him the bag of croissants and hopped into the driver's seat.

'I would love a car like this,' she said, caressing the dashboard as she accelerated past a truck. 'So, tell me. What did Marcy do this time?'

'Is it that obvious?' he asked.

She shrugged. 'I recognise the signs.'

'It's Sasha,' he sighed. 'Marcy thinks she's got obsessive-compulsive tendencies. She wants her to have therapy to address the "underlying issues" before they spiral out of control.'

Chloé nodded, eyes on the traffic. 'And you are not convinced?'

'The girl has always been meticulous. It's why she gets such good grades. We ought to be pleased about it.'

On the television screen, the ref called a penalty kick. One of the defenders had pulled down an attacker in the box. The players in yellow protested like it was the greatest outrage, but the ref was having none of it. The right call, Neil thought. The player from the black team placed it in the back of the net.

What had really hurt Neil in that fight with Marcy was her suggestion that he was resisting therapy out of embarrassment. She had told him to stop being so British about it.

'Can you believe it?' he asked Chloé, as he bit into a croissant, sending golden flakes cascading down the front of his black jumper. 'I said to her, "That's pretty rich coming from an American!" I'm telling you, their national sport isn't baseball, it's navel gazing.'

Chloé laughed her infectious laugh. 'Don't let her push you,' she said, her lips puckering on the *ou* sounds, as if preparing for a kiss.

By then the drives to and from Nijmegen were the most enjoyable part of his week. All week long he was storing up stories and anecdotes to tell her on the journey. He tried to manipulate the conversation to make her pronounce words with *ou* in them so he could watch her lips pucker. He wondered what it would feel like to kiss her. When the project fell behind schedule and the Nijmegen trips were extended to two days, a part of him was glad. The company put them up in one of the lesser business-class hotels, a nondescript, shoebox of a place off the motorway; the kind that offers a 'turn down' service, to appear fancy, leaving cheap, industrial chocolates on the pillows. The rooms were painted a neutral palette of grey, white and black and had jewel-coloured accents, and anatomical drawings of fish, plants and flowers hanging on the walls. It could be anywhere.

Dinners were with the team, at restaurants in the city centre. Afterwards, he and Chloé would stop for a drink in the hotel bar. Small shaded lamps at each table gave off warm yellow light. Easy jazz was piped in through speakers in the ceiling.

It was there, over cognacs, one evening in late autumn, that Chloé told him about Jérôme's affair.

'A neighbour,' she said. 'A friend.'

Anger rose in Neil's chest, at Jérôme, and this so-called friend. How dare they?

'And what happened?'

'It is over now, he says.'

'And your friend?'

Chloé shrugged and looked away. The pain was there for anyone to see.

'Her daughter is a friend of Aurélie's,' she said. 'They are in school together.' The downcast mouth, puckering for the *ou* in 'school'. He held tight to his glass, swirling the cognac and taking a careful sip – trying to appear sympathetic and concerned, when the only thing he was thinking about was kissing her. They finished their drinks and climbed into the elevator. Neil kept his hands in his pockets, making fists. He stepped off at the first floor, turned and raised a hand to wave. Their eyes remained locked until the elevator doors closed.

The following week was the final trip before Christmas. He looked forward to it for days. She brought biscuits in

27

the shapes of stars, hearts and stockings, dusted with powdered sugar. Traffic was light. They were riding in the middle lane, the guitar solo from 'Free Bird' blasting on the stereo. Neil, who had missed lunch, had scoffed most of the biscuits and was picking the crumbs off his clothes. Chloé called him *gourmand*. He reached across and gave her knee a good-natured tap and was slow to withdraw his hand. She placed her own hand on top of his, worming her thumb beneath his, turning it over. The moment their palms met was like an electric shock. He recalled glancing in the rear-view mirror, seeing a motorcyclist coming up fast in the outside lane.

'You have sugar on your fingers,' she said, and then bent over and licked it off, fingertip by fingertip. She traced a line from his middle finger to his wrist with her tongue. It was the most erotic thing anyone had ever done to him. He closed his eyes – only for an instant, less, a slow blink. And then she screamed.

A hundred or so metres ahead, in the far-right lane, a white saloon had lost its wheel – not a retread, not a tyre, but the whole fucking wheel. Neil pulled back his hand and gripped the steering wheel. Sparks shot into the air as the saloon's axle landed on the motorway at some hundred-twenty kilometres an hour. He thought of moving into the outside lane but then remembered the motorcycle and decided it was best to brake. The loose wheel bounced into their lane. Neil pushed hard on the brake pedal, while trying to recall whether there had been any more cars behind him, and whether anything had been following the now wheel-less saloon. He braced for impact from all sides. He and Chloé lurched forward; their seatbelts locked. The tyres screeched. Chloé screamed once more. In situations such as these, people often claim to see their whole lives pass in front of them. Neil saw only the untethered wheel rising and spinning, and as it arched in the road in front of him, he understood that he had experienced nothing, achieved nothing and were he to die on this nothing stretch of motorway, it would be without ever having lived. The tyre flattened as it touched down on the motorway, absorbing energy before springing upwards into the far lane. Neil eased his foot off the brake but just then the motorcyclist pulled even with him and on a collision course with the tyre. To swerve would be a natural, almost automatic response, and if he did Neil would not be able to avoid him. Neil's life, Chloé's too, depended on the prudence of a motorcyclist going at least one-eighty in a one-twenty zone. Neil again braced for impact and then the motor-cycle's red brake lights lit up. The driver hung on to the handlebars. The bike's rear wheel lifted up off the road. Neil passed him on the inside and then, the moment his rear wheel returned to the road, the motorcyclist tucked behind Neil.

As soon as it was safe to do so, Neil slid over into the slow lane.

'Are you all right? Are you all right?' He was shouting although she was right next to him.

'Yes, yes,' she said, hands clutching her chest, '*Mais, mon dieu!*'

He shut off the music. His mouth was sandpaper, his palms leaving patches of sweat on the wheel. The tips of his ears pulsed with adrenaline. It was another thirty kilo-metres to the hotel. When he pulled into a space in the car park, his muscles ached from clenching.

They picked up their cardkeys at the hotel's reception

and headed straight to the elevator. Chloé pushed the button for the second floor, he for the first, but when the doors opened for him, he stayed where he was. At the second floor, he followed her off. The wheels of their overnight bags hummed on the carpet as they set off down the corridor. The loose plait of her straw-coloured hair swung side to side. His heart pounded in his chest all the way to the end. Whatever happened next, he thought, was entirely up to Chloé. Part of him hoped she would close the door in his face, though if she did he thought he would die. She did not turn her head or acknowledge his presence in any way. She stepped across the threshold and held the door open. He hesitated an instant longer and then rushed inside.

Afterwards, lying entwined like two strands of the same rope, waves of white noise seeping through the window from the traffic on the A73, Neil expected to feel guilt; instead he felt only gratitude. He was grateful to be alive, grateful that a person such as Chloé, so young, so beautiful, so French, could desire such a middling man as him – a middle-aged, middle manager, with a thickening middle, thinning hair and pale skin dotted with tiny burst blood vessels, as if someone had scribbled on his face with infinitely small blue and red markers. By her grace, he could still make something out of his life.

The football match ended in a draw. Neil switched off the television and stared for a time at the darkened screen. This too shall pass, he thought. Soon, Vision 360 would be up and running; soon he would be spending more time with his children, and he and Chloé would be free to live openly as a couple. They had come so far. Just a little longer. Everything was going to plan.

Marcy

Marcy split the deck and shuffled with the standard riffle technique her grandpa had taught her. In her hands, the cards purred. Her English student, Fabrice, looked on with bemusement. She made an extra flourish, lapping up the attention as she dealt two hands of seven and placed the remainder, face down, in the centre of a small conference table. Shuffling cards was, admittedly, not much of a skill, but Marcy was starved for praise, and beggars cannot be choosers.

'You were saying, Fabrice, that your wife is an optometrist?'

'Yes,' her student replied, 'my wife, Sandrine, she work in Waterloo for an *opthalmologue*.'

'Oh, Sandrine works for an ophthalmologist in Waterloo,' Marcy repeated, as she reordered the cards in her hand.

'Yes, my wife, Sandrine, works for an oph-thal-*mo*-lo-gist in Waterloo.'

Most students only nodded at her corrections. Fabrice diligently repeated them, forcing his mouth to pronounce familiar phonemes in unfamiliar ways and place the stress on a different syllable than he was accustomed to. His face contorted with the effort. It was easy to understand why he was considered a rising star at the French pharmaceutical firm where they met for lessons twice a week. He reminded Marcy of Neil.

Not that they looked the least bit alike. Fabrice was dark, with heavy brows, and a head full of unruly curls, the opposite of Neil, but they shared a puppy-like eagerness to please and a determination to excel. There was, too, a similar earnestness of expression, a goodness. It broke her heart a little.

'Very good,' Marcy said. 'You start.'

'Okay, Marcy, 'ave you any trees?'

'No, I'm afraid I haven't any threes,' she replied. 'Go fish.'

She liked to close out lessons with this card game. After fifty-five minutes of grammar and vocabulary drills, students appreciated downshifting to something more recreational. It was good practice in standard English patterns of speech and, when combined with a little casual chit-chat, became a deceptively complex exercise in tracking multiple conversational threads.

'Optometry sounds like an interesting job,' she remarked.

'Yes,' he nodded. 'She like . . . no, she like*sss* it very much, but it is difficult because the children are small.'

'Life with small children can be hectic,' Marcy agreed, an understatement. Work–life balance was a myth. No matter how hard one laboured, how efficient one became, the pieces of the daily puzzle never fell into place. Too few hours in the day; too many moving parts. Sandrine wouldn't be the first to blame herself for struggling to square the circle.

'Fabrice, have you any kings?'

He pulled one from his hand and passed it to her.

'Please,' he said.

She opened her eyes slightly wider. He recognised his error immediately.

'Non, non, non,' he cried. 'What I mean to say is, "Erc you go."'

'That's right, Fabrice, good catch,' she said. 'Thank you very much. Do you have any fours?'

'Go fish, Marcy.' *Feesch*.

'If we have a third (*turd*) then maybe Sandrine stay at home,' he offered.

Ah, yes: the Mommy Track, temporary relief from the relentless grind, the impossible deadlines. What woman fortunate enough to have the choice could ignore its siren call?

'Have you any jacks, Marcy?'

'Go fish. And so you think that, if you have a third child, and Sandrine stays at home, then that will make things easier?'

'Yes, certainly. If it is possible, financially,' Fabrice nodded and then smiled. 'That is my hope, anyway.'

'And Sandrine? Does she want to stop working?'

He furrowed his brows and pushed out his lower lip. 'She is very tired.'

Of course she was! Modern life had turned us women into hamsters on a wheel, running as fast as we can just to stay where we are, and no one more than a young mother.

'A small break,' Fabrice said. 'And then when the children are all in school, she go back again.'

'And would the ophthalmologist be prepared to let her do that?'

'I don't know,' said Fabrice, raising both palms skyward. 'But if not, it's no problem. She is very good at her job. There will always be opportunities.'

'Ah, how fortunate,' Marcy remarked, thinking the opposite. Talent was a curse for professional women, nurturing a false impression that good jobs could be discarded and easily replaced with new ones. Too late, Sandrine might discover that careers weren't like a streaming service. One did not simply press pause, and then resume later at the place you left off. Things change; technology marches on. Life with children warps time in strange ways: minutes and hours drag on endlessly, while years and decades speed past. You blink, and there is a giant crater at the top of your CV where the career was supposed to be. You can try to paper it over with classes and spots of volunteer work, but the job gatekeepers – twenty-something recruitment officers and junior HR assistants with smooth hands and healthy pink fingernails – will notice the second they pull your CV up on their phones during the metro ride to or from work. Their young eyes are that good. At that point, you might as well stuff those applications into bottles and toss them into the sea.

'Marcy,' Fabrice said, 'do you have any tens?'

She handed over a pair of them. 'There you go, Fabrice.'

'Tank you, Marcy.'

'Pleasure,' she said. 'Sandrine sounds like a great gal. A real team player.'

'What is this "team"?' Fabrice asked, his face rumpled with confusion. 'Sandrine, she play in the badminton club, years ago.'

'Team player,' Marcy repeated. 'It's a manner of speech, Fabrice. I'm saying that Sandrine is generous to put the needs of her husband and children ahead of her career.'

'I see, okay.' His eyes brightened with understanding. 'Team player,' he repeated, mentally filing away the new vocabulary for future use. And once again she was reminded of Neil, how he'd delighted in her Americanisms: hit pay dirt; jump the shark; Monday morning quarterback.

'Your turn, Fabrice,' she said.

Beware, Sandrine! Being a team player is a twenty-four-seven gig – the cooking, cleaning and shopping; the nurturing, the 'being present', and countless other responsibilities involved when one's life is subsumed by the lives of the others. And make no mistake, subsumed it would be. There would never be enough of Sandrine to go around, but that wouldn't stop her trying ever harder, spreading herself ever thinner, to meet everyone's needs, because that was what she was there for. It was what being a team player was all about. It would be all she did and, in a shockingly brief amount of time, would be all that she was. She would say that was fine, a worthy sacrifice, noble even, until the day her teammate, the one she'd let wear the captain band because it seemed so damn important to him, stood before her, packed bag in hand, babbling about how 'we've grown apart', and 'I love you, but I'm not *in love* with you, Marcy.'

Sandrine. She meant Sandrine.

'Do you 'ave any sixes?' Fabrice asked.

Tis better to have loved and lost than never to have loved at all, she thought. Lord Tennyson's most bankable quote, recited by everyone who ever tried to console someone with a broken heart: beautiful, romantic and a load of shit. Losing someone's love was the worst, especially when you weren't done loving them.

Marcy heard a voice in her head: her mother's. 'Marsha Louise,' she said. 'You're feeling sorry for yourself.'

There was no greater sin. Reflexively, albeit begrudgingly, Marcy began counting her blessings: she had her children, and her health, of course. She had a job, and though teaching English to non-native speakers wasn't a passion in the way graphic design was, it wasn't without satisfaction. She got a kick out of seeing the faces of the motivated ones, like Fabrice, light up when they learned something new. True, the hours were irregular, and the pay less than she'd made in London, nearly two decades earlier, and with little prospect of advancement; she had to travel to her students, and unless it was the company CEO, she was shunted off into the tiniest of windowless meeting rooms – the one she was in now was a glorified broom closet – still, how could she complain? She was warm and dry. The company, perhaps feeling guilty about the broom closet, threw in a complimentary pot of coffee and plate of biscuits. Meanwhile, tens of millions of displaced people were living in camps or walking across a continent in every kind of weather in search of a safe haven. No doubt those folks had an unfulfilled dream or two and still they woke each morning to continue their journey despite not knowing where they would sleep at the end of the day, whether they would have enough food or drink, be welcomed or shunned, or where their journey would end. That was resilience. That was courage.

Her misfortunes paled next to theirs. How dare she play the victim? A week after Neil left, she walked through the house, taking stock of all they had accumulated. Goodness there was a lot of it: furniture and drapes and books and tools and gadgets and art and decorations, clothes and dishes and crockery and coats for every season and shoes and toys and puzzles and games. She went room to room, asking herself what she wanted to keep, which vestiges of this now former life would she take into the future? The answer surprised her: she didn't want a damn thing.

'Marcy? Marcy? Yoo-hoo, Marcy? Anybody's home?'

'Huh? Oh, uh, sorry, Fabrice. Now what was it you . . .?'

''Ave you any sixes?'

'Any sixes, any sixes.' She stared at her hand, wanting so much to give up a card, to give away all her cards, to be free. 'I'm sorry, Fabrice. I haven't any sixes. I haven't any sixes at all.'

The pharmaceutical company's office was in a business park near the airport. When Marcy left Fabrice, she took the outer ring road, *la grande ceinture*, in the opposite direction from home. Late afternoon was the worst time for traffic, but there were two binbags of stuffed cuddly toys in the back of her car that she wanted to drop off at the refugee centre. If children were walking from Greece to Belgium, she could spend an extra hour in the car.

It was the photo of the little boy that did it, transformed Marcy from sympathetic observer to actor. That child, practically a baby, really, lying face down at the water's edge where he had washed ashore. Chubby cheeked, arms flopped at his side, palms up, little bottom raised ever so slightly, looking all the world as if he were sleeping. Her own children had slept like that, with a kind of reckless abandon that sent her heart into her mouth.

'Want to help yourself; help someone else,' her nan used to say. Nan, who had only Poppy's small pension to live off, but who nonetheless made donations to Shriner's Hospital, the March of Dimes, the Salvation Army and a list of other charities that ran as long as her arm; Nan who bought cookies from every girl scout who came to her door, despite being a diabetic; who tossed loose change in every collection jar she came across, and ate overcooked spaghetti at countless church suppers. Nan, who was the happiest person Marcy had ever known.

Marcy could not help that poor little boy, or his brother, but thousands of others were headed north this autumn with only the clothes on their back, and at home there were closets full of things her children never wore. She had done culls before, of course, but never so ruthlessly or so gleefully: seven large binbags filled with trousers, shirts, jumpers and winter coats. She had delivered them to a smiling, effusively grateful young woman at the donations desk of the refugee charity and left with a stupid grin plastered on her face. People would be warmer, thanks to her. The sense of euphoria lingered for hours and when, inevitably, it faded, all she could think of was getting it back.

Radio Nostalgie was there to entertain her in the stop-and-go traffic and, by lucky chance, it was Eighties Hour. She knew the words to all the songs, apart from the French ones, and since the kids weren't with her, she could sing along as loud as she liked without their howls of embarrassment.

There was a sense of having turned a corner, that the hellscape of the past couple months was at last behind her. Autumn always made her hopeful. In Ohio, it was a time of blue skies, of trees aflame in yellow, orange and red. After the heat and humidity of summer, the arrival of cool, crisp mornings was like biting into the first apple of the season, fresh and invigorating; infused with all the possibility of a new school year. The feeling stuck despite seventeen Septembers in damp, colourless Brussels.

The Bangles 'Manic Monday' came on and Marcy cranked up the volume. It had been the unofficial anthem of her senior year in high school, the song belted out at every party and quoted in many a yearbook entry, her own included. She bounced in her seat, *do-do-do-dootley-dootley-do-ing* along with the song's keyboard hook before joining Susanna Hoffs singing lead. The lyrics rolled off her tongue as if it was 1987 and she was in her mother's car driving to the mall, the sleeves of her blazer rolled up, oversized bow in her permed hair, and lace, fingerless gloves on her hands. Beneath the upbeat, cheerful melody, it was the lament of a harried woman, working to support herself and a deadbeat lover. Had high school Marcy noticed? Would she have cared? It had been, she thought, a defiantly optimistic time. Reagan had declared it was morning in America and despite the steady stream of plant closings that, at one point, left her father out of a job for eighteen months, she had never doubted it was so.

All her girlfriends were equally obsessed with professional success, picturing themselves striding up Madison Avenue in a Norma Kamali dress and Reebok aerobic shoes, office stilettos in the Balenciaga bags on their shoulder, along with the Filofax stuffed with contacts and an agenda full of meetings and social engagements. Give up their career to stay home with children? Don't make me laugh! Their mother's generation had cracked open the door and they were going to blow right through it. They would have it all and do it all, all on their own. So materialistic; so shallow; so utterly convinced of their abilities.

She could laugh at it now – the breathtaking naiveté – and put it down to youth, but her daughter Sasha, currently seventeen, displayed little of that confidence, despite being smarter and more academically accomplished than teenage Marcy ever was. Belgians were so cynical!

You would have thought having the world's best chocolate, beer and frites would make people more optimistic.

She'd kill for a little of that self-belief now, the sort that could pronounce, 'This is the first day of the rest of your life!' without wanting to climb into bed and pull the covers over her head. Self-belief had got her the scholarship to the Rhode Island School of Design and the job with renowned New York design house A. G. Westin, post-graduation. She'd worked alongside some of the best in the business and burned the candle at both ends in ways that only a twenty-two-year-old could: gallery openings, book launches, theatre and parties, parties, parties. At one, in the Park Avenue duplex of a famous publisher, she had enjoyed a brief but intense flirt with JFK Jr, which formed the basis for Neil's dinner party boast that he'd beaten the heir to Camelot in the race for Marcy's heart.

'John-John Kennedy wasn't after my heart, dear,' she'd reply, 'just the other body parts.'

Like all good stories, it contained a grain of truth. In both cases, Marcy had felt an immediate attraction. Gazing into JFK Jr's dreamy brown eyes as he casually ran a hand down her bare arm had sent visions of 'happily ever after' dancing in her brain. The illusion lasted maybe five minutes, until she returned from a trip to the ladies' to observe him putting identical moves on another young woman. The woman's awed, smitten stare caused Marcy to blush at her own gullibility. She wanted to be more than just someone's chosen piece of ass for the night, even if that someone was *People* magazine's Sexiest Man Alive 1988. She preferred a man she could count on, who loved and respected her, and believed her career was as important as his own. From the moment she met Neil at a quiz night in that pub off Edgware Road . . .

Shit. She'd done it again. She must stop clinging to the legend of Marcy and Neil. The only difference between JFK Jr and Neil was time: five minutes versus twenty-five years. And as for valuing her career . . .

Marcy downshifted from third gear to second and applied the brake. Red tail lights snaked for as far as she could see. She switched the radio from Eighties Hour to the news, unable to take her teenage self's withering judgement of what she'd allowed herself to become.

The assignment in Brussels seemed like a gift. She had been three-months pregnant with Sasha, dreading telling her boss, and dreading the prospect of six short weeks of maternity leave even more. Theoretically, she had a right to fourteen weeks, but taking anything more than six was considered career suicide. A five-year hiatus – the posting was pitched as temporary – would allow her to be with Sasha and an eventual second child, for the crucial formative years. By the time they moved back to London or, fingers crossed, to the States, their (cultured, bilingual) children would be at school, and she would be free to return to work full-time. An au pair would keep up the kids' French and soften any of life's rough edges.

Top-of-the-hour headlines pulled Marcy back to the present. More bad news coming out of Syria. Conditions there had so deteriorated that journalists were reporting from the safety of neighbouring Beirut. Marcy recalled journalists reporting on Lebanon's civil war from Damascus for the same reason thirty years earlier. History doesn't repeat itself, but it often rhymes, Mark Twain said, or maybe didn't say. Probably didn't say, in fact, though people credited him with it, nonetheless, which was the sort of stuff that only happened to men. Never mind. The point being, life wasn't linear, it looped, and here she was back at square one, starting over, only this time she was an ocean away from the rest of her family, with three kids to support, and nearly twenty prime earning years lost to the wind.

'Get a grip, Marcy,' her mother's voice said. 'Not everything is about you.'

Her one big mistake had been in not looking for work when Alec entered preschool. Neither she nor Neil had considered it. An eventual transfer back to Britain or the States was still assumed. When no such transfer happened by the time Alec entered *première primaire*, Marcy had applied for jobs in Brussels. The economy wasn't great, and her CV had a couple of years' rust on it. It took months before a small design company offered her a temporary contract, covering someone's maternity leave. She accepted, convinced she could make herself indispensable, and then, a week before she was due to start, she discovered she was pregnant with Jake. Oops! Okay, make that two big mistakes. Why had she delayed getting that IUD? The rookie error set her back another four years, by which time she was of no interest to anyone, including Neil, as it turned out.

Her phone rang. Her mother's name flashed on the screen, as if she'd summoned her telepathically. Marcy's pulse spiked.

'Mom?' she said. 'Is everything all right?'

'Where are you? It sounds strange.'

'I'm in the car.'

'Oh, well call me back when you have a minute.'

'No, no, it's all right,' she said as she braked and then accelerated.

'You're not driving, are you?'

'I've got a hands-free kit.'

'A what?'

'It's a stand for the phone. I've got both hands on the wheel. Don't worry.'

The mere suggestion of multitasking while driving freaked Marcy's mother out, which was perfectly understandable, considering. Marcy could have done without the aggressive, accusatory tone, though. A convert's zeal. Before the accident, reversing out of the drive was when her mother freshened her lipstick. Marcy was twelve before she realised rear-view mirrors had another purpose. 'What's up, Mom?'

'That woman with the lake house called. She wants to know which weeks you want for next year.'

For years, they'd rented a house on an island in Lake Erie for two weeks in summer. Her mother joined them, and so did her sister and her kids.

'Summer is nine months away.'

'Don't you normally reserve a year ahead?'

They did. Or, at least, they had. It was one more thing Neil's leaving had thrown into flux.

'Sasha finishes secondary school this year,' she replied.

'What does that have to do with anything?'

'I don't know what her plans will be,' she said, trying to sound nonchalant. 'Sometimes, you know, kids take trips with their friends.'

'Can't she go any week?'

'She might get a summer job,' Marcy said. 'Things are a little up in the air for next year, is what I'm saying.' It was like being back in high school, coming home from a party with beer on her breath.

'Well, you're going to have to stay some place,' her mother said, clearly not buying Marcy's excuses. She could sniff out a lie even over the phone. 'You know I haven't got room for you here.'

'I'm sure we'll figure something out before too long,' Marcy said, not at all sure. Neil had called her job 'little' and it was, too little to afford plane tickets for herself and the children, never mind rental on a lake house at the height of summer. But she could not say any of this to her mother. Apart from a fellow teacher, Sharon, a Brit whose husband had left her a few years ago, Marcy had told no one Neil had moved out, and she was determined to maintain her silence for as long as there was a shred of possibility that he would return. This was doubly important in regard to her mother, who carried a grudge the way Lady Gaga carried a tune: forever, *con gusto*.

'Well don't wait,' her mother said. 'The woman says she's getting a lot of calls. It would be a shame to lose it.'

'I'll get to it as soon as I can,' Marcy replied.

A horn beeped and Marcy cowered, convinced it was directed at her even though she wasn't doing anything wrong, merely sitting in her lane, edging forward with the rest of the traffic.

'I'd come to see you in a minute, if I could travel,' her mother said, after a pause. 'You know that.'

'I know, Mom.' A lump rose up in Marcy's throat.

'So, how's everybody? How are the kids?'

'Everyone's fine.'

'And Neil, too? He's working hard, I imagine?'

'Of course,' she said, certain this was the truth. Neil was always working hard. 'How is your back, Mom?'

'It's, you know,' her mother made a noise that was more than a sigh, less than a grunt. 'It's okay.'

'You sound like you're in pain.'

'A little bit.' She sucked air through her teeth. 'It'll be fine.'

'Have you told your doctor? Maybe your prescription needs to be changed?'

'He won't give me any more. They've gotten very strict about them; make you fill out a hundred forms. It'll be a big production.'

'If you're in pain, though—'

'The dosage is fine. I skipped a couple, is all.'

'You're not supposed to skip them. Are you using the weekly pill boxes I gave you?'

'Of course I'm using the pill-organiser thingies. I am not an idiot, Marsha Louise. There is nothing wrong with my memory or my brain, thank you.'

'You just said you missed some doses.'

'I said I skipped them.'

'Is there a difference?'

Her mother took a deep breath and then exhaled in a rush. 'Remember how I had to have that tree in the side yard taken down, the one with the crack in it, up high?'

'I think so,' said Marcy.

'Yeah, well, Bill took it down for me. You remember Bill. Bill Schmitt? He was in school with you.'

'I don't—'

'Maybe he was a couple years behind you.'

'Okay.'

'Yeah, so that's why I'm a little short.'

'I'm not following you, Mom.'

'He's had a bad back for years, what with all the heavy lifting. I mean, it's very physical work he does; back-breaking. So I gave him four of my pills and he knocked a couple hundred bucks off the price.'

'Mom, you can't give your painkillers to other people. It's dangerous. You have no idea what's wrong with Bill Schmitt's back.'

'Sure I do. He's got the same thing as me.'

'So you're a doctor, now?'

'Don't get lippy, missy.'

'If Bill has spinal stenosis, he needs to go to his doctor and get his own prescription.'

Her mother laughed. 'Easy for you to say. He's self-employed. His insurance deductible is sky-high; co-pays like you wouldn't believe.'

'You could get in a lot of trouble, you know?'

'What are they going to do, arrest me?'

'Um, yes.'

'Give me a break. I'm sixty-eight years old. I'm not a danger to anybody.'

'It's dispensing drugs without a licence, Mother.'

'Who's going to tell them? Listen, I didn't call you to argue. I promised the lake-house woman I would remind you about reserving for next year and I didn't want to wait in case I forgot. Give my love to the kids and Neil. Call me later if you want to talk.'

The refugee charity was in an old warehouse. The woman at the front desk held the phone pinched between her shoulder and ear as she rifled through a binder full of invoices. She was not the woman who had been there during

Marcy's previous visits. She was talking at great speed. There seemed to be a dispute.

Marcy stood, a bag in each hand, and waited for her to look up.

'Donations?' the woman asked or, rather, barked, with the phone still to her ear – Marcy hoped she was on hold.

'Yes,' Marcy said.

The woman nodded towards the back. 'Bring them through. One of my colleagues will assist you.'

Marcy was only too pleased to do so. She was eager for the chance to see where her offerings were going, and to express her solidarity with the refugees. 'No need to thank me,' she would say. 'Anything to alleviate the suffering of those little ones.'

The main warehouse was two storeys high. Her footfalls echoed on the cement floor. There were four trestle tables in the shape of a U, covered in clothes that two women were busily sorting into different piles.

'Have you come to help?' the older woman asked, as Marcy approached.

'Offerings,' she replied, holding up the bags.

'Oh, well,' the woman said with weariness in her voice. 'Is it clothes?'

'Cuddly toys,' Marcy replied.

'Are they clean? In good condition?'

'Of course,' Marcy said. 'They're like new.' There were baskets of them at the house, presents from relatives, birthday gifts from school friends, gift-shop souvenirs from school trips that were quickly forgotten, an embarrassment of riches when there was so much need. Marcy imagined little pudgy hands reaching out for them, holding the soft fabric to their chests: a source of comfort.

'Over there,' the woman said, waving towards the back of the warehouse.

Marcy looked to the far wall, lined with large boxes.

'Which box?' she asked.

'All of them,' the woman replied.

'All of them?' Marcy repeated. The generosity of her fellow man was pleasing, though it left her ever so slightly crestfallen.

'I'll stay and help, if you like,' she told the women. The children could manage without her for a bit; she wanted to be of assistance.

'Fantastic,' the younger of the two said. 'Put those over with the others and I'll show you what needs to be done.'

Marcy did as instructed.

'I had no idea there would be so many,' she confessed.

'Too many,' said the younger woman, who was called Jeanine, as she dumped the contents of a bag on to the table. 'We don't know what to do with them all.'

Jeanine put Marcy in charge of the first sort: separating the clothes into piles for boys and girls. Jeanine took the boys'. The older woman, Sylvie, took the girls', for further sorting according to size and quality.

'Anything with a stain, a hole, a missing button or snap, you throw in the trash, here below.'

'That seems a waste,' Marcy said. The refugees on the television news had nothing. Surely, they wouldn't object to a missing button or stain or two?

'There is no other way.' Jeanine shook her head. 'We haven't facilities to clean them. There is more than we could ever use. Occasionally, we receive expensive things, couture brands. Those we sell to consignment shops. The rest is bought by textile merchants who send them to Africa.'

Marcy tried to think whether she had sent anything with a stain or a hole. Some of Jake's clothes, possibly.

'Does it bring in much money?'

'Pennies a kilo,' she said. 'But it is critical to our mission. Also, otherwise we would be drowning in clothes.'

'Instead, Africa drowns in clothes,' Sylvie quipped, with a dry laugh. 'They go by the tanker load.'

'Donations have increased a lot since the summer,' said Jeanine. 'It's a little overwhelming.'

'People want to feel less guilty for shutting them out, leaving them to rot in the Jungle in Calais,' said Sylvie, 'and so they clean out their closets.'

Marcy felt her face redden. She looked down and sorted faster.

'How much of what's donated gets used by the refugees?' she asked.

'Ten, perhaps fifteen per cent,' Jeanine said.

'If that,' sniffed Sylvie.

'We are, of course, grateful for all contributions,' said Jeanine. 'The sorting takes a lot of our time, though.'

Marcy had believed she was making a difference, that the things she offered would be used by the refugees themselves, but she was only making more work for the charity.

'We have clothes and puzzles and soft toys enough,' said Sylvie. 'What these people need is a roof over their heads.'

Alec

Up the stairs Alec went, passing along a dimly lit service corridor, and out through a set of double doors into daylight. For a moment, everything went white. A few blinks later, the landscape came into focus – a sparsely populated concrete concourse, dotted with benches and potted trees, surrounded by multi-storeyed buildings. He glanced right and then left, before heading at a brisk pace down the wide meandering path that was the only way out. When the main thoroughfare came into view, he began to run. He ran directly into the road, withdrew the Glock from the waistband of his jeans, and carjacked an oncoming SUV. Off he sped. Adrenalin surged in his veins as he weaved through traffic, across both sides of the double solid line, bouncing over traffic islands, across pavements, narrowly avoiding a jogger and a young woman on roller-blades.

Police cars appeared, from behind, at first, and then up ahead, on his left. He accelerated and then swung sharply right. The car skidded sideways into the opposite lane and into the path of an approaching bus. The distance between him and the bus shrank as he steered towards it in the hope of regaining control of the car: a metre, half a metre

– the grille and headlights filled his windscreen – thirty centimetres, twenty . . . black smoke from screeching tyres floated in the air. Just as he braced for impact, the car's weight distribution swung back into balance. He pressed the throttle and the car advanced. The bus clipped his rear, throwing him momentarily off course, but he recovered. He took another abrupt left only to find that his hoped-for escape route was the access road for a commuter rail station. He spun the car around just as a fleet of police cruisers fanned out across the road to block his exit. Heading straight for them as if intent on ramming his way past, he swerved at the last second up on to a train platform crowded with briefcase-toting executives, students with backpacks, old people wheeling shopping trollies, mothers pushing children in buggies. They rushed to get out of his path, but there were too many of them; he was moving too fast. Screams filled the air; the stomach-turning thud of flesh connecting with metal.

Thibaut, seated next to him on the sofa, burst out laughing, prematurely exhaling the hit off the bong he cradled in his lap like a baby. 'Ah, man, you kill me.'

Alec toggled the handset; thumbs tapping buttons as bodies became airborne. A couple landed on the bonnet; others disappeared beneath the wheels. An orange shook loose from a shopping bag and got stuck in the ridge between the windscreen and the bonnet. A smile spread across Alec's face.

'That is sick, man. Sick,' said Dhaki, giving his head an appreciative shake.

'Merciless,' Farrah murmured.

Onward Alec ploughed. He bumped down on to the tracks and entered a tunnel, speeding to the next station where he stopped as if parking on the local high street. Up he hopped, on to the train platform, and summarily shot an old man walking with a cane and a woman surreptitiously filming him on her phone.

'You are an assassin, Cowboy,' she remarked.

They called him Cowboy because he was American. Alec hated it, but he was willing to give Farrah a pass. He would give Farrah a pass on almost anything. Besides, when she said it, it sounded more like 'coy' boy, which was far closer to the mark. People thought he was mellow, zen; no one detected the mess of white-hot rage roiling beneath the surface.

Out of the corner of his eye, he saw Dhaki's arms slip around her, his nose nuzzle against her neck: Farrah, Dhaki's girlfriend of nearly a year (eleven months, sixteen days, three hours and about forty minutes, but who apart from Alec was counting?).

On-screen, Alec's avatar fought his way out of the station and ran towards the nearest road, Glock drawn, as the sound of sirens multiplied.

On the couch, the nuzzling progressed to kissing.

'Get a room, you two,' Alec said, thinking *please don't*. He shot dead a driver and stole his car.

'We've got one,' Dhaki said. 'How about it?'

She wouldn't say yes. Dhaki didn't really mean it. Their relationship hadn't reached that point: things Alec told himself as SWAT vehicles surrounded his avatar. He went down in a blaze of glory, firing out the window as police officers sprayed the car with bullets. Alec's on-screen persona slumped, motionless, over the steering wheel.

'Bad luck, Cowboy,' Thibaut said, as the screen faded to black.

It opened again moments later with a different avatar, on an airfield, running towards a small plane, automatic rifle in his burly, bare arms.

'C'est cool ça,' said Thibaut.

'Walk me to dance class?' Farrah asked Dhaki.

'It's so far,' he moaned.

'So what?'

'I've got homework.'

Typical Dhaki, Alec thought. Were *he* given the option of walking Farrah to dance class . . . In his eagerness to add an item to the catalogue of ways in which he would be a better boyfriend to Farrah, it took a moment for the significance of her words to sink in.

'Hold up,' Alec said. 'What time is it?'

'Ten to five,' Farrah said.

'Shit,' he said. 'I gotta split.'

He grabbed his coat and rucksack and ran for the tram. The lowness of the sun in the sky surprised him. A ninety-two was pulling up at the stop on the other side of the square as Alec turned the corner from Dhaki's street. He sprinted, reaching the tram just as the doors closed, and plopped into a seat, chest heaving.

One quick game and then home to study, that was all it was meant to be, taking maximum advantage of Wednesday's shortened school day to prepare for tomorrow's biology test and complete the history assignment he'd put off since the previous Thursday. Instead, he had pissed away an afternoon; worse still, he hadn't realised he was doing it. The last bit unnerved him. If not for Farrah's dance class, how long would he have continued playing?

He leaned forward, elbows on his knees, hands cupping the bridge of his nose. It wasn't that he was addicted, or anything. He enjoyed gaming. That was all. It was a way to blow off steam without anybody getting hurt, and lately that was something Alec had a desperate need for. He liked who he was when gaming – a man of action, a rebel, unafraid of breaking rules, defying authority in pursuit of what he wanted – in short, all the things he wasn't in real life. Sure, he got carried away sometimes, but he was far from the only person wasting time on electronic devices. Nearly every face on the tram was staring at a screen, every ear had an earphone stuck in it. In contrast, Alec's phone practically lived at the bottom of his rucksack. He could go *days* without looking at it. People complained they couldn't reach him; that their texts went unanswered. He couldn't win.

He should call his mother, or at least text. She might be worried. The last thing he wanted was to set her off. He reached for his rucksack only to pause mid-air. He should have been home hours ago. It was possible she was already freaking out. Which was worse, he wondered, to stress about the *possibility* he'd triggered another breakdown, or to turn on his phone and potentially remove all doubt? He let the rucksack drop to the floor.

Like water, Alec favoured the path of least resistance.

He filled his cheeks with air and then let it escape slowly through his lips: inflating, deflating; inflating, deflating; inflating, deflating.

He was the man of the house now, and yes, he was perfectly aware of how ridiculous that sounded coming from a sixteen-year-old with no job, no skills and more blackheads than facial hair, which was why he would never say it out loud. That didn't make it any less true, what with Dad gone and Mom . . . well, she was not the same;

fragile suddenly. He studied her for signs of stress. Each night he paused outside her bedroom door and listened. He had to listen hard because she was quiet, but the dumb part, the bit that made him want to kick himself, was that even when he heard her crying, he did nothing, too scared of making things worse. Instead, he carried the burden of her sadness and his uselessness with him to bed. The weight of it was slowly crushing him.

A few seats down from Alec, a small girl was playing a game on her mother's phone while the mother talked with a friend. It was a treasure hunt sort of a game. She was searching for clues and hidden items in different settings. Alec guessed the girl was around five or six, younger than Jake, anyway, and already knew her way around the phone well enough so that when the screen locked by accident, she tapped out the passcode to reopen it.

Alec's palms started to sweat. The carelessness with which people regarded their privacy was a continuous shock. How long before that kid stumbled across something – a secret, fetish or failing – that, once known, was impossible to unknow?

It had been boredom, more than anything else, that prompted him to pick up his father's phone, left behind on the kitchen table one Saturday in the rush to get Jake to speech therapy. Boredom and a vague desire to see what his father was like with other people. He'd never really expected to unlock it. How many times do people have to be warned 1-2-3-4 is not a secure passcode?

He had no suspicions, wasn't trying to unearth any deep secret, and he would have rolled right past the thread from 'Kevin' were it not for the heart emoji on the top of the message line. That didn't look right.

It was like a horror movie, when the kid who will soon end up dead decides to check out the weird noise on the other side of the house. Every sensible fibre in Alec's body told him not to tap the thread, and yet, tap it he did.

Waiting inside the apartment.
Can't stay long. Come quick, Cheri

Cheerios and milk dribbled from his mouth as he began to scroll. His father, the guy who spouted, 'Always remember: the internet always remembers' and 'Before you send a text, close your eyes and imagine the words plastered on the cafeteria wall', was sexting with Kevin! The hypocrisy blew Alec away and that was *before* he came across the nipple pic.

'Kevin' had tits.

For the briefest of instants, Alec entertained the possibility that 'Kevin' was his mother, that this was a role-playing game his parents had going to keep things fresh. That would have been embarrassing enough. But no. The tits were small and taunt. They could not possibly be his mother's. Knowing this triggered its own, separate wave of mortification; however, the worst was yet to come.

There comes a point in every boy's life when he sees his father's feet of clay. If only it had been his father's actual feet displayed, proudly erect, above the caption, 'Thinking of you'. An exceptionally bloody and ruthless session of *Call of Duty* had been insufficient to wipe that particular image from Alec's mind. His face turned the pink of a late-June strawberry when his father, upon his return, stuck his head in the TV room and asked casually if Alec had seen his phone.

'How was Madame Katy's?' Alec asked.

'I went to a café,' his father replied. 'Read the paper.'

Well, what else was he going to say: *Actually, Alec, I was off for a quickie with my lover: Kevin of the tiny nichons?* Of course not. Still, the lie jarred. Alec wouldn't claim to be a saint or to have been always, one hundred per cent truthful with his parents, but he at least felt bad when he intentionally misled them. Mr Your-Good-Name-is-Your-Most-Important-Asset didn't flinch. It made you wonder: what else was he lying about?

The tram jolted to a stop. A grey-haired man entered with shopping bags. Alec leapt up and offered him his seat.

'I can stand,' the man said, looking insulted. Sitting back down seemed wrong, like a capitulation, so Alec and the man stood close together in awkward silence in front of the empty seat until a girl about Alec's age approached. The grey-haired man signalled she should take it, which she did, with a smile and a 'merci' for the man; nothing for Alec, whose seat it was. He stewed but said nothing, just as he had said nothing about his father's texts. He had thought about it. He'd thought about it a lot. He didn't have the words, didn't even know who to tell. His father? His mother? Sasha? Kevin? It didn't take much internal debate to conclude it wouldn't be worth the trouble, not worth the risk. The thing with 'Kevin' would sort itself out. His parents got along fine. Hadn't they always been a happy family?

Alec studied them for signs of conflict or simmering resentment. There were none. That was the truth and not merely what he wanted to see. This past summer, he'd watched them, heads thrown back in laughter, over something they found funny. A couple headed for divorce would not laugh like that, he was certain, but then, a few weeks after they came home from the States, his father moved out. That night, Alec felt like the ultimate dumbass, also guilty as hell and at least partially to blame for his mother's subsequent unwinding. His cowardly silence had shielded his father. It was shielding him to this day, which was unforgivable. But Alec didn't know what else he could do. It seemed a little late to tell his mother. What if it sparked another breakdown? The truth was bound to come out sooner or later, he thought, and when it did, he would be at her side, *on* her side, supporting her. He had assumed it would be sooner rather than later but nope. The wait was excruciating, like a game of Jenga in which the final stage dragged on for months. The tower was full of missing blocks, teetering, but as long as it was still standing, there was hope. His father could still come home; the bricks could be put back and everything could be as it was before. Perhaps all his dad needed was a bit more time to figure out his family was more important than Kevin and her tiny *nichons*. Angry as Alec was with his father – and he was furious – he wanted him to come home more than he'd ever wanted anything before, and if his father did that, Alec swore he would carry his father's secret to the grave.

'Where have you been?' his sister asked as he stepped into the main living space, an interconnected living room, dining room and kitchen, elevated a civilised two metres above the street.

Sasha was at the dining table, her schoolwork spread out across four places. She didn't look up from her page, which he took to indicate that she was less interested in his whereabouts than she was in the opportunity to goad him.

'Dhaki's,' he said. 'Mom home?'

'Lessons until five-thirty,' she replied. 'She's picking Jake up on the way. I texted you, like, a million times.'

'A million. Really?' he smiled.

She looked up.

'You got your phone confiscated, didn't you?'

Their school had a strict no phones in class policy. Violators had theirs locked up in the *recteur's* office for a week.

He dug the phone out of his bag and waved it at her.

'It works better when it's on, you know,' she said.

He feigned astonishment. 'OMG, why didn't I think of that?'

'How are we supposed to get in touch with you, if we need to?'

'Such a drama queen.'

'You were gaming, weren't you?' she said.

'Maybe.' He shifted bottles and jars around in the fridge. 'Is any of last night's dinner left over?'

'Are you high?'

'No,' he replied, too fast.

She sniffed the air and gave him one of her penetrating stares. 'You're high.'

Jesus, was she part bloodhound?

'One hit,' he conceded, hardly enough for a buzz. 'There's nothing to eat here.'

She shook her head in disappointment. 'It's not a joke. You're in fourth secondary,' she said. 'The train is leaving the station, my friend. Either you're on board or you're going to be left behind.'

He rolled his eyes. She was parroting the worst of the teachers' canned motivational speeches. He didn't need reminding that the threat of failure was real. Secondary school was a war of attrition. The pace of work was brutal. Every homework assignment, dictation and control earned a score between zero to twenty (and the teachers made liberal use of the full spectrum), exams in December and June, and resits in August for the lucky slobs given one more chance to scrape fifty per cent. Those that didn't manage it got to choose between repeating the year at this school or another institution. In his first year, there had been eight classes, each averaging twenty-five students. This September, they were down to six. Sasha's sixth and final year had just three, which meant five class-loads, about one-hundred-fifty students, had either repeated a year or left for other (inferior) secondary, professional or vocational programmes. This winnowing was expected, even celebrated. His French teacher claimed he wouldn't be doing his job if everyone passed. A shameful perspective for an educator, Alec thought. Lately he sensed his own drift towards the relegation zone. Not to be paranoid, but it felt as if the teachers were gunning for him, apart from his art teacher. Madame Joelle was *sympa*: young, with a stud in her nose and hair that changed colour from week to week. Her art room was chill. She played classical music, softly, and when her students spoke, she listened, as if they might have something worth saying.

Sasha, guaranteed, had never been on any teacher's relegation list, never been lower than the top three in any class ranking. The girl was diligence personified. It didn't stop her worrying. For all her intelligence, she couldn't tell she was being manipulated. It was maddening. His sister could implement any task she was given, but never questioned why she should do it; could achieve any goal, so long as someone else defined it for her. She took Latin and Greek because that was what the best students took. She would, of course, study law or medicine at university, because that was what the best students did. He wondered if she would wake up one day, twenty-five years from now, and discover she'd been living someone else's life. He wondered if that was what had happened to Dad.

'Anything missing?' he asked. They had taken to scanning the house when they got home, looking for empty spaces on shelves and walls, gaps in the decor.

'Not that I could see.'

'Did you check in the drawers?'

'A few,' she said, 'but, by all means, conduct your own inspection.'

As an abstract idea, his sister elicited feelings of sympathy and protectiveness. As a practical one, she annoyed the crap out of him.

'Don't try to make it sound like this is coming from me. I'm not the one who went running to Dad about the TV.'

'For your sake,' she said.

They had already fought about this, but he wasn't ready to let it go. 'I don't need your help.'

'You can't go to Dhaki's house every day.'

'Who says?'

She snickered.

'There's the house computer and I've got my phone,' he said.

'You'd have to turn that on.'

He shrugged. 'Maybe I'll give up gaming altogether.'

'Yeah, right,' she said.

'You'll see,' he said.

'It was the TV, Alec,' she said. 'I mean, when she gave away the porcelain and silver, I was like, "Who cares?"'

'Only Mom,' he replied. Which was the saddest bit. Mom loved those dishes, took them out only for special occasions, and washed them by hand before returning them to the display cupboard. She kept the silver in a velvet-lined box that locked with a key.

'She could have sold them to a dealer – she's so worried about money.'

'Yeah,' he agreed, 'but then there wouldn't be refugees out there, eating off Noritake dishes with Tiffany silver.'

She smiled at that. 'But Alec,' she said. 'Where will it *end*?'

'In Molenbeek, apparently.'

'You don't think she's serious about moving there, do you?'

'Why wouldn't she be?'

'We don't know anyone in Molenbeek. I don't think I've ever been there.'

'What do you care? You'll be at university next year.'

'How can she just sell this house? It's home.'

'She doesn't have a choice. We're not made of money, Princess.'

'Does it ever seem to you that she's gone a bit' – Sasha searched for the word – 'loopy?'

'She's always had a manic side,' he said, after a pause. 'Cupcakes?'

In primary school, they celebrated birthdays in class. Most parents picked up a cake at the supermarket; theirs stayed up half the night whipping egg whites and boiling sugar into syrup, mixing and matching vanilla and choc-olate cupcakes and icings so that kids could choose from four possible combinations. 'Because there is always one kid who doesn't like chocolate,' she'd say.

'Remember the time she made you dinosaur biscuits instead,' Sasha said, smiling.

'To keep things "simple",' he added. A joke because it had turned out to be anything but. They looked too plain when they came out of the oven, so their mother had smeared them with green icing, added tiny silver balls for eyes, cinnamon sweets for mouths, and then ultimately dragged them through melted chocolate so that they looked like they'd been walking through a muddy swamp.

'She never knows when to quit,' Sasha said.

'Says the girl whose bookshelves are arranged according to the Dewey Decimal system. At least Mom is manic in a fun way.'

'Well, you take after Dad.'

People said so, because they shared the same ruddy complexion, the same rusty brown hair and pale blue eyes. Sasha and Jake were darker, like Mom. But that was just window dressing. On the inside they couldn't be more different and wasn't that where it was supposed to matter most?

'I am *not* like Dad,' he said. 'Nothing like him.'

'Okay,' she said, with wide, mocking eyes. 'If you say so.'

It was possible that his sister was shallow enough to believe he actually did take after his father, or maybe she just enjoyed getting under his skin as much as he enjoyed getting under hers. He placed his hands on the table and slid them forwards, disturbing the neat row of coloured pens she had placed there.

'Don't,' she warned.

'What?' he asked, as he gave it another nudge.

She slapped his hand. 'I think he's going to buy you a console for Christmas.'

'Great,' Alec said. 'I'll take it to the refugee centre myself.'

'You're going to have to get over this sometime. What will you do at Christmas?'

They went to their grandparents in Somerset every year.

'Maybe I won't go.'

'Don't you want to see Grandma and Granddad?'

'Of course. I just don't want to see Dad.' This was true and also false. 'You're okay leaving Mom by herself?'

'She says she's fine with it.'

For a clever girl, his sister could be remarkably stupid.

'She's lying,' he said. 'She doesn't want us to feel bad.'

'Stop taking it so personally. He left Mom, Alec. He didn't leave us.'

'He sure left us to deal with it.'

'Mom didn't exactly cover herself in glory.'

He imagined telling her about 'Kevin'; watching the smug, confident smile wipe clear off her face, but he couldn't. Angry as he was, he just couldn't do it. Video games aside, he lacked a killer instinct.

'Call yourself a feminist?' He spat the words.

'You know as well as I do, Mom can be—'

'What?' he snapped. 'She can be what?'

'Tedious.'

Killer instinct or not, his hand twitched with a desire to punch her.

Once, when he was around Jake's age, he had got an eyelash stuck in his eye, beneath the lid, on the pupil itself. The pain and irritation were like nothing he'd experienced.

He rubbed and rubbed at it. Tears streamed down his face. He could not open his eye. It was terrifying. He'd never forget his mother's calmness. She'd washed her hands, knelt in front of him – that was how little he'd been – and gently but deliberately lifted the skin of the lid.

'Now, open your eye,' she said.

And though he didn't want to open it, didn't think he could, he did open it because he knew she would make it better and she had.

'There,' she said, holding up the lash on the tip of her pinkie finger. 'It was a big one.'

'How dare—' he stopped talking as the front door opened and Jake called out. Alec put his hand on the table and in a quick, sweeping gesture, batted the row of pencils, sending them flying.

'Hey!' she cried, jumping to her feet.

'Everybody, guess what! Guess what!' Jake called, as he ran up the front steps.

The withering look Sasha gave Alec transformed into a bright, indulgent smile as their little brother bounded into the room.

'Guess what!' he cried. 'Mom has a man.'

Sasha tilted her head. 'Does she now?'

'Uh-huh. He took a boat to Greece and then walked all the way here and now he can't stay at the centre anymore because he's a grown up.'

Alec bent down, his hands on his knees. 'What's that, bud?'

They turned as their mother entered. Behind her was a young man. He had jet-black hair, was long-limbed and skinny, which made him appear taller than he was. The zipper on his tracksuit top was broken, his white sneakers had faded to grey, the laces long and droopy and frayed at the ends. In one hand, he clutched a half-full black bin bag. He gave them a shifty gaze.

'Everybody,' his mother said, 'meet Nizar.'

Neil

The Friday 15:42 Thalys to Paris left Brussels Gare du Midi on time. As it slinked through the backside of the city, Neil relaxed in a roomy leather seat, appreciating the gleam of the dome of the Palais de Justice in the mid-November sun. On the platform a few minutes before, he had pictured the sources of stress in his life as individual pieces of baggage that he purposely left behind when he boarded the train. Remarkable how heavy that shit was to carry around twenty-four-seven. He felt as if he'd dropped twenty kilos. For the next two days he wasn't going to worry about the Vision 360 roll-out, or his relationship with the kids; wasn't going to worry about money or Marcy's screwball ideas. A weekend escape was all he asked for, a momentary chance to catch his breath and recharge his batteries; forty-eight hours of only Chloé, himself and the magic that was Paris.

He reached across and gave her hand a squeeze. Not too hard; he always worried he would hurt her. Those thin hands seemed impossibly delicate and fragile compared to his own beefy mitts, physical vestiges of his peasant roots.

Zipping off to Paris for a weekend was precisely the sort of thing he had imagined doing when he moved to Brussels and it pained him to think of all those opportunities wasted, but past was past. Going forward he would do better. He had sketched an itinerary packed with shopping, museums, night-time strolls by the Seine, brunch at Ladurée and a box of macarons to take home. He had even, thanks to a last-minute cancellation, secured a table at la Carotte Mauve, the restaurant *du moment*. He would splurge for the deluxe tasting menu: nine courses, plus amuse-bouches, palate cleansers and mignardise made of the freshest seasonal ingredients, locally sourced, and a flight of natural wines with no added sulphites. This was *living*.

He took a sip of champagne, a bite of a salmon canapé, so glad he had used his loyalty points to upgrade to Premium class. No noisy school classes, unruly stag and hen parties, or other people's fussy babies.

'Isn't this nice?' he asked.

Chloé made an appreciative murmur and turned a page of the fashion magazine she had picked up in the lounge.

Trains were Neil's favourite form of travel. Many of the rails in his corner of Somerset had been pulled up in the sixties, victims of the Beeching Axe. A train trip was a special occasion. It meant adventure; comfort, too. For a child prone to motion sickness, the straight, flat trajectories and wide-open vistas were a welcome change from tootling up and down the Mendips on narrow, twisting roads in the back of his parents' Vauxhall Chevette, peering through hedges and over high stone walls in search of the horizon because his father said it would help the nausea, plastic bag clutched in one hand for the times (and they were numerous) that it didn't. For that child, the smoothness of the TGV was a source of perpetual wonder; like floating. In a few minutes, they would be cruising at three hundred kilometres an hour, which worked out to an additional kilometre every fifteen seconds between him and his worries. They would be in Paris before six, in time for a pre-dinner shag.

The door to the carriage *shushed* open behind Chloé. A young man entered, late twenties, perhaps; dark hair cut close at the sides, longer on top, razor-straight parting. French, Neil was certain, because of the confident walk and the fine weave of his black turtleneck jumper, lamb's wool if not cashmere, and torn, oil-stained designer distressed jeans that probably retailed for a couple hundred euros. The smile he gave Chloé as he strode past looked like an invitation.

'I can't wait for dinner tomorrow,' Neil said, a little louder than necessary. 'La Carotte Mauve.'

She smiled. 'Tell me about today's meeting.'

'Please, *cherie*,' he said, lifting her hand to kiss it. 'Let's not talk about work now.'

Not that he blamed her for asking. She'd been his sounding board all these months. And, of course, she had as much riding on the Vision 360 roll-out as he did. But the question set off a reel of the day's lowlights to play in his mind when all he wanted was to forget.

He had known he was in for a hard time. Country managers were notoriously difficult to please. Neil was ready when they tore into him over delays, when they roared at the suggestion that they fund some of the budget short-falls; however, he had expected more support from Monsieur G. At the very moment leadership needed to step up and push Vision 360 across the finishing line, the European president was easing off, leaving Neil to absorb the heat. The only one to speak in his defence had been Marco.

'All management consultants are optimists,' the Italian had said, with his customary over-confidence, a little presumptuously too, since, like Neil, he was at the meeting to present not participate, 'particularly when creating time-tables that other people have to follow.'

Laughs all around, and Marco flashed those super white teeth that Neil suspected were veneers. 'Let's give Neil a break,' he said almost solemnly. 'He is doing the best he can.'

Such faint praise, Neil was pretty sure he'd winced.

'Why do you scowl, *mon cher*?' Chloé asked.

'Please,' he said. 'Can we make this weekend about us, only us. Can we, *cherie*?'

'If you like,' she said, though it was clear this would not be her preferred option.

'Look at me, darling.'

Her brown eyes were enormous. He smiled, and then she smiled. His mind searched for conversation topics unrelated to work or family worries. Her face took on that skittish expression it had in meetings, sometimes, when asked a question to which she didn't have an answer. She tucked her hair behind her ear and then undid it. She was sensitive about her ears; thought they were too large. She was adorable.

'I can't wait for dinner tomorrow,' he said, again.

He picked up the champagne glasses, handed hers to her and leaned forward to clink.

'To us.'

'*Tching, tching*,' she said, lifting the glass to her lips for a microscopic sip. Her gaze shifted towards the back of the carriage. Something, or someone, had caught her attention. She smiled and raised her glass. Without looking,

Neil knew it was the Frenchman and quietly seethed – not at Chloé, of course – but at the Frenchman, for thinking it was okay to flirt with a woman when she was with her partner or, an even more irritating prospect, for not *realising* he was Chloé's partner. Neil would be the first to admit Chloé was out of his league. He had said as much more than once, but a fifteen-year age gap was hardly rare. Age, these days, was just a number. He grabbed for Chloé's free hand – too hard – she let out a small yelp.

'Sorry, so sorry,' he said, releasing it as if it were on fire. She shook the hand out, eyes narrowing into a glare. 'I'm so sorry, darling,' he repeated.

'Ah, *mon dieu*, Neil,' she said, the corners of her eyes crinkling; the glare transforming into a smile. 'You are so cute when you are jealous.'

Steak and frites for dinner, on the terrace of a café in the Marais, with the sauce of their choice, *salade verte*. A simple meal with a carafe of wine was all he needed. The heat lamp blazing overhead was more than sufficient to keep them comfortable on the clear, unseasonably warm evening.

The café's outdoor seating was full. Paris buzzed with people making the most of the glorious weather. Neil was slightly, pleasingly drunk, having consumed the lion's share of the wine, and also utterly content. On previous visits to the city he had always felt himself an observer rather than a participant. This time was different. With Chloé, a native French speaker, he had crossed the formerly impenetrable barrier that separated *vous* from *nous*.

Chloé looked incredible, like a film star, a French one, with tousled hair and smudged-on make-up, a simple white blouse, worn loose, tight jeans and tangerine-coloured high heels that drew the eye to her slim legs. It was a relaxed, effortless sort of glamour, as if she had rolled out of bed and thrown on whatever came to hand. She hadn't, of course. This didn't surprise Neil, who knew from years spent watching Marcy actually roll out of bed to get the kids off to school that it was an altogether messier, less beguiling look. Conceptually, he understood there was some artifice involved in effortless glamour, a bit of behind-the-scenes construction that took time. He hadn't expected it to consume every minute from when they arrived at the hotel until the taxi came to take them to the restaurant, and twenty-minutes more besides, botching his plans for a pre-dinner tryst. But it was all right. They'd make up for it tonight. She'd promised.

However, not before dessert. Paris had awakened his appetite. Despite polishing off his steak plus a good chunk of Chloé's and far too many fries dipped in Roquefort sauce, he was not about to forego the molten chocolate cake. It required an extra fifteen minutes to prepare but on a night like tonight, who cared? He was happy to linger a bit longer on the terrace, drinking the last of the wine, soaking up the atmosphere. The first chocolatey mouthful was a confirmation. Some things in life were worth waiting for, he thought, as the first siren wailed, quickly followed by a second. He noted the noise, but only in passing. The air was full of chatter and laughter; across the square, a street musician squeezed out the notes to 'La Villette' on an accordion.

The third siren got people's attention. They sat up; reached for phones. More sirens followed, a cacophony of them, coming from every direction and growing louder, echoing off the buildings. Police, ambulances and fire trucks passed along the boulevard, all headed north. Their flashing lights cut jagged lines in the night sky, splaying across buildings, a frightening parody of the light shows the French are so fond of. The carnival atmosphere fell away, exposing raw anxiety and nerves that had apparently been lingering just below the whole time. Something very wrong was afoot.

'Attacks,' someone announced.

'Stade de France.'

'In the tenth.'

'No, here in the eleventh.'

One or two people stood, and then quickly sat back down. A few more signalled to the waiter, but these were the exceptions. Most, like Neil, remained in their seats as if Krazy Glued to them, staring down at their phones, eyes wide with disbelief. Time was of the essence. Every second mattered. The urge to flee was tremendous but he hadn't yet paid, hadn't even asked for the cheque. He didn't know the quickest or the safest route back to the hotel. Chloé looked towards him for answers, to take charge. Of course, because that's what Jérôme would do, if he were here. Public safety and anti-terror operations were what Jérôme did all day while Neil researched the most efficient ways to shift product between factories, warehouses and shops.

The maître d', a short, stout man with an impeccably manicured black goatee, arrived and beckoned everyone inside.

'Quickly, please,' he said in French, and the again in rounded English. 'For your safety. We seek refuge.'

The restaurant's interior was about a quarter the size of the terrace, too small to comfortably hold all those now piling into it. Neil and Chloé were among the last in, squeezed into a space in front of a large window.

'We can't stay here,' she hissed. 'We'll be sitting ducks.'

'I'm sure it's just a precaution,' Neil replied. 'Police are responding.'

But, really, what did he know? Next to nothing. If the notices now popping up on his phone were correct, if gunmen really were roaming the streets of Paris, shooting people as they sat in cafés and restaurants, they'd be more like fish in a barrel. Neil looked at the outside tables: the detritus of the interrupted meals, the cutlery dropped on to half-eaten plates of food – his chocolate cake, the spoon sticking straight up in it like a candle – wine in glasses and bottles, serviettes and paper place settings blowing in the night's breeze. You didn't have to be Hercule Poirot to figure out where everyone had gone. Neil's heart thumped away, pumping adrenaline into his body. His head felt completely clear, but he was not so drunk as to believe himself entirely sober. By his calculation he'd had a couple of, let's say three, drinks too many, more than enough to slow his reaction time by half a step, which in the current situation could mean the difference between life or death. His life hung in the balance because he'd overindulged in a carafe of perfectly drinkable but by no means memorable table wine. He swore that hereafter, if he survived tonight, he would only ever drink good wine.

A hum and then the sound of creaking metal. Neil exhaled with relief as the security shutter descended slowly from above, until he saw it was not a shutter at all, but a metal grille, with rectangles of empty space easily seen through, or shot through.

People passed by on the pavement, a trickle, at first, and

then greater numbers, hurrying southbound in the opposite direction from the ambulances, fire trucks and police. Their faces were obscured in the darkness, but the jerky quickness of their movements, their crouched postures, the furtive looks over their shoulders, conveyed terror. Neil blinked and then blinked again. It was hard to believe any of this was real.

He kept his eyes trained northward, scouting for danger, the fight or flight mode still doing its thing despite neither being a realistic option. He was effectively cornered. He might die here. Tonight. In this space. It seemed important to acknowledge the possibility; to name it, if silently, to himself. Chloé slid her narrow body behind his; her fingernails dug into his arm. He hoped that, should the situation call for it, he would have the courage to shield her with his body; that his final act would not be one of cowardice. Thoughts of his children, and Marcy, too, put an ache in his chest. A sudden chilling notion: he had made the most awful mistake.

A hand on his shoulder. The maître d' eased him to one side. Waiters set about removing the place settings from tables, pushing them together in a double row in front of the window. A pair of waiters lifted another table on top of the row. Others stepped forward with more tables. They built a second level, laid chairs on their sides across the top, in the spaces between. Neil grabbed a few chairs and stacked them in an unfortified area at the side of the window. Soon, a makeshift barricade covered floor to ceiling.

They turned off the lights at the front of the restaurant and on the terrace, though the gas heaters continued to burn, orange beacons glowing in the dark. They left on the kitchen lights and one over the bar. Patrons and waiting staff crammed together like rush-hour commuters on the metro; couples huddling in one another's arms, everyone on the phone, sending texts or frantic calls to loved ones. Chloé was having trouble getting through to her mother. Neil sat on the floor, staring at his phone screen. Around him, the room erupted in emotion – joyful, heart-warming cries at every successful connection; yelps of alarm whenever a call went to voicemail, or the network failed, which it did more and more. Neil imagined the same scene repeated all over the city. The spike in data traffic must be enormous. Chloé dialled and redialled her mother's number. Neil's thumb hovered over the screen. He fiddled with his wedding ring. Maybe he ought to write to Marcy, to let her know, in case anything happened, how grateful he was – how grateful he had *always* been – that she was such a good mother, and that he knew their children would be safe in her hands. This was followed by a second thought, that it would be better to write directly to the kids, and then a third, more of a recollection than a thought: no one knew he was in Paris. He hadn't thought to tell them, which now seemed a rather glaring omission. He longed to hear their voices, make contact, but wouldn't it be selfish when they'd only worry? He went back and forth about it for a while before writing a banal post to his two older children.

Terrible news from Paris

Alec ignored him, but Sasha answered:

Horrible

76

The one-word response sparked joy within him.

I love you both. Jake, too.

He typed, adding:

You three are my greatest treasures

The blue circle on his screen spun and Neil began to regret the overt sentimentality of his message, wishing he could edit out the soppiness while retaining its meaning, make it cooler, less Dad-like. The circle stopped spinning. The message sent.

'I'm fine, Maman. I'm with a friend,' he heard Chloé say, using the slang, *mon pote*, instead of more common words like *copain* or *ami* that would reveal the friend's gender.

The cold light emanating from smartphones gave everyone's face a ghoulish tint; the news displayed therein only added to it: gunfire, explosions, a hostage situation, a death toll that kept climbing. They scrolled through their feeds, shouting out the contents of the latest report, statement from police, or politician; hitting 'refresh' as the network slowed further. The news simultaneously revolted and compelled. They needed answers. How many dead? Where? When? Was the night's horror over, or might there be more to come?

Sasha wrote back:

Dad, are you in Paris?

The blood drained from his head. Beads of sweat formed

at his hairline. His fingers typed too quickly. He made mistakes and had to hit the backspace.

What makes you think that?

The circle turned and turned as his heart beat in his ears. He stared at the screen, waiting for the message to send and the rolling dots to reappear. It took forever. A woman sitting on the floor near the bar had not been able to reach her daughter, who had been meeting friends near the scene of one of the attacks.

Next to him, Chloé was telling her mother to put Aurélie on the line, though the child had to have been in bed for hours.

Neil looked up. 'Honestly, darling . . .'

On his screen, dots rolled and then stopped.

'Wake her up, *alors*!' Chloé insisted.

He shook his head and mouthed: 'Don't. Alarm. The child.'

'I want to speak to my daughter,' she snapped at him, in English, before switching back to French to address her mother. 'What is that, Maman?' she went quiet. 'No, I suppose not. Yes. No. Yes, I'm safe, Maman. I swear to you.' Her voice cracked. She sniffed. 'All right, Maman. I will call when we are back at the hotel. *Moi aussi, je t'aime.*'

The dots under Sasha's name rolled again.

No reason

She wrote. More rolling dots followed below. He waited, heart in his mouth.

Water from the exhaled breath of two dozen lungs condensed on the restaurant's front window. The people inside burned through data and credit and roaming charges, watching the latest interview with survivors, reading the latest live update. Outside, a state of emergency had been declared, presidential campaigns suspended, borders closed. Twenty minutes' walk from where they were sitting, preparations were being made to storm the Bataclan Theatre. As phone batteries ran low, chargers appeared, pulled from backpacks, briefcases, and handbags. The maître d' went to his office and came back with an extension cable. They charged their devices in turn, everyone careful not to take more time than they needed, just enough juice to keep the phones going until it was safe to go home, whenever that might be. The room erupted in cheers when the woman finally heard from her daughter, who had lost her phone while fleeing the scene. By then, they were well into the third hour.

The maître d' took orders for coffees and drinks; '*offert*,' he said. People left money on the bar, anyway, piles of it, far exceeding the price of the drinks. On this evening of barbary, there were many acts of kindness. Online, people opened their homes to strangers stuck in the city when the trains shut down. People threw down bed sheets to cover the bodies of the dead. Graphics saying 'Pray for Paris' popped into his feed. Neil showed them to Chloé.

'Nice,' she said.

'They're so much more than nice. See how they're evolving?' he said, pointing to the incorporation of the French tricolour, the use of the Eiffel Tower for the A in Paris, overlaying it with hands clasped in prayer or encircling it to make a peace sign. Artists were pulling ideas from one another, taking inspiration, modifying, improving. It was collaborative and clever. He was moved. 'So many layers,' he observed, 'in such little time, and for no commercial gain.'

Chloé smiled politely and then returned her attention to her phone.

It was Marcy who had taught him how to appreciate graphic design, and about the exploration and expansion of message that underpinned it. The urge to contact her returned, not to talk about the damn graphics, necessarily, just to – he wasn't sure – say thanks for the good times, and also sorry for having caused so much pain these past few months. He was sorry. Very.

Instead, he went to the bar to accept a beer from the maître d', and a sparkling water for Chloé. He made small talk (in French!) and added euros to the pile on the bar. Chloé was on the phone when he returned, listening intently, nodding along, a finger in her other ear to block out the chatter. When she eventually spoke it was in rapid, slang-filled French he found difficult to follow.

'Who is it?' he mouthed, though he knew or at least had a strong suspicion.

She put her finger to her mouth in a shushing expression and turned her back to him.

'How far?' Chloé asked.

It had just gone one in the morning. They were heading back to the hotel, on foot, a trip of well over a mile, possibly two, by Neil's estimates.

'Down here a bit, and then we turn left,' he said, leaving it at that. He wasn't sure how she would manage in heels and he was afraid of discouraging her.

'Ugh,' she groaned, and then shivered. Temperatures had fallen, and she had only a light wrap.

He removed his jacket and draped it over her shoulders. It was the only thing he had to give. He was shaking anyway. Nerves. He felt unsafe, no longer sitting ducks, but slowly waddling ones; easy pickings. The buildings lining both sides of the boulevard had tall windows facing the street, any one of which might contain a sniper. It was an absurd thought, and yet, he reasoned, no more absurd than what had actually happened this night. Chloé navigated the cobblestones so slowly, flinching a little with each step. He clenched his teeth to keep them from chattering. The journey would take ages at this pace. He put an arm around her to gently urge her along.

'Don't push me,' she said. 'If only you hadn't had that stupid *gâteau moelleux*. We would have been back at the hotel before any of this started.'

'Or we might have ended up closer to the attacks,' he countered, 'with no place to shelter.'

Her mouth made a little twist of disgust, which irked him. His irritation built as they advanced in baby steps. She wasn't the only one with something to complain about.

'You called Jérôme, didn't you?' he said. 'Back there, in the restaurant.'

He wasn't sure what he expected in reply. An apology would have been ideal, though he believed he would have been content with far less – a simple acknowledgement of wrongdoing, some nominal sign of remorse or, at the very least, a trace of discomfort in having been found out. There were no words to describe his feelings about her indifferent shrug. He reacted with a single, biting syllable.

'Ha.'

'What is "Ha"?' she snapped. 'What does "Ha" mean?'

There was fury in her tone. Wholly unmerited. He was the aggrieved party, the one prepared to protect her with his life, and she had turned to Jérôme, a man whose myriad acts of insensitivity and neglect Neil could recite in minute detail. Had she phoned Jérôme early, when the situation was fluid, the sense of danger palpable, and the urge for final confessions perfectly natural, he would have understood. But they were long past the crisis point when she dialled. Even then, Neil would have found her actions easy to forgive – after all, he had considered phoning Marcy – had she not turned her back to him, shutting him out. He felt well within his rights to storm off, let her find her own way back to the hotel, and yet he remained.

'I'm sure you would have been perfectly fine with me phoning Marcy,' he muttered.

'Does Marcy have inside information about the attacks?' she asked.

He stopped and turned to her. 'Do they suspect a Belgian connection?'

She furrowed her brows as if he were a simpleton.

'Of course there is a Belgian connection.'

He left Paris late the following afternoon. There was no point staying. The museums were closed, the shops and restaurants, too. There would be no dinner at La Carrotte Mauve, no brunch at Ladurée, not even a little box of rose-flavoured macarons to take away. A moonlit walk along the Seine felt inappropriate, disrespectful, and, most of all, irrelevant because there was no Chloé.

She made clear her intention to return to Brussels before they reached the hotel – in the end the walk back had taken over an hour, with Neil carrying her, piggyback-style, the last hundred or so metres – furthermore, she made clear she would not be going by train. He couldn't blame her. Jérôme said all leads pointed to Molenbeek – and as she rightly noted, they had already proved they could attack a train.

Understanding her wishes was easy; fulfilling them was another matter entirely. Neil checked every travel and car-rental app and website. He slipped the hotel's concierge a twenty. In vain. Not a single car was available for rent in all of Paris for the next forty-eight hours. Chloé took the news better than he feared – a brief twist of the mouth to signal displeasure, and then she phoned her father, who was on the road within half an hour; in Paris before noon. She offered Neil a ride, though they both knew he couldn't accept. The drive from Paris to Brussels meant three hours of small talk, putting months of careful planning at risk. This was not how he wished to be introduced to Chloé's father, a man who, for years, had taken annual fishing trips with Jérôme.

Security had been beefed up all over the city. Armoured vehicles lined streets; barriers appeared around potential targets. At Gare du Nord, soldiers patrolled in full combat gear, their fingers on the triggers of automatic rifles. The lines for the baggage X-ray and metal detectors threaded back and forth across the hall, advancing with sloth-like speed. No one complained. Not a single murmured '*putain*', nary a Gallic shrug. It was most un-Parisian.

On board the train, the porters' and attendants' smiles were chiselled on to their faces as they went through their paces, pretending it was any other day, while stopping to ask:

'Is that your bag?'

'Is that your coat?'

'Is that your umbrella?'

'This is a security announcement . . .'

The display of complimentary newspapers in the Premium-class carriage sat untouched, full of pictures and blaring headlines of the very thing no one wanted to think about, at least not before their safe arrival in Brussels. He studied his fellow passengers with greater than usual interest, taking note of which bag belonged to whom, and where on the rack they placed it. He made eye contact with others in the carriage and he noted others doing the same. 'I'm watching you,' they all seemed to be saying. He gazed out the window and his own haggard reflection gazed back. Indian Summer was replaced by November gloom. Every time the door between the carriages shushed open, all within gave a collective jump.

Was this how it was going to be from here on out? Was the possibility of being gunned down in the street or blown to bits by a suicide bomber part of normal daily life? The thought caused a commotion, a shudder, deep within him.

He must not exaggerate. There had been literally thousands of IRA bombings and assassinations when he was growing up in England. Nobody allowed themself to be paralysed with fear. True, his village was far removed from the violence, but he had gone to London after university and experienced his share of bomb threats; actual bombings, as well. He and Marcy had been newlyweds, living in a one-bedroom flat in Notting Hill when half a block of South Quay was destroyed one Friday evening. It hadn't stopped them going down to the pub that night, and for a curry after.

They hadn't had the kids, though. That altered the equation. Knowing that Monday morning his children would be riding the tram to school made his pulse ring in his ears

'Champagne, Monsieur?'

The attendant's hand trembled as she poured; the glass overflowed, adding to a sizeable puddle on the tray. Neil gave her a smile of encouragement, grabbed a cocktail napkin and wiped the bottom of the glass.

It was normal. They were all on edge. That's how it was with things like this: people got over-excited but then they settled down. Life went on. He sipped from his glass. Champagne bubbles crackled inside his dry mouth.

One thing about the IRA, though: they took care to avoid killing the general public. When they put a bomb in a public space, they gave fair warning, using special code words so the authorities knew it wasn't a hoax.

He took another mouthful of fizz. Jesus, how fucked up was the world when the IRA looked like a paragon of comity and civility?

He needed to chill. None of this was new. It had been going on since before 9/11, which still held the record for audacity, and deaths (by a factor of ten). But New York was so far away. Al-Qaeda talked about challenging 'the West' but they clearly meant America. Also, the sheer scale of the destruction had seemed, in a weird way, insurance against future attacks, as if in succeeding tactically beyond their wildest dreams, bin Laden and his lot had guaranteed strategic failure. It was Marcy's theory, actually.

'Mark my words,' she had said, while the fire still burned in the asbestos-filled wreckage of the twin towers. 'Terrorists everywhere will rue this day.'

She didn't normally go in for that sort of Dirty Harry

jingoism. Neil had been willing to overlook it, considering the circumstances, only that wasn't what she'd meant at all.

'They've destroyed hijacking forever,' she said. 'Passengers will fight back from now on. They've got nothing to lose. If the hijackers don't kill them, they'll be shot out of the sky. Think about it: one of the most popular and effective terror techniques of the past five decades made obsolete in less than an hour.'

If he hadn't known better, he might have suspected she felt sorry for future terrorists.

'What's next?' she asked. 'Do they bomb an embassy? A shopping mall? Public transit? There is no second act to this. Everything looks small in comparison.'

Unconventional arguments, Marcy's specialty, and yet there was a certain logic to them, self-serving, because what possible targets did Brussels have to rival the Twin Towers or the Pentagon? But these guys were different. There didn't seem to be much of an end goal apart from killing people any way they could. He lifted his glass to his lips with both hands.

His brain started to spin. Jérôme had told Chloé some of the terrorists were thought to be western-born veterans of the civil war in Syria. Since 2011, thousands of European-born Muslims had slipped across a porous Turkish border to fight and now, it seemed, some were slipping back. Last night's atrocities, the bloke who attacked a train on this very route a couple of months ago, and the one who shot up the Jewish museum this past spring: they were all connected, part of a larger plan by ISIS, Daesh, or whatever they called themselves, to open a western front. If true, it meant there were potentially hundreds of Jihadi-trained killers with Belgian passports, and a fair few of them called Molenbeek home.

Neil put down the glass and wiped his sweaty palms on his trouser legs. He longed to see his children. Problems with Vision 360 had kept him in Nijmegen the previous weekend, when he should have had them. Extraordinary Wednesday meetings had become routine, had prevented him from picking up Jake at his swimming lesson the past two Wednesdays. Had he died the previous night, would his kids have remembered him as a devoted and loving father, or the selfish bastard who put his career and frolicking in Paris with his mistress ahead of them?

Chloé was probably correct that Marcy had no intention of moving to Molenbeek, that it was a ploy to get the house, but maybe that didn't matter. He needed to make a sacrifice, something tangible to show the children their welfare was more important to him than anything. The cost of a house was a small price to pay in exchange for their safety.

'That one, over there,' Neil pointed to the taxi driver. 'The one with the For Sale sign on the balcony.'

He told the driver to wait and he approached the front door. He had always thought it looked like the entrance to a church, the way the panels came together in a pointed arch at the top; imposing in its glossy blackness, its brass fittings in need of a polish. His hand slipped into his pocket, as if expecting to find a key. He withdrew it, pressed the bell and took a step back. He put both hands back in his pockets, took them out and clasped them in front of him, and then finally let them hang simply at his sides. Who would open the door, he wondered? Jake would give him the most enthusiastic greeting, for sure, but Neil hoped it would be Alec. He didn't care if Alec reacted with disgust, didn't care if he laid into him. It had been months! The door opened. It wasn't Alec or Jake on the other side. It was a kid he'd never seen before.

'Good evening,' the boy said, very formal, in French with an accent Neil couldn't place, and suspected was put on.

'Bonsoir,' Neil replied. 'Is Marsha in?' He didn't know why he used Marcy's full name. She never did.

'It is on behalf of Monsieur . . .?'

'Neil,' he replied, sensing mockery in the boy's formality. Was this kid a friend of Alec's? Had his son put him up to it? 'I'm Alec's father,' he added.

The young man nodded and stepped back. He made a sweeping gesture with his hand, as if he were a butler. 'Please,' he said. 'It is a pleasure to meet you. I am Nizar.'

'Thank you,' Neil replied, more convinced than ever that Alec was directing the scene; taking the Mickey, and such was Neil's desire to mend fences with his son, he played along. He followed the boy up the marble steps that were lined with his children's shoes. His heart filled at the sight of Alec's man-sized Timberlands, Jake's ridiculously over-sized satchel. They passed into the upper hall.

'Wait here, please,' the boy said, stepping into the living room and closing the door behind him.

When had they started shutting the living room door, Neil wondered? The kid was pushing it; even so, Neil remained patient. He studied the tiled floor: his most successful DIY project ever. It had been in a terrible state when he discovered it beneath a god-awful bit of puke-green and gold carpet. It had taken hours to remove the grime and sticky carpet glue from them. He had hunted reclamation yards for tiles in the distinctive inter-woven blue and brown vine pattern to replace cracked and broken ones, and spent untold hours re-laying and re-grouting.

The door to the living room flung open.

'Daddy!'

Jake dived into Neil's arms with seven-year-old abandon.

'Hey there, old chap,' Neil said, burying his face in Jake's hair. 'Old chap.' Few things in the world beat seeing your child's face light up at the sight of you; feeling their arms and legs wrapping around you.

'We're playing UNO,' Jake said, wiggling to the floor, keeping hold of Neil's hand and pulling him towards the living room. 'You can be on my team, Daddy.'

'There is nothing I'd like better, old chap . . .'

'Daddy isn't staying, honey.'

Marcy placed her hands on Jake's shoulders, steered him back into the living room, and closed the door behind him. Neil smiled warmly. Her face was emotionless.

'I have a taxi waiting,' he said, stupidly.

'Then you should go.'

'I was just, ah, in the neighbourhood.'

'You can't just drop by, you know,' she said.

'Of course,' he said. 'I apologise. I ought to have called and asked before I came over. I wanted to check in on the kids – on all of you, actually – make sure you were all right.'

'We're fine, Neil. Why wouldn't we be?'

'I just—' he had no explanation. 'Awful about Paris, don't you think?'

'Terrible,' she agreed. She studied him in a manner that, though not menacing, per se, was unnervingly intense.

'And, well, it got me thinking,' he said, 'about your plans to move.'

She shook her head. 'Not this again, Neil.'

Which is what he normally said to her.

'Hear me out.' He lowered his voice to a whisper. 'I have it on good authority that police are pursuing a Molenbeek link.'

'Who is this "good authority?"' she whispered back, a stage whisper, as if this were a bloody comedy sketch.

'I'd rather not say,' he replied.

'Why? Top secret, is it?' She chuckled. 'It's not exactly breaking news, Neil. Everyone suspects a Molenbeek connection. Haven't you watched the news?'

'Then why in heaven's name are you considering moving there?'

'It's convenient: near the refugee centre, on a direct metro line for the kids' schools and, crucially, because I can afford it. Besides, you can't condemn a whole neighbourhood for a couple of bad apples.'

'Marcy, we're talking about a potential terrorist cell—'

'If I'd avoided every block where there'd been a murder when I was living in New York, I would have had to live in Poughkeepsie.'

The reference to New York caused Neil to bite his lip.

'Wouldn't you rather stay here, though?' he asked. 'In this house,' he added, pointing to the floor he had restored, lest there be any confusion.

'You know that's not possible,' she said.

'Perhaps it could be,' he said.

'And how would that happen, Neil?' she smiled. Her demeanour transformed, like a flower turning towards the sun. The emotional detachment that had made him so uneasy these past weeks was gone. Her eyes were almost flirty.

'We could simply agree that you can stay here for a set amount of time,' he explained, 'until Jake finishes secondary school, for instance.'

'That would be,' she began, and then seemed to stall. 'Kind,' she said, softly. She looked disappointed, crestfallen.

'This would be irrespective of any other financial settlement,' he added.

'I'll think about it,' she said, the detachment back.

'What is there to think about?' he wondered aloud.

'Lots of things,' she replied. 'I can't make plans on vague promises.'

'There is nothing vague about my offer, Marcy,' he said. 'Do you need it written in blood?'

'Of course not,' she said, smiling once again but this time it was a completely different sort of smile. 'Ink on paper, signed by a notary is fine.'

Which was just what Chloé would have told him she'd say.

'If you'll forgive me, Neil,' she said as she opened the living room door and called inside, 'Would someone go upstairs and tell Alec dinner is almost ready?'

She started walking him towards the front door. The kid from before emerged and headed up the main stairs.

'Thank you, Nizar,' Marcy said.

'It is my pleasure,' the boy replied, in the same odd accent.

'Who is this kid?' Neil asked.

She had to say it a couple times before he understood.

'Have you lost your mind?' he cried. 'After what's just happened in Paris?'

'Well, obviously, Neil, I didn't know there would be a terrorist attack in Paris this weekend.'

The whole point of offering her the house was so she wouldn't move to Molenbeek, but it seemed she had already moved Molenbeek to the house. Why hadn't he been informed?

'You have no right to bring a man into the house without—'

'He's barely a man. I mean, in the legal sense he is, of course, but by any practical measure, he's just a boy. That's the whole problem, you see. He was a minor when he got here; only recently turned eighteen. It's so cruel, Neil. One day he has his own social worker, a right to schooling and housing and support and the next, poof, all gone.' She waved her hands dramatically to illustrate the word 'poof'.

'Nevertheless, Marcy, you had no right to bring a stranger in here without my permission. I won't allow it. I forbid it.'

'You *forbid* it?'

She let the word hang in the air. He felt his face redden.

'Think of the children, Marcy. Think of their safety.' He couldn't believe she needed this explained.

'Nizar is a boy. And he's been through something horrific. He needs our support. And it's good for the kids to see how fortunate they are.'

'They're saying some of the terrorists came through Greece, you know? Passed themselves off as asylum seekers. What do you say to that?'

'Whoever *they* are,' she said, with a flick of her wrist. 'A lot of rumours flying around.'

'You dismiss it because it doesn't fit your narrative.'

'Nonsense. It's possible some western fighters pretended

to be refugees to sneak across the border. But they wouldn't have applied for asylum.'

'You say that with utmost confidence, but you can't know, can you?'

'Well, no, but that would be stupid, wouldn't it? They'd be found out. There are all kinds of verifications, documents that need to be provided: birth certificates, passports, fingerprinting . . .'

'How can you be so cavalier?'

'How can *you* be so insensitive? Imagine there was a civil war here. What if Alec, what if Jake, had to flee alone to a foreign country, with a language they barely spoke? Wouldn't you hope a family would welcome them in, offer them shelter and food and a place to sleep and kindness instead of anger and fear? Wouldn't you want that for them?'

'That's hardly the point, Marcy.'

'It's precisely the point. Do you expect people in other countries to be better than we are? Who will do this if not us?'

'What other countries, Marcy? There is no civil war! We are not at war!'

'We could be, though. Peace has never lasted this long in Western Europe. We're living in a fluke of history and we've no right to be selfish.'

He placed the tips of two fingers against his forehead where the blood was pulsing. He concentrated on speaking slowly, enunciating.

'There is a great deal of difference between welcoming people, offering a helping hand, and inviting a stranger into a home where there are young children,' he said. He was trying to keep the lid on his emotions but it was infuriating having to explain what ought to be bloody obvious to anyone with an IQ a few points above plant life, and after a few more attempts, he snapped. 'You know what? *Don't* think about my offer. I retract it! It's officially off the table. Go ahead, move to Molenbeek. See if I care! But you're not taking my children with you. I feel the need to warn you, I will be seeking legal advice on this matter,' he said, wagging his finger at her like a damn scold.

She nodded. 'Will you be picking Jake up from swimming on Wednesday?' Her face was expressionless. 'Or have you got a meeting in Frankfurt? Dusseldorf?—'

'Nijmegen,' he muttered, through clenched teeth.

'Of course,' she nodded. 'Thank you for letting me know in advance.'

'I'll be here next weekend.' It came out sounding like a threat.

She blinked slowly, as if she were a cat. 'The children will look forward to that.'

Alec

The tram was crowded. It always was after the schools let out. Alec stood with Sasha in the articulated space between the carriages, rocking side to side as they sped past the traffic on the R21 ring road, towards home. His sister turned to him:

'Do you think *he'll* be there?'

This wasn't really a question so much as an invitation to grumble about Nizar, an invitation Alec was only too happy to accept.

'Of course,' he said, 'sipping tea with three sugars.'

'Out of a glass rather than a mug,' Sasha added.

'Smoking on the terrace.'

'With the door open, so the smoke floats back inside.'

Nizar rolled his own and favoured a particularly pungent blend of tobacco.

'Maybe he'll be wearing his new suit?' Sasha said with a smile.

It was Black Watch tartan, with wide lapels and bell-bottom trousers. Nizar had plucked it from the toss pile at the refugee centre.

'They were going to throw it away; can you believe it?' Alec said, mimicking Nizar's astonished tone. 'Why, yes, Nizar. Yes, I can.'

The floor beneath their feet pivoted as the tram rounded a bend.

'You just know that thing was lying in the back of some dead *mec*'s closet since forever,' Sasha said. 'Why does he choose such crap?'

'The price is right, I guess.' For every box of stuff their mother carted to the centre, Nizar came back with a carrier bag or two of other people's junk. And it really *was* junk. Alec wondered why their mother allowed it. 'He must have a dozen old mobile phones by now. What's he going to do with those?'

'Fix them up and resell them, he says.'

'Well, good luck to him.'

'He fixed the spotlight in the kitchen,' Sasha said.

'And doesn't it seem too bright now?' The light had been broken for years. They'd all forgotten it was there.

Sasha shrugged. A seat opened up. Alec insisted she take it. He stood next to her, hand on the grab rail, rucksack between his feet, nodding along as she vented.

'He's just *there* all the time,' she said, 'sucking up the oxygen. I mean, he's got a room of his own. Not that I'm saying he has to go to his room or anything, but you'd think he'd want a break from us every once and a while.'

'I know I could use a break from him,' Alec quipped.

It wasn't entirely fair to say Nizar was there *all* the time. Most days he went to the centre, where he performed odd jobs for pocket money and took classes (he was preparing to sit the secondary-school leaver's exam). By 9 p.m. he had usually retired for the night; however, in the prime hours of the afternoon and evening, he stuck around the family living space, joining Sasha at the dining table while she studied, messing with her system; hovering over Alec's shoulder as he worked on art, asking irritating questions that sounded like thinly veiled criticisms. 'Is that a man or a woman?' he'd asked, pointing to a sketch of Dhaki. 'Does the shirt really fall flat like that? Should it not be fuller?'

'Skyping with some relative on the living room Mac,' said Sasha.

Alec nodded. He didn't mean to eavesdrop on Nizar's private video chats, but the conversations were hard to tune out. Thanks to the forty-two-and-a-half-inch screen Mom bought for graphic design projects, Nizar's mother and sister's distress was beamed into the living room at two and a half times the pixel density of full high-definition. Alec felt sorry for them. Judging from how close their heads were pressed together, the screen on their end was significantly smaller. They could not know that their every pore, wrinkle and blotch was being magnified to ten times its natural size. A zit on Nizar's sister's nose was the diameter of a euro cent. The harsh consonants and unfamiliar inflections of Arabic wormed into Alec's ear. He didn't understand a word; he didn't need to. The sadness came through loud and clear. At some point, the mother would start crying. She held nothing back, wailing with a sorrow Alec felt in the pit of his stomach. Nizar and the sister pleaded with her – at least, that's what Alec gathered, given how their voices turned soft and whiny. There was a cousin in Sweden, also, with whom Nizar chatted regularly. They spoke much more softly, practically in whispers. Amazingly, that was every bit as distracting as his mother's howls.

'Always hopping up to help with the dishes or sort the recycling,' Alec continued. The tram journey was only six stops and there was a lot to gripe about.

Sasha gave a snort. 'Because you so enjoy sorting rubbish!'

'No one enjoys it,' he replied. That was the whole point. Nizar was stealing his right to complain about it.

'He's nice to Jake,' she allowed.

This was another irritant. Nizar rarely passed up the chance to join their little brother on the floor when he pulled out the Lego or a board game. He was making them look bad.

'What about that new friend of his, Tarif, is it?'

'Tahrir,' Sasha corrected him. 'Like the square in Cairo.'

'Tahrir then, whatever. What do you think of him?'

'Creepy,' Sasha said.

Alec flexed his biceps and grimaced in imitation of Tahrir's burly silence. The tram accelerated.

'I miss bacon,' Sasha said. Their mother had stopped cooking it, so as not to make Nizar uncomfortable.

'Meatloaf,' he replied.

'Pulled pork.'

'I miss speaking English,' Alec said.

Another rule instituted for Nizar's comfort.

'I can't bear Mom's French. It's just embarrassing.'

'Have you noticed the way he sniffs his food before tasting it?' Alec asked, eager to bring the focus of their grievances back where it belonged: on Nizar.

'It was so irresponsible, what she did,' said Sasha. Their mother hadn't mentioned anything about taking in a refugee when she'd set off for work that morning. 'She leaves with a sushi roller, a quesadilla maker, and a set of cooling stones; comes back with a human being.' The absence of communication, coupled with the scramble for fresh towels and bedding to make up the guest room, led

Alec and Sasha to conclude it had been a spur-of-the-moment decision. 'Zero forethought.'

Alec nodded. 'She picked him up like he was a chocolate bar in the rack at the supermarket checkout.'

His sister made a disapproving cluck with her tongue. 'That's racist,' she whispered.

'Would a pack of mints be better? A shitty magazine? Feel free to substitute the impulse item of your choice.'

'I prefer a puppy she saw in the pet-shop window.'

This was not the first time Sasha had made the analogy. She did it on purpose, because she knew it stung. Alec had longed for a dog ever since a classmate showed up to *maternelle* with a silken-eared, brown Labrador named Toblerone. Over the years, he had begged, cajoled, hoped. Their parents never said no outright. They left the possibility dangling, making it seem as if, under the right conditions, they could be won over. It ought to be illegal, stringing a kid along like that.

'Getting a dog is a big responsibility,' he said in a low voice full of mock parental solemnity. 'It's a long-term commitment, not something that should be entered into lightly.'

'Whereas adopting a refugee can be decided on the fly,' Sasha added.

The crowd on the tram thinned. More free seats appeared, further down the carriage, but Alec remained at his sister's side.

'To be fair, she hasn't adopted him,' he said. 'And Dad was the one always lecturing about responsibility and commitment.'

'You always find a way to defend her.'

'Just setting the record straight.'

The tram braked suddenly and came to a stop in the

middle of an intersection. Turn traffic was blocking the rails. The tram driver rang the warning bell. It was a light trill rather than a menacing honk and so seemed suggestion rather than order.

'It's not Dad's fault we're stuck with Nizar. You must have heard him the other night? He's furious.'

'Dad is in no position to give his opinion.'

'Well I am,' Sasha said. 'Don't get me wrong. What's happening in Syria is a tragedy and it's a scandal that western governments are spending more energy and resources keeping people out rather than helping those in need, but haven't we been through enough?'

As was befitting for the president of their school's Club for International Justice, Sasha prefaced critiques of Nizar with bromides of support for refugees in general. The phrase *Everything before the but is bullshit*, popped into Alec's mind and he almost smiled, but he said nothing, which probably made him as much a hypocrite as his sister. The truth was, he needed an ally.

As did Sasha. Why else would she have waited around his locker at the end of the day, when hers was on another floor in the opposite wing? It was not their habit to travel to and from school together and yet this was the third time this week she had sought his company. Given that his final class of the day, history, was in the school's satellite building, a five-minute walk away, she must have been waiting a while, and Sasha hated to wait, hated anything that messed with her schedule.

The tram stuttered forward in pulses. The driver leaned on the bell.

'The guy isn't going to move any faster because of the silly bell,' Sasha said.

'Yeah, he should just ram his ass off the road,' Alec said. 'That's what I would do.'

Sasha smiled, thinking he was joking.

It was nice having someone to complain to, someone who not only validated his feelings but shared them. He felt closer to her than he ever had before, which was good but also dangerous. A couple times, he had been tempted to tell her about Dad and 'Kevin'.

The path cleared and the tram advanced to the traffic light across from their stop.

'Are the lights on?' she asked.

Alec craned his neck in the direction of home. 'I can't see yet.'

'He won't talk about how he got here, have you noticed?' she asked. 'Even when you ask him a direct question, he'll look away and pretend not to hear.'

They were talking faster, determined to squeeze in a few more complaints before they had to get off.

'He says some weird shit,' Alec noted. '"Enthusiasm is my horse"? What does that even mean?'

'"Your mother should be the light of your life",' Sasha added, miming sticking a finger down her throat.

That particular phrase had irked Alec, too, not the suggestion that his mother was worthy of reverence, but the implication that he needed reminding of the fact.

The tram advanced across the intersection.

'Lights,' Alec said, looking up at the large, central window to the elevated main floor. 'Are on.'

Take a seven-year-old with no concept of time and a mother who can never recall where she left her keys and the result is unlikely to be seamless, tension-free punctuality, which was why Alec laid low on Saturday mornings until his mother and Jake left for his brother's speech-therapy session. Consequently, he was the last to hear the news. Descending the stairs at half past nine, dreamily rubbing the few whiskers on his chin with the back of his fingers, he found the rest of the household watching from the windows of the first-floor study as a convoy of army personnel carriers rumbled up the boulevard towards the city centre.

'Guess who hasn't checked his phone,' said Sasha, at the sight of his gobsmacked expression. 'Unbelievable!'

'Speech therapy is cancelled,' Jake announced. 'There are no trams.'

'There are some trams,' his mother corrected. 'But not ours. Not in time, anyway. The metro is closed, so the speech therapist couldn't get to work. It's a security alert.'

'Category Four: *Cat. Quatre!*' Sasha exclaimed, her voice gaining in velocity and frequency as she went along. 'First time ever. It means an attack is imminent. All public buildings are closed. Concerts, sporting events cancelled. We're supposed to avoid large gatherings.'

'Calm down,' Mom said, unhelpfully.

Sasha was but a nudge away from spinning out of control, a nudge that, as her brother, Alec felt duty-bound to supply. Unfortunately, he had to weigh the ramifications on their alliance, on Jake, and, crucially, on his mother.

'I guess if having Europe's most wanted man hiding out in the city doesn't qualify for a Category Four, you sort of have to wonder what would,' he said, reluctantly opting for deflection and distraction. He hated having to be the reasonable one. The grown-up.

'They say they're acting out of an abundance of caution,' said Mom.

'National pride is on the line,' he added, with another rub of the whiskers. He was playing it cool, though the news was causing his own heart to skip. 'They know the French blame them; think they're incompetent.'

'Never mind *their guys* waved him through two security checkpoints on his way back to Brussels,' Sasha remarked.

Voilà, deflection and distraction achieved. His sister was so predictable.

'Reminds me of when martial law was declared in Poland in the nineteen-eighties,' Mom added, dreamily.

'You were in Poland in the nineteen-eighties?' Sasha asked.

'They ran the same clip over and over on *Good Morning America*,' Mom explained, ignoring the question's underlying snark. 'Tanks rolling along incredibly wide boulevards, each one travelling the same speed, an equal distance between them. It looked choreographed. Like a tank ballet.'

'A tank *ballet*?' Sasha exclaimed.

'There goes tonight's party,' Alec said.

'Oh, you never know,' said Mom. 'This could be over in a couple hours. They're acting on very strong leads, I expect.'

To Alec, this sounded wildly optimistic, even for his mother.

'Will we go to Dad's after all, then?' Jake asked.

'Next weekend, sweetie,' she replied, giving Jake's hair a ruffle before turning towards Alec, as if he'd asked for an explanation. 'We agreed to swap. It makes sense. The pool is closed; the cinema, too, and, of course, all Jake's toys are here.'

Another last-minute cancellation. Well, fuck him, Alec thought.

'Why are the soldiers wearing green-and-brown camouflage?' Sasha asked. 'It is literally the opposite of camouflage. They stick out rather than blend in.'

'It is on purpose, a show of force,' said Nizar.

Alec startled and then did his best to disguise it as a stretch. He hadn't noticed Nizar standing there, back from the window.

They migrated on to the main floor with a new-found sense of purpose. This wasn't going to be just any weekend. The air buzzed with the expectation that something momentous was about to happen. His mother went to the kitchen to take an inventory; Jake carted down his duvet and pillow and an extra box of Lego blocks. Nizar rolled a cigarette and went out on to the terrace to smoke it, staring out at the tiny courtyard with self-important pensiveness. Only Sasha kept to her usual Saturday schedule of studying at the dining table. Her phone buzzed every couple minutes with a message or news alert she read aloud like a town crier.

'"Brussels Lockdown" is trending on Twitter,' she announced. 'They say it's going to last the weekend; maybe beyond.'

'I'll go check what we've got in the freezer,' Mom said.

'Alec?' Jake called. 'Make a Lego house with me?'

'In a little while, bud,' Alec replied. He really needed to study. He had fallen behind in several subjects and teachers were taking note. If he didn't turn things around, he'd flunk the year, a prospect that filled him with the wrong sort of anxiety: paralysing rather than motivating. Today, he promised, would be different.

Nizar finished his cigarette and came back inside. He approached Jake with that quiet stride of his. Alec loathed the economy with which the guy moved.

'May I join you in your game?' he asked.

The wanker.

He sat on the floor beside Jake, knees lying flat thanks to his weirdly flexible hips, and unravelled the scarf around his neck. Mustard yellow, it was another 'steal' from the reject bin at the centre. It appeared to be homemade, the work of some novice knitter who couldn't quite figure out how to finish it off. Soon, the air was full of the crunching churn of plastic as Jake and Nizar trawled through the box for blocks.

'Searches ongoing in Molenbeek, Schaerbeek and Charleroi,' Sasha announced.

'Round up the usual suspects,' Alec chirped.

'Arrests made; AK47s and explosive belts found!' Sasha.

Alec stared down at his physics notes, bewildered by the gibberish contained within. He could ask Sasha for help, but if past experience was any guide, it would only end in frustration, with him asking, 'But why?' and her replying, 'You just have to know it', over and over again. He'd have more luck watching tutorials online. He booted up the Mac with the best of intentions, only to click on Minecraft instead of YouTube. Six months ago, he believed he'd outgrown the game, but the loss of his PlayStation had caused him to re-evaluate. He built things and then blew them up. It was a good way to let off steam. He was in a rush today, so he skipped the building part. He chased a cow around a field, boxing it in with explosives, and then detonated. White, grey and brown clouds billowed up into the air and when they cleared there was a zigzag of craters. That was meant to be it; time to switch over to physics videos. Instead, he carved the craters into a long trench, added water to make a river, and then a waterfall. His phone pinged constantly with notifications. Most was dross – Instagram photos of classmates and friends of classmates, people he didn't even know, in pyjamas, relaxing at home. Nonetheless, he stopped to look every time because each new notification had the potential to be a blockbuster: arrests, gunfights, terrorists rounded up. Next thing he knew, Mom was giving them the ten-minute warning for lunch.

Normally they made their own lunches on Saturdays, but on this day Mom served tomato soup with tiny meatballs and toasted cheese sandwiches.

'I used all the bread,' she said. 'We're low on milk, as well.'

'I'll go shopping after lunch,' Alec volunteered.

'Absolutely not,' she said. 'Not until all this has settled down. I found a shoulder of lamb in the freezer. We'll have stew with white beans. There'll be enough to last us days, if needs be.'

'I thought you said it would be over in a couple of hours?' Sasha quipped.

Alec turned to his sister, 'And I thought you said they're extending it to the end of the weekend, maybe beyond.'

'We'll be fine,' Mom insisted. 'Whatever happens.'

The sound of synthesised bubbles and wind chimes filled the air: the video-call app ringtone.

'It's Daddy,' Jake said, running towards the computer.

But the voice they heard belonged to Nana.

'What's happening over there?' she called. The image was three-quarters wall and ceiling and, in the bottom quarter, Nana's brassy curls and sun-spotted forehead. 'Is everyone all right?'

'We can't see you, Nana,' Jake said.

'Huh?'

'The camera, Nana!' Jake cried. 'We can't see your face.'

'Well all right, wait a minute.' Nana's forehead disappeared as she leaned forward; the screen filled with curls the colour of new pennies. 'Hold on, now.' The image shuttered and jerked. Everything went blurry, there was a clatter, a close-up of the keyboard. 'Wait a minute.'

The picture blurred and jerked again and then Nana's face came into focus.

'Better?' she asked.

'That's good. Keep it just like that,' Mom said. 'You're up early.'

'They say Brussels is on lockdown!'

'Not really. They've closed the metro and public buildings. There isn't a curfew or anything.'

'It's on the news over here: Lockdown in Brussels. I was telling your sister. We saw the Grand Place on the news, last night. I said to Jan, I can't believe it. Your father and I had lunch right there on the corner. Police everywhere, carrying machine guns. Right next to the Christmas tree.'

'They make it appear more dramatic than it is,' Mom said.

'Streets deserted. Tanks!' Nana cried.

'Things are calm in this part of town. It's kind of like snow days back when I was a kid.'

'What happened to martial law in Poland?' Sasha muttered into her soup. Mom turned in her direction to signal she'd heard.

'Some snow day,' Nana said. 'I hope they don't decide to come over here. The terrorists, I mean,' she clarified, in case there was any confusion.

Alec and Sasha exchanged looks.

'You know, I hate to say it,' Nana continued, 'but that Trump is right. We need to be stricter about who we let in here. It's just too risky.'

'There are mass shootings in America practically every week,' Mom said.

'Where?'

'Everywhere. Malls, schools, cinemas. Churches.'

'Well, I don't count that.'

'Why not?'

'Because I don't and I don't think anyone else does, either.'

Alec was going to turn to physics. Just as soon as he researched the best design for a bridge across his Minecraft waterfall. He had it narrowed down to truss or cantilever when he received a text saying the party had been cancelled. This was not a surprise given the metro was closed, but it was a disappointment. Alec wasn't what you'd call a party guy. He was the sort who held up the wall while others danced but Farrah had promised she'd be there. At the previous party, she had worn a gauzy turquoise dress with gold thread woven into the fabric that caught the light when she danced.

People who never spoke to him kept interrupting him with messages of solidarity and encouragement. 'We heard the news,' his cousin in the UK wrote. 'Keep calm and carry on.' 'Stay safe,' wrote his American cousins. 'We're praying for you,' said his aunt. Sod off, he thought. They only cared because Brussels was in the news and knowing him put *them* a bit closer to the action.

He had just started a physics tutorial when Nizar's mother and sister made a surprise video call from Turkey.

The mother's wails could be heard before the video even kicked in. She held a balled-up tissue in her fist and when Nizar moved closer to talk to her she leaned forward and kissed the screen. Her squished lips looked like an apple-sized blood clot.

'Eew,' said Jake, from the other side of the room.

'Shhh,' said Mom. She walked up, behind Nizar, calling out a friendly 'Hellooo', waving with both hands and laughing as if she were already part of the conversation and responding to something funny one of them had said. 'It's so nice to put a face to the name.'

'You are most gracious,' Nizar's mother replied, in accented French. 'Thank you for taking in Nizar.' Her lower lip trembled.

'Oh, don't,' Mom said, batting away the idea with her hand. 'We are lucky to have him. He is a joy to have in the house. Did he tell you he fixed the light in the kitchen?'

Sasha snorted because Mom had used the verb *fixer* instead of *réparer*, which sort of suggested Nizar had hung the lamp rather than repaired it. Nizar's mother looked perplexed. Alec didn't think it was due to his mother's choice of verb. Nizar's mother said something in Arabic to her daughter and then they each said something to Nizar who replied. They went back and forth for a while and then he turned to Marcy.

'They are worried,' he explained, looking embarrassed. 'They heard about the security warnings.'

'Oh my goodness!' Marcy cried. 'All the way in Turkey?'

Sasha rolled her eyes and muttered, 'Turkey is closer than Ohio.'

'We're perfectly safe.' She laughed an exaggerated laugh. 'Having a cosy weekend at home.'

As the sky turned from grey to black, his mother's stew simmered on a back burner of the stove; buttermilk biscuits rose and browned in the oven. Sasha topped off her sixth and final hour of revision.

Jake carried his Lego creation aloft to Mom. It was a three-storey chateau of white bricks, a pair of black chimneys sticking out of either end of a red roof with latticed eaves, red shutters, and a manicured lawn with flower beds and a fountain.

'Stunning,' Mom said. 'You did such a good job, Jake.'

'Thanks,' he replied. 'Nizar helped, too.'

Nizar stood a few paces back, hands folded in front of him, in all modesty. Alec imagined kneeing him in the groin. His own day had disappeared into Minecraft, the bridge growing into a half-assed replica of Frank Lloyd Wright's Falling Water. He hadn't watched a single physics tutorial.

'An operation is underway in Central Brussels,' Sasha announced, just as Nizar headed off for a pre-dinner prayer.

'See, what did I tell you?' Mom said.

'Police have roped off the area and are asking people not to tweet about it. People are advised to remain indoors, at home, if possible; stay away from the windows.'

'Why do we have to stay away from the windows?' Jake asked, eyes large with alarm.

'Um—' said Sasha. 'You know, Jake? I'm not entirely sure.'

This was a hard sell, even to Jake who, though not yet eight, knew that Sasha was rarely unsure.

'I think we could all use a break from social media,' Mom announced. She made everyone shut off their phones and put them in a fruit bowl on the sideboard. Even Nizar had to do it when he came back downstairs, and he didn't even have a smart phone. 'Let's take this chance to have an evening together.'

'We've spent the whole day together,' Sasha groaned.

'Not really,' Mom said. 'We've been beside one another but not *together*.'

For the first couple of minutes, it was hard not to think about what might be going on in other parts of the city. Things, it seemed, were finally coming to a head. With time, and Mom's dogged determination, they settled into a conversation.

'How nice to speak to your mother and sister today, Nizar. That must have been a wonderful surprise.'

He smiled and looked down at his bowl.

'Have they been living in Turkey long?'

'Since two years,' Nizar replied, bending over his bowl to sniff the stew.

'Uh huh,' said Mom, 'and do you still have family in Syria?'

'One uncle in Damascus,' he replied, 'and one aunt, also. She went to live with him after the war started.'

'So why didn't you do that?' Alec asked.

'Aaa-*lec*?' his mother said, turning his name into a question that was actually a warning, before turning to Nizar, 'We are awfully glad you're with us, Nizar, aren't we kids?' Alec gave a half-hearted nod because his mother was watching him, even though he was manifestly *not* happy Nizar was with them; moreover, he thought it a stupid thing to say.

'We must go north, because of the fighting,' Nizar said between spoonfuls of stew. 'We left late. My mother did not think it would get so bad. We thought, maybe there will be some trouble in the Kurdish areas. Either Assad will crush it, or he will be toppled, like Gaddafi.'

'So you would have been okay if the attacks had been limited to Kurdish areas?' Alec asked. This earned a second warning from his mother, a look, this time. Nizar only shrugged.

'It's the Kurds,' he said. 'Never we think there will be trouble in Aleppo. Is Syria's biggest city. The centre of business and the banks.'

'Assad is such a monster,' Sasha said.

'He certainly is,' Mom agreed.

That his sister and mother showed such little concern for the Kurds surprised Alec, but he let it pass, lest he draw a third warning from his mother.

'We did not like him,' Nizar explained. 'But we went along. To oppose him was trouble. We hoped he would be better than his father. They said he was a reformer.' Nizar stared at a piece of biscuit he held between his thumb and forefinger. 'He looked harmless, an eye doctor from London. No chin.' He ate the piece of biscuit.

'Do they live in a camp?' Sasha asked. 'Your mother and sister, I mean.'

He shook his head. 'They live in a, how you say, a garage?'

'Do you mean a converted garage?' his mother asked in her teacher voice, 'a garage that has been rebuilt so that it is suitable for a home?'

Sasha clucked her tongue and glanced at the ceiling.

'Not so converted,' said Nizar, with a shy smile. 'They have rugs, a small stove. It is very . . .'

'Snug?' Mom offered.

'Expensive,' Nizar said.

'Is that even legal?' Sasha asked.

Nizar looked puzzled. 'There are many people in need of a place to live.'

'It's got to be better than a tent,' Alec said.

'Yes,' Nizar agreed.

'Your mother and sister should come to live in Belgium,' Jake said.

'I think they would like that very much, Jake.' Nizar gave Jake's hand a tap, a gesture that might have annoyed Alec less had Nizar not been sitting in their father's place. 'However, I am eighteen so is finished, family reunification. They must remain in Turkey, I am afraid.' He frowned at his bowl.

'Why didn't they come with you?'

'It was not possible,' Nizar said. He bent further over his food.

'Why not?' Alec asked.

Nizar shook his head and put another spoonful of stew into his mouth.

Sasha asked, 'Would you be interested in speaking to my international justice club sometime?'

'Oh,' he said, smiling, weakly. 'I would not know what to say.'

'People would love to hear your experiences.'

'I don't—'

'Like how it felt to flee your home, the journey to Belgium. We read things in the press. You've lived it.'

The spoon slipped from Nizar's hand. It landed in the bowl, sending flecks of stew splattering across the tablecloth. He blanched and dabbed at the nearest stain with his napkin.

'Not to worry,' Mom said, jumping up for a damp cloth. 'It will come right out in the wash.'

Alec planned to get cracking on physics after dinner, but

Jake pleaded for everyone to watch *The Lion King*. Alec set it up on the computer. Mom made popcorn and hot chocolate.

'See?' she said. 'Who needs a television?'

Jake nestled in the middle of the sofa with his duvet and pillow, directing everyone.

'Nizar, come away from the window,' he ordered. 'You sit here, next to me. Mom can sit on the other side. Sasha you sit on that pillow, and Alec, you can sit on that one.'

'I can only watch for a little while,' he told his brother.

But he had forgotten how great a film it was; he was soon drawn into the story. By the time it finished it was nearly nine. Jake went to bed; Mom, too. Nizar went on to the terrace for a smoke and then retired, wishing the peace and the blessings of Allah upon them. Sasha retrieved her phone from the fruit bowl. Alec couldn't face homework. He was surprisingly worn out from the day. Better to get to bed early and make a fresh start tomorrow after he'd done the shopping.

'Arrests stand at nineteen,' Sasha announced. 'Abdeslam was spotted in Liège, driving a BMW towards the German border.'

Alec grabbed his phone. He'd just check the headlines while getting ready for bed. He scrolled through the feed as he climbed the stairs, as he brushed his teeth, undressed, and got into bed. He hit refresh, clicked on articles and short videos. Through the wall, he heard Nizar moving around and wondered whether he was praying. Didn't they have to do it five times a day? He hit refresh again and then once more. News of arrests could come any second, a dramatic but successful conclusion to the day. Resolution was around the corner. He could feel it.

He woke the next morning with the phone still in his hand. The previous night's reports had been uniformly false. No explosives were found, no men with bombs, no guns. The man driving the BMW in Liège towards Germany was not Abdeslam, just some random dude going about his evening. Of the nineteen arrested, eighteen had been released without charge. Alec had expected more after twenty-four hours of lockdown.

On the bright side, it lent an air of excitement to the morning's grocery shop: brave Alec, hunter-gatherer, putting the needs of the family above his personal security. He wasn't scared. Part of him wondered whether dying in a terrorist attack would be all that bad. His picture would be splashed across social media, in newspapers and magazines, possibly even television. He hoped they'd use a good one, not the lame one from school. Media in the UK and US would claim him as their own. Everyone would say what a great guy he was; Farrah would probably cry. Dad would feel a right shit, as well he should. Riding this tide of morose satisfaction, Alec descended the stairs and on to the main floor where he saw the fresh bread and croissants on the dining table.

'Nizar found an open bakery,' Mom gushed. 'Isn't that terrific?'

Nizar was on the terrace, smoking. Sasha was out there too, seated cross-legged in a chair; jumper stretched over her legs for warmth. With one hand she was gesticulating expansively the way she did when making a point. The other hand held tea. In a fucking glass.

'I said I'd go!' Alec cried.

'I wasn't going to drag you out of bed,' his mother said. 'You like to sleep in on Sundays.'

'But I said I'd do it!'

He seethed at having been robbed of his chance to step up, to be denied this sorry excuse for an adventure; seethed at the sound of his own pathetic mewls.

'I'm sorry,' his mother said, sounding not the least bit sorry. 'I didn't realise it meant that much to you.'

'Fine. I'll go for a walk, then.'

'You will do no such thing. The advice is to stay at home, whenever possible.'

So it was okay for Nizar to go out but not him?

'I'll go crazy if I stay here another minute,' he announced.

'Don't exaggerate, Alec. Most weekends you have to be dragged out of the house, kicking and screaming.'

Talk about exaggerating, he thought, as he turned on his heels and stomped every step of the three floors back to his room and dropped, theatrically, on to his bed. He lay there, scanning through his phone at all the people from school whose #brusselslockdown experience looked more fun than his, and wondered why he hadn't just walked out. His mother could not have stopped him.

Twitter was full of cat tweets: cats Photoshopped into Star Wars stills, dressed as jihadis, snipers, regular photos of cats in all their adorable catness. Asked by police to refrain from posting details of security operations, Belgians had responded with cat pictures, and the world's press, with little actual news to report, had pounced. The cats of '*cat. quatre*' were the feel-good story of the lockdown, showcasing Belgians' dark but irrepressible wit, their linguistic dexterity. A country with three official languages was conducting wordplay in a fourth, something that Alec, even at his most cynical, had to admit was pretty cool. Farrah had posted a drawing, her own, he was sure, of a cat in a suit and bowler, in the style of Magritte's *Fils d'Homme* (Son of Man), only instead of a green apple covering its face it was holding an iPhone with the Apple logo on it. It had over a thousand likes from all over the globe. Alec thought of the perfect reply: a lounging cat in the shape of Magritte's pipe and beneath it, in script, the words: *Ceci n'est pas une opération de securité* (this is not a security operation). He scanned back through the feed to see if it had already been done. It seemed so obvious. With his mother's graphic design software, he could replicate the texture, shape and palette of the original painting. The only problem was the software resided on the downstairs computer, in the very room he'd just stomped out of in a fit of pique. He sulked upstairs until he deemed a suitable amount of time had passed and then skulked back.

He couldn't make the picture on the screen match the one in his mind's eye. There was more to the software than he realised, and he wasn't about to ask his mother for help. Instead, he dabbled on Minecraft, surfed the internet and social media. Physics? He'd get to it soon. Maths? Gonna start that in a minute, right after this funny video and one final check of email, and WhatsApp, and Insta, and the group chat and Twitter and, oops, here was a new funny video. The internet knew what he wanted before he knew it himself. All he had to do was look away, disconnect, turn off the computer; he couldn't. He was flailing as the weekend slipped away.

'Haven't you got any homework?' his mother asked him. They had just cleared the dinner plates, and Sasha had commandeered the dining table. She was helping Nizar with his secondary-school leaving exam preparations. They'd become downright chummy.

Maths, Alec thought, *biology, French, chemistry* . . . 'Art,' he replied.

'Better get cracking, then.'

He shuffled to the sideboard where he had left his sketchbook, his pride wounded by his mother's order. Procrastination in his other subjects was understandable; he *liked* art, especially still lifes. He liked how grouping random things together got people making associations between them, constructing connections, concocting back stories. Friday afternoon he started one featuring a pencil sharpener, a broken ruler, a tangled ball of earbuds and a half-eaten packet of Mentos: the first four things he pulled from his rucksack. It had been coming together just fine. He was excited about it, even, and yet he hadn't touched it all weekend.

The moment Alec picked up his sketchbook he knew something was off. It felt odd, lighter. He flipped it open and found a chunk of pages missing. They had been roughly torn from the back; whoever did it was in a hurry.

'Jake,' he called, 'have you been in my art paper?'

'Nope,' Jake replied. He was lining up his Playmobil knights outside the Lego house.

'Well, someone has.' Alec popped open his pencil set. 'Are you serious?' he shouted. 'Come on, Jake! How many times have I told you my art pencils are off limits?'

'I didn't play with your art pencils,' his brother said, dipping the head of a Playmobil horse down to graze on the green Lego lawn.

'Calm down,' his mother said.

The instruction was every bit as helpful as it had been to Sasha the previous morning. Alec was ready to blow. 'No!' he shouted. 'There's like one, two . . .' he counted, 'six. Six pencils missing: 3B, 4B, H1, H2 . . . all the best ones!' He threw his hands up and then let them fall on to the table with a thud.

'Quit it,' Sasha said.

'Could you have left them at school?' Mom asked.

'I was using them Friday before dinner!' He covered his face with his palms. Sasha wouldn't have touched them, obviously. His mother would have admitted to it from the get-go. Jake would have fessed up by now, tearfully and with remorse. 'Hey, Nizar,' Alec called, 'you didn't use some of my art paper, did you? Borrow some pencils from my case?'

'I did not,' Nizar replied.

Alec was sure he was lying. He looked at his mother, and then at Nizar and then back at his mother.

'I need them for class,' he said.

His throat ached, his eyes stung, at the injustice, but also the embarrassment that such a small thing was bringing him to the verge of tears. 'Are you sure, Nizar? Because you were at the table Friday, when I had them out.'

'He said he didn't take them,' Sasha said.

'Alec,' his mother said, 'be polite.'

'I am being polite,' he replied. He'd said *borrow* when what he meant was *steal*. 'Do you remember being at the table, Nizar? I do. I remember that.'

'I am sorry I cannot help you,' Nizar said. He took a sip of tea and stared down at his book. Those long lashes of his formed a dark curtain.

For the second time in a day, Alec stomped off to his room. This time he slammed the door and then, for good measure, gave it a kick. He flopped on to his bed, facedown, and screamed into his pillow. When his throat got sore and he began to tire, he rolled over on to his back, breathless, and waited for his mother. That she would come, he did not doubt, and when she saw how sad he was, she would be sorry. He listened for footsteps. He waited a long time and then, finally, he heard them. He knew just how it would go. His mother would knock quietly, ask to come in. She would sit at the edge of the bed. 'You seem pretty upset,' she'd say. 'Want to tell me about it?' The footsteps rounded the corner to the final half flight of stairs. He counted the ten steps; now they were on the landing. Alec waited for the knock. Instead, the door to Nizar's room opened and then shut. Alec heard him moving around inside his room, humming a strange tune.

The weekend was a total bust for Alec. But it was an even bigger bust for the Belgian government. Forty-eight hours after shutting down their capital city, without a single significant arrest or breakthrough, officials had no choice but to extend the closure of schools and the metro into the next week. Alec had been given a lifeline. He swore he would not waste it. Which was why, even though he could have slept in Monday morning, he was downstairs before his mother left for work. He went straight to his still life, determined to finish it, making do with the pencils he had. But when he opened the case, all the pencils were there, freshly sharpened.

'There now,' his mother said. 'You were probably just looking in the wrong place last time.'

He stared at her, incredulous, but she was hunting for her car keys and took no notice.

'Now when Nizar gets back this evening—'

'He's gone?' Alec asked. Finally, a bit of good news.

'He went to the centre,' Sasha replied.

'But there's no metro.'

'He cycled,' said Mom.

'He has a bike?'

'He took yours,' she said, wandering out to the hall to root through coat pockets.

'He what?' Alec shouted.

'I would have dropped him off, but my lesson is in the opposite direction. Where could they be? Traffic is going to be terrible.'

'He could have asked,' Alec said.

'I had no idea it was that important to you,' Mom called back from the hall. 'When was the last time you rode it?' A rhetorical question, as she immediately began muttering about how she ought to have been on the road ten minutes before. Alec was going to call her out for insincerity, but then she started raking her fingers through her hair. Sasha saw it, too, and leapt up from her seat. They both started searching for the keys, Sasha in the dining room and kitchen, Alec in the living room, where he discovered them lying beneath one of Jake's jumpers.

'Thank you, sweetie,' Mom said, placing a hand on his cheek. 'Be nice to Nizar today, won't you?'

'Did he complain about me?'

'No. He would never do that. But we need to be kind. Think of what he's been through.'

Alec waited for his mother to close the front door before saying to Sasha, 'Can you believe her?'

'Well, he kinda *has* been through a lot,' Sasha replied. 'He had a nice life before the war – a big apartment, a maid and a cook and a chauffeur. That's why his mother wouldn't go until the bombs were literally falling. He and his sister were begging her to leave. They've lost all their savings. His sister is working after school in a slipper factory for extra money.'

'Sounds more like his sister has been through a lot,' Alec muttered.

'And he feels terrible,' Sasha said. 'Their father died when he was twelve. He's supposed to be the man of the house.'

The phrase hit a little too close to the bone for Alec. It made him want to punch something. He turned to walk out so that the something wasn't his sister.

'Off to your room for another sulk?' she asked.

'No,' he said, though that was exactly where he'd been headed. 'I left something up there.'

He took care not to stomp on the stairs, so as not to prove Sasha right, and when he reached his floor, the door he opened was Nizar's.

The room looked different. It smelled different, there was a cloying sweetness. The bed was pushed against a wall, there was a prayer mat at an odd angle – facing Mecca? The stuff from the refugee centre lined another wall, still in the bags they'd arrived in: old lady teacups and saucers, mugs with the decorations worn off them, plates in various sizes, ceramic bowls, a gravy boat, pots and pans with stained bottoms and mismatched lids, a pressure cooker, wooden salad tongs, a toaster, an electric kettle, utensils, souvenir teaspoons, a barometer, towels and sheets, candlestick holders and was that a fax machine? There were bags of food, too, which Mom didn't allow upstairs. Most of it was long-life stuff – individually-wrapped biscuits, juice cartons, UHT milk, dried fruits and nuts. There were fresh apples, also, and pears and bananas, some of which were over-ripe. That explained the smell. Alec smiled at the sight of old mobile phones lying in pieces atop the chest of drawers. Nizar's phone restoration project appeared to have hit a snag. He rifled through drawer after drawer, finding nothing but clothing, a hodgepodge of formerly owned items in shades of plum, russet, tangerine, marmalade and olive. With growing frustration, he pulled open the bottom drawer, pushed aside a few bags of nails and a brick of clay, and there it was: a stack of sketch paper. The uneven tear marks told him all he needed to know.

'Bastard,' he seethed.

Some of the pages, *his* pages, been drawn on. Worse still, the drawings weren't half-bad. In fact, they were rather striking. A mangy, possibly dead, dog, with a dirty snout; a sandaled foot sticking up out of rubble; and a young man sitting on a beach, staring out at the sea. Alec took them downstairs and dropped them in front of Sasha.

'I knew he was lying,' he said. 'He stole *my* paper.'

'Okaaayy?' she replied. Was she really that clueless?

'They were in his room, in a drawer.' He poked at the air with his finger for emphasis.

'Jesus, Alec.'

'I know, right? Wait till Mom sees it.'

'Why are you making such a fuss over a couple sheets of paper?'

'Not a couple. Like fifty.' It was maybe half that. 'And my pencils.'

'Heavens, the pencils!' she cried, melodramatically. 'You got those back.'

'Only after I complained.'

His sister took a deep breath and expelled it slowly. 'Have you considered that maybe Nizar was scared to admit he took paper without asking?'

'I don't care. He's a thief and a liar.'

'Says the guy who just admitted to breaking and entering.'

'I took back what was rightfully mine.'

'Do us all a favour,' she said, 'put them back where you found them.'

'He's got food in his room, you know.'

'Go on, now. Go!' She waved him off, dismissively, as if he were an underling. 'I'll buy you another sketchpad if it means that much to you.'

He scooped up the pages and left.

'There's a good boy,' she said.

'Fuck off,' he replied.

He put the paper and drawings back in the drawer, apart from the one of the boy on the beach, which he slipped into his art portfolio. He preferred the mangy dog, but he knew he could never pass it off as his own, too edgy; its setting too obviously foreign. He resolved to look for ways to incorporate that kind of grittiness into his own work.

'There's been an announcement,' Sasha said when he returned.

'Did they get him?' Alec asked.

'Nope. School is going to be closed all week,' she told him.

'Seriously?' he cried. 'This lockdown is a joke.'

'I thought you'd be happy about it.'

'I'm sick of being stuck in this house. How is it they haven't caught the guy? He's just one guy.'

'They say it isn't only about him,' Sasha said.

'Because they haven't a clue where he is. If they found him, this whole thing would be over.'

'They can't really lower the threat until there's a breakthrough,' Sasha said. 'Not after making such a big deal out of it.'

'Great. We'll never leave the house again. The guy's probably back in Syria by now.'

'Surely they can't let this drag on too much longer,' she said.

And indeed, within the hour, officials backtracked. Schools would reopen on Wednesday.

'Lamb stew again?' Alec asked, later, as his mother ladled out the steaming bowls for the third time in as many days. 'It's like *Groundhog Day* around here: can't leave the house, and then lamb stew for dinner.'

'For me it tastes better each time,' Nizar said, brown-noser.

'Well thank you, Nizar,' Marcy replied. 'I think so too. And you're in luck, Alec. Your father has taken tomorrow off to spend with the three of you.'

'Youpie,' cried Jake.

'So we can sit around his place? No thank you,' Alec said.

'Everything is open outside the city,' Mom said. 'He said he'll take you swimming or to Technopolis.'

'That'll be a hard pass from me,' he replied.

'But you love Technopolis,' Sasha said.

'Yeah,' said Jake. 'There's the airplane you can fly, and the bicycle on the tightrope wire high above, and the play shop with money they print with your own picture on it.'

Alec did love Technopolis, but he wasn't going to come when his father called. He wasn't a dog.

'I'll have the house to myself,' he replied.

'I will be here as well,' Nizar said.

'You aren't going to the centre?' Alec asked.

'I do not work Tuesdays,' he replied. 'Tuesdays, I am free from work.'

The prospect of spending an entire day with Nizar, just the two of them, was almost enough to make Alec reconsider his plans. His mother gave him one last chance the following morning.

'I'm sure your father would like to see you.'

He couldn't believe she actually wanted him to go. It was a test, he decided, one he would pass with flying colours.

'I have to study,' he said. 'Also, we're out of milk again, and coffee and eggs and bread, and there's nothing for tomorrow's pack lunches.'

'I would be pleased to do the shopping,' Nizar said.

'I said I'd do it, Nizar,' Alec said. He turned to his mother. 'And don't tell me I need to stay inside. The lockdown is over in all but name. You're going to work. Nizar goes out every day and tomorrow we're going back to school.'

'I will accompany,' Nizar said. 'To help carry.'

'Okay,' Mom said. 'So long as you go together.'

Why did she think he was a baby?

'Dad's here,' Sasha announced.

'Get your coat, Jake,' said Mom. 'Alec, do you want to come and say hello?'

'I'm good,' he said.

'I would very much like the chance to see *my* father again,' Nizar observed, when they were alone. 'And I am certain your father would be pleased to see you. He who wishes to enter paradise through its best door must please his mother and his father both.'

'Who said anything about entering paradise?' Alec asked.

'When shall we go to the shops?' Nizar replied, in that way he had of changing the subject when he didn't like a question. 'I will speak to my cousin at noon. For thirty minutes, and I must check the toilet upstairs. It go—' He made a shushing sound. Jesus, was he a plumber as well as an electrician?

'Whatever, Nizar,' he said. 'We have all day.'

Nizar's cousin phoned at twelve on the dot, but the call ended abruptly a few minutes later, when a man off-screen started shouting. Nizar looked flustered, also guilty as hell.

'What was that about?' Alec asked.

'He had to go. His father needed him.'

'You mean your uncle?'

'My uncle?' Nizar asked.

'Yeah, your uncle,' Alec said. 'Your cousin's father is your uncle, right?'

'Oh, yes,' Nizar said, after a beat. 'My uncle. Shall we go now? I will get my coat.'

The coat was a trench with wide lapels and frayed cuffs. It smelled of mothballs and – to Alec's mind – death, so much that, as they waited at the traffic light opposite the Syrian Embassy, he stood downwind from Nizar.

Alec pointed across to the embassy where a man was pacing back and forth in front of the gate. The man wore a black suit and white shirt, no coat, despite the damp cold.

'Convenient for when your passport needs renewing,' he remarked.

Nizar stiffened. 'I do not think I will be going there.'

'Take it easy. I was joking. Stick around and you'll see some protests, though. And not just the Kurds, but real Syrians too.'

Nizar looked uneasy, which was all the encouragement Alec needed to continue. 'Anyhoo, the legal protests take place over there.' He pointed to a small park to their right. 'The ones in support of Assad are the best. There's music, dancing and they have enormous banners and posters of Assad's face. All identical. It looks really authentic, totally grass roots.'

The light changed and they stepped out on to the pedestrian crossing. Nizar stared at the ground and hunched up his shoulders. 'Shhh,' Alec thought he heard him say.

He raised his voice instead. 'Illegal protests take place at night and are less civilised, we're talking break-ins, smashed windows, paint bombs. A few years ago, a bunch of guys climbed the gate in the middle of the night. Police chased them out. It was winter and there was snow on the ground, one of them tripped and the cops beat him with batons. I saw it from my bedroom window.'

The man from the embassy was staring at them.

'Bonjour,' Alec said.

'Bonjour,' the man replied. He had thick dark hair and a moustache.

'Nizar, don't be rude,' Alec said. 'Say, "Bonjour" to the man.'

'Bonjour,' Nizar muttered, into his scarf.

The man nodded, gravely, and stared at them as they passed, uphill towards the supermarket. At the top, where the street cut perpendicular with Avenue Louise, an armoured personnel carrier full of soldiers went by.

'Only been a couple days and already no one bats an eye,' Alec remarked.

'One can get used to extraordinary things,' Nizar muttered.

Alec agreed. Traffic was practically back to normal. Tomorrow, schools and the metro would reopen, but nothing had changed. Adults were shit at solving problems.

In the supermarket, Alec snapped pictures of the fish laid out on the crushed ice, close-ups of their dead eyes and open mouths. He bought bacon, though it wasn't on the list and then, at the checkout, he handed Nizar the basket, so he'd have to load it on to the belt.

'I have some business,' Nizar said when they were back on the street. 'I will meet you at the house.'

'I'll come along,' Alec replied.

'But the juice cartons,' said Nizar. Alec was holding a tray of them, some twenty-four individual boxes. 'They are heavy.'

'Not too heavy for me.'

A look of confusion flashed across Nizar's face but then he shrugged and started walking. Alec followed him to a hardware store and then around the tightly arranged shelves while Nizar picked up a fill valve for a toilet, a set of small screwdrivers, a soldering gun and two bags of large nails. Alec remembered the nails in Nizar's drawer, which made him think of the drawing of the boy on the beach. He wondered whether Nizar had noticed it was missing. If he had, he would surely know – or at least highly suspect – Alec was the one who'd taken it.

'A curious collection of items,' Alec remarked.

'I fix the toilet.'

'You need a soldering gun and nails to fix the toilet?' Alec asked.

Nizar shook his head and smiled a weak smile. 'They are for something else.'

'Like what?' Alec asked, but Nizar had turned to the

cashier to pay. He took all the bills from his wallet but was five euros short.

'I have it,' Alec said.

Nizar held up a hand as if to say, 'halt'. He withdrew a pint-sized, cloth drawstring purse, full to bursting, and proceeded to count the small change, arranging it into neat, one-Euro piles. Behind Alec, a customer sighed impatiently.

Back at home, Alec fried the bacon with the kitchen fan on low so that the smell wafted to the top floor. He did homework at the dining table, leaving his art portfolio lying open beside him. All Nizar had to do was turn over a single page and he'd find his drawing of the boy on the beach. Alec wasn't afraid. He wanted him to see it. It was unlike Alec to be brazen and yet he felt entirely in control. Invincible, even, until Sasha and Jake returned from Dad's and Sasha yanked him out of his chair by the arm.

'Cut it out,' he said, rubbing his shoulder. She did not appreciate her own strength.

'Come with me,' she whispered.

Had Nizar ratted him out? They'd probably been texting one another all afternoon. Well, Alec wasn't going to apologise, he thought, trudging reluctantly behind her, up the stairs to her room, and she couldn't make him. He picked up a glass owl from one of her shelves and passed it from hand to hand.

'To what do I owe the honour?' he asked.

'Could you put that down, please?'

He did, but in a different spot to where he'd found it.

'Will you stop being an asshole?' She jumped up and returned the owl to its rightful place. 'This is important.'

'All right.' He sat down on her bed. She stood in front

of him, neutralising his height advantage. He looked up and waited for the scolding lecture to commence.

She twisted her hands together. 'I don't know how to say this, so I'm just going to say it,' she declared, which was not the opening he expected. 'Don't freak out but—' She paused and then blurted: 'Dad is having an affair.'

For a moment, Alec was speechless.

'I've suspected for a while,' Sasha continued. 'I didn't want to say anything until I was sure. At Technopolis, I overheard him on the phone, calling someone *cherie*, and just now when we stopped at his apartment, I went through the cupboards in his bathroom and found makeup and tampons and a hairbrush with long blonde hairs in it.'

Alec nodded. Sweet relief flowed through his body. The secret was no longer his alone to guard. A burden shared truly was a burden halved.

'I feel sick,' said his sister. 'Poor Mom! I mean, sure, she *has* let herself go a bit.'

'She's old,' Alec said. 'She can't help it.'

'Oh my God, what if Dad marries her? What if they have kids!'

'Let's not get ahead of ourselves.'

'Do you think Mom knows?'

'Don't tell her,' he cried. 'It'll be a disaster.'

'So you think I should confront Dad?'

'God no!'

This was exactly what Alec had feared; exactly the reason he hadn't told her about Kevin with the tiny *nichons*. Sasha was a weak link, a blabbermouth. She was going to wreck everything, send the Jenga tower tumbling.

'You don't seem surprised,' she said, taking a step back. She crossed her arms over her chest, stuck out her chin.

'Well, you suspected it, didn't you?' he said. 'I mean, why else would he have left?'

Her eyes narrowed. 'You knew already, didn't you?'

'What makes you say that?'

A stupid thing to say.

'How long have you known?'

Cornered, he blustered and babbled.

She repeated the question through clenched teeth: 'How. Long. Have. You. Known?'

Marcy

The call from the estate agent came during Marcy's nine o'clock session: a last-minute viewing at eleven. She raced back to the house, grabbing shoes off the hall steps, as many as she could carry, filling her arms, and then running to the closet under the stairs to heave them in. It took four trips to make them disappear, an exercise repeated before every visit, although usually with a bit more warning. 'Think: IKEA showroom,' the estate agent said. With four young people living in the house, it was a Sisyphean task. Those shoes would be back on the steps by the end of the day, tomorrow at the latest. Marcy shut the closet door and ran to the top of the house, going room to room, descending, scooping up clothes, loose papers and family photos and shoving them into drawers and cupboards, under furniture. She filled the clothes hampers with towels and stray socks, checked that the toilets were flushed, the lids closed. She hesitated before entering Nizar's room, not wanting to invade his privacy. She left the stacks of bric-a-brac where they were, and draped a cover over the mess on the chest of drawers. She hoped he wouldn't mind.

Back on the main floor, she put the mugs, the crummy plates and cutlery into the dishwasher, put away the honey, the jam and the butter, wiped down the counters. She had learned shortcuts and tricks to hide piles of clutter. Sasha's books and study materials were stacked on a chair that was tucked under the dining table; a box of Lego was slid behind a planter in the living room. She was stuffing super-hero figurines beneath throw pillows on the sofa when the estate agent rang the bell.

'Merci, Madame. Thank you for making time,' the estate agent said in her gravelly smoker's voice. 'Last minute, I know, but demand has not exactly been high. We must seize every chance we get.' She walked through the house, switching on lights. Her smile was as natural as her bottle-blonde hair.

'Of course,' Marcy said. 'You'll lock up when you leave?'

'Do not worry yourself,' said the estate agent, already at work rearranging furniture, setting the stage. She did not want Marcy around; likewise, Marcy didn't want to be there. Selling a house was like uploading a picture to Tinder, or so she imagined. It was putting oneself on display for the world to judge, and the world was swiping left. Not a single offer, despite dropping the price. Neil complained about it in a way that made her feel he blamed her for it, and maybe he was right. She had chosen the colours and the decorations, decided where each piece of furniture would be placed, where comfort was more impor-tant than elegance, and warmth trumped style. She loved this house. But it had to go. She could never truly claim to be standing on her own two feet until it did.

Despite the zeal with which Marcy culled other possessions from the house, she left Neil's personal things undisturbed. The coats he had left behind still hung in the front hall;

toiletries, shaving creams and shampoo bottles cluttered the bathroom they had shared, and she hadn't once opened the door to his wardrobe. So when she laid on her bed, focusing on the family that had arrived at the refugee centre that day so as not to slide into self-pity, you best believe she kept strictly to her own side.

There were five of them in the family: a set of parents and three little girls, all of them looking like they'd been through the wringer which, of course, they had.

'Welcome to Belgium,' she told them, grasping their hands in both of hers. 'I'm so happy you're here.'

She gave each girl a sweet. She had taken to keeping them in her pockets, brightly coloured sourballs wrapped in clear cellophane.

The oldest girl had plucked one with her forefinger and thumb with a delicate grace that made Marcy think of the sugar tongs in her grandmother's silver teaset. A string bean of a child, Jake's age though she looked younger, with curly black hair that hung the length of her back. Her lips moved in thanks, but no sound came from her mouth. Marcy's heart lurched to think how little this girl had, while Marcy lay in a bed so big she used only half of it.

When she started volunteering at the centre, Sylvie had warned her not to expect gratitude from the refugees. Marcy tried not to laugh. She didn't want their gratitude. She wanted to be of service, to hear their complaints when the daily bread delivery was late, or that the meal she had helped prepare didn't appeal to their tastes. She gladly helped mothers sort through piles of clothing and shoes for items that suited their family members. No request was too small! So long as she was focused on someone else's problems, she was all right and moving forward. It was the quiet moments, while driving between classes, or late at night, here in her bedroom, that the backsliding happened, when the words echoed in her head: that cheerless chant, the mournful mantra:

He's gone.

He's gone

He's gone

The small stabbing sensation in her chest, combined with – and this was the dangerous bit – morose satisfaction, the kind you get when picking a scab. It hurts but you keep going back for more.

She rolled on to her stomach, plumped her pillow. She'd read that the death of a marriage is like the death of a loved one: it's not something you get over; it's a thing you get used to. She saw how that could be true. In the days after her father died, part of Marcy's brain had clung to a fantastical hope it had all been some terrible misunderstanding, that someone would call and say, 'We're awfully sorry for the confusion; please disregard our most recent message.' But the sight of him in the casket, face covered in thick pancake make-up to conceal the worst of the burns from the airbag's deployment, simultaneously there and not there, had been too material to deny. There was no equivalent moment of truth for the death of her marriage and so hope, that thing with feathers, lingered, fluttering upwards at the lightest breeze.

She stuck one leg out from under the duvet. She would get through it. She must. For the children's sake as well as her own. The key was to stay busy, keep moving, keep focused on the next thing and the thing after, and the one after that. Also, stay sober. However appealing the thought of unwinding over a beer, a glass of wine . . . a fifth of Jack Daniels, she dared not, lest it end in a tearful late-night phone call to Neil, begging him to come home. Desperation wasn't a good look on anyone, and on a woman in her late forties, it was downright pathetic.

She could not afford to be pathetic. Not now. Despite having slid into a traditional gender role, there was still time to become the self-sufficient, independent badass she knew in her feminist heart she had always been. The first step was financial independence. She must start paying her own way. And if doing so required scaling back her needs to fit her reduced means, so be it. She'd been poor before.

Which was yet more reason to stay away from alcohol. It would save her hundreds, perhaps thousands, of euros. A penny saved is a penny earned. Buy the supermarket brand of butter instead of the Kerrygold? She'd save twenty-five pennies. Take coffee to work in a thermos instead of picking one up at Starbucks? Two-hundred-fifty pennies. Packed lunches earned even more. The six-euro lunch vouchers her language school provided could then be spent on groceries.

She let go the cleaner; lowered the house temperature by five degrees, counted twelve euros, fifty-three cents – more than two lunch vouchers – in pots of loose change lying around the house. She stopped using the dryer, except for the towels, which turned scratchy when line dried. She clipped coupons, expanded meatless Mondays to meatless Mondays, Wednesdays and Fridays, saving money, the environment and their health. It was a contest with herself, a competition, to see how much excess could be squeezed from her budget.

A competition, but also a performance for the children,

Sasha especially. She could not afford to look weak, not after the spectacle she had made of herself the night Neil left – she shuddered whenever she thought of it. What sort of example had she set? That a woman was nothing without a man? That the proper response to adversity was collapse? She was heartbroken, of course she was; nonetheless, she must accept things as they were, not wish for how she wanted them to be. In a few years, she'd look back and say it was all for the best.

And yet, she could not let go of hope or, more precisely, hope would not let go of her. It bloomed whenever his name popped up on the caller ID. She'd answer expecting to find the old Neil, the dear one, her partner, not this stranger, this *other* who treated her as if she were nuts when *he* was the one acting out of character: one minute threatening to sue for custody of the kids, cancelling dates with them the next; absurdly insisting they hadn't been happy for years, decades. It took all her willpower to remain calm. She would not demean herself – not any further than she already had, anyway – by pointing out the obvious: that discarding all they had built together was not merely foolish, it was wasteful. Neil had always abhorred wastefulness. He was the guy who ran around the house turning off lights, saying, 'spare a thought for the polar bears'; who cluttered the fridge with nearly empty Tupperware containers because heaven forbid two teaspoons of perfectly good pasta sauce went down the drain. What kind of person saves a thimble's worth of Bolognaise and tosses away a successful twenty-two-year partnership, tosses away a *family*?

It made no sense; ergo, there was a chance it was a passing phase. It would not be the first for Neil, who'd once declared a desire to stand for the European Parliament, despite not belonging to a political party, or being very political. Another time, he had set his sights on becoming an innkeeper in Vermont, a state he had only ever seen in pictures. For weeks he had combed online real-estate listings and local schools for the kids. They would keep goats to make cheese, he said, get season passes at the local ski area and spend winter afternoons on the slopes. Those ideas fizzled and were forgotten. Why not this one as well? One day he would call and ask to come home or, better yet, she'd open the door to find him standing there, bag in hand. 'I've been such a fool,' he'd say.

She got up to pee. She ought to hate Neil for the pain and suffering he was causing, but all her brain did was churn out memories of past kindnesses: Neil bringing her coffee in bed; Neil driving with the hazards on when they took Sasha home from the hospital; Neil's eyes filling with tears as she recited her wedding vows. He was a good man.

She washed her hands and drank a glass of water. Thank goodness for Nizar, whose presence reminded her of the insignificance of her own misfortunes. Through him, the children were learning a valuable lesson in how to deal with adversity with grace and fortitude. Jake adored him and, after a predictable period of scepticism, so did Sasha. Alec was still a bit standoffish, but Marcy had no doubt that in time he and Nizar would become, if not like brothers, then cousins or at least very good friends. Nizar's helpfulness had rubbed off on Alec who, she'd noticed, no longer needed to be asked twice to unload the dishwasher or take out the rubbish.

Nizar was settling into life in Belgium. His French had improved, and he was working so hard to make up the schooling he'd missed due to the war. Four years was a lot, and yet he was determined to become a doctor, as his father had been. And he was making friends. Well, one friend, at least. Tahrir was older by quite a bit, Marcy assumed, though she hadn't asked. What did it matter? Tahrir wasn't what you'd call handsome. About the best thing you could say about his square head was that it suited his stocky build. Worry had furrowed a deep crease across his brow. He kept to himself. Marcy had never heard him speak. He shook hands with Alec and nodded respectfully at Marcy and Sasha before quickly averting his eyes. Marcy wasn't offended. She could imagine that someone raised to observe strict gender roles would find our everyday interactions with members of the opposite sex difficult to navigate. Culture shock. She could relate. She never remembered which cheek one was supposed to kiss first, or figure out how an acquaintance graduated from *vous* to *tu*. Who was she to criticise?

She climbed back into bed and her thoughts turned back to her marriage.

It would be a lie to claim she'd never considered leaving. There were moments spent curled in a ball, weeping on the kitchen floor as R.E.M.'s 'Imitation of Life' blasted because she had no life of her own; she merely facilitated other people's lives. Seventeen years of doctors' appointments and school runs, speech therapy and laundry, ironing and grocery shopping – *I got a Master's degree for this?* – cooking and washing up and helping with homework had swallowed her whole. In those low moments, and they came hard and fast after her fortieth birthday – midlife was a bitch – the thought of running away was tantalising. She'd gone so far as to check flights online, but even with the cursor hovering over the 'Purchase' button for a one-way ticket to New York, she knew it was fantasy.

She had been aware their marriage was in a valley. Peaks and valleys was how her soft-spoken father had described marriage. 'Hold on to your head in the good times; your faith in the bad' had been the entirety of his wedding speech to them. The brevity led some on Neil's side to suspect, incorrectly, that he didn't approve of the match. Most of their marriage was spent on a grassy upland of gently undulating hills, so it seemed only natural to Marcy that another peak awaited them, just around the corner. Instead, it was a cliff above a rocky ravine.

In bed, she tossed and turned. She and Neil didn't really have a faith. Perhaps that was the problem. The only thing they'd had to hold on to was each other and that proved insufficient when the terrain got rugged.

The thought brought a fresh stab of pain. Sadness, sure, but also humiliation. Marriage and family were her life's work. She hadn't planned it that way. It hadn't been her intention, but there it was, and to have failed utterly made her want to lie in a warm bathtub and open a vein.

Not really. She wasn't melodramatic and she hated the sight of blood. But it sucked pretty bad. It was about the suckiest thing she could think of.

Irises, she had read, were symbols of hope, but she thought a more apt floral representative was the dandelion: humble yet sturdy, able to flourish anywhere and built to endure. No matter how many times you ripped them out, they pushed their way back up through the soil and flowered anew. Because the roots went deep.

She turned on a light, got out of bed again and opened Neil's wardrobe. She wasn't sure what she expected, dust bunnies and empty, mismatched hangers, she supposed. Instead, it was half full of the plain, classic button-down shirts that were, until recently, a staple of his wardrobe. The suit he'd worn to their wedding was there, which hurt, though not as much as the old rugby shirt. It had been his favourite Saturday shirt when they met, old even then, its navy blue long faded to dirty grey, the collar separating at the seam. She put it on and climbed back into bed. A cast off in a cast off, the frayed cuffs growing damp with her tears.

Winter was on its way. The sun was a low-watt bulb in the flat grey sky. Marcy pulled her coat close to keep the damp chill at bay and walked faster. The restaurant was on the corner where Boulevard Winston Churchill meets Chaussée de Waterloo, at the spot where the tramline bends. Just there, set back from the road, one of those brasseries that serve shellfish on ice platters, with wedges of lemon, crustless fingers of buttered brown bread and tiny bowls of vinegar.

Neil and she had come here with the kids this past spring. They sat outside under the awnings. Jake ate profiteroles for the first time, to his everlasting delight. That was another lifetime, before she started measuring the cost of things in lunch vouchers. She arrived early and was escorted to a table in the main room, beneath an awesome stained-glass dome the perfect shade of yellow – warm, not jaundiced. When she was a teenager, she had thought the faux Tiffany lamps and brass rails of the TGI Friday's in her local mall the epitome of cool. Here the art nouveau was its authentic self; no need to clutter the walls with kitsch or festoon the waiting staff with pieces of flair. If she was going to blow a hole through her budget, at least this place was the real deal.

The maître d' pulled out a table with a quick flourish

and Marcy sat on the bench behind it. He asked if she'd care for an aperitif. She started to shake her head no, and then thought, what the hell? A glass of Chardonnay would be worth a voucher if it calmed her nerves.

That she should be this nervous about meeting a colleague for lunch was a bit embarrassing. It felt adolescent, immature. But if things went well, Sharon might become a friend, and Marcy could really use one of those right now.

Such a thought would have seemed incredible to the Marcy who had first moved to Brussels. That Marcy had picked up friends wherever she went: French class, the American Women's Club, the Childbirth Trust. Together they had navigated expat life, discovered the best hospital to give birth in, which local cheese could be substituted for cheddar, which was the least bad television service provider. With them, she had explored Manneken Pis's closet full of elaborate outfits, ogled at houses designed by Horta, and marvelled at the carpet of flowers in la Grande Place. They had planned bar crawls for themselves and their husbands and strolled together through the inner ring's tunnels on Car Free Sunday.

She'd had little in common with most of these women, apart from a mother tongue, but that had been enough, somehow; more than enough. It was momentous. Thanks to them, the daily struggles and humiliations with the unforgiving French language became a source of hilarity instead of despair. Each interaction with a snobby salesperson or unsmiling official was fresh material.

Like the time Kathy meant to compliment a carpenter on his work but instead declared she loved him.

Or when Marcy, in conversation with her doctor five days past her due date with Sasha, mispronounced a single vowel in a conversation and instead of conveying how relaxed and laid back she was, accidentally inferred she was having suicidal thoughts and possibly in need of urgent psychotherapy.

Or when Heather, who studied French at university and spoke it better than all of them, brought the car in for servicing and, blanking on the French word for steering wheel, had launched into a lengthy explanation of its function ('the round thing you hold and use to turn the car in the direction you want it to go . . .').

How they had all howled at that one.

Marcy's wine arrived on a silver platter accompanied by a tiny glass bowl of pretzels. The wine was cool and dry, with a strong minerality: delicious.

Kathy had been the first friend to leave; one of only three Americans and the only fellow Midwesterner. Kathy and her husband Rick threw a raucous party during which they drank all the booze that couldn't be shipped back and then some. The gang chipped in for a lace tablecloth, handmade, not the cheap stuff hawked to tourists. A few days later, Marcy helped Kathy sweep the empty apartment, shared a litre of Chouffe that they swigged straight from the bottle. When the taxi arrived to take Kathy to the airport hotel, they had sobbed like a couple of heartsick teenagers.

More departures followed with more house parties and gifts of tablecloths, tapestries and coffee-table books on Magritte, Horta and Brel. Promises were made to stay in touch, that there would be visits, joint holidays, but apart from one hastily arranged dinner in London and a brief meet-up at an adventure park outside Chicago, these had come to nothing.

Fresh arrivals took the places of those who left. But

connections with these people never ran as deep and, after a while, there seemed little point getting to know someone who would likely be gone in three to five years. The kids and the house kept her busy, so did the efforts to kick-start her career. Occasionally, she and Neil went out with couples from his work. Not one of the wives had been in touch since Neil left. It was only to be expected, Marcy supposed. She hadn't noticed how isolated she'd become.

'Am I that late?' bellowed a voice. 'Or are we going to get on famously?'

Sharon was pointing to Marcy's empty glass and smiling.

'My eleven o'clock cancelled,' Marcy said, 'a last-minute meeting.'

'Don't you just hate that?' Sharon clucked, as she dropped into the chair opposite. 'And ten to one the meeting's been in the diary for days. At least you can bill him for it.'

'A call would have been nice; saved me forty minutes' drive,' Marcy said.

Sharon flagged down the waiter to order wine. 'You'll have another, yeah, or should we get a bottle?'

She shouldn't. A bottle would cost her at least three more lunch vouchers; nonetheless, she agreed.

'Fourth time he's cancelled in as many weeks,' she added.

'See, I tell any student like that to leg it. A waste of time, they are.'

'He's the managing director.'

'Argh! They make the worst students,' she said, signalling to the waiter to open the bottle. After he'd topped up their glasses and placed the remainder in an ice bucket, she continued. 'They couldn't care less, and you *can't* drop him because the school sees him as a pipeline to more students.'

'He wants to reschedule for Thursday, after lunch.'

Sharon rolled her eyes and opened the menu. 'What's good here?'

'The homemade meatloaf is popular; the steak tartare, as well.'

'So what did you tell him?'

'I said I had to check my calendar.'

Sharon gave her a disappointed look.

'I need the hours,' Marcy said.

'Don't we all? First week of December they start deffing off, like the year's already over. Happens every June as well. Summer hols.'

'This is a great job for someone who doesn't need the money,' Marcy said.

Teachers at their school were independent contractors, paid for hours taught, plus mileage but not time spent in transit.

'Ar,' said Sharon, 'busy work for la-dee-dah wives of executives.'

The waiter took their order. Marcy wanted the meatloaf but ordered the steak tartare because it was three euros cheaper. Sharon had half a roasted chicken. There was a small kerfuffle when she tried to place her order in Flemish, which, the waiter replied, in French, he did not speak. The matter was quickly resolved by switching to English, but Sharon was not best pleased.

'Sorry I had to have a Benny there,' she said. 'The city is supposed to be bilingual.'

'I don't think he's Belgian,' Marcy said. 'Spanish, maybe? Portuguese?'

'Doesn't matter. You won't find a waiter in Flanders who isn't trilingual: Dutch, French and English. If my daughter were here, she'd walk out.'

'How old is your daughter?' Marcy asked. She had no desire to wade into Belgium's linguistic swamp. She wondered why Sharon cared. She was from somewhere around Birmingham, if Marcy was remembering correctly.

'Fourteen,' Sharon said, 'but she's precocious.'

'Mine, too,' Marcy replied. 'Precocious, I mean. She's seventeen.'

Sharon took a big swig of wine. 'I dread when Aafje turns seventeen. Already she knows everything.'

Marcy smiled. 'The way my daughter rolls her eyes, I sometimes worry they're going to roll right out of her head.'

'We can do nothing right. It's amazing, honestly, we've survived so long.'

Marcy nodded. 'What did you do before teaching?' she asked. They had all started out in other careers or used teaching to supplement less lucrative occupations. Frank was a potter; Alice had once been a member of the corps de ballet at the Royal Ballet of Flanders; Marianne had once worked in marketing.

'Journalism,' said Sharon. 'I was going to bring down Thatcher. Instead I wrote about tunnels and tunnelling.'

Marcy smiled. 'I was going to be the next Alan Fletcher.'

'Still, teaching has been a godsend ever since Jost ran off with his secretary,' Sharon continued. 'Talk about a cliché. Aafje blames me, of course. She adores her father. I'm the bitch who chased him away. She thinks I'm the reason she isn't living with him.' Sharon snorted. 'I love her dearly. Sometimes, though, I just want to say, "Darling, you have no idea."'

'How awful,' Marcy said.

Sharon took another gulp of wine. 'Her school ski trip

costs six hundred euros and the man won't contribute a cent. "That's what child support is for," he says. Tells me I need to learn to budget. The cheek.' Sharon took another swig and refilled both glasses, though Marcy hadn't taken a sip since the waiter refilled her glass. 'Don't tell me you're one of those civilised divorced couples,' she said, putting air quotes around the word *civilised*, 'who spend Christmas and birthdays together and never quarrel.'

'We're not—'

'Thank God!' Sharon cried. 'Here's to good old-fashioned acrimony.' She raised her glass in a toast.

Marcy clinked glasses, not wanting to be rude. Still, she felt the need to clarify. 'I mean, we aren't divorced. Not yet, anyway. It's all very recent.'

'But you've filed.' It was more comment than question.

Marcy shook her head. 'Not yet.'

Sharon's face lit up like a firecracker. She put down her glass, placed her palms on the table and leaned in. 'You can file in the UK!'

'I'm not British,' Marcy said.

'Doesn't matter. He is, right? And the children too, I assume. And you lived there for a time. The first to file gets to pick jurisdiction.'

Sharon paused as the waiter arrived with their food. When he'd gone, she picked up again.

'Britain is heaps more generous to dependent spouses. It's not even close, darling. I should have, *would* have, done that had I'd known what Jost was up to. The sneaky bastard.'

'I'm not going to file,' Marcy said.

'Don't let him just walk all over you,' said Sharon as she sawed into the chicken. They're surprisingly stingy here, you'll find. Shockingly so. You'll get child support until the sprogs are eighteen, and a bit more if you haven't worked, but it's capped at a third of his income, and never lasts indefinitely.'

Marcy lifted a forkful of tartare. 'I'm not going to file. Not in the UK, not here.'

'You're not one of those born-again Christian types, are you?'

'It's not religious. I don't want a divorce. I don't want to *be* divorced.'

'I know exactly how you feel,' Sharon said, laying down her fork and knife to take a sip of wine. 'I was like that, too, in the beginning. Believe me, that will change. When Jost first left, I would have done anything to get him back, even though this current girlfriend – may the Lord crush her blackened soul – is but the latest of a loooong line and, deep down, I always knew.' She leaned in. 'Is there someone else?'

Marcy dabbed at her lips with her napkin and shook her head. 'I don't think so.' Sharon responded with raised eyebrows. It was difficult to explain to someone who didn't know Neil. 'A few years ago, one of his colleagues, his mentor, actually, had an affair with a woman he managed. Neil was disgusted. I mean *really* upset. He kept saying: "How *could* he? This isn't the man I know." He must have said it a hundred times. At one point I had to say, "Honey, it's not like he's cheating on you."'

'You sure he wasn't looking at it as a how-to guide?' Sharon smirked. 'You know what they say: the wife is always the last to know.'

Marcy dipped a *frite* in mayonnaise. 'Believe me, I'd rather there was someone else. At least then he would have left me to go towards *something*. Instead . . .' The tears came fast, catching her by surprise. 'We were good together, you know? On all the most important issues, we agreed.'

'You are not blaming yourself,' Sharon announced, jabbing a fork across the table at Marcy. 'I forbid you to blame yourself.'

Her stridency, the funny way her face scrunched with anger, made Marcy laugh. 'I'm not blameless,' she replied. 'How could I be? There were two of us in the marriage and I haven't been my best self these past couple of years. My dad died, unexpectedly, right around the same time as my career. I should say, around the time I realised my career was dead. I was slow to admit defeat. Neil had his share of professional disappointments, too, I know. I could have been more understanding. I regret teasing him about his shirts.'

'His shirts?'

'Custom-made, from a shop over near Louise. It was weird. For as long as I've known Neil, he's only ever worn solid white or light blue dress shirts and then suddenly he's Jay Gatsby – a rainbow of colours, bold prints, florals. They come in pale pink boxes, with black lettering. I asked how much they cost and he told me and then I said, "For that price they ought to come with washboard abs." It was a joke, you know. He looked so hurt. They're beautiful shirts. I wish I'd told him how beautiful they were.'

'Well, no wonder he left!' Sharon said, with a roll of the eyes that made Marcy think young Aafje had studied at the foot of a master. 'Good grief! Men always need to have their egos stroked and be told what good boys they are; how handsome, how virile.'

'I just . . .' Marcy held another *frite* in her hand as she waited for the lump in her throat to recede. 'It's really rough, you know?' She shook her head and glanced at the ceiling. 'I thought we were a team.'

'How long did you say you were married?' Sharon asked.

'Twenty-two years.'

'And you're, what, forty-seven?'

'Forty-eight,' Marcy said.

Sharon's eyes flickered upward as she made a quick calculation. 'Well that's not bad. He'll probably have to pay at least until he retires, and whatever you get will be indexed to inflation, so there's that. You'll get more if he gets a raise or inherits, but if he loses his job, which, if he's like my tosser of an ex, he'll do on purpose, it can be reduced. The UK is a much better bet. Take my advice, lawyer up, hop on a Eurostar and file. I can give you some names. Or you could really go brass knuckles and file in Canada.'

'I'm American,' Marcy said.

'Oh,' Sharon said. 'Why did I think you were Canadian?' Marcy shook her head. 'I get that a lot.'

'So then go back to America.'

'This is where the children were born,' she said.

'The children will adjust.'

'And now there's Nizar to think about.'

'Is that your dog?'

'No,' Marcy laughed. 'He's a refugee from Syria.'

Sharon looked as if Marcy had announced Nizar was a pet boa constrictor that roamed free around the house.

'You must sleep with one eye open at night,' Sharon remarked.

'Nizar is wonderful. He's like a member of the family. So kind and helpful.'

Sharon shuddered. 'If it were up to me, they'd all go packing, back where they came from.'

'They never wanted to leave. They're fleeing for their lives.'

'At least, that's the script they recite,' Sharon replied. 'We have no way of knowing whether it's actually true.'

'I don't believe that's the case.'

'If they really are fleeing for their lives, why are so many of them young, single males?'

'Because they're fit and strong enough to make the journey.'

'Why not stay and fight for the country they supposedly love so much?'

'Maybe they don't know which side to fight on? Maybe they don't like any of the sides? Many are professionals. They were the ones who could afford to pay the smugglers.'

'You know who else has money? Terrorists.'

Marcy's face must have registered her disgust because Sharon immediately began backtracking.

'I'm not saying they're a majority or anything, but even one is too many. That's how the Paris killers got through, you know.'

'They were all born in Europe.'

'Which is exactly my point,' said Sharon, not pounding the table, more like tapping it with the palm of her hand. 'Don't tell me no one knows where Abdeslam is. That whole neighbourhood is helping to hide him. There are enough right here who hate our way of life. Why add to the numbers? And yet, once again, the government just throws open the doors.' She threw her arms open.

Marcy's heart sank. 'We're hardly throwing—'

'They'll settle in Schaerbeek or Molenbeek and we'll never get rid of them. We'll be supporting these people and their children for the rest of our bloody lives.'

'A lot have professional degrees: dentists, lawyers, business executives. Nizar is studying for his leaving exam. He wants to be a doctor.'

'Be honest with me, now. Can you truly say you aren't worried about having a grown man, a stranger, from a very different culture, in the house with your seventeen-year-old daughter? He's probably been raised to believe any woman who doesn't wear a veil is no better than a prostitute.'

'Syria was one of the more secularised countries in the Middle East,' Marcy said. 'I wish you could meet Nizar.' The last part was a complete lie. She would never expose Nizar to this vile woman.

'Where is his bedroom in relation to hers?'

Marcy pretended she hadn't heard the question. To respond to it would be to dignify it and she would not do that. She quietly ate her tartare, dipping *frites* in mayonnaise; Sharon stripped the chicken carcass of meat and refilled her wine glass twice. Marcy considered asking whether she was driving, but then realised she didn't care. She had no wish to say anything more to Sharon. Not today, not ever again. Still, the silence was intolerable. Marcy believed in building bridges instead of walls.

'The steak tartare is wonderful,' she said. 'And goose-fat *frites* are divine.'

Marcy lay still in her bed, listening, searching for the source of whatever had roused her from sleep. All was quiet inside the house and in the street beyond, no car alarms, drunk students passing by or protesters at the Syrian Embassy, not even the buzz and shush of the tramline, which meant it was sometime between one and five in the morning, certainly not a time to be awake. It had been the house settling, perhaps, or a neighbour, or maybe she had dreamt the whole thing? She closed her eyes and rolled over and then, there it was, overhead: footsteps in Sasha's room.

Her first thought was of Nizar preparing tea for Sasha as she tutored him in chemistry after dinner, the careful way he measured out the loose leaves and the sugar.

Her second thought was to curse Sharon for planting foolish ideas in her head.

A third thought: perhaps she ought to investigate, all the same?

She pictured Sasha opening the door, finding her mother standing there, in the middle of the night, dressed in her father's old rugby shirt, wanting to know if everything was all right. The look of withering contempt such a scene would provoke. If only Neil were there. Without question, he would have felt it his responsibility to check on Sasha.

But, really, what was Marcy afraid of? She was on the receiving end of her daughter's contempt every day. Pretty much everything Marcy said or did was a disappointment, an affront. It was a phase, Marcy understood, a necessary step in Sasha's forging of her own identity. She ought to be glad, and maybe she could have been glad, were each look of contempt not a reminder that, on the night Neil left, when her children needed their mother, Marcy had instead forced them to mother her. It had been a fundamental test and she had failed. The boys would forgive her, but Sasha never would. And Marcy couldn't blame her because she wouldn't forgive herself either.

However, the truth was Marcy had been failing to live up to Sasha's high expectations since the day that child was born. Such a pernickety baby, crying whenever the slightest bit wet, her sensitive skin unable to bear anything but the softest natural fabrics. When she grew older, she would not sleep until her stuffed toys were lined around her bed, each in their allocated place. Marcy had had to draw up seating plans for babysitters.

More footsteps: Sasha's, Marcy was sure of it. Alec scuffed his feet when he walked; Jake's strides were shorter and harder on the heels. Sasha walked the same way she did everything in life: with steady purposefulness. Marcy did not know what Nizar's footsteps sounded like.

Stop, she told herself, lying back and covering her head with the pillow. She could not do this; could not allow herself to be so easily swayed by suggestion, particularly from people whose opinions were loathsome.

Marcy worried about Sasha. Not because of anything to do with Nizar, but because she was so highly strung, so fixated on following rules and colouring within the lines; because she worked too hard at school and ate too little. The perfectionism that had brought her academic success was unlikely to bring her joy in life; it might even prove a hindrance in her career. But these words of wisdom would, coming from Marcy, at best, fall on deaf ears; Sasha was likely to double down on her current strategy.

And Marcy was hardly in a position to lecture anyone about eating enough. Her own appetite had followed Neil out the door. She had shed so much weight she was now beneath the mythical target weight she'd chased for decades. Sadly, the effect wasn't the ethereal beauty she'd always envisaged. Her face was wan, possibly haggard; her breasts sagged; her bra cups were half-full of air.

Footsteps again. This time in the hall and then on the stairs. These were different, staccato, accompanied by the sliding sound of a small hand gripping too tightly to the rail: Jake. On the landing, he broke into a trot. Marcy felt the duvet lift, and a small, taut body slide in next to her, planting cold feet on her warm calves.

Never mind. She was glad to have him. Sure, he kicked and thrashed in his sleep and took up an outrageous amount of space relative to his size but, feet aside, he was a warm body. His presence was a buffer to the sadness and regret lying at the end of every chain of thought; it was a defence against the notion she had wasted her life.

He was so different from Sasha, shambolic and disorganised; happy go lucky, for the most part, although he had burst into tears earlier tonight, when she'd asked if he was prepared for tomorrow's dictation.

He was tired. Neil had picked him up at swimming today and taken him to dinner. It was nearly bedtime when they began ninety minutes of homework. The fatigue would roll into tomorrow and into the rest of the week. Marcy reached out and lightly ruffled her son's hair. He was already asleep, the way only children could. He sighed, mumbled something unintelligible and then flipped on to his belly.

Unless she was mistaken, his last night-time visit also occurred after he'd been with Neil. She wondered if she ought to start keeping a record of these visits. But to what end? Neil, he would say she was out to discredit him; it would become one more thing they bickered about, and that certainly wouldn't put Jake more at ease.

She babied him. She had done from the start, carrying him around in a sling for the first three months after an article she'd read suggested the closeness would boost his self-confidence. Her back had never been the same.

That was the way it was, wasn't it? You tried your best

as a mother, employing the best practices doctors recommended, only for future scientific research to reveal you'd been endangering them all along.

When she was pregnant with Sasha and Alec, doctors said eating peanuts could give them life-threatening allergies; by the time she was pregnant with Jake they said eating them was the best way for him to avoid developing an allergy to them.

Cot bumpers went from essential safety feature, to safety hazard. An occasional glass of wine, from harmless to borderline criminal.

She introduced solids at three months for Sasha, in accordance with her doctor's advice. When Alec came along, eighteen months later, the doctor said to hold off until four. And with Jake, solids were out of the question in the first six months. All from the same doctor. Her mother said she worried too much about such things.

'Christ, I smoked a pack a day when I was pregnant with you and drank a cocktail every night.'

'*Trésor*,' said Jake, clear as day, with a perfectly trilled *r*. He kicked her thigh and then pushed off it as he turned perpendicular.

Mothers always got blamed for any trouble or defect and yet, the older her children grew, the more convinced Marcy was that most of their character was baked in from the start. The personalities of each of her children had manifested themselves strongly and distinctively, from their first breaths. Sasha had been angry and petulant because she was not in control of her own birth. Jake had needed help turning. Alec slid out after four pushes. An infant Sasha wailed when left in her Moses basket, demanding attention. Alec would lie tranquilly, staring at the ceiling,

157

for the longest time, occasionally making small 'Eh, eh' sounds, like the clearing of a tiny throat.

'Sometimes, I forget he's here,' Neil had confessed.

Alec didn't make waves, gliding along with minimal exertion. In swimming lessons, one of the early tests is for the child to jump into the deep end of the pool and totally submerge. Sasha entered the water like a whirligig, arms and legs pinwheeling, fighting every inch of the way. When it was Alec's turn, he disappeared beneath the water with barely a ripple. Down, down he went and then – whoosh – he resurfaced. He was the goldilocks child, that just-right blend of scholarly acumen and creativity. Alec would always bob to the surface.

The footsteps again. What was Sasha doing up at this hour? Marcy hoped it wasn't more homework. That kid would do whatever was required to excel. At some point, she would come up against a problem that couldn't be solved by working longer and harder. What then? Sasha had never had to dust herself off and start again. She had no experience of failure. Marcy worried that, when the moment arrived, her daughter would crumble.

Neil

Neil slipped the microphone headset over the top of his skull while the techie, a skinny kid, dressed head to toe in black, clipped a battery pack on to the back pocket of his jeans. The opening notes of the Mahler symphony, soft and tremulous, reverberated in the glass and metal foyer of Marsh Inc's Europe, Middle East and Africa headquarters, where a temporary stage had been constructed for the big launch. The techie gave Neil a thumbs up. He looked about sixteen, a constellation of bright pink pimples dotting his pale chin. More and more, the world seemed to be run by adolescents. Neil's hand shook as he lifted his thumb in return. Three hours' sleep and twelve cups of coffee will do that, he thought, and then opened his mouth to explain. The kid shushed him, which would have been insulting enough, but the manner in which he did it – miming slitting a throat in a series of angry, authoritative motions – crossed a line.

'Now see here,' Neil said, stopping at the sound of his own voice booming through the hall. The kid shook his head and pointed to the mic. Mahler filled the silence, melancholic and suddenly full of foreboding.

He closed his eyes and went over the instructions from this morning's rehearsal: at the kid's cue – right after

Mahler hits crescendo – he was to stride through the curtain and to his mark, positioned slightly to the left of centre stage, face the audience, make a few brief remarks before introducing CEO Benny Marsh, who had flown over especially. Easy peasy lemon squeezy.

That crescendo was still a way off, more than three minutes in – three minutes, twenty-six seconds, was it? Twenty-eight? Forty-eight? He looked around for the Big Man, who had been touring the office since touching down in the company jet that morning. Benny Marsh loved glad-handing staff, everyone's buddy – 'How ya doing?' 'Good to see you!' – like a politician, albeit one with a very safe seat, who never had to worry about being re-elected. Neil had probably shaken his hand half a dozen times in his early years with the company. That sort of thing left an impression; a good one. The Benny Marsh Neil saw in meetings was less ebullient, easily bored, often irascible and prone to lash out at negative news. Nonetheless, Neil was proud the CEO knew his name.

Neil touched the earpiece; he touched the headset's band. The Mahler was stirring stuff, he had to admit, though absolutely the wrong choice for a theme song. Neil had requested something short, punchy and familiar, something people could sing along to. 'Born to Run' would have been perfect, though he conceded licencing would likely be exorbitant. The Mahler was beautiful – complex, haunting, romantic; but nothing about it said, 'streamlining information across countries and platforms'. As with so much related to Vision 360, the theme song seemed to over-promise, lifting expectations beyond that which a suite of software – however interactive and 'postmodern', whatever that meant – could deliver.

'It's the cogs and wheels that make the clock hands turn,' he explained, arguing for a lower-key celebration. 'The best possible outcome is if nobody notices it's there.'

'All the more reason to make a big splash,' Marco said. 'It would be a shame not to get credit after all your hard work.'

Yeah, sure, Marco, Neil thought.

Neil saw now that the die had been cast from the beginning. If not Vision 360, they would have invented something else to launch: the Big Man was coming to town, Monsieur G wanted a show.

No expense was spared. A media company was brought in to design and build a stage with a countdown clock, and an enormous, glittery, game-show-sized model of a switch for Benny Marsh to 'throw', putting the system officially online, and a pair of confetti canons to shower the audience and stage with glitter and bits of coloured paper.

'If you're not comfortable with the role of emcee,' Monsieur G said, 'I'm sure Marco would be willing to step in.'

Neil was sure Marco would be, but Neil was not going to let that happen, which was why, despite his misgivings and the knowledge he was not a natural public speaker, he stood behind the black velvet curtain, caffeine pumping through his veins, preparing to step out on to the stage.

He was hollow with fatigue. The past two weeks were an insane scramble to make up the delays that had beset the programme from the start. Neil had asked for the ceremony to be pushed back a week – Vision 360 was already three months behind, what was another week? But that would interfere with the Marsh family's annual visit to their ski lodge near Whistler. Neil and his team worked feverishly, eighteen-hour days to get the job done, but Monsieur G seemed more excited about the organic olive oil Marco had sourced from Tuscany to go in the commemorative gift bags along with the company-branded notepads, pens and memory sticks. 'I want something European,' he'd said, 'something that isn't chocolate.' Marco got a small-batch producer to label three hundred bottles with the Marsh Enterprises logo.

'Because Vision 360 is the grease for the wheels and the cogs that keep the clock running,' Marco announced, smiling smugly.

Neil would bet anything the oil producer was a friend of Marco, if not a relative. A knot formed in Neil's gut. Fucking Marco.

Next thing he knew the techie was frantically signalling 'go'. Neil rushed through the curtain, Mahler hitting crescendo, all minor chords and doom.

'Ackk,' he said, clearing a sudden tickle from his throat. 'Ladies and gentlemen,' he croaked, as the muscles in his throat contracted and his eyes watered. 'European country managers, friends, honoured guests . . .'

The heat from the lights overhead warmed the top of his forehead. Had they been this hot at rehearsal? The collar of his mock turtleneck was constricting. He couldn't see the audience beyond the blinding lights; couldn't tell how they were reacting.

'We know that the world is becoming more integrated. And here at Marsh Enterprises, we have planned for an integrated future in which we integrate data across multiple touchpoints.'

*Shit. Too many integrate*s.

'We're future-proofing our business model to retain our competitiveness.'

So much bullshit. Neil licked his lips and swallowed. Both actions were picked up by the mic. In need of a friendly face, he searched for Chloé in the shadows. With all the work on, they'd hardly seen one another outside the office in three weeks. He spotted her four or five rows back, in the middle and tried to make eye contact. She was leaning towards Joe from the Dusseldorf office.

'Vision 360, the culmination of eighteen months of work that will transform the way we do business—'

He shifted into the sales pitch he had been giving for months:

'Seamlessly integrating forecasting,' blah, blah, blah, 'vital parts of our business', blah, blah, blah, 'advanced integration', blah, blah, blah, 'three dozen countries', blah, blah, blah, 'twenty-three languages', blah, blah, blah. 'For whatever—'

He was rounding the final corner, bringing it home, when he saw Chloé's head dip, the white of her mobile screen refract in the lenses of her glasses. She was on her phone!

During an over-long pause, he fiddled with his wedding ring while his brain raced through the major touch points: future-proof, seamlessly integrating . . . oh, yes.

'For whatever the future has in store.'

After another short, torturous silence, the crowd applauded.

'And now, it gives me great pleasure to introduce to you today the man without whom this great enterprise would not be possible. He is the grandson of our founder, the son of the man who launched us into Europe. The man *Forbes Magazine* recently named one of the twenty most important innovators. Ladies and gentlemen, all the way from Wisconsin, our CEO, Mr Benny Marsh.'

They played more Mahler as Benny Marsh strutted on to the stage, pumping his fists like a prize fighter.

'Is this guy wonderful or is he wonderful, huh?' he asked the crowd, as the music faded out. 'How about we give a nice round of applause for Nigel, here?'

There were a few nervous titters, an audible gasp or two and then the applause began. Benny Marsh walked back and forth across the stage like a caged animal, or someone who'd just done a line or two of cocaine.

'Last week I was talking to G on the phone, I said, "G, the US has been up two weeks already. What's wrong with Europe?" and he says, "Benny, you've got to be patient. Things in Europe move a little slower than they do in the US." I says, "Asia is going to be up soon, too." He says, "We do things differently, over here. We like our holidays; like our thirty-five-hour workweeks. Europe," he tells me,' and he stopped pacing and faced the audience, '"is like a fine wine." And I says, "G, I don't got to be patient. I didn't get rich being patient." And he says—'

The wild, rambling tangent that followed began with the day he took over the family business, jumped back to his childhood in 1950s Detroit, forward to Reagan during the Cold War before somehow arriving back at the present day, the beauty of 'this project', the brilliance of its design, which, incidentally, was his idea, and how it was going to lift the company to greater heights. Neil stood on the stage, wooden and mute, a pathetic Steve Jobs wannabe in a mock turtleneck, trainers and shapeless dad jeans. Benny Marsh gamely tugged on the switch with both hands, pretending it took great strength, and smiling with boyish delight when the canons exploded. Mahler returned. Benny threw an arm over Neil's shoulder.

'Come on, Nigel,' he said, and together, arm and arm, they left the stage.

Neil never considered not going to his parents for Christmas. It was his mother's favourite holiday. Her plum pudding was the best. She made it after breakfast on Christmas Eve. Everyone took a turn stirring the batter for good luck. It steamed all day in the Aga, infusing the house with holiday spices.

Neil hadn't missed a year, though some years he went more gladly than others. They'd almost skipped the Christmas when Marcy was pregnant with Jake, deciding to chance it at the last minute, packing a bag with Marcy's prenatal records and registering the route between his parents' and the central maternity hospital on the sat nav, just in case. In the end they'd had a wonderful visit and made it back to Brussels with a week to spare before Marcy's waters broke.

After the strain of getting Vision 360 off the ground, he was looking forward to the country air and his mother's cooking.

It was going to be a brief visit, just three days instead of the usual ten; shorter than he wanted, but Marcy deserved a chance to celebrate Christmas with the children. She could have put the kibosh on his trip, if she'd wanted, or made demands in exchange. She hadn't. In fact, she acquiesced so readily he wondered how much further he could have pushed it. Might a request for the whole two weeks have earned the same distracted nod? The same, airy, sing-songy, 'All right'? But his conscience would not permit him to take advantage of her passivity; besides, he wanted to spend New Year's with Chloé.

The mid-afternoon sky was a pink-infused grey as his car joined the river of red tail lights, three lanes wide, bound for Calais. Sasha was in the passenger seat, head nodding gently to the rhythm piped in through her earbuds: physically present, but in all other respects a million miles away. Jake had the back to himself. Until the last minute, Neil had held out hope that Alec would join them. It seemed logical that any sixteen-year-old boy would prefer to spend Christmas in the English countryside with people who loved him than at a refugee centre with a bunch of strangers, but Alec had his pride to consider. May it bring him comfort, Neil thought, come Christmas Day, when he was spooning mashed potatoes out of a tray with an ice cream scoop.

The drive from Brussels to Somerset was eight hours in the best of conditions which, two days before Christmas, they were never going to get. Thankfully, Neil had an onboard entertainment system in his car and the complete works of Pixar in his glove box. He reckoned he could have driven to Inverness before Jake got bored or restless. Whoever it was who'd thought of imbedding television screens in the back of headrests deserved a Nobel Peace Prize. If only they'd been around when Alec and Sasha were younger and quarrelling about who was encroaching on who's space; who held claim to the last fruit roll-up, the last Lu biscuit, while Jake, a toddler, kicked continuously at the back of Neil's chair. Neil became adept at tuning it out but there was one time on the way to the South of France when they'd kept it up for a hundred kilometres. He had lost his cool and started issuing threats about turning the car around.

He reached across and tapped Sasha on the shoulder; waited for her to unplug an earphone and look at him.

'Remember that time I threatened to turn the car around? You and Alec were fighting.'

'Which time?'

'What do you mean, which time? I only did it once. Jake was kicking my seat.'

'You did it all the time.'

'No, I didn't.'

'Okay,' she said. 'If you say so.'

But it was only the once. He was sure of it. He remembered the moment distinctly, his patience wearing progressively thinner as he focused on the road while his ears and body were repeatedly assaulted. Marcy had tried to calm everyone down with a game of I Spy. It was the arrhythmia of the kicks that had sent him over the edge. The sourness after his explosion had lingered for the rest of the journey, though that night, in the master bedroom of the dreadful house they'd rented, with a too-soft mattress that made them roll towards one another, they had giggled over it: the emptiness of his threats; the chirpy faux-enthusiasm in Marcy's voice:

'I spy with my little eye something beginning with T.'

He chuckled thinking of it now. He turned again towards Sasha. She was staring ahead at the road, the earbuds back in her ears. He glanced at his rear-view mirror and tried to make eye contact with Jake.

'You okay, old chap?'

His son stared at the screen, eyes wide, lips open part way, skin tinted an unearthly iridescent blue-white.

'Don't forget to blink,' he said. Jake didn't respond.

Was a little connection too much to ask? He was reduced to the role of chauffeur. Better to be ignored than kicked in the back, he thought. In the silence, Alec's absence was all the more noticeable.

Knowing how attached Alec was to his grandparents, particularly his granddad, Neil had assumed the threat to stay home was an empty one. He'd done what any sensible parent of an adolescent does: called his bluff. And now his family was splintered. At Christmas.

Of course, these things are inevitable when a couple separates. Neil saw now that he hadn't given the matter enough thought, preferring to focus on a more appealing – and ultimately fantastical – notion that Chloé would be joining them, and that her first impression of his home village would be of it sparkling under hoar-frost or a dusting of snow, the morning mist rising, the old pub all cosy and welcoming, a fire crackling in its great stone fireplace. He had looked forward to sharing with her the awesome majesty of the carol service at the cathedral in Wells and his mum's plum pudding.

Foolish optimism. He'd known since at least mid-July that EEFS would miss the deadline, and with Christmas falling on a Thursday, it was always unlikely they'd arrive in Somerset in time for the carol service, which was held a few days before.

Neil had expected elation, post-rollout – liberation at last! – instead, there was only exhaustion.

'So,' he said, driving Chloé back to her car after the launch party.

'So,' she said.

He had invited her to stay the night but was relieved

when she said she had to get home to Aurélie. Had she stayed, there would have been an expectation of sex and he didn't have the energy for it. *This is it*, he thought, eyeballs stinging with every blink as they made their way through the tunnels on Avenue Louise. He would introduce her to his children, and he would meet her parents, extended family, and eventually (gulp) Jérôme. This was the moment they'd been waiting for, what they'd been working towards all these months.

'No more trips to Nijmegen,' he said.

'Thank God,' she replied.

'It'll be good to get back into a normal rhythm.'

'Yes,' she agreed, repressing a yawn.

'If I can remember what that is,' he joked.

She laughed, but not one of her spontaneous laughs.

'For all that other stuff, you know, the us-moving-in-together stuff, the big decisions stuff,' he said, 'all that can wait until after the holidays.'

'There is no rush,' she agreed, a bit too readily.

'I mean, we know what we want, right?'

'Absolutely.'

'And that's to be together.'

'Of course.'

He ought to have left it at that, and he probably would have if not for the way, before answering, she'd hesitated. Not long, a fraction of a moment, a micro-moment. Long enough.

'So, what do you reckon we aim to have it all sorted by February?'

'Why do you do that?' she asked. 'Always pushing?'

'I'm not pushing,' he replied. 'I don't push.'

'We just agreed we would take our time.'

'It isn't pushing to set a timeline—'

'Can't we just have a minute—' It was dark inside the car, but he could tell she was twisting her mouth that way she did when annoyed.

'A very *rough* timeline,' he clarified. 'It could even be March.'

He was just tossing it out there and, for God's sake, March was months away, a quarter of a year. She inhaled sharply and then exhaled slowly. It reminded him of the count-to-ten trick Marcy had employed when the kids were little and drove her around the bend.

'Where will Aurélie sleep?' she asked, finally.

Aurélie, of course. Where else would she go? Thoughts of Aurélie triggered flashbacks of his own children's toddlerhoods. It might be more apt to say feelings, because he felt them in his shoulders, neck and arms before his brain summoned specific examples of Jake padding down the stairs for a beaker of water, a cracker, or because he heard a noise, but really because he hated going to bed before everyone else; of reading *We're Going on a Bear Hunt* to Alec for the one-thousand-and-seventh time; rooting through bags, under sofas and between cushions for Blue Elephant, Patchwork Octopus, or Squeaky Lion for Sasha. There was sweetness in all these memories, and yet, the truth was that young children had a way of sucking up all the energy around them. They dictated the agenda, not in a bad or malicious way, but because they were needy and relatively helpless. He was sure Aurélie was a wonderful, charming little girl, but he'd already had three rides on that particular carousel and that was plenty.

He glanced over at Chloé when they were stopped at a light. That smooth, untroubled forehead, a merest trace of crinkles at the corners of her eyes, and only when she smiled. She was so young. Was is possible she'd want more children? She had never said so, but nor had they discussed it. Not really.

'Better to get things right,' he agreed.

He was almost fifty.

'Exactly,' she said.

'I'm sorry you have to spend Christmas with your in-laws.'

'I am not looking forward to it, believe me,' she said, with another twist of the mouth, 'but it will be good for Aurélie.'

'Next year you two will come with us.'

And there it was again, that same split-second of hesitation before she smiled and said, 'Yes. Of course.'

'I'm hungry,' Jake announced. The film had finished. 'What is there for snacks.'

'Err,' said Neil. There had been so many things to remember: the train reservation, the passports, the pounds sterling left over from his last trip, the chargers and plug adaptors for various electronic gadgets, the case of Belgian beer – a sampler of different brands – wine for Christmas dinner, chocolates, of course, and the biscuits his father liked, presents for Sasha and Jake, his parents, his brother, his sister-in-law and their two children – who were spending Christmas at her parents in Scotland, this year, and so wouldn't even be there – DVDs for the trip, the European Health Insurance Cards, even Jake's inhaler – the boy hadn't had an asthma attack for years, but why risk it? – all these he'd remembered.

'I've got mints,' he offered.

'You didn't bring any snacks?' Sasha asked. It was remarkable what children heard and didn't hear through their earbuds.

'We'll get something in the terminal.'

'How far is that?' Jake asked.

'Coming up to it now, old chap. Right around the corner.'

'I want a Mediterranean bowl,' Sasha said.

'Fried chicken,' said Jake.

'There's no reason we can't get both,' Neil said. 'There's plenty of time.'

'Can I watch another video?' Jake asked.

'Darling, we're nearly there.'

'Can I, though?'

'Only a few minutes more.'

'Can I?'

'Fine, Sasha, would you mind?'

'*The Incredibles*,' Jake called.

Sasha swapped out the DVD and opened the twelve-disc container. '*Toy Story 2*?' she called, flipping through the discs, '*Monsters University?*'

'We'll be through in two ticks,' Neil said.

'*The Incredibles*,' Jake repeated.

'You'll barely get through the opening credits,' Neil warned, just as the car in front of him braked. The queue for check-in extended far beyond the corral built to contain it.

'What's happening?' Sasha asked.

'Must be extra security,' Neil said. As soon as the words were out of his mouth, it made perfect sense. He was glad he'd left a bit of extra time. 'And that's a good thing.'

They advanced in car-length increments, with the car's stop-start system switching off the engine in between.

Stop-start, stop-start. Neil said a silent prayer of thanks-giving for the gift of rear-seat entertainment. *The Incredibles* was halfway done by the time they reached the check-in window. They then proceeded on to a second queue for security. They were inspecting every vehicle. A white Vauxhall Corsa up ahead appeared to have been selected for extra scrutiny. Officers were conducting internal inspec-tions in the front and back seats, a third was lifting the carpet in the boot, testing the area beneath it. The car's contents were stacked on the ground not far from it. It was an impressive load relative to the car's size: luggage and shopping bags, cartons of cigarettes, dried fruits, cases of fizzy drinks. A trio of brown-skinned men stood a short distance away, smoking cigarettes and shuffling their feet in the cool night air, their blousy shalwar kameezes hanging below thinly insulated black nylon winter jackets. An officer beckoned Neil forward into a square outlined in yellow paint on the pavement. He tapped on the car boot; Neil released the catch. The officer flashed a torch around the suitcases and bags that Neil had rearranged numerous times to make them fit. The officer took a swab of the upholstery with a handheld, electronic device and then went off, presumably to have it tested, leaving the top open and cool air blowing in on them. Another officer circled with a mirror attached to a long pole, inspecting beneath the car. When he was done, he waited, arms crossed on the pole, for his co-worker, who returned with a slip of paper whipping in the wind. Neil held his breath as the pair huddled in consultation. Over by the Corsa, the men continued to smoke and shuffle their feet as a female secu-rity officer went through a large suitcase. Neil looked at the dashboard clock. He imagined the contents of his car spilt out on to the concourse and then having to fit it all back in again when the inspection was done, in front of a large, impatient audience. The boot closed shut with a *thunk*. The officer in front waved him on. A grateful Neil thanked the officer effusively.

'Why are you thanking him?' Sasha asked.

'Just being polite,' he replied. 'Right, who wants some food?'

But when they got to the roundabout, an attendant waved them instead towards the trains.

Sasha was upset.

'I've no choice, darling,' Neil said, following instructions. 'If we miss our train, we'll lose our slot.'

'But what will we eat?'

'There'll be food on the other side, I'm sure.'

'Will they have Mediterranean bowls?'

'I don't know, darling. We'll see.'

They were held in a queue for half an hour before being allowed to board, and then forty minutes inside a car inside a train inside a tunnel: Neil and two hungry, disgruntled offspring.

'Would you have been happier if I'd brought snacks but forgotten your presents?' he snapped at Sasha at one point.

'That's a false equivalency,' she replied. 'It's not as if you had to choose.'

The tension built throughout the trip and then, just as they announced the train was approaching the station, Jake burst into tears.

'Sasha, help him,' Neil said. He tried to offer soothing words from the driver's seat. Jake bawled throughout the off-loading, the drive along the slip road, and out on to the motorway.

'*Mais arrêtes*, Jake,' Sasha cried, sounding a touch hysterical, herself, '*ça suffit*!'

Jake, however, was beyond reason. Only exhaustion would stop him now. Neil tried to block it out. He needed to concentrate on driving. Operating a left-sided car on UK roads always took a little adjusting. Traffic on this side of the Channel was no lighter than it had been on the other side. A steady rain demanded yet more attention. It was a very long ten miles to the first motorway service centre, where Neil bought ham and cheese sandwiches – the best of the tired remnants of the day's selection. By then Jake was no longer crying, merely snuffling each time he inhaled.

'The lettuce and tomato are *dégeulasse*,' Sasha declared. 'The buns are soggy. Eew.'

True on both counts and yet Neil was offended. He had overpaid for them, throwing in a large bag of crisps and a family-sized packet of bourbon cream biscuits as a gesture of goodwill. He would be digging crumbs out of the back seat for weeks. Not a word of thanks.

'If you lot don't cut the crap,' he thundered, 'I'll turn this car around.'

He was awfully glad neither child called his bluff. Sasha put another film on for Jake and then returned to her phone. Jake's snuffles gradually calmed. Neil tuned in to Radio Four. The familiar format and tone were comforting, until the weight of the subject-matter started to accumulate. Civil war in Syria, migrants drowning in the Mediterranean, terrorists using cars as weapons of mass destruction, austerity cuts, a double-dip recession: an unbroken string of doom and gloom from Folkstone until he left the A303, just past Stonehenge.

The darkness of the regional roads was its own challenge. The windscreen wipers thumped out an allegretto. Even at their quickest setting, they had trouble clearing the rain from the windscreen. Neil looked to the cat's eyes in the middle of the road for guidance. Radio Four moved on to female-genital mutilation, regional flooding and, finally, for lightness, Neil supposed, a review of a novel about three friends on a gap year in Thailand who get mixed up in human trafficking. It was as if the producers were vying to see who could bring their listeners down the hardest before the holiday. The car's headlights reflecting off the wet leaves of the hedgerows made the road appear even narrower.

But, oh, how wonderful to wake up the next morning to robins' song instead of car alarms and bleating sheep instead of bleating horns; in bed sheets that had spent time in the airing cupboard. A fresh pot of coffee awaited him in the kitchen. There was brown toast with thick-cut marmalade and lots of butter and his mother, in front of the Aga, asking how he wanted his eggs. As if she had to ask! His mother's fried eggs were the standard to which all other eggs were measured: the yolks deliciously runny, the whites fluffy, without a hint of gag-inducing, uncooked goo. This was just what he needed.

'The kids up?' he asked.

'Jake had some cereal, just now,' his mum said. 'He's off watching the cartoons. Sasha took a coffee back to her room.'

'Says she's got studying to do,' his father, added. He was at the kitchen table, standing, reading the newspaper spread flat in front of him. 'If you can believe that. First day of her holiday.'

'Bless her,' said his mum.

'She's a studious girl,' Neil said, stretching his arms, giving his shoulders a scratch.

'Awfully thin,' his mother said.

'Ah, she's all right,' Neil said. 'What time are we making the Christmas pudding?'

'Oh, a bit later, I expect,' his mother said.

'I thought we agreed we weren't going to do a big hulla-baloo?' his father said.

'But it's tradition,' Neil said.

'Jimmy, see what dried fruits we've got in the larder.'

His parents exchanged looks.

'Jimmy, if you don't get the dried fruits from the larder, I'll get them myself.'

His father strode off to the larder, returning moments later holding a few mostly empty bags.

'That looks like plenty of currants, but we'll need more raisins,' Denny said. 'No cherries?'

'This was all I found.'

'Were there ground almonds?'

'I didn't see any.'

'We'll have to go to the shops after breakfast.'

'Today? You've got to be kidding. It'll be a right palaver.'

'I'll go,' Neil said.

'I bought a pudding last week,' James said. 'One of those celebrity chefs. Got a whole orange baked into the centre.' Debate closed, he returned to his newspaper.

Neil's heart sank. He looked out at the breezy, yellow morning. 'Then I think I'll head out for a walk.'

His father turned a page of the newspaper. 'Going to rain, they say.'

'Oh, dear,' his mother cried, in a tone that suggested calamity. 'I've broken the yolks!'

'Don't worry,' his father said.

'I'm sure they'll be fine, Mum,' said Neil, because he didn't want her to feel bad, though he was a bit disappointed.

'No, no, they're ruined!' she shouted, with an intensity of feeling that was most unlike her and wholly disproportionate to the situation.

'It's all right, love' his father said, patient, soothing, as if her overreaction was the most normal thing ever.

His mother lifted the frying pan off the burner. It shook and swayed in her hand and then bumped hard against the stovetop. His father leapt to her side.

'I've got it, James,' she shouted.

'Of course you do, darling,' he replied, taking hold of the handle and steadying it.

'You're always in the way,' she said.

'Guilty as charged.'

She scraped, clumsily, at the pan with a faded old spatula. 'They've all come apart!'

'It's fine, darling,' he said. 'Tastes the same, either way.'

'No!' she cried, throwing down her hands in frustration much as Jake did at the start of a tantrum, before he outgrew them. 'You've interfered and now it's all a mess.'

'My fault entirely, Denny darling,' his father said. 'How can I help?'

'Fetch the bacon and sausages in the top right door,' she snapped.

Neil rose out of his chair. 'I'm happy to—'

'Sit,' she commanded, her back still turned to him. Neil sat back down. 'Mushrooms and tomatoes are in the next one up.'

His father opened and closed the Aga doors, spooning

and forking things on to a plate. His mother stood slightly apart, staring at her left hand, turning it one way and then another, as if it were a curiosity and not part of her body.

'There you are, see?' his father said. 'Everything right as rain.' He slid the plate in front of Neil. The eggs were a half-cooked jumble of chunks and goo.

'Looks delicious,' Neil lied. It looked like something a person with lung disease might cough up.

'It's revolting,' Denny said, still staring at her hand. 'It's horrid.'

Neil searched for one of the better cooked pieces, scraped transparent goo off its top and, popped it in his mouth.

'Mmm,' he said, pursing his lips together, locking down the gag reflex.

'Derek and Lisa all right?' he asked, convinced a change of subject would be welcome to all.

'Right as rain,' his father said. 'I wonder you two don't keep in touch more.'

'We do sometimes,' Neil said. Perfunctory emails and texts exchanged at birthdays and other special occasions. 'He's busy, I know.'

'I think I'll have a lie down,' his mother announced in a voice that was suddenly, harrowingly quiet.

'Darling, I'll—' said his father, rushing to her side.

'No,' she snapped. 'I can make my own way, James.'

'Of course, Denny.'

She moved slowly towards the doorway, left foot dragging along the floor and then rising into the air on each step. His father followed behind, at a distance, vigilant, arms out to catch her if she stumbled.

'I know you're there, James,' she said.

'I left my glasses in the bedroom, I've just realised.'

When they were out of sight Neil scraped the eggs into the food waste bin. He sliced a thick piece of bread and then toasted it on the top of the Aga. He spied a stack of store-bought mince pies and, on the far side of the room, tucked behind a door, a wheelchair.

His father came back into the kitchen a few minutes later and poured himself more coffee.

'Top up?' he asked.

'Cheers, yeah,' Neil replied.

His father returned to his newspaper.

Neil watched him while buttering the toast and spooning on marmalade. He wasn't hungry any more, just going through the motions. Why hadn't he been told any of this? He wanted to ask but he never knew how to begin with his father. His mother liked to say they didn't speak one another's language.

'Dad?'

'Hmm?' his father said, eyes on his paper.

Neil drew a deep breath, opened his mouth:

'Mind if I have a section of the paper?'

'Take what you like, only leave me the sport.'

The sport, of course. His father loved all sport; rugby above all. He was president emeritus of the local club, a popular presence on the touchline. His portrait hung on the clubhouse wall and the trophy awarded to the best all-round player bore his name. Neil's mediocrity at the game might have passed unremarked if not for whose son he was, whose brother, too. Derek, two years younger, had been a standout.

Neil reached across and took the Saturday section because it was nearest.

'Tummy Slimming Exercises for 40-Plus,' his father read aloud. 'Well, there you have it.'

'There are walks and weekend getaways, too,' Neil replied – although, truth be told, the cover story was what had caught his attention. A small podge around his middle was of increasing concern. 'The best wines . . .'

'Hmm, and a sex column, as well,' his father added, 'if memory serves.'

How Marcy would have laughed at them both. He could hear her now:

'Nope, no elephant in this room. Not under the kitchen table, not behind the door. Why always the elaborate dance? Why can't you get to the point?' As far as she was concerned, there were no boundaries. 'We ask because we're *fam-i-ly*,' she'd say. 'We ask because we care.'

Which, Neil would argue, was every bit as good a reason to *not* ask. No need to mortify one's nearest and dearest. She would have interrogated James before he had both feet back in the kitchen and he would have allowed it, too. Her directness disarmed and charmed him.

'You Yanks,' he'd say. 'Always saying what you mean and meaning what you say. There's just no understanding you.'

'I'm sorry, Dad,' Neil said, the words coming in a rush before his courage failed him. 'I had no idea.'

'No idea of what, dear boy?'

'That things were this bad. You said everything was under control.'

'Everything is under control,' his father said, giving the newspaper a snap.

'Mom seems—' He knew he must choose his words carefully. 'Well, she's not exactly herself.'

'She gets frustrated. You would too, believe me.'

'Of course.'

'She was up too late last night, waiting for you lot, and then insisted on getting up to cook a proper breakfast,' he said. 'It's always worse when she exerts herself.'

'What are the indications for things, going forward, I mean? Have the doctors said?'

'She keeps up her exercises, eats right, needs to avoid overdoing it. And that is all there is to it.' He put down the newspaper and walked over to the dishwasher and started to unload it.

Neil nibbled at a corner of toast. 'I noticed the wheelchair,' he said.

'Oh, that.' His father sighed, withdrawing the cutlery basket and carrying it over to the drawer. 'We take it on shopping trips, anywhere she'll be on her feet for a long time. She hates it but, you know, eventually—'

'What can I do?' Neil asked.

'Nothing,' his father snapped. 'There is nothing to be done. We just have to live with it. Make accommodations.'

'I'm sorry, Dad. This has to be hard for you.' Neil tore off a piece of toast and played with it. 'You're in such good health, yourself. You didn't sign up for any of this.'

'Mind your words, son,' his father replied in that tone that made Neil sit up straighter. 'This is precisely what I signed up for.' The dinner plates clattered as he placed them in the cupboard.

'I didn't mean to suggest—'

'Going on fifty-two years, now,' he said, coolly. 'A damn good bargain, far as I can tell.'

His father returned the pots, pans and associated lids to their proper places with brusque, angry efficiency. Neil pushed away the toast and stared at the illustrations of the exercises in the Saturday section as if they were the most interesting things in the world. His face burned. Rain started to fall on the roof overhead; a few drops at first and then louder, sustained.

'Ah,' said his father. 'Right on schedule.'

It turned out to be only a passing shower. When it cleared, Neil put on his old wellies, took the knock-off Barbour from the peg in the mud room, slipped his phone into a pocket and headed out the back, through a kissing gate at the bottom of the garden and started climbing the hill behind it. Phone reception was rubbish at his parents' house.

He hadn't spoken to Chloé since he'd left Brussels. They kept missing one another. Their text correspondence looked something like this:

Arrived at last
Relieved to hear it.
xox
xx
Can u talk?
I'm wrapping gifts
. . . preparing lunch
. . . sitting down to eat
. . . putting Aurélie down for a nap
Later?

The hill was steeper than he recalled. The weather didn't help. The air was humid and far too warm for Christmas. He was soon huffing and overheating, so much that he had to pause part way up. What had happened to him? He recalled sprinting up the previous year, heart pounding, yes, but mostly in anticipation of hearing Chloé's voice. The view from the top had been achingly beautiful: the cloud-shaped silhouettes on the flat patchwork fields and grassy hillocks that stretched to the Bristol Channel.

'You should see it,' he had told Chloé. 'Honestly, I'm almost in tears.' The photos he took to show her didn't do it justice.

This year, a wall of cloud blotted out most of the prospect. In the drab light, even the grass seemed grey. Chloé's phone went straight to voicemail. He left a friendly message.

'It's me; just want to say Happy Christmas. No need to call. I'll try again tomorrow.'

It was probably just as well he'd missed her, he thought glumly. Lately all their conversations drifted in unpleasant directions. He did think it rather odd she hadn't picked up. He had texted before leaving the house. The previous year, she had been waiting by the phone and was nearly as breathless, without having climbed a hill.

He took the path that led down the other side and came out near the pub, trudging with heavy feet. Must not read too much into things. Last year, their relationship had been in its heady early days. Such intensity of passion could not possibly be maintained. No one would get anything done. They had been through a lot, lately, what with the launch, and of course Paris. All would be well once he got back to Brussels.

There was no fire blazing at the pub; too warm for it, but there were red tinsel garlands and gold plastic bells, and an artificial Christmas tree with twinkle lights and beer coasters tied to the branches with bright bits of ribbon. A group of men played darts at the far end of the room.

Neil almost tripped over a black and white spaniel standing next to his master.

'Well, look who the cat dragged in,' a voice called from the end of the bar, nearer the darts. 'If it isn't Neil Yardley!'

A large man, with a ruddy, weathered face was looking at Neil and laughing. Neil peered across the bar, his mind was blank, and then, like a gumball falling out of a machine, a name dropped on to his tongue:

'Trevor Holler?'

Trevor smiled, and Neil exhaled.

'A pint for my old friend Neil, here, Hamish, if you will,' Trevor called to the young barman.

They had been together at the village primary school, which was so small it had only one class for each year, and sometimes those classes were very small. Contrary to what Trevor said to Hamish the barman, they had never been particularly friendly, even less so when they moved on to secondary. His father had a dairy farm, down the road a way. Neil recalled Trevor driving to the year-ten leaver's ball in a tractor – one of several farmers' sons who had done so. Their picture was printed on the front page of the local newspaper.

'Haven't seen you for donkey's years,' Trevor said, making room for Neil to stand.

'Cheers,' Neil said, accepting the pint of bitter from Hamish.

Neil and Trevor traded a few self-deprecating comments about their respective girths, Trevor's being the more impressive, and the greyness of each other's hair or lack thereof.

Trevor held the pint glass to his lips and took a noisy slurp of cider.

'Where you residing these days, Old Neil?'

'Brussels,' Neil replied, taking a swig from his own glass. He was wary without knowing why. Old time's sake, perhaps. Back in secondary, Trevor had ridden in the back of the bus, cracking jokes with the lads. Some of those jokes, Neil was sure, had been about him, sat up front to minimise the motion sickness.

'Ah,' he said. 'Europe's most boring country, innit?'

'According to the English,' Neil replied.

'Never been there, myself. Is it nice?'

'It's all right,' Neil said, wary. 'It's a city. There's traffic and people.'

'Doesn't smell of shite, neither, I bet.'

'Mostly not, no,' Neil agreed, with a chuckle. His mouth filled with the sour taste of hops. He'd missed it. 'Lots of Eurocrats, though.'

'Whatcha think, are we going to have a referendum?'

'Don't know if Cameron can avoid one,' Neil said. 'He promised.'

'Suppose you're right.' Trevor paused for a swallow of cider. 'Which way you think it'll go?'

'Can't imagine us leaving,' Neil said.

'I wouldn't be so sure.'

'It would be terrible for your business.'

'Don't get me wrong,' Trevor said. 'I believe we should stay. Only there's a lot of folk who think we'd be better off on our own.'

They took a few swallows, elbows on the bar.

'You'll vote to stay in, I expect,' Trevor said, finally.

'If I'm allowed,' Neil replied. 'I couldn't vote in the last general.'

'That so?'

Neil nodded. 'They strike you from the register after fifteen years away.'

'Hmm,' Trevor said, resting his other elbows on the bar. 'Didn't know that. Mind you, seems fair enough.'

'How is it fair?'

'Well, you're not living here, are you? Don't pay taxes here. Don't see why you should still get a say in what happens.'

'I might have to come back if we vote leave.'

Trevor laughed. 'You might at that.' He took another slow swallow and placed his empty glass on the bar. 'Mind you. Probably won't come to that.'

'No, probably not.'

'You'll have another, Trevor?' the barman called out.

'I will, Hamish.'

The barman had already pulled the tap in anticipation.

'Let me get it,' Neil said, when Hamish came with fresh pints.

'Much obliged,' Trevor said. 'To your health.'

'And yours.'

Trevor tilted the glass back. When he righted it again, a third of the pint had disappeared.

'Didn't I hear you married an American?' he asked.

'That's right, yes.'

'Well, that's you sorted, isn't it? You can go off to America if we vote to leave. Would have thought you'd have shoved off a long time ago.'

'Me too.'

'Why didn't you, then?'

'Dunno. The opportunity didn't come up.' The inside of his mouth was lined with bitter. He smacked his lips. 'Anyway, we're separated now.'

'Ah, crumbs, I'm sorry to hear that.'

Funnily enough, he sounded as if he genuinely was.

'Kids?' Trevor asked.

'Three,' said Neil.

Trevor shook his head. 'It's rough on the kids, isn't it?'

Neil nodded. 'Sometimes, though, it just doesn't work out, does it? It's not anyone's fault. Couples grow apart.' Why was he saying this stuff to Trevor Holler, of all people?

'We expect a lot from marriage, these days, don't we?' Trevor said. 'I don't imagine any of us can live up to it. I know I didn't.'

'You and your wife split up?' Neil asked, unable to think of Trevor's wife's name, if he'd ever known it.

'Nah, my Sandy passed away. Last spring, it was.'

'I'm so sorry. I had no idea,' Neil said.

'No, I don't suppose you would have. It was quick,' he said, taking a large swallow. 'Brain cancer, it was. They said a year, maybe eighteen months. She lasted three days, poor lass. Your parents came to the funeral. It was very good of them.'

Neil had a vague recollection of a phone call with his mother, half-listening as she droned on about the death of a young woman whose name meant nothing to him. The suddenness of it, and how nobody had known. God, he was such an arsehole.

Trevor stared into his glass. 'Was a blessing, I suppose. Hardly time enough to brood or suffer.' He swallowed the remaining third of cider in one. 'Well, Yardley, I'd best be getting back to me girls.'

'Of course,' Neil said. 'How old are they now?'

Trevor gave a great laugh. 'Talking about me cows, eejit, aren't I? Got to get on with the afternoon milking. Sandy and me, we never had kids.'

Denny woke mid-afternoon, stiff and in need of her husband's help to get moving and do her exercises. There was no time to cook the roast she'd planned, let alone the plum pudding.

'I've got these lattice beef burger things in the freezer,' his father said. 'They're quite tasty.'

'Of course,' Neil said. 'Whatever suits.' It shamed him that his first thought had been for the implications on their luck in the new year without a turn stirring the batter.

They had mozzarella in them, the beef burgers, and a tapenade of sundried tomatoes and his father opened a bag of chunky frozen vegetables.

'So,' his mother said, 'Alec didn't come in the end.'

'No,' Neil said. 'I told you he wouldn't.'

'I thought he might have a change of heart,' his father said.

'He and Marcy are spending Christmas at a refugee centre,' Neil tried to explain. His father's remark annoyed him, even though he'd thought the same. It felt like a criticism. 'She's been doing a lot of work over there, volunteering and such.'

'What do Muslims care about Christmas?' his father asked.

'Some of them are Christian,' Sasha said.

'It's a wonder you bothered to come for just three days,' his father said. 'It's an awfully long way. Brutal, this time of year. I never thought you'd be here so late last night.'

'I don't blame Alec wanting to stay with his mother,' Denny said. 'Doesn't want her to be alone on Christmas, does he, bless him?' She pulled a crumpled tissue from the sleeve of her jumper and dabbed at her nose.

'She's not alone,' Jake said. 'Nizar is there.'

'Who's Nizar, then?' his father asked.

'Nizar is from Syria,' Jake announced, mouth full of burger.

'Chew with your mouth closed, please, Jake,' Neil said.

'He came in a boat and then walked from Greece to Germany,' Jake continued. 'All the way. And he has a friend named Tahrir.'

'Did he now?' Neil's father asked, head tilting back to look at Jake from the lower part of his progressive lenses. 'And does Nizar visit often.'

'He lives with us,' Sasha said.

His mother blinked several times.

His father cocked his head and said, 'He does, does he?'

'When did this happen?' his mother asked, turning to Neil, eyebrows arched.

'It's not what you— He came over as an unaccompanied minor but then aged out. Marcy offered to take him in until his papers come through.'

'This Nizar fellow,' said his father. 'Is he one of the Christians?'

'I, ah, I don't believe—' Neil began.

'He's Muslim,' Sasha confirmed. 'His name means "a glance".'

'Well now,' said Denny, smiling stiffly. 'That's lovely, isn't it? A glance.'

'And Tahrir means "pure",' Jake added.

'Virtuous,' Sasha corrected him.

'Indeed!' said his mother full of exaggerated interest and surprise.

'So, what do you think of these beef burgers, then?' his father asked. 'Not bad, eh?'

*

It was the wettest Christmas on record, a newsy nugget repeated by every weather presenter. Too wet to leave the house much. Jake woke at six. Sasha stayed in her room until after nine.

'Are you not concerned?' his mother asked.

'What, about Sasha? Not in the slightest.'

Neil tried to help with the Christmas dinner, but his mother insisted on doing everything. She wore herself out and then went to bed without eating. They made for a sad tableau, four people, sitting around a table that, the previous year, had held fifteen.

'We few, we happy few,' his father quipped.

His mother joined them for plum pudding, which was nowhere near as good as her own, Neil told her. He thought it would please her, but it only seemed to make her sadder. After the Queen's speech, Sasha and Jake video chatted with Marcy and Alec while Neil cleaned the kitchen. Looking on the bright side, it was a much quicker job than in previous years. Most of it fitted in the dishwasher; just a few roasting trays and the pots and pans that needed doing by hand. Neil was standing at the sink when his father appeared, a dishtowel draped over his shoulder.

'So, this Nizer person,' his father began.

'Nizar.'

'All right. Nizaaaaar, then.'

'Just so you know, I had nothing to do with it. It was all Marcy's idea. I was dead against it. I even consulted a lawyer. Apparently there has to be evidence, or the children have to say they are afraid, to claim child endangerment.'

'Well, quite right,' his father said.

And that was the end of the conversation.

By early evening, Neil was more than ready to call it a day, when he got Chloé's text:

Talk in half an hour?

He didn't want to go out. All the food and wine had left him sluggish, but he went to the mud room and got his jacket and wellies.

'Where are you going, at this hour?' his mother asked.

'Taking a walk.'

'It's pitch black out there, and there's fog.'

'I'll bring a torch.'

'The ground's so uneven. You'll fall and hurt yourself.' The thought clearly alarmed her. This was new. He had taken countless walks at night over the years; his mother had never batted an eyelid before.

'I'm forty-nine years old, Mum. I'll be fine.'

What appeared to be fog was actually rain. Tiny droplets of water covered every cubic millimetre. It was like walking through a cloud. Within ten steps of the back door, Neil was soaked. He climbed the hill into a crosswind, following the torch's beam. Water dripped off the hood of his jacket, and his face, off his chin and earlobes. He leaned into the slope, not trusting the traction, all the way to the top, where he waited for her to call.

'*Joyeux Noël*,' he said, cupping the phone to deflect the wind.

'Happy Christmas,' she answered.

'How was yours?'

'Nice,' she said, exhaling in a long hiss. Was she smoking? 'Aurélie's cousins are here. Jérôme's brother dressed up as

Père Noël. They have a suit and take turns. My mother-in-law and I took a walk this afternoon.'

'But you don't like her.'

'When did I say that?' she said. 'I never said that.'

'All right, have it your way.'

She had, though, shortly before Christmas, last year. It was after the second time they slept together, the one that proved that the first hadn't been a fluke.

'It's not "my way", it is the truth.'

'Is Jérôme there?'

'Of course,' she said, making a faint whistling sound as she exhaled. She *was* smoking. 'It is his mother's house.'

'Well how should I know? He could be working.'

Jesus, he sounded peevish.

'He has a shift early tomorrow.'

'Where are you staying tonight?' He shielded the mic with his free hand.

'It's easier if we stay here. It's late; we've been drinking.'

'And Jérôme? He's staying as well, I presume?'

'Neil.'

'What?'

She exhaled sharply. 'It was sweet, at first, your jealousy. I was flattered. But now—'

'Just answer the question. Yes or no. Has he moved back home? Are you together again?'

She said nothing. Neil was determined not to fill the dead air with his own voice. The hood of his jacket flapped and fluttered.

'It was always a fantasy,' she said, finally. 'This thing with us.'

'I don't know. Seemed pretty real to me.'

'Jérôme is my husband.'

'Who hurt you and took you for granted.' He pivoted a quarter turn and then a half, trying to escape the wind.

'Yes, and I wanted to punish him, so that he would know what it feels like to hurt.'

'So you used me to get back at your husband, is that what you're saying?'

'Please, Neil. Why must we do this?'

'I deserve to know. Did you sleep with me to get back at Jérôme?'

She inhaled deeply and held it for a few seconds before exhaling. 'If I did, it was not my intention.'

'Not your intention? What does that even mean?' Such bullshit. 'For God's sake, Chloé, we made plans. Quite a lot of them.'

He couldn't hear what she said next on account of the wind.

'Speak up,' he said.

'I never told you to get the apartment.'

'I did that for us! You were tired of going to your friend's, you said—'

'Well, yes, but—'

'But what?

'Never mind. This is crazy. We lost our heads. I was low, and you were so sweet. You made me feel beautiful and desired, but Jérôme is my husband. He is Aurélie's father. She deserves to be with her father.'

'What about my kids, Chloé? Don't they deserve a father?'

'Certainly. I am not keeping you from them.'

'You could have told me all this before I left my family.'

'No. Do not try to make that my fault. You used me.'

'I think we just agreed it was you who used me.'

'I was the crutch you needed to leave Marcy. You said yourself you should have done it years before.'

He couldn't say how long he stayed there after they'd rung off. Wind and rain lashed his face; he was soaked through. What did he care? Standing at the top of a hill, in the dark, in the middle of a gale on Christmas Day, he must've looked like a madman. He was mad. He'd dreamt of bringing her here, to this exact spot. In his imagination, it was always a lovely, clear night, ten thousand stars twinkling in the sky in a way you never saw in Brussels – too much light pollution – the clusters of warm yellow light of the street lamps in the towns and villages below. He had imagined snow, too: a Christmas card come to life. How often did snow fall in Somerset, in December? Once a decade? Once every fifteen years? He shook his head and laughed.

Last Christmas, when he wasn't sneaking off to call Chloé, he had been daydreaming about her. Marcy had noticed the inattention and had asked what was wrong.

'You're brooding like a teenager,' she said. No. 'A lovesick teenager,' she had called him.

He tried to laugh it off, but she kept pressing and eventually he shrugged and said, 'Work.'

'You need a break,' she'd told him. 'This is time for family.'

How irritated her response had made him, seeing it as yet further proof his wife had become an incessant nag. But, really, her only fault had been to accept his lie at face value. There had been little Marcy said or did or wore or ate that hadn't annoyed him back then. He had kept meticulous track of it all to share with Chloé. These, along with each new illustration of Jérôme's callous indifference, had sustained them on the long drives between Brussels and Nijmegen. He'd bet Chloé liked hearing how much more sympathetic she was than Marcy, how much more understanding. She probably liked it as much as he liked hearing Chloé say that Jérôme didn't appreciate her the way he did.

Neil wasn't used to screwing up. Derek was the naughty one, the one who failed tests, got into fights, crashed the car. Neil was the straight arrow, the standout student, the dependable worker, the devoted son, father and husband. This was a new feeling and not a good one. This wasn't a mere cock-up. It was an epic cock-up. Derek totalled a Ford Fiesta. Neil totalled his marriage; he totalled his family, and for what?

His fingers were numb; his teeth began to chatter, his legs shook.

'How could I have been so stupid?' he raged at the wind. 'So fucking stupid?'

Tiny rivulets flowed across the path. The wet grass glistened in the torchlight. He stepped on what looked like a rock. It turned out to be a small mound of mud. His foot slid forward. He scrambled to get his other foot back on the ground, but that one slipped too and so he returned to the first foot as he tilted ever more out of balance. His arms flailed; the torch flew from his hand. Faster and faster, a hamster on a wheel, a cartoon character, running backwards in place, whirling and grasping and when he inevitably fell, he landed bum first on the slick grass and shot down the hillside as if he were on a carnival slide. He fought to slow his descent, clawing at the ground, grabbing blindly in the dark for clumps of grass. He slammed into a mound and bounced into the air, landed on his side and began to tumble, and as he tumbled he heard his mother's voice telling his father, 'I told him. I told him he'd fall and hurt himself'. On he tumbled until somewhere near the bottom, where the ground was level and sodden, he rolled to a stop.

Marcy

Had the estate agent phoned five minutes earlier, Marcy would have let the call slide to voicemail. She was in the rear of the refugee centre's warehouse, rooting through donated furniture in search of a coffee table for a family. The wife had a reputation for being difficult. They'd been there over an hour, pulling tables from the stack, until they'd found one that's dimensions, style and condition she deemed acceptable.

'She is a holy terror, that one,' Sylvie said, sympathetically, as the husband and son carried the table off, the wife walking behind, shouting instructions. 'You don't want to know how long I looked for a winter coat the right size and shade of pink for her daughter.'

'She never would have got this far without being difficult,' Marcy replied. 'She'd still be in a camp or worse.'

That's when the estate agent rang. Marcy considered ignoring it. She did not want to have to rush home to prepare for another last-minute visit. The kitchen had been a mess when she left that morning, and Alec was probably still asleep.

She picked up anyway.

'Good news,' the estate agent chirped in a friendly tone

unlike any of their previous dealings. 'We have received an offer on your house.'

Marcy was stunned. Who buys a house in the week between Christmas and New Year's?

'I'll have to speak to my husband,' Marcy said.

'Yes, yes, of course,' the estate agent replied. 'But it is a matter of some urgency. We do not want to delay.' And there it was: the hard edge beneath the thin veneer.

'He is on the road today. He won't be contactable for hours.'

'It is fine to take a few days,' the agent said. 'But I must caution you,' she said and then again, 'I must caution you. I do not think we can expect a better offer.'

Marcy texted the offer to Neil together with the words:

Your thoughts?

And then, fearing she sounded cold, or bitchy, she added:

Hope you had a nice time with your parents.
Safe travels back. Tell the kids I can't wait to see them.

She didn't expect a reply until he got to the Eurostar terminal in Kent, and then she figured it would be only a quick text, telling her to accept. Instead, he phoned from the road a few minutes later. He was outdoors. His voice had to compete with the sound of the wind and cars rushing past on the motorway.

'Where are you?' she asked.

'Just past Stonehenge.'

'At a rest stop?'

'Of course I'm at a rest stop.'

'Oh, well, I'm glad for that.'

'So finally, an offer.'

'Yes.'

'It's lower than I expected.'

'Me too. Maybe our expectations were unrealistic?'

'Yeah,' he said. 'Maybe. I dunno. It's a good house.'

His voice sounded rough, tired.

'It is,' she agreed.

'I mean, there's a lot of house there for that price.'

'I know. But the agent doesn't think we'll get a better offer.'

'Did she say that? Were those her words?'

'Yes,' Marcy said, feeling her defences rising. 'Do you think I'd make that up?'

'No, of course not,' he said.

'Anyway,' Marcy said. 'Do you want to accept?'

'I dunno. It feels really . . .' He took a deep breath and then exhaled sharply. 'Really . . .' Traffic drowned out his voice.

'Sorry, Neil. I didn't catch that last bit.'

'I need a little time. I'll think about it on the train. We can discuss it when I drop the kids off. I mean, if you're free, that is.'

'Are you all right, Neil?'

'A bit tired.'

'How's your mother?'

'Not great, Marce.'

She heard the strain in his voice and pictured his Adam's apple bobbing up and down, the way it did when emotions threatened to escape.

'I'm sorry to hear that. We'll talk when you get here. I'll be home. Be careful on the road, will you? Precious cargo.'

*

They walked down to Flagey, to the bar in the former radio station, an art deco masterpiece with its large windows in their curved wooden frames and comma-shaped zinc bar. The place was full of students, young professionals and people with young children. They wended their way through the crowd, to a narrow table in the middle. They ordered coffees.

'When did everybody get so young?' Neil remarked.

'I think you mean: when did we get so old?' she joked.

He shrugged. He looked worn out.

'So. The offer.'

'I still think it's low,' he said.

'The estate agent doesn't think we'll get more.'

'That's not what she said when she was trying to get us to list with her.'

Marcy shrugged. 'Does it really matter? There'll be more than enough for a deposit and, with your salary, you'll have no problem getting a mortgage.'

'Is that what you think? That the money is all I care about? It feels insulting that someone could buy the house for so little.'

'At the end of the day, it's just bricks and mortar.'

'It's not, though. It's the only home Sasha and Alec remember, and the only one Jake has ever known.'

'I'm not saying it's not special to us,' she said. It was strange for him to bring up the sentimental value of a house he'd left voluntarily, but now seemed the wrong time to point this out. He looked like he was about to crack in half.

'Tell me more about your mum.'

'She's using a wheelchair for shopping trips but around the house she won't use it, or a cane or anything, but she needs a cane or a walking frame or something. Dad hovers, thinking he can catch her if she falls but he probably can't.'

'How is James holding up?'

'You know my dad. I think he starches that upper lip of his. He sends his regards, by the way. He always liked you, Marcy. He'd talk to you about things he'd never say to me, not in a million years.'

'Fathers and sons,' she said.

He flinched and she regretted her choice of words.

'I miss Alec,' he said. His Adam's apple did that thing it did.

'He'll come around,' she said.

Neil shook his head. 'I've made so many mistakes, Marce.'

'Haven't we all?'

They finished their coffees and ordered wine.

'It was this project, I think.' he said. 'It really did my head in, I mean. And now, with the offer on the house, it all feels as if things are moving so fast. Too fast, all of a sudden.'

Marcy nodded, more out of empathy. It had been nearly six months. 'We can say no,' she said.

'That would be stupid, wouldn't it? We've waited so long for an offer.'

'Then we should accept.'

'I wonder if we're,' he paused, 'if *I*, actually . . .' He brought his hands together. The fingers of his right hand fiddled with his wedding ring. 'If I haven't been rash.' He shook his head. 'I'm so sorry, Marce. I fucked everything up.'

What could she say? It was true.

'We don't have to decide on the house right now. The buyers are away until the second of January. We can take a few days to think about it.'

He nodded, glumly, spinning the ring on his finger, rubbing it like it was a genie's lamp. He looked miserable.

'How about we each mull it over and in a couple days,' she offered, 'you can drop by for coffee or a drink? I'll make sure Alec is around so you can see him, and we'll make a decision then.'

He made a frowny smile.

'Would New Year's Day work?' she asked.

'Anytime, really. My schedule is wide open.'

'So how about New Year's Eve?'

She meant it as a joke, but he smiled and said, 'New Year's Eve works fine.'

In an outdated, brutalist shopping centre in the Bascule neighbourhood of Ixelles, connected to a branch of the Inno department store via a windowless arcade of snack bars, cobblers, second-rate jewellers and shops selling novelty T-shirts, is a nondescript franchise of a national supermarket chain which contains one of the best fishmongers in Brussels. The book of orders for Christmas and New Year is brick-thick with commands for smoked salmon, oysters and langoustines. On the afternoon of the Saint-Sylvestre, the queue stretched through the dairy and foreign foods sections, back nearly to the main entrance.

Marcy and Sasha were keeping themselves entertained while they waited by picking out people in the crowd and dreaming up secret histories for them. Of a man in a tan cap, Marcy said, 'By day, he drives a delivery truck, but by night he writes romance novels.'

'Under the nom de plume: Eloise la Fleur,' Sasha announced as they inched past the Marmite.

'Nice one,' Marcy said, elbowing her gently. 'Your turn.'

Marcy's mood was buoyant, largely because playing the game had been Sasha's suggestion. They were talking and joking as they used to. Her daughter was treating her as if she was a sentient being. Also, they were going to ring in 2016 together as a family. She tried not to think beyond that, worried about getting her hopes up. If Neil wanted to come home, all he had to do was ask, but he *would* have to ask.

Sasha strained her neck and stretched on tiptoe to see over the crowd until a little old woman in a mink coat and matching hat nudged her aside with her cane to grab a pot of whipping cream. 'She is a spy,' she mouthed as the woman toddled away.

Marcy nodded. 'Retired, of course, with a hollow molar in the back of her mouth. She used it to smuggle microfiche prints of state secrets.'

'What's microfiche?' Sasha asked.

'Really? That's the part of the story that attracts your attention? Not the hollow tooth?'

'I know what a hollow tooth is,' she said.

'Microfiche is a flat piece of film storing microphotographs, usually of newspapers and magazine, it's . . .'

But Sasha's interest had already waned. 'Your turn,' she said.

Marcy scanned the crowd. Her eyes fell on a middle-aged woman in a neat dress coat with a large gold brooch pinned near a shoulder. She was carrying a Styrofoam saucer of shellfish tied with a large red presentation bow.

'Patricia?' Marcy said.

The woman started. Her eyes widened briefly, before returning to their normal size.

'Marcy?'

Patricia was a fellow American, from somewhere mid-Atlantic, Baltimore or DC, Marcy thought. Her husband worked at Neil's company. They had met at company events where they got on well enough to talk about getting together for lunch, although they never had.

'Happy new year,' Marcy said.

'Happy new year to you,' Patricia replied. 'Wow! What a surprise running in to you here.'

'It's been a while.'

'Ages.'

Most years they met at the fancy Fourth of July party that Monsieur G hosted at his villa in leafy La Hulpe. Marcy had missed the most recent one to attend the second wedding of an old school friend.

'How was the speech this year?' she asked. 'Anything revolutionary?'

In the evening, before the fireworks, Monsieur G would raise a glass and give a lengthy toast in honour of 'America's first and greatest friend', the Marquis de Lafayette, with whom he just so happened to claim shared ancestry, albeit through marriage.

'I missed you that day,' Patricia said. 'There was nobody to roll eyes with.' She laid a manicured hand on Marcy's forearm. 'Listen, I feel awful I haven't called. I had no idea you were still in Brussels. I thought I heard you were in the States?'

'For a wedding,' Marcy said. 'We had a holiday booked for later in the month. I flew out a couple weeks ahead of the family.'

'I just assumed, you see.' She pursed her lipsticked lips.

'I meant to get in touch,' Marcy said. 'Life has been a little,' she paused, searching, 'chaotic.'

'Of course it has, hon.' She squeezed her arm tighter and gave it a little shake. 'It's my fault. I should have reached out. Now I feel terrible. At times like these a girl needs a friend, a compatriot.'

The thought put a lump in Marcy's throat, even though they weren't close. Patricia leaned in, conspiratorially. 'It won't last, you know,' she said.

'Oh, I know,' Marcy said, because that was the nature of grief, wasn't it? She thought of her father's death. 'The first year is always hardest.'

Patricia gave a little snort. 'If they get *that* far. Pierre says the smart money in the office pool is months, if not weeks.'

'Wait, what?' said Marcy. The sly smirk on Patricia's lips disappeared, her eyes widened in horror as a manicured hand rose to cover her open mouth. 'Oh,' Marcy said, almost to herself. She thought she'd die.

'Patricia,' she said, astonished her mouth managed to form the words. 'Have you met my daughter, Sasha?'

Watching the blood drain from Patricia's face brought a sliver of satisfaction, and after the briefest of chit-chat, Patricia sashayed away. Marcy stared straight ahead, marshalling all her energy to pretend she hadn't just been run over by a bus, her heart tossed in a mulcher, as if her life was still as it had been two minutes earlier.

She shuffled forward. The numbness of the initial blow began to fade, allowing the true extent of her humiliation to take shape. Of course there was someone else, you fool. Men Neil's age don't fall out of love. They fall *into* love with someone else, someone with less baggage, smoother skin, whiter teeth and fewer, if any, grey hairs. Marcy longed to escape her body, to slip her mortal coil the way patients who flatline on the operating table sometimes report having done; to hover above it, observing with serene detachment the spectacle of her utter devastation. But there she remained, beside the chilled racks of butter and margarine, growing ever smaller. Her arms were cold. She hugged herself to keep from shaking.

She took a furtive, sidelong glance at Sasha, careful to avoid catching her eye, and was relieved to see her tapping at the screen of her phone with both thumbs. Maybe she hadn't been listening? The idea seemed at least plausible. Teenagers had little interest in adult conversation. She could have been texting friends, exchanging cat videos or posting pictures of the queue.

Replacement was so much worse than rejection. How could she have ever imagined otherwise? And everyone at the office knew.

It was ages before they arrived at the front of the queue, but when they did, things went quickly. Marcy told the man her name. Some attendants rifled through the stacks of Styrofoam saucers for hers. He handed it to her, and she smiled, stretching her face muscles as far as they would go. She and Sasha continued their shop, placing duck breast and foie gras into her trolley, asparagus and waxy potatoes, champagne and a good merlot, chocolate truffles.

By the time they were halfway home, Marcy believed she'd regained enough control over her emotions to point to a tall man walking an Afghan hound and say to Sasha, 'He knits tea cosies.'

Sasha rounded on her. 'I cannot believe you! You're going to smile and pretend nothing happened, just let yourself be a laughing stock? Have you no pride?'

The fury, the venom, pouring out of her daughter knocked the wind out of Marcy. Why such anger?

'I felt sorry for you,' Sasha went on, livid. 'I was on your side, but you won't even defend yourself. You have no self-respect. Honestly, no wonder Dad left you. You're a joke!'

Such disdain. A phrase popped into Marcy's head: *No one can make you feel inferior without your permission.* Who had said that? Eleanor Roosevelt, was it? Seemed like something she'd say, the kind of advice that is supposed to make a person feel better but actually makes them feel worse, spinning what ought to be a simple case of cause and effect – responding to a hurtful act by feeling hurt – into a character flaw. Not a person, a woman. We women are trained to own our misfortunes, she thought, take responsibility for them. It was pure victim blaming.

'I was trying to protect you,' said Marcy, hoping her daughter would understand. 'No kid deserves to learn about their father's affair from an idle gossip.'

It wasn't fair to call Patricia an idle gossip. She had been as mortified as Marcy.

'I already knew!' Sasha cried.

Marcy had never hit any of her children. Indeed, so intent was she on protecting and nurturing their budding psyches, she avoided raising her voice or saying no to them. Not that she always lived up to these lofty ideals – she was human, after all, and so were her children – but on those occasions when she fell short, she apologised and redoubled her efforts. This is all to say, to underline, that physical violence was antithetical to her parenting philosophy. She abhorred it and, at this moment that felt pivotal, the one positive she had to cling to was that her hands were full of groceries. Otherwise, surely, the urge to slap her beloved daughter into next week would have proved irresistible.

She counted to ten and then to ten again. She took deep breaths. When they got home, she put away the food, rearranging the refrigerator like someone from the bomb squad diffusing a bomb, with that sort of focused intensity. Sasha, perhaps regretting her choice of words, stood at her right hand, silently passing one item after another, while Alec and Nizar hovered close by. When all the bits and pieces were made to fit and the refrigerator door closed, Marcy turned to her and said, 'I expected more from you, Sasha. I don't know what your father promised you in exchange for your silence.'

'Nothing,' Sasha replied, mouth falling open, at the audacity of the suggestion. 'He doesn't—'

'Please, don't interrupt,' Marcy said. 'It was very disloyal. You are a bright, intelligent woman. You must see how hurtful it is that you kept your father's secret while living with—'

'Alec's known longer,' Sasha blurted out, pointing to Alec. 'He's known for months, nearly a year.'

Marcy whipped around to her son. 'Is this true, Alec?' The words came out in a whisper.

'Umm.'

His expression said it all.

'And you never thought to tell me?'

'Well, I . . .' He swallowed hard; stared at his foot as he shuffled it.

'That was important information. Vital.' So much betrayal all around her. She would drown in it. 'You had no right to keep it from me; to let me carry on, day after day, not knowing.'

'I did it to . . .'

'Please,' she said, resenting the tears pricking at her eyes. Even her own body was betraying her, robbing her of dignity. 'Please don't say you wanted to protect me.'

There was earnestness in his face and fear in his eyes.

'I am *not* a child, Alec. I am the adult here,' though she sure didn't sound like an adult, shrieking like a banshee. 'You lied to me.'

'I didn't.' He tilted his head in a certain way and he looked just like Neil had when she had first known him. That sweet, kind man she had believed would never hurt her. She collapsed on to the kitchen counter, grabbed a fistful of her hair and yanked.

'This is why I didn't tell you,' he cried. 'Exactly this. I knew you'd freak out, like be—'

Before he could finish the word, Marcy popped up and slapped his face. She did it with a quickness bordering on automatic, the way a ping-pong player returns a volley.

'Go to your room,' she said, holding away from her body the hand that had done the slapping as if it was dirty, infected.

Alec didn't move, not even to touch the spot on his cheek where she'd struck him, the spot that was now blooming red.

'Get out!' she shrieked.

What followed was a blur.

Neil

When Neil returned from his parents', he found a golden puddle on the stovetop. It was about the size of a fifty-pence piece, settled into a depression beneath the grate of the left back burner. He wiped it clean with kitchen roll but by the following evening it was back, significantly smaller and yet unmistakably present. He couldn't figure out where it came from. He hadn't used the stove. This admittedly small mystery took up outsized space in his brain for the lack of other, better distractions, and Neil needed distractions. He was alone, with nothing to do, and still three days until New Year's Eve. He wished the office was open. In the office, there were always things in need of his urgent attention, emails piling up in his inbox, and meetings in which his presence was required. In the office, he was kept so busy, he hardly had to think at all.

He wanted to reject the offer for the house. Not because he hoped for a better price, but because he didn't want to sell it, full stop. The thought of strangers living there, repainting walls and filling its rooms with their furniture, was intolerable. He knew this meant he'd have to make sacrifices, meant being stuck in this apartment for the foreseeable future and probably trimming his spending somewhat, as well. That was all right with him. The hard part was not phoning Marcy to tell her. He expected the news to please her; also, open-ended situations made him uneasy. He wanted the matter settled. But he resisted the urge to call her. It wouldn't be fair of him to intrude on her time with the children. The news could wait until he saw her.

The previous New Year's Eve they had made raclette and Alec, displaying the bottomless appetite of a growing boy, had devoured copious amounts of grilled cheese, charcuterie, and boiled potatoes. Jake had fallen asleep on the couch, and he had carried him upstairs to bed. Neil had taken advantage of the moment to squeeze in a quick call to Chloé.

With every passing day, he felt a bit more foolish about the Chloé chapter. He bore her no ill will, was grateful for her discretion and pragmatism. In cutting things off, she had done him a service. A great service, and the next time he saw her – which could be a while given their departments were on different floors – he would thank her. But talk about clichés! Everything but the red convertible – and the truth was he had been considering a cabriolet to replace his current company car when the lease was up this coming spring.

He had been in a deep fog. That was the only way to explain it. He hadn't been thinking straight. Heaven only knew how much damage would have been done if they'd had to wait until he came to his senses. He might have ended up like Gerry Fisk, with one set of kids in college and another set in nappies, which would have been a disaster, and not just financially. It was irresponsible to take on a commitment that the actuarial tables say you're unlikely to fulfil. A child needs their parents around. Marcy had been forty-five years old when her father died, and it was still devastating for her.

The first time Neil saw Marcy was during a quiz night at a pub off Edgware Road. A guy he knew from uni had dragged him along.

'Just so we're clear,' Marcy had said when she took the seat next to him, 'any questions about football are strictly your responsibility. The only thing I know about "football",' she said, putting air quotes around the word, 'is Pelé.'

So she knew nothing about football, but by golly, she knew a lot about a lot of things, random and disparate things such as: which country is home to the highest waterfall? (Venezuela) and, what nation's flag is not rectangular (Nepal). The more obscure the question, the more likely it was that she knew the answer to it. What was first read in Troy, Ohio in July 1974 off a pack of Wrigley's Juicy Fruit gum? A barcode. A bloody barcode! To be fair, the feat seemed a tad less amazing after she explained that she'd grown up in Ohio, less than two hours' drive from where the eventful scanning took place – at a Marsh supermarket, she added. No relation to Marsh Enterprises.

Impressive though she was, a team of old boys from Haberdashers' Aske's, oozing that public schoolboy confidence, toffs every last one of them, took the lead from the opening round and never let it go. They looked in control until, with less than a minute remaining, Marcy named 'Cassandra' as being the B-side song to ABBA's last single release, 'The Day Before You Came', putting their team to within five points of the lead. Better still, it got her a bonus question worth ten.

'Your question subject is,' the pub quizmaster announced, pausing for drama, 'football.'

Neil remembered how she'd winced and shaken her head. The guys from Haberdashers' Aske's cheered. They pounded the table. No conferring was allowed on bonus questions. Victory hinged on a woman's, an *American* woman's knowledge of football, and they liked their chances. Neil took a nervous swig from his pint.

'No pressure,' he told her. 'It's all good fun.'

The quizmaster drew out the question in dribbles of two or three words. 'Which footballer . . . was named . . . after . . . the famous American inventor . . . Thomas . . . Alva . . . Edison?'

Marcy looked at him. He made a small shrug. He had no clue.

She threw her hands in the air and said: 'Pelé?'

He made sure he got the seat next to her when they went out for a celebratory curry. They laughed at their incredible luck and at how the Old Habs' table had gone dead silent upon hearing the answer was correct. He was besotted with the sound of her voice. Her accent sounded friendly. She delighted in learning new things and saw no reason to hide it. Her natural optimism and openness to the world was the sort of thing that made people think Americans were naive or stupid. But she was clearly not stupid – she won the pub quiz for them. And as for the charge of naivety, she'd lived in New York City. The Big Apple. Her positive outlook was a welcome change from the practised cynicism displayed by everyone he'd met since Freshers week at university. It was pretentious performance art. There was a moment when she reached across for the plate of onion bhajis; she had turned in his direction and their eyes met, and he could swear he felt his life shift on to a new path.

He'd insist on staying to do the clean up after they rang in the New Year and then he would make a full confession, tell Marcy everything, the whole, sad tale of how he'd lost his way in the fog and how sorry he was for having caused so much pain. He would beg her forgiveness. He didn't expect her to give it right away. She had every right to be furious. He would wait as long as it took, having faith that, in time, her compassion would win out.

The golden puddle kept reappearing on the stove. There were other things, too. The windows that he had found so charming, originals, in lead casements, were the perfect conductors of cold air. The kitchen fan was inadequate, and the oven door was flimsy. In the bathroom, part of the silicon liner around the tub was black with mould. The water pressure was far from ideal and he had to place his feet at an awkward angle when shaving and brushing his teeth due to a loose tile in front of the bathroom sink. How had all this escaped his notice? And he was bored. So bored.

To break up the monotony, he took long walks around his neighbourhood. Apart from the café he and Chloé and frequented, which no longer held the same appeal, he had barely explored the quartier since moving in. He wandered up Chaussée de Waterloo towards the open-air Marché du Parvis and strolled around the stalls, making purchases in embarrassingly small quantities: a lemon, two apples, a thin slice of paté. It was hard to avoid comparing it to the markets at Flagey and Boitsfort where he'd gone for years, knew the vendors and where they set up their stalls. On the third day he recognised the man selling quiches was the one he'd previously bought from in Boitsfort. Neil walked over, eagerly.

'I'll take a quiche Lorraine, please.'

'It's cheaper if you buy three,' the man said, showing no sign he recognised Neil.

'One is all I need, thanks,' Neil said.

'They can be frozen.'

'I'm aware. Just the one, thanks.'

The man wrapped the quiche in paper, launching into instructions for its reheating and general care while he did so.

'Preheat the oven to 190 degrees. Cut the quiche into quarters.'

'Yes, I know,' Neil said.

'Place them tip first on the grille,' the man said, and then again. 'Tip first on the hot grille.' He mimed the action, the tip of the quiche slice making contact with the grille. 'Heat for eight minutes.'

'I've been buying these from you for twelve years,' Neil said.

'Instructions are printed on the wrapper,' the man continued. 'In case you forget.'

The man would have remembered Marcy, Neil thought. Everyone remembered Marcy because she was interested in everyone. Aristocrat or working class, long-time friend or stranger, she wanted to know what made you tick. She believed not only that everyone had a story, but that everyone wanted to tell that story. Shyness or reticence did not deter her. Like an oystercatcher with a fresh mollusc, she pried stories out of people. Once, at the wedding of a friend from university, they were seated next to the most boring man in Shropshire, or so it appeared. From the starter through main course, he was a dark cloud hanging over the table, sitting glumly, taking no interest in the conversation. It was so bad, Neil began to feel self-conscious, wondering what offences he had committed against the bride to have drawn such a table companion. It could have been a terrible evening if not for Marcy. She peppered the man with questions, searching for his passion until, as dessert arrived, she found it: tractors. How she hit upon it, Neil would never know, he'd tuned out long before, but damn if the chap didn't open like a flower. His whole demeanour changed, and he became quite chatty. Later that night, in their room, Marcy had remarked: 'Did you know the word tractor comes from the Latin *trahere*, meaning, "to pull"?'

When Wendy from HR called about an emergency meeting on Tuesday, Neil went in gladly. Marco Skyped in from somewhere in the Italian Alps but most of the rest of the group showed up. Helen from coms was there and Wendy, looking tired. The meeting started at eleven. Monsieur G glided in at ten seconds after.

'When Benny Marsh visited us in December,' he began, 'he brought with him a plan for the future. To make Marsh Enterprises a leaner and meaner company, fighting fit for the twenty-first century. We're going to uncomplicate our org chart, flatten the hierarchy. Obviously, in the best of all possible worlds, all of this would be done organically, by attrition, but Wendy and I have crunched the numbers, and this alone will be insufficient to hitting our targets.'

'I don't understand,' Jones from marketing said. 'Revenue was up six per cent last year.'

'We're looking to the future. I'm calling on each of you to open the hood and inspect the machinery of your teams. Think about critical processes, skills and capabilities we need, and then we will match employees with the most suitable skills.' He looked towards Wendy and nodded. 'HR reminds me to remind all of you that this it is not about individuals but to matching skillsets to future needs. This is an opportunity.'

'How many will need to be cut, chief?' Marco asked.

'I don't like to reduce people to mere numbers. The goal of the re-org is to shave thirty million from the worldwide budget.'

There was a collective gasp.

'How many from each department?' Helen asked.

'Depends on the department. I want you all to think outside the box. Be innovative. Do more with less.'

'What just happened?' Neil asked, stunned, as he walked to the car park with Helen. 'I'm all in favour of increased efficiency, but thirty million is a huge cut when we're making a profit.'

'Haven't you heard?' Helen asked. 'Benny Marsh is divorcing his wife.'

'Let me get this straight. We're squeezing cash out of the business so he can pay her off? You can't be serious.'

'And it's going to be costly,' Helen nodded. 'I suspect we'll have to sell off a division or two.'

Neil whistled. 'What, no prenup?'

'It's a family business, that makes it communal property, and they've been married over thirty years.'

'Man,' Neil said, shaking his head. 'Any ideas who you're going to cut?'

She stopped walking and turned towards him. 'Seriously, Neil?' Her voice was cool, and her eyes, icy.

'What? What'd I say?'

'Your line of questioning is totally inappropriate.'

'Helen. It was an innocent question. Forget it, okay? I take it back.'

She shook her head and then walked to her car.

It was a silly, stupid mistake. In a moment of inattention while mincing an onion, Neil sliced into his middle finger. One of those beautiful Japanese knives cut through nail, skin and flesh with shocking ease. Blood dripped over the board and got soaked up by the onions. Neil had no gauze and so he wrapped the wound with kitchen roll and then, when that soaked through, a dish towel. When the dish towel soaked through that, he got a hand towel and headed to urgent care.

The hand specialist on duty said it wasn't as bad as it looked. 'Superficial,' he said. 'No apparent nerve damage. You'll lose the nail, of course, but that can't be helped. A couple of sutures ought to do it.'

He prepared an injection of local anaesthetic and while waiting for it to take effect, he tapped Neil's wedding ring.

'That has to come off,' he said. 'It's restricting the blood flow. Your finger is slowly dying.'

Five neat stitches and two quick clips from a pair of pliers, and Neil's hand was his own again.

The ring's print remained on the finger, the skin beneath it a ghostly white. The doctor laid the pieces out on the table, placing the segments together: a broken circle of unequal parts.

The following morning was Saint-Sylvestre. Neil took the tram to Sablon so he could stroll around the antique markets. He was searching for something for Marcy, a hostess gift. What exactly he was looking for, he couldn't say, only that he felt certain he would know it when he saw it. In each shop he entered, he was drawn towards the velvet-lined glass cases where the jewellery was displayed, even though he suspected jewellery would be inappropriate. There was a marvellous platinum and diamond brooch. It had distinctive art nouveau swirls that Marcy would love, sprinkled with diamonds. But jewellery would be moving too fast; even worse, it would suggest he thought Marcy could be bought with a trinket. And then he spied a vase. It was made of green glass and enamelled with pink poppies and a gold filigree of foliage at the lip. Seeing it made him think of the field in the Bois de la Cambre, where Marcy had taught the children to do cartwheels. It was a Sunday afternoon. The Bois was full of the lunch crowd and there was Marcy, past forty, barefoot in the grass, turning head over heels, as tight-laced bougie Belgians gawped. He couldn't tell whether they were aghast or impressed.

'Muscle memory,' Marcy explained.

When she'd first told him she'd been a cheerleader in high school, he hadn't believed her. Not because she didn't look the part – she was beautiful and fit – but because it seemed too incredible that he would be dating a cheerleader, even a former one. On a visit to her parents, she dug out her old uniform to prove it. He'd begged her to put it on. She complained it was tight; it was. In all the right places. This had been on his first trip to the States, a magical ten days in which everything – from the interstate they'd driven from Detroit to Toledo, to the stacks of pancakes at breakfast, and the stars and stripes flying atop every flagpole – had been dream-like. He'd whispered to himself, over and over, 'I'm in the heartland.' Still, the moment with the cheerleading uniform was in a class all its own. In her bedroom, wearing a blue jumper with SPARTANS emblazoned in gold across her chest, a short, pleated skirt and no knickers, she performed a cheer for him. His teenage fantasy come to life, Neil would say, except teenage Neil wouldn't have had the boldness to aspire to such a fantasy. The jumper got stuck as he lifted it over her head. They laughed so hard his stomach muscles were sore the next morning, as if he'd done too many sit ups. When had they stopped laughing?

He bought the vase, and the brooch as well because he was afraid, if he didn't, someone else would buy it and he couldn't bear to think of someone other than Marcy owning it. He would set it aside and wait for the right time to give it to her.

He took the tram home and was carrying his purchases upstairs to the fourth floor. It was barely 2 p.m., still loads of time for a shower and a shave. He would wear his blue suit with a light blue shirt and a brown and white striped tie. It was a long trudge back up to the apartment; hard to ignore the dinginess of the walls or the narrowness of the staircase.

His phone rang. It was Sasha.

'Hey, Sash,' he said, brightly.

'Has Mom called you?'

'No,' he said. 'Does she need me to pick something up for tonight?'

'You'd better not come, Dad. Mom knows.'

'Sorry, Sasha. I don't understand what you're talking about. Knows what?'

'About your affair, Dad. She knows everything and she's going ballistic. Please don't come tonight, Dad. We can't handle any more drama.'

Alec

For once, Alec welcomed the end of the school Christmas holidays. He was a white-hot sack of grievances: angry and sad; disgusted and more scared than he wanted to admit. He wasn't speaking to his mother, wouldn't look at Sasha and hated Nizar more than ever. School was a haven by comparison. He would knuckle down in all his subjects and take risks in art, really stretch himself. Such was the resolve with which he set out that morning from the house now officially 'under offer' and therefore already a bit less like home. It lasted all of two periods. Enthusiasm seeped out of him as his maths teacher monologued on the finer points of polynomials. Seated in the back row, next to the window and a radiator throwing out heat like a sauna, his breathing slowed, his head nodded, the lids of his eyes grew heavy and then – BAM! Something hit the window. Hard. Alec's heart went into a sprint. Students scrambled to their feet to see what it was. The teacher, moving with the stealth and efficiency of the ex-military man he was, got there first.

'Only a bird,' he said. Alec noticed his jaw go slack with relief.

'*Le pauvre!*' cried the girls, seemingly in unison.

'It is fine,' the teacher said. 'Stunned. It will rest and, in a minute or two, it will fly away.'

The bird, a crow, did not look fine. It had landed on its back in a pile of leaves over a grate. A single wing flapped jerkily as it tried to right itself; its neck lay at an unnatural angle.

'Everyone, back to your seats,' the teacher ordered. 'You have ten minutes to begin the homework. I am happy to answer any questions.'

Alec tried to concentrate on maths, but the sporadic rustle of leaves drew his attention. Bursts of rustling were intercut with moments of silence as the bird struggled. The rustling was unbearable; the silence was worse. When the leaves were rustling, Alec wished for it to stop, and when it stopped, he prayed for it to start again because that meant the bird was still alive. It wasn't its fault it had flown into the window, which must have been reflecting the sky. How was a bird supposed to know the difference between a reflection and the real thing? The silences grew longer; the rustlings became weaker and shorter, until they stopped altogether. Alec ached for the bird. When his lunch break came, he walked outside to where it lay, partly buried beneath the leaves, toes curled, one wing out, its crow eyes staring at nothing. He took out his phone and photographed it from different angles, using a stick to change its position. He would include it in his next still life.

A Beethoven violin sonata was playing when Alec got to the art room. He went to his workstation, next to Farrah's, and took out the drawing he'd started on New Year's Eve, soon after Mom drop-kicked a hundred euros' worth of shellfish into the courtyard.

'Another still life, Alec?' Madame Joelle asked, as she

made the rounds. She had returned from Christmas break with hair the colour of candy hearts. Today it was pulled back from her face with a black chiffon scarf, knotted at the top. She looked like the Rosie the Riveter poster in his grandparents' garage, a Warhol version.

She studied his pencil drawing of cracked oysters, mangled langoustines and red mullets sitting in crushed ice flecked with dirt, spilt from a tilted Styrofoam saucer with a boot-tip sized hole. Alec watched her eyes to see if they'd widen, which they did whenever they detected something worthy of remark.

'The lines are too heavy,' she said, eventually, and then frowned slightly. 'I had thought you were pushing out in another direction. The drawing of the boy on the beach was good stuff. More of that, please.'

Alec's face burned. Accepting compliments was difficult for him, even when deserved, which in this case they weren't. The worst part was that he had thought he *was* pushing out in another direction. The wrecked seafood platter had felt powerful and edgy. The heavy lines were intentional, to convey his anger. He was taking a painful moment from his own life and transforming it into art. He meant for it to be as poignant and shocking as Nizar's drawing of the foot sticking up out of the rubble: a depiction of regular, ordinary life destroyed.

Madame Joelle moved on to Farrah. 'Another portrait in charcoal?' she asked. 'Your technique is always solid, but you are too comfortable. We are here to stretch ourselves.'

'Don't listen to her,' Alec whispered, when the teacher moved on to another workstation. 'That portrait is amazing.'

It was of one of her great-aunts. Farrah had a lot of relatives, all of them willing to sit for their portraits. She had captured every wrinkle and fold of the great-aunt's skin, the irregular bone structure in her nose, even the light in her eyes.

'Thanks,' Farrah whispered back. 'And I adore your still lifes.'

He blushed for a second time, not because he believed her – she was too talented an artist herself to fail to note the paltriness of his abilities – but because it showed she cared enough about him to pretend otherwise. For the next half hour or so, working silently beside her, he was entirely focused on drawing. Not once did his thoughts drift to the hurtful words that had preceded Mom's drop kick, or his parents' divorce that was really, seriously, actually going to happen and there was nothing he could do to stop it.

Halfway through the class, Madame Joelle rang a little bell she kept on her desk and called them to the centre of the room. While he had been focused on lightening lines, adding shading and contouring, she had taped a large sheet of paper to the concrete floor and set out small pitchers of paint in various colours. The class took up positions around the paper. There were only fifteen of them, art being the least popular of the school's five options of specialisation, the one considered a doddle and probably a dead end; there was plenty of room.

'Up to now,' Madame Joelle began, 'we have focused on realism, on acquiring techniques to render the three-dimensional world on to a two-dimensional plane. But is that all there is to art?'

She wrote on the blackboard in capital letters: ACTION PAINTING – ABSTRACT EXPRESSIONISM

'Action painting is a movement that started in the United States after the Second World War. Rejecting composition and form, the action painters approached the easel not with an image in their mind, but with material in their hands and the intent to do something to the other piece of material in front of them. The canvas was not a space in which to reproduce, re-design, or analyse, but an arena in which to act.'

Alec nodded. He had never had much patience for composition and form, preferring to leave it to the viewer to decide for themself how the items in his still lifes related to one another. Composing was the same as contriving which, in a way, was the same as lying. How can a lie be art?

'For these artists, art is a moment, an action,' Madame Joelle continued. 'Each action exists independently. A sketch is one action, a painting another. One action cannot be "better" or more complete than another.'

'But that is nonsense, non?' asked Camille, whose specialty was watercolour paintings of flowers. 'Not every drawing or painting can be "art". There must be trial and error and exploration to discover what works best.'

'What is the point of an act if you already know what it contains?' Madame Joelle replied, with a hint of defensiveness. 'Action painters believed art must be a surprise.'

She picked up a cup of red paint and poured a vivid streak across the white canvas. The class gasped.

'Critics called it lazy,' she said.

'Of course,' said Guillem, the only other boy in the class. 'What do you expect from a bunch of Americans?'

Madame Joelle shot Guillem a warning look and continued. 'But the famous essayist Harold Rosenberg argued it was "a desperate recognition of moral and intellectual exhaustion".'

Alec could relate. He was exhausted, morally and intellectually, and desperate for someone to recognise it.

'For artists like Jackson Pollock, Franz Kline and Norman Bluhm, action painting was the embodiment of freedom,' the teacher said. 'The painter releases himself from values – political, aesthetic, moral – to embrace his true identity, his true self.'

Could it be true? Alec wondered. Was feeling guilty and responsible preventing him from embracing his true self?

Camille snorted. 'It's an excuse for bad behaviour, an invitation to be selfish and mean and call it truth.'

'Perhaps,' the teacher replied. 'But an action painter would argue action is not a matter of taste. You don't let taste decide the firing of a pistol or the building of a maze.'

Yeah, thought Alec.

Madame Joelle picked up a jug of blue paint. 'Action painting is automatic, instinctive, responsive, chaotic,' she said, doing a little skip as she poured a thin line of paint across the canvas. 'Pollock was known to dance around as he created his masterpieces. The art was the process. He never even touched the canvas.'

She set down the blue jug and scooped up a pot of green with a large brush stuck in it, twirled and then held it out to Alec. He accepted it and lifted out the brush.

'Pollock never even touched the canvas,' she repeated.

Paint dripped from the end of the brush on to the paper. Alec gave his wrist a flick and as the explosion of green dots splattered in an arc across the paper, he felt a shock in his limbs, violent and satisfying.

*

Madame Joelle was naturally dynamic and enthusiastic, but the module on action painting sent her into a whole other gear. In her lessons, she spoke louder and faster. Her eyes grew bigger and more expressive; her mouth widened. She arranged a lunchtime trip by tram to the Musée des Beaux Arts to see the Hans Hartungs.

'Pictures and slides cannot convey the energy,' she said, adding with a small sigh. 'Pity there are no Pollocks.'

Her hair became a Pollock unto itself. A week into the module, she dyed it every colour of the rainbow. Action painting was her passion, you could tell, maybe even the reason she'd become an art teacher, and Alec could see why. It was liberating, exhilarating. For once, he didn't look at his work and count the ways it failed to match the image in his mind or the efforts of his classmates; he wasn't afraid of making a mistake. Each painting represented an action, a mood, an emotion: truth – and therefore the only way an action painting could be a failure was if the painter failed to bring his authentic self to it. Alec literally poured his heart on to the canvas. When Madame Joelle hung their initial pieces around the studio, she put his at the front of the class, the place of honour.

When he talked about it at dinner and breakfast *he* spoke faster and louder.

'We're going to have a triple class,' he enthused. 'Painting outside in the *cour polyvalent*, rain or shine.'

'It's so good to see you smile,' Mom said with a smile of her own. 'I've missed that guy.'

She brought home an enormous flip-chart one of her students gave her, a leftover from a brainstorming strategy meeting. It felt like it might be a peace offering.

She constantly reminded them they were downsizing to a small apartment and needed to sort through their stuff.

'Halve it and then halve it again,' she said.

Meanwhile, Nizar hauled junk into the house by the bagful, but never mind.

Alec's mother said he could paint in the *sous-sol*, so long as he laid down newspaper and a plastic tarpaulin to protect the tiles. Alone in the basement, after everyone had gone to bed, he sometimes danced as he drizzled, dribbled, dripped and flicked paint on to the page. For Mother's Day in May he would buy the biggest canvas he could afford and create an amazing painting for his mom. He imagined it hanging somewhere prominent in their new apartment.

'Isn't it marvellous?' his mother would say when visitors remarked upon it. 'Alec made it for me.'

Sasha had been selected to represent the school at the city-wide Latin competition that would be held in March at the Université Catholique de Louvain. It was a great honour. She and another two students the school had put forward met with the head of Latin after school nearly every day to prepare. Alec didn't miss her company in the afternoons and evenings. He was still sore at her for throwing him under the bus with Mom. 'I'm sorry,' she'd said. 'I panicked.' He'd forgive her, eventually, but he thought it only fair she stew in her guilt a bit longer. Nizar wasn't around much, either. If he wasn't at work at the centre, he was off with Tahrir. Alec came to expect having the house to himself. He'd make cinnamon toast and tea the proper way, in a mug, with milk. And then one afternoon, he came home and saw Nizar's coat was hanging on a peg.

'Alec,' Nizar said. 'May I make you a glass of tea?' He stood at the stove, heating water in a pan.

'No thanks, Nizar. I'll make my own.' He hit the switch on the electric kettle and threw some bread into the toaster.

'Suiting yourself,' Nizar replied.

Alec took a mug out of the cupboard and tossed in a tea bag. He was happy with an uneasy silence, but since when did he ever get his way?

'Alec,' Nizar said. 'I have been sensing your anger toward your mother.'

'What ever gave you that idea?' Alec asked.

Nizar added crushed cardamom and a spoonful of tea to the saucepan of boiling water. 'It pains me to see the discord between you.'

'Does it?' he asked. 'Does it pain you?'

'Your feelings have been hurt, I realise.' Nizar added sugar and lemon juice 'But you must be gracious. When you are dead, your sister's tears will dry as time goes on, your widow's tears will cease in another's arms, but your mother will mourn you until she dies.'

'Why am I always dead in your scenarios?'

'It is nothing,' Nizar said, with a wave of a hand. 'A manner of speaking only.'

'A gruesome way of speaking.'

Nizar strained the tea into a small glass. The toast popped.

Nizar lifted the glass to his lips and took a tiny sip. Alec wondered how he did it without burning his fingertips.

'You think I do not understand your position,' Nizar said.

'What I think,' Alec replied, scraping and scratching the toast with the butter knife, 'is that you ought to keep your nose out of other people's business.'

'I know what it is to feel guilt,' Nizar said in a low voice, almost a whisper. 'I told my mother a lie. I said I wanted to come to the Europe to study medicine because I knew if I told her that she would give me the money, but I never had this intention. My sister is very clever. She is like Sasha. It is she who should be a doctor, like our father, and if not for the war, she would have been. I took all my mother's savings, everything she had in the world, to pay the smuggler.' He lowered his head. 'I was selfish.'

Alec had thought he couldn't possibly hate Nizar any more than he did already. The interloper had bested him in every conceivable way. He was a superior handyman, a better brother, a more talented artist. The least, the *very* least, he could do was leave for Alec the superlative of bearer of the heaviest burden of guilt. Apparently not.

'There is just no way to top you, is there, Nizar?'

'Pardon?' Nizar asked.

Alec was saved from further explanation by a timely video call. He walked over to the computer, hoping it would be Nana. It was from Sweden.

'It's your cousin,' he said.

Nizar stiffened. 'Let it ring. I will call him later.' He took his tea and tobacco pouch out to the terrace.

Marcy

Marcy felt bad for having had such a go at Alec. It wasn't his responsibility to tell her about Neil's affair. That was on Neil. Her son had wanted only to protect her which, paradoxically, was what outraged her most. He hadn't protected her, he had left her totally exposed, parading her ignorance for the world to see. It was the nightmare of being naked in public come to life. Of course, slapping him had been way out of line. Her fingers retained the memory of contact with his face, the little bristles of whiskers on his chin: small patches of man, and yet still so much boy. She could not bring herself to apologise. She was done apologising, done trying always to accommodate the feelings of others, to cause no trouble, be the person others wanted her to be. Alec would have to get over it. After years of being cautious, afraid of offending the world, afraid of being an Ugly American, Marcy did not give a fuck. Did. Not. Give. A. Fuck.

She stopped asking the kids about homework, or if they had a clean kit for PE. She bought dinner from the friterie in Flagey. For Jake's birthday in the second week of January, she skipped the homemade cupcakes and sent him to school with a boxed supermarket cake and a party-sized packet of M&M's. No one died. For his actual birthday, which fell on one of Neil's Saturdays, she booked a party at an indoor playground in Waterloo and invited twelve children, three of whom had ADHD, for three hours of fun on four football pitches worth of obstacle courses, ball pits and tunnel slides, housed in a former factory with terrible acoustics. Neil was still battling the resultant migraine when he dropped Jake off, Sunday evening.

She hoped that she and Neil could settle the divorce without lawyers. Just to be safe, she got the name of a killer one from Sharon, who, despite being a racist, had nevertheless responded to the news of Neil's affair with kindness and understanding.

'Denial ain't just a river in Egypt, my dear,' she said, and she offered one additional piece of unsolicited advice. 'Go out and get shagged.'

Marcy was thinking about it.

She gave Neil's coats, old work shirts and the suit he'd worn to their wedding to the refugee centre, though she kept his old rugby shirt. She tossed out the nearly empty bottles of shampoo and bath gel, the crusted-over containers of creams and toothpastes, the shaving foams and old toothbrushes, electric shavers, a curling iron, a hair straightener, the caffeine shampoo Neil had bought for his thinning hair. And then she moved on to the bookshelves, pulling every professional advice and self-help title: *The Entrepreneur's Secret*: gone; *Kickstart Your Career at Forty*: gone; *Thirteen Fool-Proof Ways to Grow*: gone, gone, gone. Next went the novels she had abandoned part way through, and then those she had never got around to starting, even those she'd adored but was unlikely to read again. She understood how Gandhi came to embrace life with just a dhoti and shawl. Possessions were a burden. To own nothing was the ultimate freedom.

She wasn't going to take it that far. Still, the short, neat stacks of T-shirts and jumpers in her wardrobe were mighty satisfying, so too the space between the hangers on which her clothing rested, and those rows of folded socks and overlapping triangles of underpants, their vertexes uniformly pointed north, suggesting a mind similarly in order.

Her mind was not in order.

She couldn't remember the last time she had felt hunger. She survived on pots of yoghurt, nibbles of toast. She wasn't sleeping, either, lying in bed, head spinning, every cell humming.

A doctor offered sleeping pills, but Marcy declined, fearing she would come to need them. Breathing and relaxation techniques helped sometimes, and Jake's night-time visits were a comfort, if an unpredictable one.

She used to be an excellent sleeper, snoozing through thunderstorms and tornado warnings as a little girl. On a train trip through Italy, Neil had marvelled that she could board a train, take her seat and be asleep before they left the station. He called it her superpower. He'd been too wrapped up in his boyish wonder of trains to close his eyes. Maybe that was what had allowed her to do it: knowing he was watching over her, sure to wake her in time for them to get off?

Neil's mistress was stalking her in her dreams. Not every night, but often enough to be a source of anxiety. The dreams varied in inconsequential ways but hewed to the same general script. Marcy is minding her own business, going about her day, when there, across a room or in a public space, she sees her. Marcy calls her Betty Boop, even though she looks nothing like the cartoon character. She has a pointy chin, the thinnest of lips, and large, snake eyes. She stands there, just stands, oozing the blasé mien the French have perfected – Marcy had seen four-year-olds in *maternelle* employ it to devastating effect – and it sends Marcy into a rage.

'Whore. *Pute*,' Marcy screams, words she abhors because they demean all women.

Betty Boop's snake eyes blink nonchalantly and Marcy starts punching. The mistress doesn't fight back; doesn't even attempt to block the punches. Her head swings like a pendulum, a punching bag on a stand. It's a beating, a pummelling and all the while, Marcy is screaming foul words she would never utter. Slut. *Salope*. Cunt.

She punches and screams to the point of exhaustion and Betty Boop stands there, unmoved, unaffected, untouched. Marcy wakes breathless, furious and debased.

'Marcy, if you had any fours, and I asked for them, would you give them to me?'

The subject of today's lesson was the conditional tense. They were trying to extend the exercise into their end-of-session card game. It wasn't easy. The language didn't flow naturally, but it was useful practice.

'Had I any fours in my hand, Fabrice, I would most definitely offer them to you now. Sadly, I do not, and so my reply would have to be, go fish.' She fingered the tops of her cards. 'But I would also feel compelled to add, nicely stated, Fabrice.'

Fabrice grinned as he leaned in to pick up the top card from the pile between them. It was the smile of someone accustomed to praise.

'Suppose I were to ask whether you had any queens?'

'If you were to ask whether I had any queens, I would reply, go fish, Marcy.'

Marcy picked a card up from the stack. 'I think you're getting too good at this, Fabrice. We're going to have to take things up a notch. Let's see,' she tapped her fingers on the desk: 'If you won the Lotto, Fabrice, what would you do with your winnings?'

'Buy a Lamborghini.'

She wagged her finger at him. 'Uh-uh-uh. Full sentences, stay in the conditional tense.'

'If I won the Lotto, I would buy a Lamborghini.'

'Would that be all?'

'I would also buy ponies for my daughters, and a diamond necklace for Sandrine. Oh, and I would hire a nanny and a maid,' he said, taking to the game. 'What would you do, Marcy, if you won the lotto?'

'Hmm. If I won the lotto, I would . . .' Though the question was predictable, her mind was blank. 'Pay off the mortgage on my house,' she said, eventually.

'Would that be all?' he asked. His disappointment at her lack of imagination was clear.

'It would not, of course not,' she replied, but every other idea that popped into her head – expand the refugee centre, feed the hungry – sounded pretentious, as if she were rubbing Fabrice's nose in her altruism, when there was no other way to answer the question except with consumer greed. But all the money in the world couldn't buy Marcy what she wanted. So what? No one said she had to be truthful. This was an exercise in language, a game. No need to over-think it. She could say anything: take a cruise around the world; buy a house in Hawaii, a Birkin bag.

'I would buy a diamond as big as the Ritz,' she said. 'And I would build a mansion on top of it.'

'Would you happen to have any sevens?' he asked.

'Nice enunciation on those *h*s, Fabrice,' she said. 'As it happens, I do have sevens, a pair of them, and I would be happy to give them to you here.' She put extra emphasis on all the *h*s.

His eyes twinkled with joy.

'Fabrice, have you ever been in a situation in which you are the only person who doesn't know something? There is a secret that everyone around you keeps from you? They are all in the know and you are alone in the dark?'

He furrowed his brows. '"No" as in opposite of "yes"?'

'No, know as in knowledge.'

'And I am in the dark?'

'Yes.'

He snapped his fingers. 'It is an idiom, yes?'

'Well done, Fabrice. What a good memory you have.' They had discussed idiomatic expressions and aphorisms before Christmas, making comparisons and contrasts between the French and English ones.

'Is same as we say in French, "*dans le ciel*"?'

'Not quite. "In the sky" implies inattentive, dreamy; "in the dark" means ignorant, out of the loop.'

'Out of the loop?'

'Another idiom.'

'He nodded. 'In the dark and out of the loop are synonyms.'

'Pretty much, Fabrice. Good work.'

'Would you have any twos, Marcy?'

'If I didn't have any twos, I would say, "Go fish, Fabrice."'

He smiled at her, 'But you do have some twos.'

'I do have a two, and I would be pleased to offer it to you now.' She handed over the card. 'Now, back to my question. How would you feel if you were out of the loop? If everyone around you was keeping a secret from you?'

Fabrice shrugged. 'We have an idiom in French, "*On rit mal des autres quand on ne sait pas d'abord rire de soi-même*: we laugh badly of others when we cannot laugh at ourself."'

'Ourselves,' said Marcy.

'Ourselves,' Fabrice repeated.

'Yes, but my question is a little different. A person can't really laugh at himself, or herself, if he or she is not in on the joke, that is to say, he or she does not know they *are* the joke?'

'So many persons and tenses!' he exclaimed. 'I cannot follow!'

'I'll rephrase. Let's say there was a secret that everyone around you was keeping from you, a secret that concerned you most of all. Would that be funny, or would it be hurtful?'

'I think it would depend. A good secret – a party of surprise, for a birthday, for example, would be funny.' Fabrice pronounced birthday like 'bird's day'.

'A surprise party for one's birthday would, of course, be amusing. It would also be a very nice gesture. But what if the surprise were less nice, or not nice at all. Let's say you were ill, seriously, gravely ill, so ill you were going to die, and everyone knew apart from you. Wouldn't it anger you that everyone was keeping this secret from you? Wouldn't it make you feel ashamed?'

He tilted his head thoughtfully. 'I think I would feel ill and so maybe at such a time I would not be thinking about what people were thinking or knowing. I would be preoccupied.'

'Okay but—'

'Also, if I were at the end of my life; if I were dying, I would probably be aware of it. Studies have shown it.'

'So maybe that wasn't the best analogy. What if you had a work partner, someone with whom you had collaborated on many things, and there was a big project coming up and you believed that you and your collaborator would do this project together because you always had but . . .' She rambled on, her hypothetical situation growing ever more convoluted, the thread of her logic ever more tenuous. Fabrice's expression went from puzzled to perplexed to uneasy.

'Marcy,' he asked, softly, almost pleadingly. 'Would you have any kings?'

Fabrice was Marcy's last session of the day. Afterwards, she drove to one of the airport hotels and walked into the bar. She sat down next to a clean-cut man in a suit, ordered a glass of chardonnay and struck up a conversation that quickly turned personal. The man was going through a divorce, as well. At least, that was what he said, just before he asked if she was staying at the hotel.

'Just passing through,' she replied. If she had to guess she'd say he was about five years younger than her.

'I have a room,' he offered. 'In case you're curious what they look like.'

Had men been this transparent when she was young? She could have sworn this particular dance was more nuanced, back in the day.

'We could watch TV,' he said. 'See what happens.'

'See what happens?' she repeated.

'It's an offer not a threat,' he reassured.

She took a sip of wine, hoping to drown the butterflies fluttering in her stomach. The man was charming and seemed nice enough, but she had no particular attraction to him. It had been twenty-five years since she'd had a new partner. Twenty-five years since she'd invited Neil up to 'see' her bedsit above the tanning salon.

She took a larger sip of wine, a gulp. Her sensuality was waking from a long nap. This would be a declaration of independence from Neil, the first strike towards evening the score and, perhaps, just a touch of payback. Her heartbeat rang in her ears.

'I appreciate the offer,' she said, finally, 'but it wouldn't be fair to you.'

'I don't mind,' he said, his grin downright puckish.

'But I do.'

She walked into Jake' school and up two flights of stairs. The classroom door was closed and so she knocked.

The teacher opened the door. She was an Amazon of a woman, with narrow hips and waist coupled with large breasts, something of an anatomical mystery. Like a Barbie doll. Marcy wondered how she stayed upright, particularly in the high heels she favoured. Also, Marcy loathed her.

'*Madame*,' Madame Vanderloo said, placing a cool, limp hand in Marcy's.

'*Madame*,' Marcy replied, resisting the urge to squeeze it hard. 'So nice of you to join us.'

Neil was already there. His eyes widened when he saw her, like a deer caught in a car's headlights. He had nominally handled interactions with the teacher since the previous school year, after Marcy and the teacher tangled over the quantity of assigned homework.

The teacher motioned to the child-sized chair next to Neil. She sat in her own, adult-sized chair.

'I'm concerned about Jake,' she began. *Shjake*. She and Neil ought to have given more thought more to how their son's name would be pronounced by the French. 'He seems easily distracted and he has cried three times in the past week.'

Neil looked in Marcy's direction, giving her first crack at a response, but Marcy refused.

'Well. . .' Neil said, pausing to clear his throat and cast another, cautious glance at Marcy. 'We recently separated.'

'I see,' the teacher said, with a small frown that Marcy assumed was ironic. 'Many of his classmates have had the same experience. It's a stage. They come out on the other side. In the meantime, we must ensure he does not fall behind. His points in dictation, in particular, are worrisome.'

'And what do you advise?' Neil asked. He put his hands on the table and Marcy saw his wedding ring was gone.

'A more disciplined study routine,' she said. 'Many parents find it helpful to conduct practice dictations at home.'

'There is already a lot of homework,' Marcy said. 'You want to add practice dictation, too?'

'The choice is yours,' Madame Vanderloo said, with an indifferent shrug, 'but without fundamental changes, his struggles will only increase.'

'Have you considered not giving them a dictation every day, or reducing the homework?' Marcy asked.

'The programme is designed to created good habits, rigour,' Madame Vanderloo said, pushing back her shoulders and looking down her nose at Marcy. 'If you find it too difficult,' she added, 'there are other, *slower* schools.'

Neil's jaw dropped but Marcy was ready for it. The gloves were off.

'I was wondering, *Madame*,' she said, 'which course you flunked before deciding to become a teacher?'

Madame Vanderloo blinked a few times. 'Pardon me?'

'Clearly, it wasn't your first choice. I've seen how you wince at the children. This was obviously plan B. What was plan A: medicine? Law?'

'*Madame*, that is highly inappropriate.'

'I'm going to say law,' Marcy continued. 'You don't look like the science type. I'll bet you saw yourself over at the Palais de Justice in a robe and a wig.'

'I will not sit here . . .' Madame Vanderloo shuffled the papers in front of her.

'Fighting the good fight,' Marcy continued, undeterred. 'But it didn't work out.'

'Marcy,' Neil said, putting a calming hand on Marcy's shoulder.

'Couldn't keep all those statute numbers in your head.'

'Marcy, *please*,' said Neil.

'Maybe you should have tried practising dictation.'

'Well,' Neil said, when the classroom door shut firmly behind them. 'That was quite a performance.'

Marcy laughed. 'Did you see her face? I think I hit a nerve.'

'But what objective did it serve, Marcy?'

'Come on, Neil, the woman's a harpy. This place is badly in need of reform. I bet the curriculum hasn't changed since nineteen twenty.'

'We could have sent the kids to the British or the international schools. You rejected that.'

'I had no idea it would be this rigid, this old-fashioned.'

'Do you think you helped Jake going forward?'

'Probably not. But it felt good. You must understand that, Neil? Sometimes you just have to do what feels good and fuck the repercussions.'

He sighed. 'Look, Marce, you have every right to hate me.'

'When someone starts a sentence like that, they're always working up to a but.'

'There is no but,' he replied. 'I took you for granted. I lied to you and betrayed you and I am incredibly sorry.'

'Well, thank you, Neil.'

'Give you a lift home?' he said.

'No thanks. I'll walk.'

He sighed. 'I am trying, Marce.'

The sun had set and fog clung near the ground, diffusing the light from the street lamps, blurring the edges and shapes of things. Marcy progressed along the wide pavement running next to the abbey. A pair of black figures emerged up the staircase and out the abbey gate: students from the art college, wearing cloaks down to their ankles and each carting a portfolio nearly as big as they were. They turned left, in the direction Marcy was going, heads together in conversation. Marcy was watching in admiration when something moved at the edge of her field of vision. Not something, someone. A man, lurking in the shadows. She picked up her pace and veered away from the abbey. The figure did the same. He was headed straight towards her. The orange ember of a cigarette glowed in the grey darkness. Maybe she should have taken Neil up on his offer of a ride. Her heart beat faster as the figure drew close, close enough for her to smell the cigarette. The unusual blend of tobacco was familiar.

'Nizar?'

'Hello Marcy,' he replied.

'Goodness,' she said. 'I was scared there for a moment.'

'It is only me.' He smiled in that shy way of his. 'I am meeting Tahrir.'

'Wouldn't you prefer to wait for him in the house where it's warm?'

'I like the fresh air. I like to see the art students.'

A few more of the students passed by, headed to the bus and tram stops; one of them had a mop of bright green hair with yellow tips, another wore paisley-printed harem pants, the crotch hanging below the knee.

'God love them,' Marcy said, nodding in their direction. 'It's amazing they survived primary school, let alone finished secondary. I want to grab these kids by the collar and say "Good for you! You made it!"'

'Do you think it's a good thing for them that they are this way?'

'The people on the edges are what make a society move, Nizar. Don't ever forget that.'

'But can a person just do as they choose? Customs, culture and religion are also important, are they not?'

'Indeed, they are,' Marcy said. 'So long as people's spirits aren't trampled.'

Nizar smiled but she wasn't sure he understood what she meant.

'Ah, here is Tahrir,' he said.

Tahrir appeared out of the darkness, dressed entirely in black and scowling.

'Tahrir,' Marcy said. 'Nizar and I were just discussing the importance of artists in any society.'

Tahrir grunted.

'Are you an art lover?' she asked.

He shot a nervous look towards Nizar.

'He is a butcher,' Nizar said. 'But he is also a lover of art, and artists as well. Isn't that so, Tahrir?'

'Yes,' Tahrir said after what appeared to be an internal struggle.

'We must be going, Marcy,' said Nizar. 'I will return before ten tonight, if that is all right with you?'

'Of course,' Marcy replied. 'Should I save you some dinner?'

Nizar looked at Tahrir before answering.

'No,' he replied. 'That is not necessary but thank you for your kind gesture.'

Alec

The week before the scheduled outdoor painting session, Madame Joelle showed up to class with chocolates.

'Take as many as you like,' she said.

Alec took two, not wanting to be greedy. The girls limited themselves to one. Guillem grabbed a handful.

Once everyone was eating, Madame Joelle announced it was her last day. As they stared in shock, she told them how much she had enjoyed teaching them and that she hoped they would continue to pursue their art with a creative spirit.

Alec was gutted. How could she leave them like that? Walk away before the outdoor-painting session she'd promised?

'Where are you going, Madame?' Farrah asked.

'I'm not sure,' she replied. 'I'm looking for a new position.'

The chocolate turned to mud in Alec's mouth. Had Madame Joelle been sacked? Rumours flared on group chats that night: it was because of her nose ring and audacious hair colour, parents had complained; she had been caught *in flagrante delicto* with a student. Alec was sure that one was a lie. The truth was more banal and outrageous. She had been bumped to make room for a more senior teacher from another school in their district, a teacher who was *nommé*.

Farrah had to explain it to him.

'Teachers who are *nommé* have a guaranteed job until they retire. If there's a *reáffectation*, like, say, a school closes or drops their course, the administration has to find them a place in the same subject, within the same geographical zone.'

'But there wasn't a position here,' Alec said.

'If there aren't any open positions in the zone, the teacher who is *nommé* can take the job of a teacher who isn't. The school has no choice; it has to give it to them.'

The pitch was underhanded, a great lobbing moon ball, that arced two metres in the air. Alec knew instantly it was not worth a swing and watched, with satisfaction, as it passed the strike zone, high and outside.

'Strike one,' the teacher announced.

Usually, Alec enjoyed PE. There was no homework, no pop quizzes, no interrogation, and it offered a chance to blow off steam. Except when they played *le baseball*. The teacher's call, so obviously wrong, filled him with fury. He did his best to hold it in; push it down. There was nothing to gain by questioning the teacher's judgment or his skill. In addition to umpire, the teacher was also serving as the pitcher. And, anyway, an inability to distinguish a ball from a strike was hardly the teacher's most egregious offence against America's national pastime. They ran clockwise, instead of anti-clockwise, around six bases instead of four – a pentagon rather than a diamond. They weren't bases at all, but florescent traffic cones, too small to tag, slide into, or steal. They didn't even have a baseball, for God's sake; they used a tennis ball instead. Alec wasn't a quibbler or a purist; however, when you keep tinkering with the rules of any game, at some point, it ceases to be that game and becomes a totally different one. Why insist on calling it baseball?

The teacher bounced the tennis ball against the macadam surface of the school's courtyard the way tennis players do in preparation for an overhead serve.

Alec pursed his lips together, tapped the tip of the aluminium bat on the ground, twice, before resuming his stance. The bat hung in the air above his shoulder, buffering slightly in the winter breeze, so much lighter than the ash Louisville Slugger his mother had used to teach him the game. The real game.

The next pitch was lower and flatter. Alec uncoiled his swing, but the lightness of the bat – it was like holding air – threw off his timing. He was done swinging before the ball reached him.

'Strike two,' the teacher said.

'Come on, Cowboy,' someone called out. 'You're supposed to be good at this.'

The comment earned snickers from his fellow players. His being American lifted expectations; unreasonable ones, he thought. Backyard lessons with his mother and grandfather aside, he'd only ever played a few pick-up games, tagging along with his cousins and random kids during holidays on the island in Lake Erie. They cut him slack because he was 'foreign' and stuck him out in right field where he would do the least damage. He spent the time daydreaming and praying he'd never have to actually field a ball. Okay, it was more experience than anyone else could claim, but it hardly made him an expert, and besides, that was in real baseball, not this fanciful bastardisation of it.

'Why so serious, Cowboy?' Dhaki asked, tugging on the thread of a conversation that had begun in the locker room. Earlier, in geography class, the teacher, illustrating the difference between population and population density, had said, 'We know that Belgium is a small country, only nine million people, whereas the United States is much bigger: three-hundred-twenty-three-million people. But the territory of the United States is even more vast than its population is large, only thirty-five people per square kilometre whereas in Belgium, we have three-hundred-seventy-four. For the United States of America to have a population density equal to ours, it would need three point three billion people. Which, I think we can all agree, would be far too many Americans.'

It wasn't his classmates' outrageous laughs that upset Alec. He had expected them. However, the teacher smiling at his own joke was gutting. Alec liked the geography teacher. In four years, he'd never known him to mock or humiliate a student the way some teachers did. Alec stared down at his desk, and when it was finally over and he got up to leave, he could not meet the teacher's eye.

'It was only a joke,' everyone said.

'How would you have felt if he'd said that about Morocco?' he'd asked Dhaki. 'Or Israel,' he said, to Felix, who was Jewish.

'But that would be racism,' they both said. 'It's completely different.'

'How?' Alec asked, emotion rising in his throat despite his efforts to hold it back. 'How is it different?'

'It is,' they replied with shrugs. 'America isn't a race.'

'Unless you're a Native American,' Felix added.

'Yeah,' Dhaki said. 'Obama isn't the same race as you. How can America be a race if your president isn't the same race as you?'

Dhaki had been in a pissy mood all week. He had fooled around with a girl from Troisième C at a party the previous weekend, and now Farrah wasn't talking to him. Alec said the right things, made the right sympathetic noises, but inwardly he rejoiced that their romance had run its course.

Alec choked up on the bat and adjusted his stance, squinting at the yellow tennis ball in his teacher's hand as the teacher's arm drew back and then swung forward, palm opening to release the ball. The yellow orb moved through space, slow and straight. His Gramps had a name for pitches like these: meatballs. They're so mouth-wateringly good, a batter can't resist taking a bite out of them. Gramps had thrown plenty of meatballs for Alec, in the backyard of his house, when Alec was little. Mom stood behind Alec, a foot planted on either side of his, hands atop his own, to guide and steady each swing. Alec recalled his first hit, the satisfying crack as leather connected with ash; Gramps calling out:

'That's it, Allie-oop! Now run! Run to first.'

Alec waited until the ball crossed in front of him before he unwound, striking it square on. A ping. The bat rever-berated in his hands. The ball flew high and long. The teacher and the boys on the field looked up and watched it. It curved up and over the back fence and bounced off the roof of a parked car and then into the road. Alec dropped the bat and ran towards first base.

'The other way, Cowboy,' they shouted.

*

The gym teacher held them too long, forcing them to run to the changing rooms, Alec more than the others as he had to go from the basement changing rooms to the art room on the top floor. He barely rinsed off in the shower and was sweating again as he rushed out.

'Hey, Cowboy,' Dhaki called, 'wait up.'

Alec slowed, though he had no time to waste.

'I need a favour, bro.'

Alec closed his eyes, knowing what was coming.

'Talk to Farrah, would you? Tell her this is all a misunderstanding. Say nothing happened with the girl from Troisième C.'

'You're asking me to lie?'

'Hey, man, you weren't there.'

'Come on, D. Everyone's talking about it. There were witnesses.'

Dhaki shrugged. 'If I can get with a girl, I'm going to. You know how it is.'

Alec nodded, but the truth was, he had no idea 'how it is' or was. 'Farrah isn't just any old girl,' he said.

'I know. Don't you think I know that? The *pute* from Troisième C didn't mean anything.'

'You can't treat her like that.'

'I know, and I won't; not ever again. You need to talk her into taking me back,' Dhaki said. 'Farrah will listen to you. She respects you.' Dhaki gave him a brotherly punch on the arm and sauntered off to economics, his backpack draped over one shoulder. 'Thanks, Cowboy. You're the best.'

Alec took a breath and continued rushing up the stairs, his portfolio catching the air like a sail. When he reached the studio, he was panting.

The change in atmosphere was immediately apparent.

The new teacher, Monsieur Renard, had heavy bags under his eyes and stringy, mostly grey hair. The action paintings that had covered the classroom walls lay in a pile on the floor in a corner. In their place, posters of the Madonna and Child and the Joconde hung together with posters listing the rules of classical geometry and symmetry, the rule of odds and the rule of thirds. On a table at the centre of the class was a bowl filled with fruit.

'I will call you up, one by one, and look through your portfolios,' the teacher said. 'In the meantime, I want your rendition of this fruit bowl.'

'Great,' Alec whispered to Farrah.

'I'd have thought you'd be happy,' Farrah murmured. 'You like still lifes.'

'I've gone in another direction,' Alec said.

He hadn't agreed to Dhaki's request, but he knew Dhaki assumed otherwise. He wished he wasn't such a doormat; wished he would learn to say no. For minutes, he vacillated about whether to speak on Dhaki's behalf, and then launched into a half-hearted effort. 'Listen,' he began. 'Dhaki is really broken up.'

'Don't, Cowboy,' she said.

'It's just. He's devastated.'

'He ought to have thought of that before.'

'He can't sleep; can't eat.'

He made this last part up, to prove to himself he wasn't going about it half-heartedly. Farrah wasn't buying it.

'Yeah. He's positively wasting away.'

'Give him a chance.'

'We were doomed anyway.'

'How?' he asked, hoping to hear something like, 'Because I never loved him.'

'My parents claim they aren't religious and yet. . .' She let it trail off.

'You're both Muslim, though, aren't you?'

'Yeah. He's Sunni, though.'

'So?'

'So, I'm Shia. My parents would rather I dated you than a Sunni.'

Alec couldn't ask why that was because hearing her outline a hypothetical in which they were a couple momentarily deprived him of the ability to speak, and then the teacher called his name. Alec went forward with his portfolio. The teacher flipped quickly through the pages of still lifes. He paused, very briefly, at Nizar's drawing of the boy on the beach. Once he got to the action painting section, he closed the book.

'*Pas terrible*,' he said with a grimace. 'But not original, either. Six out of ten, maybe.'

Alec walked to the tram, despondent about a future in which he couldn't even look forward art class. He was nearly incandescent with rage and in need of distraction if he was going to avoid having the uncoolest of tantrums on the tram platform. He took out his phone and googled: Sunni vs Shia, wanting to understand the conditions that made him a more suitable boyfriend than Dhaki in the eyes of Farrah's parents. A video about the rightful heir to the Prophet was dry and dull, but the next one, about geo-political issues, was marginally more interesting, and the one about power struggles more interesting still. He watched more, watched all the way home, videos about power struggles, regional crises and centuries of strife. The tone of each was a bit more strident than the one before it, a steady upward progression of passion. When he got home, Alec went straight to his room and kept watching. The focus of the videos shifted from facts and history to grievances and justifications; angry men waving swords as they railed against false prophets and idolatry, and swore revenge against infidels. Alec responded to their anger if not their words and kept clicking, until he came to the one of the man in the orange jumpsuit, handcuffed and kneeling in the desert, a masked man in black, and the close-up of a sharpened knife glistening in the sun. The internet knew what he wanted before he did.

That night at dinner, his mother had an announcement.

'I've seen an apartment I think could work,' she said, 'and that's within my budget, but I need to ask you a favour, Alec. Would you mind sharing with Jake?'

Share a bedroom with an eight-year-old? Have his room filled with Lego and Playmobil? He was aghast.

'It would only be temporary,' she said.

'How long is temporary?'

'At least until Nizar's application is complete. Normally, that's not supposed to be more than six months, but they're backlogged because there has been so much demand. It could be nine months.'

His mother was going to make him share a room with Jake so Nizar could have his own? It was an outrage. He seethed but replied with an indifferent 'whatever'.

After dinner, instead of doing homework, Alec made a list of people he blamed for ruining his life. He typed it in the Notes feature on his phone, under a title, 'Those Who Must Pay'. Dhaki was on it, for cheating on Farrah, and Farrah for still being in love with Dhaki despite claiming otherwise. His geography teacher made the list, so did his gym teacher for not knowing baseball. Monsieur Renard was a new entry, for sucking the fun out of the only class he enjoyed, and Madame Joelle for having abandoned him to Monsieur Renard, even if it wasn't her fault. And while he was at it, add whoever it was who set up schools to suit teachers instead of students. Nizar was on the list, of course, and Sasha for throwing him under the bus. Regretfully, his mother was there, too, for not understanding he had only wanted to protect her. She was, however, several places below Kevin with the tiny *nichons*, whose name, he now knew, was Chloé, who was second, right below the man at the top, her partner in crime, the guy who had wrecked it all: his father. And yet even as Alec was writing his father's name in capital letters, he understood his list was a lie, a misdirection, a deflection. The person he blamed most, the person he despised, was none other than himself. He loathed his weakness; his way of keeping quiet when he ought to speak up, for behaving like water, taking the path of least resistance because he was too cowardly to go his own way.

The canvas wasn't a place to produce a product, Madame Joelle taught him. It was an arena in which to act. The time had come for Alec to act. The school would be his canvas. He thought of Pollock's *Number 17A* – its energy and passion. He would create his own *Number 17A*, Yardley *Number 1A* on the windows of the art room, though even in his most feverish rage, he doubted he'd be able to reach the third floor without a catapult. The main entrance would have to suffice: an explosion of primary colours; a statement of his *colère*.

He took the paint he had bought for his mother's canvas,

and found some balloons in a drawer, left over from Sasha's birthday two years before. They were purple and had *Joyeux Anniversaire* written in large white letters on them. With the funnel they used to pour dirty frying oil back into their original bottles for recycling, he slowly filled a balloon with paint. He worked in the old soapstone utility sink in the basement and was glad he did because he filled it too much and it burst when he tried to lift it.

Ideally, he would have filled dozens of balloons, but there were only six in the bag, and he had ruined one. The next one he filled halfway, leaving lots of slack at the top for the knot. Red, yellow, blue and another red: four balloons covered the bottom of the shopping bag he took from the closet. He decided against adding the last one for fear it would burst and he'd have a real mess on his hands. The bag was heavy enough as it was. Quality over quantity. On impulse, he filled his Super Soaker water gun with white paint for a detailed flourish. He carried the bag and water gun to the front hall and then went up to his room, creeping extra softly when he saw light glowing beneath the doors of both Sasha's and Nizar's bedrooms. He put on black jeans, a long-sleeved black T-shirt and his black Adidas hoodie, which he put on inside out so that the logo didn't show. He held the rail as he descended the stairs in the dark, stepping wide to avoid a squeaky floorboard on the landing outside Sasha's room. He misjudged. His heel hit the ground harder than expected. He froze, too afraid to breathe. He stared at the doorknob, willing it not to turn. He counted: one Mississippi, two Mississippi, three Mississippi, exhaled, and then he continued on his way.

A tram approached as he was lacing up his boots. He

stuffed the water gun underneath his hoodie, though he couldn't prevent its bright yellow barrel poking up through the collar. As quietly as possible, he opened the front door and closed it behind him, turning the lock twice to engage the bolt, as the tram departed. Holding the water gun beneath his hoodie with one hand and the bag in the other, away from his body so as not to disturb the balloons, he walk-waddled to the shelter where the tram schedule was posted, only to discover he had just missed the last one. He could not believe it! School was at least three kilometres away, too far to walk. He could cycle, but the balloons were fragile. The bag was heavy. He'd have to leave the water gun behind. The anger that he had channelled into this project suddenly threatened to boil over. He wanted to kick the bag, to scream into the night so that his voice echoed off the buildings. He was a teenage artist with a bag of paint and no canvas. He stomped his foot and paced the platform, turned and saw the answer illuminated in the night: the Syrian Embassy.

The first balloon, when he lifted it out of the bag, was as unwieldy as a snake, the paint rolling and shifting within. He needed both hands. A smaller balloon would have been better, he thought, and then stopped himself.

He must *not* think. He remembered Madame Joelle's words. 'Leave behind the self that wishes to choose its own future,' he whispered.

He approached with his back to the embassy gate, cradling the balloon in his arms like a baby. He squatted and then swung the balloon from between his legs, up and over his head like an old-timey basketball player shooting, granny-style, from the foul line, only backwards. The balloon wobbled, topsy-turvy, head-over-heels up over the spikes of the wrought-iron fence and burst against a first-floor window, an explosion of blue.

Pollock didn't even touch the canvas.

He pumped the barrel of the Super Soaker. Jets of paint streamed through the bars of the gate, adding a thin line of white to his masterpiece. He scooped up another balloon. He took up the same position, but at the moment of release, a shadow appeared to his left, to block. The balloon burst in the air above him; red paint rained down, streaking Alec's head, his hair, shoulders, dripping down his pant-leg and on to the pavement. *No point in an act if you already know what it contains.*

He turned towards the shadow, expecting to find a police officer or a security guard.

'Fucking Nizar!'

Neil

Had he given the matter any thought, Neil would have dressed with a bit more care. As it was, he'd gone from his bed to his car in minutes – seconds, perhaps – throwing a pair of tracksuit bottoms on over his sleepwear before rushing from his apartment as if from a burning building. And, yes, perhaps he'd overreacted. He'd definitely overreacted. The closest thing he'd ever come to a brush with the law was receiving a handful of parking tickets. Who wouldn't be alarmed by a call from police in the middle of the night informing them their son was in custody? But now, standing beneath a fluorescent light that did his complexion no favours, sliding his identity card through the hole in the Plexiglas screen to the female officer at reception, it occurred to him that an extra five minutes to put on a pair of jeans and a proper shirt would have been time well spent. He hadn't been thinking of himself, only of Alec.

'When can I see my son?' he asked her, pulling close his trench to cover the T-shirt that announced: *This guy needs a beer.*

'Take a seat,' she said, pointing with her chin. 'The inspector will be with you shortly.'

Neil sat on a moulded plastic chair in a small waiting area. 'Three-twenty-eight,' said the digital clock on the opposite wall; red lights on a black background. 'Three-twenty-nine.' The colon in the centre blinked with each second. 'Three-thirty'. He bent to lace his shoes and tug the hem of the tracksuit to cover his bare ankles.

At three-forty-two a plain-clothed policeman came around the corner.

'Monsieur Yardley?' he said as Neil jumped to attention. 'Inspector Wouters.' The inspector took Neil's hand in a vice-like grip. 'Please. Come this way.'

Neil followed him down a hall with several doors. The inspector threw one open and signalled for Neil to enter. 'Please,' he said.

It was a small room. In its centre was a rectangular table and on the far side of that table, looking utterly miserable, sat Alec. Neil gasped when he saw his hair, matted with what appeared to be blood. 'What have you —' *What have you done to my son?* He was going to ask but then he realised it wasn't blood but paint.

'Oh, Alec,' Neil cried, after Inspector Wouters closed the door, leaving them alone, 'what on Earth have you done?' It was a literal question. He'd been given a rough idea. It just didn't make sense.

'I desperately recognised my moral and intellectual exhaustion,' his son mumbled.

'What the hell is that supposed to mean?'

'I knew you wouldn't understand.'

'You're damn right I don't understand.'

'Then why did you ask?'

Neil flinched under his son's cool gaze. In the past two months Neil had grown accustomed to being in the wrong.

It took a moment to recall that, in this instance, he held the moral high ground.

'Look here. You called me in the middle of the night, and I've come. A little gratitude is in order, don't you think?'

Alec pushed a little air out his nostrils and gave his head a microscopic, insolent shake. 'Would you mind holding off on the lecture just a little bit, Dad?'

As a matter of fact, Neil *did* mind. If ever there was a time for a lecture, this appeared to be it. His own father would have boxed his ears had Neil showed one tenth of Alec's cheek. Still, Neil wasn't going to bang on about it.

'I'm glad you called me, son,' he told him. 'You did the right thing.'

'Yeah, well I didn't want to cause Mom any more pain,' he muttered.

'No, ' Neil agreed, devastated. 'No, of course not.'

Inspector Wouters returned with another man, younger, broad-shouldered, and with a jaw that could have been chiselled from granite. 'My colleague, Inspector Dumont,' he announced.

Inspector Dumont opened a file and began reading from a report. 'This morning at approximately one-thirty, the Syrian Embassy was attacked with paint bombs. We are consulting with the embassy for a copy of the tape from their security cameras. Your son and another suspect were discovered in front of the embassy gates and near them was a bag containing several more paint bombs and a water gun, also filled with paint.'

'Paint,' Alec said. 'Meanwhile, Assad drops barrel bombs filled with chemical weapons on his own people.'

'There are peaceful ways of protesting,' said Inspector Wouters. 'We have laws in this country.'

Neil frowned to convey the seriousness with which he regarded the situation, but inwardly, he felt only relief. Vandalism, even of an embassy, was a misdemeanour charge. There'd be a fine, a little community service, maybe a written apology. Nothing on Alec's record. And the experience would likely deter him from doing anything stupid in the future.

'Actions have consequences, Alec,' Neil said, mostly for the police officers' benefit. They'd be out of here in half an hour. With a little luck he could get another hour of sleep in before he had to get up for work. 'This will cost you. A hefty fine, I expect. And make no mistake, it is going to come out of your pocket money.'

'There is something else,' Wouters continued. 'We wanted to speak with you because we are concerned for Alec's welfare.'

'His welfare?' Neil repeated.

'Has Alec been spending more time alone in his room?' the chiselled jaw one asked. 'Isolating himself from family and friends?'

'Doesn't every teenager?' Neil remarked, with a nervous laugh.

'Does he ever appear to speak from a scripted speech?'

'Not to me,' Neil said, neglecting to mention that, up until five minutes ago, his son hadn't spoken to him since last July.

'Is he unwilling to discuss his views?' Chiselled Jaw continued.

'Err,' Neil said, 'not that I'm aware of.'

'Suddenly become intolerant of the opinions of others?' Wouters asked.

The officers were fishing for something, what exactly Neil could only imagine, but he knew he must choose his words with care. He was treading a fine line. At what point does replying narrowly to a question become lack of candour or evasiveness?

He turned towards his son. 'I think we'd better call your mother, don't you?'

He and Alec were in the waiting room, on the moulded plastic seats, when Marcy swept in, eyes full of anxiety at six past six. She put her arms around Alec, and Neil watched as their son, who stood a head taller than his mother, melted as she gently rocked him back and forth. When she deemed him sufficiently comforted, she handed him a comb and sent him to the toilet to wash the paint out of his hair.

'What's going on?' she asked Neil.

'Alec threw a paint bomb at the Syrian Embassy. He isn't under arrest, but police say they're worried for his welfare.'

'What does that mean?'

'It's not entirely clear.'

'Do we need to talk to a lawyer?'

'To come in guns blazing won't serve our interest, I don't think,' he said. 'This isn't America.'

'I never said it was.'

Neil watched the minutes click past: six-eleven, six-twelve.

'Have you finished your list?' she asked.

The list of things he wanted from the house. It was required for the divorce petition. Marcy wanted to file as soon as possible.

'Not yet,' he said.

'I sent you the inventory. All you have to do is check off what you want.'

'I know,' he said, 'and I'm sorry. Things are crazy at work.'

'When aren't they?'

'This is different. There's a reorganisation.'

He was going to tell her about the hundreds losing their jobs on account of Benny Marsh's divorce and then thought better of it. Chloé was part of the first wave. Neil had had an uncomfortable conversation with the head of HR who was trying to gauge the company's potential exposure to charges of sexual harassment or retaliation.

'Honestly, Marcy,' he said, 'you can have everything. Take it all.'

'Even the mantel clock?' she'd asked. The clock had belonged to a great-aunt and was over a century old. 'Wouldn't your mother mind it leaving the family?'

The thought of Marcy no longer being part of his family filled him with sadness.

Shortly after Alec returned with his now wet hair combed and parted, Inspector Wouters invited them back to the interview room.

'We appreciate that adolescence can be a trying time for parents and children, particularly sons,' he said, with a sympathetic smile for Marcy. 'It's important for us to have any relevant information so that we may save Alec from himself.'

'Madame Yardley,' Inspector Dumont began, 'do you monitor your son's online activities?'

'Absolutely not. I believe he has a right to his privacy.'

'Have you noticed increased levels of anger in him?'

She paused. 'Well,' she began.

'So you have noticed some troubling behaviours of late?'

'He's an adolescent boy.'

'Has he become secretive about his internet use?'

'Not that I can recall,' she said. 'Previously we've had discussions about video gaming.'

'Which aspects?'

'The violence and the time spent on them.'

'And which would you say concerned you most? The violence or the time?'

'Both were a concern,' she said. 'But I would say primarily the violence.'

'How was the situation resolved?'

'I gave his console away.'

'Has Alec expressed to you a feeling that he doesn't belong?' said the other cop, Dumont.

'Hasn't every teenager since the dawn of time felt they didn't belong? And, well, he *is* an outsider. We're foreigners, all of us. I know I feel I don't belong sometimes. Often, in fact.'

Neil would have hedged out of fear of getting Alec into more trouble, but Marcy always looked for a way to understand others. She might be the most empathetic person he knew.

'Are you aware of his preoccupation with violence and death, that there is evidence he has engaged in the torture of animals?'

'What?' all three cried out in unison.

'I never,' Alec exclaimed.

'We found these pictures on Alec's phone,' Inspector Dumont said as he took a sheet of A4 paper from his file and slid it across the table. There were close-ups of dead fish, crushed shellfish and a dying crow captured from various angles.

Neil gasped, 'Alec!'

'It flew into a window at school,' Alec said. 'You can ask my maths teacher!'

'But why photograph it?' Inspector Wouters asked. 'That is the question.'

'For art,' Alec replied.

'Do you care to tell your parents about the hit list, Alec?'

Alec looked down.

'It was on his phone,' Wouters said. 'You are at the top, Monsieur Yardley. Madame Yardley, you are on it as well, albeit further down.'

'It didn't mean anything,' Alec said, looking up. There were tears in his eyes. 'I was angry. I would never. . .'

'Has Alec ever expressed sympathies for Daesh?' asked Inspector Wouters.

'Hang on,' Neil said. 'That other suspect that was caught with you,' he said to his son, 'that was Nizar, wasn't it?' Neil didn't know why he hadn't thought about it before. 'Has he been filling your head with stories of injustices?'

'Why are you bringing Nizar into this?' Marcy asked.

'He was with you tonight, wasn't he?'

'Dad,' Alec pleaded, 'would you just shut up?'

'Wait, Nizar was with you? Where is he now?'

'We're here for our son, Marcy. Stop worrying about Nizar. There's a good chance he has corrupted Alec.'

'So, Monsieur Yardley,' said Chiselled Jaw, 'you admit to having concerns that Alec is being radicalised?'

'He wouldn't know,' Marcy told the inspectors. 'He hasn't seen him for months.'

'What if I told you, Madame Yardley, that Alec has been visiting radical jihadi propaganda sites; watching videos of executions?' Wouters asked.

Marcy's eyes narrowed. 'Inspector, as far as I know,

curiosity about the world is not a crime. He has friends who are Muslim. He hears about these things all around him. I'm glad he's seeking out answers to his questions. I trust my son to know right from wrong.'

'Have you any idea how quickly boys like Alec have been radicalised?' Wouters asked. 'For many parents, the first warning of a problem is a call from the battlefields in Syria.'

'I'm sorry,' Marcy said. 'Which department did you two say you worked in?'

They exchanged glances. Wouters nodded to Dumont.

'Counter-terrorism,' he said.

Marcy stood up. 'I think we're done here.'

'Not so fast, Madame,' Wouters said. 'Recent changes in the law give us tools to fight terrorism and potential threats to public safety. Based on the evidence, we can make the case that Alec is at risk of flight to Syria. We can have his passports confiscated.'

'That's absurd,' Neil said. 'He's a citizen of the European Union.'

'He could even be banned from the kingdom of Belgium,' Chiselled jaw added.

'Without due process?' Marcy asked.

'He is a minor,' Neil cried. 'He's British!'

'Furthermore, we might be forced to share these details with the US government as part of our ongoing security cooperation. His name could be added to the no-fly list.'

'We won't be saying anything further until we consult a lawyer,' Marcy said.

Neil got the name of a reputable criminal law firm from the head of legal at his company. The female lawyer who arrived at the precinct a few hours later wasted no time spelling things out.

'Legally, they could hold Alec another two days, but they're willing to release him provided he surrenders his passports and agrees to join the anti-radicalisation programme.'

'For throwing some paint against a wall?' Neil said.

'It is fortunate he is still a minor,' she told them.

'Don't get me wrong: what Alec did was stupid,' Neil said. 'Phenomenally stupid, but it was naive teenage angst.'

'That embassy gets attacked all the time,' Marcy said. 'We know. We've seen.'

'Yes,' Neil agreed, 'and much worse than this. There was the time the windows were smashed. They got inside; ransacked the place.'

'It's even been paint-bombed worse before,' Marcy said. 'This barely made a splatter.'

'The damage to the embassy isn't the point. None of this would have happened if Alec hadn't given them permission to look through his phone.'

'I didn't think I had a choice,' Alec said.

'You always have a choice, unless they have a warrant,' the lawyer said. 'Any sixteen-year-old from Molenbeek, Schaerbeek or Anderlecht would have known that.'

'So this is all my fault?' Alec asked.

'Your parents should have refused to talk to them without a lawyer present. All this stuff about a friendly chat. There is no such thing as a friendly chat.'

'It's all circumstantial evidence,' Marcy said.

'They don't need proof, Madame. Alec isn't being charged with a crime,' the lawyer said. 'They are covering their backsides. It is easier to pull in the boy who landed in their lap to fill this anti-radicalisation programme. Even better, Alec gives them cover to say they aren't racial profiling.'

'You mean they don't actually believe what they're saying?' Neil asked.

'We cannot know what they believe,' the lawyer said. 'I would say it's a possibility.'

'So the threat of kicking him out of the country or getting him added to the no-fly list, you think that's a bluff?' Marcy asked.

'We cannot know, and it is my advice that you not test it, not if Alec wants to visit his American family in the future. The government is scared of a Paris-like attack and they have egg on their face because Abdeslam slipped through their net. Imagine, how would it look if it turned out they had a future terrorist in custody, and they let him go? In some ways, the ones who come back from Syria are the least of their worries. They know who they are. It's the ones they don't know that they are losing sleep over. People radicalised over the internet are like needles in a haystack. A boy like Alec, white, dual UK, US national, with a clean record, is a diamond to the terrorists. And he ticks a lot of the boxes: family in difficulty, having trouble at school, is a bit of an outsider. The photos suggest he's obsessed with death. Searching websites. And there is always the possibility that they're right and Alec is being radicalised.'

'Has Nizar been trying to recruit you?' Neil asked Alec.

'Why do you keep trying to blame Nizar?' Marcy asked.

'Don't be stupid, Dad,' Alec muttered.

'What if we refuse,' Neil asked the lawyer.

'Then you must be prepared for Alec to spend the next two days – maybe more – in jail, waiting to come before a judge who might not be disposed to take his side.'

'It's madness. It's unjust.'

'Monsieur, believe me, I see far worse every week. Are you truly surprised that injustice exists, or is the surprise that your son is experiencing it first-hand? If Alec keeps his nose clean, in a few months he will most likely be deemed not dangerous. At that point his record will be wiped clean and he will not suffer any adverse consequences.'

Wouters and Dumont could hardly repress their smug smiles.

'Should you need to travel as a family, either of you may ask for Alec's passports and you will have them back within twenty-four hours. Alec is expected to attend weekly meetings and the family agrees to participate in any supplementary sessions deemed necessary, understood?'

'Can you assure us he won't be placed on a no-fly list?' Marcy asked.

'That is a matter for the US government, Madame,' Wouters said, 'and if I were you, I would do all I could to keep them out of this.'

'He's never even had detention at school!' Neil remarked.

A uniformed police officer stuck her head through the door. 'Jérôme?' she called.

Dumont looked up and Neil's heart rate jumped from zero to sixty. His palms began to sweat. Jérôme was a common enough name for a man of this guy's age, Neil told himself. Besides, this guy was called Dumont, Chloé's last name was du Pré.

'Have you got the dossier on Van Nyes?' the woman asked.

Dumont nodded, pulled a dossier from his pile and held it out for the officer to take and as he did so, he turned towards Neil. Did he imagine it, or did Dumont nod at him?

That's when he recalled that Belgian women often used their maiden names professionally.

Wouters's phone rang.

'Wouters,' he said.

He listened with his head down.

'*D'accord*,' he said and then again, '*d'accord*.'

He hung up and turned towards Neil, Marcy and Alec.

'My colleagues have executed a search warrant on your home. They found bomb making equipment and plastic explosives.'

Marcy

The therapist's waiting room was narrow and cramped, with rickety wooden chairs lining both sides and beneath a sash window, a play area, with a toy basket and a mat in bold primary colours. A toddler was on the mat and in front of him was a toy barn. He was opening and closing its doors, which made a mooing sound whenever they opened. A woman, the child's mother, presumably, sat nearby, staring at her phone.

Phew, thought Marcy. They were on time, before Neil, even. It hadn't been easy, but she had made it home from her lesson and ensured the kids had what they needed to stay the weekend at Neil's. At least she had got this one thing right.

She sat down, placing her handbag on the chair next to her. Jake made a beeline for the toy basket. The pickings looked slim: a baby doll in a threadbare dress, its pallor grey from countless sticky fingers, and some plastic building bricks, warped and faded, but Jake, ever-hopeful, kept digging. Sasha and Alec went to sit on the other side of the room, as far away from Marcy as they could get. Sasha took out a vocabulary list for Ancient Greek, lips moving silently as she committed the words to memory; Alec stared at the tips of his trainers, that disconsolate expression on his face. 'You okay?' Marcy wanted to ask but didn't for fear of irritating him further. No answer he gave would put her at ease.

Jake found a spiny-backed dinosaur figurine in the basket. He put it on the mat and made it hop around. 'Oink-oink,' he said. 'Oink-oink.'

The barn doors went *moo* and the toddler laughed.

Neil arrived a few minutes later.

'Old chap!' he said, as Jake ran to embrace him. He kissed Sasha on the cheek and patted Alec's shoulder. Marcy moved her handbag from the seat next to her, a gesture of goodwill, but he waved it off and chose another seat. Her face burned. She had thought they would put on a united front, for Alec's sake. Obviously, he was still angry with her.

Jake went back to making the dinosaur hop.

'Oink-oink,' he said. 'Oink-oink.'

'That's some pig you've got, old chap,' Neil said, his thumb touching the spot on his finger where his wedding ring used to be.

'It's not a pig. It's a dinosaur,' Jake replied. 'Oink-oink.'

'Did dinosaurs oink?'

'They *could* have,' Jake replied. 'We don't know how they talked.'

The barn doors went *moo* and the toddler giggled with delight.

'Maybe we should leave the toys for the little kids,' Neil said.

'I *am* a little kid,' replied Jake, making the dinosaur hop across his father's shoes. 'Oink-oink.'

The edges of Alec's mouth lifted in a faint smile, one

274

of the first Marcy had seen in the ten days since what they were obliquely referring to as 'Alec's act of creative expression'. Her heart fluttered. *Oh, Alec!* she thought.

The consulting room was sparsely furnished. The counsellor was young – well, young-*ish*, mid-to-late thirties, if she'd had to guess, which, admittedly, wasn't so young. What she really meant was that he was younger than her. Also, he dressed like a barista: a red-and-white lumberjack shirt, skinny jeans rolled to the top of his Doc Martens and a beard, perfectly groomed and waxed.

'I am Michel,' he said, exuding empathy and calm. He had arranged chairs in a circle. Jake played shy, sucking his thumb, staring at the floor. He clung to Marcy and tried to crawl into her lap.

'Jake,' Michel said. 'There's a seat for you. Right next to Maman. You can hold her hand, if you'd like.'

Jake sucked his thumb two beats longer, in contemplation, and then gave his wet hand to Marcy, the other hand still clutching the dinosaur.

'Jake, can you tell us why you have all come here today?' the therapist asked.

Jake looked down and shook his head. He posed the dinosaur on his knee.

'All right. Who will go first? Sasha?'

'Shouldn't Alec go first?' Neil asked.

'We'll get to him,' Michel said. He rested one foot casually on the opposite knee and propped an A4 legal notepad on his thigh. 'I suspect Alec has been the central focus recently. I'd like to get a picture of the household.' His voice was soothing.

Sasha took a deep breath: 'Alec threw some paint at the embassy and downloaded some jihadi propaganda and now the police think he could be a terrorist or a future terrorist so we've all got to go to therapy so he doesn't get kicked out of Belgium or land on a no-fly list,' Sasha said, in the tone and tenor of one replying to a teacher's request for a recap of the previous lesson.

Alec folded his arms across his chest, his face stricken. It made you want to hug the kid, but Marcy couldn't reach him without leaving her seat and Jake, who in addition to holding her hand, was now leaning on her.

'Okay. That's a start,' Michel said, nodding his head. He uncapped a pen and made a note on the pad.

'For now, at least, I want to set aside what Alec did. I'd like to talk about all of you. The family.'

He asked the ages of the children and how well they got along, before moving on to the question Marcy, and probably Neil, too, had been dreading.

'And I understand there is a rupture, that you recently separated?'

She cleared her throat.

'That's correct,' Neil said.

'And would you say it was amicable?'

'For the most part,' Neil said.

Michel turned towards Marcy and she nodded.

'And was it by mutual consent?'

Neil made a little open-palmed wave, offering the floor to Marcy. She refused. The silence dragged on for a few seconds.

'It was my decision,' he announced, finally.

'He was sleeping with his secretary,' Marcy added, the words slipping out.

'I see,' said Michel.

Neil coloured. 'She wasn't my secretary,' he said.

'Whatever,' Marcy replied. 'She reports to you.'

'No, she doesn't.' He turned towards Michel. 'We worked on a project together.'

Michel nodded. 'And on that project, was she subordinate to you?'

'I don't see what relevance that has,' Neil replied.

'Interesting,' said Michel, making another note. 'And why do you think that?'

Neil flustered and fidgeted in his seat. 'Do the children really need to hear this?'

'Oh, that's rich,' said Marcy. 'As if the kids haven't been covering for you for months.'

'They weren't covering for me,' he replied. 'I didn't know they knew.'

Sasha bit her lower lip. Alec chewed on a nail. Jake returned his thumb to his mouth.

'Hmmm,' said Michel, stroking his beard. 'So, Neil, why do you think you kept the truth from Marcy and your children?'

'That's a good question,' Neil said. 'I've asked myself that a lot lately and—'

'Oh, please,' Marcy said, with a little snort. 'He didn't want work to find out. But work knew; the kids knew. Everyone knew apart from me.' She was aware of the anger rising in her, and the danger that she would lose control of it.

'The end of a marriage is always a *bouleversement*, particularly in situations such as this when there are children and the marriage has been a long one,' Michel said, 'but when one party doesn't know the whole truth, it makes everything more complicated. Without the facts, closure is not possible.'

'It was a mistake,' Neil said. 'I regret it. If I could turn back time, undo it all, make it all go away, I would. I wish I could heal my family, more than anything.'

'Really, Neil,' Marcy cried. 'Now *that's* something the children don't need to hear.'

'Are you saying you wish to reconcile?' the therapist asked Neil.

'No,' Neil cried, with a vehemence that made Marcy's skin prickle. 'I mean I *did*,' he said. He paused for a deep breath that he exhaled in a rush. 'We were headed there. At least I thought – that is, I *hoped* – but then she learned about the affair before I could tell her. By the second week in January, she'd accepted an offer on the house and sent me forms for a divorce by general consent.'

'Marcy, is that a fair description of events?'

'Well,' she said, dragging out the word to give herself time to collect her thoughts and keep a lid on her temper. 'I'm not prepared to be sloppy seconds. Fidelity matters to me. I thought it mattered to Neil. I thought it was something fundamental we agreed on. And I know you people think it's very square and backward and *Anglo-Saxon* of me to get hung up about an affair, but I can't help it. I'm not French, *excusez-moi*.'

Michel made another note. 'Madame, we are not French, either. We are Belgian. I know it can be difficult for the English to tell us apart.'

'I'm not English,' Marcy replied.

'American,' said Sasha.

Michel looked surprised. '*Chapeau*, Madame. Your French is very good.'

'Thank you,' she replied, ignoring Sasha's slight guffaw.

'And if I may say, with respect to your comment on

278

affairs,' he continued, 'perhaps it will not surprise you, but in my work, I meet many who have, or have had them. With very few exceptions, these people did not believe themselves capable of such an act. It was unthinkable to them. When asked to explain themselves, they talk about dissatisfaction, not with their partner or their marriage, but with themselves.'

'Yes,' said Neil, quick to agree. 'I would say that was true for me.'

'I bet they say that,' said Marcy, 'after they've been caught.'

Michel pivoted. 'Alec, how long did you know about your father's affair?'

'Um,' Alec said, looking at the floor. 'A while.' He swallowed hard, debating, gathering courage, before looking up. 'About a year, I think.' The sentence ended on an upswing, like a question.

'That is a long time to carry such a burden. It's not surprising, in such a situation, that one would want to lash out,' Michel grabbed at the air. 'Just to relieve some of the tension.'

'Yes.'

'Why the embassy?'

'I was going to my school, but I missed the last tram.'

The therapist stroked his beard again. 'You told the police that Assad was a monster.'

'Well, he is,' Alec said.

'Did Nizar suggest hitting the embassy?'

Alec shook his head.

'Is that a no?' Michel asked.

'No,' Alec said, speaking into the cuff of his hoodie.

'Alec,' said Michel, 'you seem reticent to be completely honest. Is it to protect Nizar?'

Alec smiled at his feet. 'I couldn't stand the guy.'

'Please, Alec,' Michel said. 'I am here to help you and I will be better able to do that if you are truthful.'

'I *am* being truthful,' Alec insisted.

'Did you sympathise with his anger?'

'I didn't know he was angry, but I can't say I blame him.'

Marcy gasped but not as loudly as Neil.

'Why?'

'It's obvious, isn't it? His childhood got stolen, his home destroyed. He's been left with nothing. We could have done something to help but we didn't.'

'We gave him refuge,' Sasha said.

'Yeah, but only him. His mother and sister are stuck in Turkey. Forever. If I were him, I'd . . .'

He paused.

Michel let the silence hang in the air for a few seconds. 'You'd what?' he asked.

'Nothing,' Alec said.

'Would you say that violence is sometimes justified?'

'Not justified. No, but understandable.'

'Interesting.'

'None of this would have happened if his mother hadn't invited a terrorist into the house without asking or consulting me,' Neil said. 'I warned her it was dangerous. I tried to do something about it, and I might add, your legal system was of little help. The lawyer I consulted practically called me a racist.'

'I still can't believe Nizar would do anything evil,' Marcy said.

'Marcy,' Neil exclaimed, 'they found traces of explosives; bomb-making equipment.'

'I know. I know. I just can't believe it.'

Neil rubbed his forehead with his fingertips.

'Was there nothing about him you found suspicious?' Michel asked.

'No. Absolutely not,' she said. 'He was courteous, helpful. He fixed things around the house; he took out the rubbish and recycling. He was lovely in every way.'

'Sasha, were you ever suspicious about Nizar?'

'A little, at first,' Sasha admitted. 'Alec and I both were. He was cagey.'

'What do you mean by cagey?'

'He didn't like to answer questions or talk about the camps or how he got to Belgium, but then I got to know him a little better and I just figured he stayed quiet because it was too traumatic.'

'Did he ever say anything radical or political? Did he ever tell you how you should dress, for example?'

'No. He talked about his sister and his mother. He felt guilty about leaving them in Turkey; and also about the secondary-school leaving exam. We're both taking it this year. He wanted to study medicine at university. I didn't say anything, but he has no chance. He is so far behind in his studies.'

Alec snorted. 'He never wanted to study medicine.'

'Well, obviously,' Neil said, looking nervous. It was odd. Marcy would have thought the change of focus from his affair to Nizar would have put him at ease. Instead, he looked as he did in pictures of his parents' fiftieth anniversary party, when he had known that, after dinner, he was going to have to sing 'The Confrontation' from *Les Misérables* with his brother: an impending sense of doom.

'And Jake, how did you feel about Nizar?' Michel asked.

Jake started to talk about the games Nizar had played

with him and the chateau he and Nizar had built with Lego during the lockdown, describing it in elaborate detail until their session was over.

'So, we agreed you'll bring the kids back by seven on Sunday,' Marcy said to Neil, as they filed back out to the waiting room.

'If I could have a word,' he said, and then he turned to the children. 'I'm just going to talk to you mother about something, won't be a moment.'

Neil took her elbow and steered her to the most remote corner of the room, withdrew an envelope from his breast pocket and handed it to her.

'Is this the list of things you want from the house?' she asked.

'Open it,' he said.

As she tore a corner from the envelope, he rubbed his jaw. 'I had no choice, Marcy,' he said. 'You left me no choice.'

It was a copy of a letter his lawyer had sent to the family court. Marcy's eyes scanned the page, but the words wouldn't sink in – such heavy, formal French gobbledegook and her heart was going like a freight train. Something about a petition and an audience with a judge and then the words: *garde exclusif.*

'You're suing for sole custody?' she asked him.

'You endangered the children. You all could have been killed, if not intentionally, then by accident. I mean, the guy was building bombs in his bedroom and you had absolutely no idea.'

'You've had this with you the whole time? You've been sitting there, waiting to spring this on me at the last moment?'

'I wanted you to hear it from me, so you knew I was sincere and that this was not in any way a cheap shot.' His tone was pleading, as if he were the victim in all this.

'How is this not a cheap shot?' she asked.

'I could have filed an emergency petition for immediate custody. That's what my lawyer advised I do, but I don't want to go down that route. I'll bring the kids back Sunday evening as we agreed. With Nizar in custody, there's no reason not to let this play out in the normal way. I'll use the time to get a bigger place that can fit us all.'

'I can't believe you're doing this to me.'

'I have *agonised* over this, Marcy, but I have to put the kids' safety first.'

On the walk home, Marcy compiled a list in her head of all the reasons why no judge was ever going to grant Neil sole custody. He had walked out on his children, whereas she had remained. She did the school runs, teachers' meetings, doctors' appointments and after-school activities. She prepared nutritious hot meals and packed lunches, laminated their schoolbooks, and cared for them when they were ill; she read them *Babar* and *Le Petit Prince*; *Goodnight Moon* and all nine books in the *Little House* series; taught them to ride bikes, to ice skate and do cartwheels; drilled them on multiplication tables, the animals of the farm, the varieties of trees, the parts of the fucking flower. Meanwhile, Neil headed off to work each morning and returned ten or more hours later. That is, unless he had a business dinner or a work trip. It wasn't possible that a man who consistently put work ahead of family, who regularly cancelled or rescheduled visits with his children at the last minute, could be deemed the more responsible parent; that her decades of good mothering were negated by one supposed mistake. An act of kindness. No harm had come to the children from having Nizar in the house. They'd carry the scars of Neil's affair forever. How could potential harm be worse than actual harm?

It couldn't, obviously, and yet this did not reassure. A clever lawyer could make her fostering Nizar seem like an act of gross negligence. They would cite things she had said and done at her worst moments to paint her as reckless, undependable, crazy. It wouldn't be hard and she couldn't count on the kids to defend her. Sasha would probably relish a chance to recite her mother's many faults to a judge. Poor Alec had enough on his plate right now. It would be cruel to add another pressure and Jake was too young. Marcy wouldn't allow him to testify.

She'd need a clever lawyer of her own. Monday she would call the one Sharon recommended. He was bound to be expensive, eating into her share of the profits from the house. She hoped theirs wouldn't be one of those cases that dragged on unresolved until all resources were exhausted. Her little pot of money was shrinking. Already, she'd had to revise her apartment search from four bedrooms to three, and if Neil succeeded in winning custody, there would be no child support.

The creak of the front door reverberated as it swung open. Her footsteps on the hall tiles resonated. Tonight would be her first night alone since they had brought Sasha back from the hospital nearly eighteen years before. How many times since had she pictured, fantasised, about an evening such as this, where the only needs she had to meet were her own? It had to be hundreds, perhaps even thousands. Solitude was a treat doled out in limited quantities:

the length of a nap or half a school day, its supply so wholly inadequate to the demands of daily life that indulging in anything for her own pleasure was a dereliction. She could indulge all she wanted now: take a long soak in the bath, paint her nails, curl up with a book and eat ice cream for dinner, straight out of the carton, but there was no joy in it. The weight of five floors of empty house pressed down upon her, the silence insufferable. A mere taste of the future, as certain as night followed day. Even if Neil's petition failed, Sasha would be gone in months; Alec was right behind her, lined up, ready for take-off. Knowing how time accelerated as it went along, the eight remaining years with Jake would pass in a blink of an eye. What then?

If, when she was a teenager in Ohio, a fortune teller had whispered in her ear that she would live her adult life in Europe, she would have imagined glamour, rubbing shoulders with great artists and thinkers, like the Lost Generation they'd studied in English Literature. But living in Europe wasn't an automatic ticket to the cool crowd. She wasn't hanging out with her generation's Hemmingway and Fitzgerald in Les Deux Magots and Café de Flore. There were no glitzy dinner parties, little sparkling conversation. Nothing about her everyday life glittered. The daily hassles and challenges she faced were the same she would have had if she lived in the US: school runs, laundry and trips to the grocery store. Only she had to navigate it all in her second language, often blind to unspoken rules, perpetually a bit gauche. What the hell was she doing in this country that wasn't hers?

Maybe it was time to go home; to make a fresh start in the land of second chances. But was the US even home anymore? On recent trips, she'd roam the aisles of grocery stores in a daze, overwhelmed by the choice of shampoo and lady shavers, by entire aisles devoted to frozen pizza, just frozen pizza. And the cars were so big! When she'd left, American cars had been only a bit larger than European ones. She and Neil had learned to drive in the same model car, a four-speed, stick-shift Chevy Chevette, though Neil's was technically a Vauxhall. These days, taking a car like that out on the SUV-filled roads would be a death wish. One fender bender and you could be squished like a bug.

In a weird way, she felt more American when she was in Europe than she did when she was in America. Here, her Americanness was a second skin, intrinsic to her identity. She served as a permanent ambassador for her country, unpaid (naturally), a human counterpoint to the often cartoonish portrait painted by nightly news programmes and documentaries featuring the craziest, most outrageous characters and situations. In her bones, she was American.

But so much had changed. When she was a kid, football games hadn't begun with a salute to the troops; there weren't F-16 flyovers at road races; people hadn't felt compelled to stop every soldier they came across to thank them for their service. The veneration of the military didn't sit right with her. It felt knee-jerk and, given less than one half of one per cent of the population chose to serve, a smidge insincere. There were practical considerations, too. Twenty-five years out of the US was twenty-five years of not paying into social security and she didn't even want to think about the cost of health insurance.

She wandered into the kitchen. It was a little past five, cocktail hour. She could have a drink. A whisky sour, she thought, but there was no simple syrup. A Manhattan, then? But they were out of vermouth. A gin and tonic? But the tonic had gone flat. It was her life in microcosm: the constant lowering of expectations, bargained downward. She would give up. Climb into bed and call it a day, if only she could be sure sleep would come.

The ringtone for the video app broke the quiet. Marcy moved in the direction of the computer on a hunch, soon confirmed, that the caller was Nizar's mother. She had phoned every day this week. That cousin of his in Sweden, who used to call all the time, hadn't called once. But maybe the cousin was part of whatever it was Nizar had been up to? Maybe he, too, was in jail? Perhaps he wasn't a cousin at all? And what about Tahrir?

Oh, God! Was Neil right? *Had* she been irresponsible, negligent?

She let the app ring out. She could not bear to see Nizar's mother's pained face, the inevitable worry in her eyes; could not bear to hear her wails. She had enough shit to deal with. She bore the woman no ill will. On the contrary. How terrible it must be to have a child imprisoned in another country. That poor woman, who had sacrificed to send him here for a better future, in the belief he would be safe. Whatever barbarous acts he might be accused of planning, or plotting or *thinking*, he was still her child, her world.

But there was no point answering. Marcy could not help her in any way. She did not know where Nizar was being held, whether he was in the general prison population or solitary confinement, or even which one of those options would be preferable. She couldn't say what sort of defence his lawyer planned to argue; wasn't clear on the charges he faced.

The computer made a 'bloop' of disappointment as the link cut. Marcy sighed, knowing full well this was not the end. Not by a long shot. That woman would walk through fire, spend her last cent in an overpriced internet café so long as there was a chance to talk to her son. Because a mother never gave up.

She went upstairs to Nizar's room. She had not been there since the police searched it. Sasha said they'd dressed for the job like scientists entering a clean room: gloves and rubber boots, jumpsuits and hats, which spurred thoughts about contamination and evidence tampering. Irrational thoughts. They had carted away anything remotely suspicious – the pressure cooker, the mobile phones, the bags of nails – each bit of evidence individually sealed in its own plastic bag. The things that remained after they'd emptied drawers and closets, pulled back the bedding and searched under the mattress, were of no consequence: clothing and papers, packets of dried food and bric-a-brac. She sifted through a pile of pencil drawings left on the bed. She had not known he drew so well. His mustard yellow scarf was wound around a bedpost. She smiled, thinking how often he'd worn it these past months, even in the house. It was normal, she supposed. He was used to a warmer climate. If only she knew where he was being held, she'd bring it to him, but surely scarves were banned in prisons. She'd bet Nizar was missing his mother right now. Wasn't that the way? Our mothers drive us batty but when things get tough, when we're lost or hungry or scared, they are the ones we yearn for.

Marcy stood up. She rushed down the stairs and went straight to the computer and dialled her own mother's number and when her image appeared on the screen – a from-the-eyebrows-up angle that included mostly ceiling – she began to weep and to tell her everything, starting in the middle and working back from both sides at once.

The following morning was cool but fine. Marcy walked down the hill to Place Flagey. The daffodils were out around the ponds. The trees had pale green leaves. She stopped at the café for a croissant and a cappuccino before browsing the stalls of the market, selecting a *chèvre*, *demi-frais*, vegetables for a ratatouille and a bouquet of multi-coloured tulips, the buds closed up tight. She dropped into the old radio station and picked up a brochure on upcoming events. In the afternoon, she went to the art-house cinema to watch a film that had won a prize at an obscure festival. In the evening, she poured herself a glass of Pinot gris, tossed a *salade frisée*, warmed a slab of *chèvre* on toast under the grille and then drizzled it with honey. She ate on the terrace as the light faded. When the doorbell rang, she assumed it was an online delivery for an absent neighbour. It happened more and more, especially in the late afternoon or early evening, when the drivers were desperate to empty their trucks. Instead she found a pair of young men. One of them was Tahrir. He stood, feet apart, arms crossed over his chest like a bodyguard or a bouncer. The other, head down, lips slightly pursed, peering at Marcy through the veil of his super-long lashes, was Nizar.

'Hello, Marcy,' he said, softly. 'I've come for my things.'

Alec

Their father drove past the turn on to their street, through the intersection; he slowed along the abbey side of the boulevard, looking for a place to park.

'You can just drop us off,' Sasha said.

'Yeah, just drop us off,' Alec echoed. It was the first time since Friday afternoon they'd agreed on anything. She'd driven him crazy with her complaints about having to share Dad's one-bedroom apartment with three males. She had the pull-out sofa to herself; he was stuck on an air mattress with a slow leak.

'No, your mother and I have some things to discuss,' Dad insisted. He was grinning the same grin he'd had plastered to his face since Mom's call. It was a grin of determined positivity in the face of all contrary evidence, a grin that declared: this is *not* an absolute clusterfuck.

But, of course, it was. He must regret putting Mom's call on speaker phone, though, to be fair, one side of the conversation would have been sufficient to get the gist.

They exited the car, pulled their backpacks from the boot and started walking in the direction they'd just come from. Waiting at the light, the sense of doom was palpable. Alec's eyes drifted back and forth between the Syrian

Embassy and the SOLD sign hanging from the first-floor balcony of home: a panorama of regrets.

Jake ran in, gave Mom a hug and announced he was going to play with his Lego. He wanted no part of whatever was about to go down. Alec considered following him upstairs, but he stuck around, curious. He hoped Dad would extend an olive branch. His father walked through the door first, blocking Alec's view of his mother, so he didn't catch her expression.

'I assume you retracted your petition?' she said.

Nizar's release demolished his case for custody. Now, instead of appearing a responsible father concerned for his children's welfare, he risked looking like a dick trying to lower his monthly support payments.

'Just so I'm clear on what happened.' Dad said. 'They dropped all the charges against him?'

'Well, they must have, mustn't they?' Mom replied. 'People charged with terrorism don't get bail.'

'How did he look?' Sasha asked.

'All right,' Mom replied. 'A little tired, maybe, and quieter than usual.'

'But you asked him, correct?' Dad asked. 'He confirmed that they'd dropped all the charges?'

'Yes,' Mom said.

'On what grounds?'

'He said it was all a mistake,' said Mom.

'A mistake! They had evidence, Marcy. Hard evidence. Explain that.'

'I don't need to explain it,' Mom replied, opening her arms. 'That's what the police and the courts are for.'

'Did you call the police to say he'd come by?'

'Why would I do that?' Mom asked.

Dad laughed a dry laugh. 'I would think the answer to that would be obvious.'

Mom tilted her head to one side and smiled. 'You aren't seriously suggesting he escaped from prison and then swung by to collect his stuff before heading out on the lam? You think a prison break wouldn't have made the news; that police wouldn't have come here straight off?'

It was a bit disappointing to see his father cling so tightly to a moral high ground that had already crumbled beneath his feet.

'Maybe they screwed up,' Sasha suggested. 'Maybe they violated his rights and had to let him go on a technicality?'

'Before a trial?' Dad asked.

'Is he coming back to live with us?' Sasha asked.

'I should think *not*,' Dad said.

'I told him he was welcome,' Mom told Sasha. 'He didn't decline outright. That friend was with him, the grumpy one, you know, Tahrir. Between them, they took what they could carry away. I feel bad. The police left that room in a state. I should have cleaned it. It looked as if we didn't care, as if we'd forgotten him.'

'Right, well I'm off,' Dad said. 'I haven't got your unlimited capacity to empathise with the downtrodden, Marcy.'

'You say that as if it's a bad thing,' Alec said.

'I'm exhausted, that's all,' his father replied, 'and I can't help feeling there is more to this Nizar story.'

That feeling grew stronger after his father phoned the police, who confirmed Nizar had been released without charge on the twenty-fifth of February, a full week before his visit to the house. Where had he been in the meantime? Where was he now? Questions multiplied and there was nowhere to go for answers. The police wouldn't comment further, citing privacy protections, as did the lawyer helping Nizar with his refugee application. Nizar's phone number was disconnected. His mother's calls suddenly stopped, and no one at the refugee centre had seen or heard from him or Tahrir since Nizar's release. It was a true-life mystery and the primary topic of conversation amongst the family for days. Until Nana showed up, giving them something else to talk about.

She appeared out of the blue one morning before school. Alec found her on the doorstep in yoga pants and a bright pink fleece, lugging a sturdy suitcase nearly as big as she was.

'You!' she squealed, clapping a hand on either side of his face and squishing his cheeks together. 'I could chop you up into a dozen pieces, for what you did. Help me with this, would you, honey?' she said, pointing to the case, which could have been designed for intergalactic travel. 'My back is killing me.'

Alec heaved the case up the marble steps. It was as heavy as it looked. 'Mom,' he called, 'Nana's here.'

'Nana's what?' Mom called back.

'He said I'm here,' Nana shouted, gripping hold of the brass rail as she lumbered up the steps behind him. Alec assumed his mother had either deliberately kept Nana's visit a secret or had forgotten to mention it. Both seemed plausible; however, one look at her face as she rushed into the hall made clear she was every bit as surprised as he was.

'What are you doing here?' she asked.

'If the mountain can't go to Mohammad, Mohammad must go to the mountain,' Nana announced. 'Too soon?' she asked, cackling. 'Too on the nose?'

'What are you doing here?'

'I told you I'd come.'

'I didn't think you meant it literally.'

'Why wouldn't I mean it? When my grandson is in trouble? My daughter in distress? I wouldn't joke about coming. I'm not a monster, Marsha Louise.'

For the second time in less than a minute, Alec had to re-evaluate his assumptions. He thought of himself as a B-list grandkid, the supplementary or special-guest grandkid; nice to see at major holidays, milestones and summer vacations; useful for filling out family photos, but not worthy of the same love as his cousins who lived close by and in whose lives Nana participated twelve months a year. That she had come all this way for his sake touched him deeply.

'Now, I've just got to lie down a bit,' Nana said. 'My back is seizing up.'

'That's why you're not supposed to fly,' Mom observed.

'It wasn't too bad.' Nana placed her hands on her lower back and slowly straightened. 'I had a rum and coke at the airport and a couple Vicodin on the plane. Slept the whole way.'

'Where did you get the money for a ticket.'

'Never you mind that.' She shuffled over to the sofa and stretched out flat. 'I'll be fine. Don't you worry. I just need to rest here a bit until the muscles loosen. Sasha, how about a kiss for your old nana? I hear you're in a Latin competition. Congratulations, what an honour! Like being named head cheerleader in Ohio. Where's Jake? Jakey! Come and say hello to Nana!'

'How long are you staying, Nana?' Sasha asked.

'I fly back the twenty-second.'

'That's nearly two weeks!' Mom exclaimed. Shrieked, more like.

'I got a good deal,' she replied, letting out a small grunt as she readjusted her position.

'Ah, it's a shame you're selling this place. I'll miss the old railroad apartment,' she added.

'It's not an apartment, Nana,' Jake said. 'It's a house.'

'I know, Jakey. It's just an expression, the way the rooms line up in a row, like an old railroad car.'

'It's not a railroad apartment,' Mom said. 'It's *trois pièces en enfilade*.'

'Too fancy for me,' Nana said. 'Was there always an echo? Where did everything go? Did Neil take it? There's one thing I won't miss: climbing all the way to the top of those goddamned stairs. I'm not looking forward to that, I can tell you. Please tell me your next place has fewer floors.'

'There's only one floor,' Jake said. 'Alec and I are sharing a bedroom. But we'll have our own rooms at Dad's house. He promised.'

'And we know your dad is good at keeping promises,' Nana said.

'Mother,' said Mom.

'What? Can't anyone make a joke?' Nana asked.

'I need to go to work, Mom, and the kids need to get to school,' Mom said. 'Will you be all right?'

'Of course. I'll be up in no time.'

A prediction that proved wildly optimistic. Nana was still on the sofa that afternoon when Alec and Sasha got home from school. She remained there until Mom was ready to serve dinner. Nana needed help to rise to a standing position and walk to the table. She eased herself into a chair with remarkable slowness but, once there, was chatty enough, catching her daughter up on the news of former neighbours and friends.

'Do you remember Darlene Sinowitz?'

'I don't recall . . .'

'She's driving Uber.'

'Okay.'

'Kenny Wayland died. Overdose. His parents are beside themselves.'

'Gosh, that's terrible.'

'I ran into Mary Coswell the other day. She wanted to be remembered to you.'

'How nice.'

'Her grandson OD'ed twice in a single day. The cops saved him with Narcan. Miracle drug, Narcan. One sniff brings them back from the dead, which brings its own problems. The druggies shoot up in public, now, because they know all first responders carry it. We had a young man crash his car into a telephone pole on Main Street, the other day, with the needle still in his arm!'

'A needle?' Jake asked.

'Mind you, it's not pleasant,' Nana continued. 'Sends them straight into withdrawal. They don't thank you for it.'

'A needle?' Jake repeated.

'Remember, Jake and Sasha and Alec: just say no to drugs.'

'Ugh!' said Mom. 'Is there any good news?'

Nana paused, fork hovering over her plate as she considered the question. 'Gina Kowalski married a nice man who owns a Seven-Eleven down in Maumee,' she said. 'They're living over there. She seems very happy.'

Nana didn't think she could make it all the way to the top floor, so Mom offered to take the spare room but Nana asked her to stay in case she needed to get up in the middle of the night. It did not go well.

'Your mother was fighting dragons last night,' Nana announced at breakfast the next morning. 'I feared for my life.'

'It was a bad dream,' Mom explained, slicing carrots into sticks for the lunch boxes.

'No kidding! You almost knocked my teeth out.'

'I'm sorry. I apologised.'

'I guess I'll have to hike it up to the guest room after all,' Nana announced.

'I'll go,' Mom said.

Alec expected Nana to refuse or at least feign reluctance to accept, at first, but she accepted immediately. Her back continued to bother her. Mom said she should see a doctor. Nana said she didn't think she could make it into a car and walk to a hospital. Mom said SOS Médecins would make a house call. But Nana was afraid of the expense, even after Mom assured her it would only cost fifty euros and she'd pay. Instead she spent the next few days lying on her back, irritable from the pain and the lack of a TV. She called Alec the 'juvenile delinquent'; told Sasha she was too skinny, and Jake that he was too old to play with Lego. She said Mom's jumper made her look like a potato pancake.

She and Mom bickered over everything: who had lived in which house in the neighbourhood when Mom was growing up, the colour of the car they'd had when Mom was a kid, the cost of tuition when Mom went to college. Sometimes when Nana talked, Mom made faces and rolled her eyes the way Sasha did when Mom talked.

'I wish I'd had sons,' Nana remarked. 'Every young man wants to replace his father. No young woman wants to be her mother.'

Mom scoffed. 'I'm hardly *young*, Mother.'

Alec's anti-radicalisation meetings were held at a centre for at-risk youths. The centre was an inconvenient trip from school, requiring a metro, a bus and an uphill walk, and, despite leaving school as quickly as he could, he arrived late to his first meeting. Every head turned in his direction as he walked into the room. He heard the whispers, felt their eyes following him as he made his way to one of the open seats, all of which were in the front row.

'S'up, my *rebeu*,' the kid next to him called out, to general laughter. Many of the others actually were *rebeu*, European-born children or grandchildren of North Africans. Alec's pasty, freckled skin shone under the florescent lights like a light-emitting diode. This was going to be torture.

The leader introduced the speaker, a woman in a light-blue hijab who walked to the front of the room. She held up a picture of a pudgy, pie-faced brown boy in a Belgian national team jersey: her son. He was mad about football and ice cream, she said in broken French. The jersey, which she said had Eden Hazard's name and number on the back, was his favourite sixteenth birthday gift. He struggled at school because he was dyslexic, she said, but was kind and gentle, especially to his little sister. She said that she and her husband were strict. Her son was not allowed to hang out on street corners with the other boys in the neighbourhood and because of this he had few friends. 'More than anything,' she said, 'he wanted to belong.'

He'd showed little interest in religion until a month or so before the day, the previous April, when he skipped school and flew to Turkey. From there, he crossed into Syria and joined up with ISIS. She spoke of her shock and confusion at receiving the text telling her where he was, and started to cry when recalling the visit from the anti-terror squad during which she read his conversations with a recruiter he met online.

'He went to build a caliphate to the glory of Allah,' she said. 'Lies. My son was not there long before he saw the truth.' She choked back tears. 'He said, "Maman, I am like the boys in *Pinocchio* who go to Paradise Island, turn into donkeys and are sold to work in the salt mines."

'He told me, "I want to come home, but I can't." A boy from Canada had tried to escape. He was captured, tortured, and shot.'

At the start of her talk, everyone was slouched back in their seats, laughing and exchanging looks, but as she got going, they fell quiet. By the time she told them that her son was believed to have died in an allied air strike in November, they were leaning forward on their desks, hanging on every word.

'Thank you, Madame,' the leader said. 'I'm sure many of the boys will want to ask questions, but first I want to welcome a new member to our group. Alec, why don't you present yourself.'

Alec rose and faced the rows of desks, full of dread. 'I was born here,' he began. The boy next to him sneered at the sound of his 'proper' Belgian accent. 'I've lived here my whole life, but I'm not Belgian.

'My mother tongue is English – American, actually,' and here he paused to clear his throat. 'But I speak with a weird accent no one can place. My American relatives say I'm British, because that's what my father is. The British relatives say I'm American. I don't belong anywhere.

'And whenever America does something – invades a country or defends Israel at the UN, I have to answer for it even though I've never lived in America, and I'm too young to vote.'

The boy seated next to him looked him up and down. 'What do you know?' he said, leaning back to peer at him. 'You *are* a *rebeu*.'

'An American *rebeu*,' said someone behind him.

'A Yankee Doodle *rebeu*,' said another.

By the time the meeting finished, Alec was hungry. The aroma of newly fried potatoes emanating from the *frites* stand he passed on his way to the tram stop beckoned. He bought a cornet with spicy samurai sauce, and had just dug out the first forkful when he saw him walking in the other direction. Though it was twilight, Alec recognised the stride immediately, the economy of movement: Nizar. Without a second thought, he grabbed his things and hurried to follow, keeping a discreet distance, ready to duck into a doorway or plaster himself against a wall should Nizar turn around. He was doing his best James Bond impersonation – if James Bond had to lug a backpack, a bulky portfolio and a cornet of *frites* he ate straight from the cornet, hands free. The samurai sauce burned his lips. After a couple of hundred metres, Nizar disappeared into a building. The door was battered and badly in need of a fresh coat of paint. There were two rows of four buttons on the buzzer outside. Nizar's surname, Al Sami, was nowhere to be found. He studied the post boxes and found it written, by hand on paper, covered in clear tape, next to the name Aad. Alec matched the name on the buzzer and waited. Nothing happened, and so he pressed it a second time. A few seconds later, the door opened.

Assuming the placement of the doorbells mirrored the placement of the apartments, Alec guessed the flat was on the ground floor. He went through a hallway out to the back. There was an open door. Alec took his chance and walked through it.

'Hello?' he called.

It was a studio, one large room with a concrete floor and a kitchenette in one corner, and a bed against the opposite wall, unmade. The back opened out to a small, sad courtyard, paved, with high concrete walls. Nizar was out there, with a steel helmet on his head and a lit blowtorch in his hand, bent over a bench vice attached to a worktable. He jumped when he saw Alec; extinguished the blowtorch and flipped up the helmet. A single word escaped his lips.

'How?'

'I saw you in the square just now,' Alec replied. He took a few steps towards him.

'Frite?' he asked, holding out the cornet.

'No thank you,' Nizar replied.

Alec gestured with his chin. 'What are you making?' A nail in the vice was turning from orange to brown as it cooled. There was a hammer, a pair of long pincers and a delicate tangle of melted nails. 'Is that a bird's nest.'

'What do you want?' Nizar asked.

What *did* he want? Why had he followed him? He hadn't had a plan. 'My mother worries about you,' he said.

'I am well,' he said.

'She would love to see you.'

'Your mother is a good woman. I am grateful for her kindness.'

'I'm afraid I wasn't very kind to you,' Alec said. Why was he saying these things? 'I should have told police you didn't do anything, that you had been trying to stop me.'

'I do not think it would have made any difference.'

'Well, I wasn't very nice before that night, either. I'm sorry.'

'The envious person is a sad person.'

Alec bit his lip. This wasn't making him like Nizar any better. 'Yes, well—'

The buzzer sounded. Nizar rushed past Alec to a receiver hanging on the wall near the open door. Alec seized the chance to eat a few frites and look around. There were other nail sculptures – a spikey globe, what looked like a bunch of wildflowers, a cross. He was admiring its intricacy when Tahrir entered. He circled Alec like prey, eyes narrowing. He and Nizar exchanged words in Arabic.

'Can I offer you some tea, Alec?' Nizar asked.

'No thank you. I should be getting home,' he replied. He very much doubted Tahrir and he had been discussing tea. 'Can I just ask: why did they let you go?'

'Because he is innocent,' Tahrir said.

'They found bomb-making equipment,' Alec protested.

'A false positive, traces of soap in some dishes he got from the centre,' Tahrir replied. The guy's French was better than he let on.

'Soap?' Alec asked.

'Glycerine.'

'And the plastic explosives?'

'Modelling clay,' Nizar explained. 'For sculptures.'

'You've got to be kidding.'

Nizar turned his palms upwards and shrugged.

'Oh, I have something of yours,' Alec said. He opened his portfolio and withdrew the pencil drawing of the boy on the beach.

Nizar removed his gloves and took the drawing in both hands. He nodded and smiled. His hand caressed the page.

'It's your cousin, isn't it?' Alec asked. 'The one in Sweden.'

Nizar bit his lower lip and nodded. 'He's not my cousin,' he said, softly.

Tahrir moved close to Nizar and peered over his shoulder at the drawing. They exchanged looks. Nizar blushed, and then handed the drawing back to Alec.

'You may keep it,' he said, looking again at Tahrir. 'I don't want it any more.'

Alec took in the room. The building must have been built for an industrial purpose and then later carved into flats. The floor was concrete. There was a kitchenette against the back wall, with rickety cupboards. A round table with a pair of chairs sat near the centre, an easy chair lined-up directly in front of a flat-screen television and, in the back corner, the unmade bed, a double.

'Please don't say anything,' Nizar whispered. 'If my mother knew . . .' he trailed off. 'I took her money, Alec. Everything she had. But I had to escape.'

Tahrir put an arm around him. 'We will pay her back.'

Armed soldiers boarded the tram at Louise. They fanned out along the cars in pairs, checking identity cards, part of the security patrols stepped up since Abdeslam's fingerprints were found on a glass in an apartment in Forest earlier in the week. The soldiers took care to balance the requests to young brown and black men and women in headscarves with those to old white ladies and men in suits, but no one was fooled. The soldiers rode for a few stops and then got off. People took their presence in their stride. The reaction was quite different from what it had been in November. Alec was reminded of Nizar's remark back then, that people could get used to extraordinary things.

'Where have you been?' Nana asked.

'Re-education class,' Alec said.

'Why don't you ever answer your phone?' Sasha asked him.

'I didn't hear it.'

'There's a police operation ongoing in Molenbeek,' Sasha said. 'The police say it's terror related.'

'Were you afraid I was involved?'

Marcy

Marcy's mother was always the last to wake, padding downstairs for breakfast in her pyjamas and robe just as Marcy rushed to get out the door with Jake, wanting to know whether they'd left any coffee for her. But today she was fully dressed, lacing up her shoes in the hallway.

'Can I get you some coffee?' Marcy asked. 'How about a slice of toast?'

'Neither. I'll eat at the airport,' her mother replied. 'I'd like to get going. Is Alec awake? Alec!' she called up the stairwell. 'Bring down my case, would you?'

'We have plenty of time,' Marcy said.

'Three hours before an international flight,' her mother snapped back. 'It says right on the ticket.'

Marcy had tried to explain several times that since her mother's flight was connecting through Heathrow, this first leg was technically a European flight, and so an hour and a half was plenty of time to clear security, but her mother would not be moved. Some residual stress remained from last night's online check-in experience. The printing of the boarding passes had hit a few snags and her mother's anxiety had hit the roof. Alec got it to work, eventually, but by then her mother was in a state, convinced her request for special assistance had been ignored. Marcy had had to contact the airline to confirm all was in order.

The children came downstairs to say goodbye. Marcy reminded Jake that his father would be coming by to take him to school and that he needed to watch the clock and make sure he was ready.

Marcy lifted the suitcase into the boot and they set out for the airport.

'I hope we don't hit traffic,' Mom said.

'We won't,' Marcy said. 'It's still early.'

'Still,' her mother said. 'You never know.'

'True,' Marcy said, shifting gears both literally and meta-phorically, 'Well, Mom, we're really going to miss you.'

The lie felt heavy on her tongue. Marcy wished the ends of visits with her mother didn't always feel like missed opportunities, that her primary reaction to her mother's departure wasn't relief. Her mother had said she'd come to help but her only contribution was making dinner one night, tacos with minced beef and seasoning out of a packet with a side of Ambrosia, a concoction of coconut, mandarin oranges, maraschino cherries and whipped cream that she insisted, against all evidence, was a fruit salad.

'Your cousins love it,' she had said with a frown when none of the kids wanted seconds.

'Let's cut to the chase,' her mother said now. 'You need to have a plan for what you're going to do next.'

How typical of her mother to spend two weeks under her roof and wait until they were driving to the airport to say her piece.

'And I suppose you have some thoughts on the matter,' Marcy said.

'I do, but you won't like them.'

'Try me.'

'All right. Either get back together with Neil or come home.'

'Well the first is not going to happen.'

'Why not? I think he'd jump at the chance, if you gave it to him.'

'He cheated, Mom.'

'So he made a mistake? Big deal.'

'It's not just the cheating. He lied about it. For months.'

Her mother cackled. 'Well, honey, what did you expect him to do? You would have done the same if the shoe had been on the other foot.'

'How can you say that?'

'Because you're human. Everybody lies about cheating. And can you blame them? It's embarrassing.'

'Excuse me. I was the one humiliated.'

'We've all got to eat our pound of dirt, honey.'

'Mine feels like more than a pound.'

'Marsha Louise, you still think that if you can just be a little better, try a little harder, nothing bad will happen to you.'

'I don't think that.'

'Yes, you do. I blame Gloria Steinem and the feminists, filling you with a load of hogwash and false expectations, and the nuns, too. I would have thought that after what happened to your father and me it would have put such thoughts to rest. Sometimes shit happens and that's all there is to it.'

'Well shit has undeniably happened.'

'And you know what?'

'Do not say I'm feeling sorry for myself.'

'That's exactly what I'm going to say. You think you've

been humiliated? Look at your hero, Hillary Clinton. That woman was humiliated in front of the whole world and look at her now: she's going to be president; God help us all.'

'Don't you want a woman to be president?'

'Of course,' her mother said. 'Sarah Palin would have been fantastic.'

Marcy gripped tighter at the wheel.

'And you know I'm a Democrat,' her mother added.

This was too much. 'You haven't voted for a Democrat since Jimmy Carter in seventy-six.'

'It's not my fault they haven't put up any good candidates. And I have so. I voted for whatshisname on the city council.'

'That doesn't count.'

'It counts. It most certainly counts.'

'What do you have against Hillary, anyway?'

'I never warmed to her. But I give her credit for staying with her husband.'

'I didn't know you were such a traditionalist.'

'I believe in what works. All this talk about fulfilment, "Love, pray, eat", and all that jazz. Give me a break! It's not all about you.'

'This is the only life we're getting, Mom. People don't want to waste it.'

'Hogwash. People are lazy. They don't want to put in the work. It's a throwaway society. Marriage is about working through things. We don't always get what we want, but we get what we need.'

'Thank you, Mick Jagger.'

'What do you expect? I was a flower child.'

'Of course you were, Mother.'

'What's that supposed to mean?'

'Nothing,' she sighed. 'I just feel that it's time for me to stand on my own two feet. I don't need a man.'

'What tripe! Of course you need a man. Jesus! Parenting is a thankless job. It's hard enough when there are two of you, especially since you went and had a third. What did I tell you about allowing yourself to get outnumbered?'

'If I could just bring us back to our original discussion: am I not entitled to feel a little bit sorry for myself? When I sacrificed my career for my husband and then got kicked to the kerb when I got too old?'

'Cry me a river. You can get your husband back if you want. And as for your career, what's wrong with being a teacher? It's a noble profession. A good teacher makes a big difference in people's lives. You wouldn't be where you are today without that art teacher of yours. Think what she did for you.'

'What I do is hardly in the same league, Mother. I help executives advance their careers, and their kids get better grades in school.'

'You can be hard to read, Marsha Louise. You talk so fancy. But whenever you call me Mother at the end of a sentence, I always know you're talking down to me. What's wrong with helping executives and their children? Not enough prizes? Not enough accolades from the committee?'

'I'm so alone, Mom. I thought the kids, at least, would always belong to me, that we'd be a team, but we aren't. They're like aliens. I don't understand them.'

'Honey, welcome to the world. I don't necessarily believe in God – don't tell your sister that, by the way – but I believe life tests us. And one way it does is by giving us children we don't understand.'

'This is different, Mom.'

Her mother popped open a pill container and shook a couple of pills into her palm.

'What are you taking?'

'Baclofen,' she said, with the pills in her mouth. 'It's a muscle relaxant.'

'On an empty stomach?'

'I'm not a child, Marsha Louise.' She lifted a water bottle in Marcy's drinks holder. 'How old is this?'

'It's fine. I filled it this morning.'

Her mother took the cap off and proceeded to drink. 'Most kids go through a weird stage. Remember when you used to stick safety pins in your ears for earrings.'

'I did that maybe twice.'

'Your favourite lipstick shade was black.'

'When was my favourite shade of lipstick black?'

'Black fishnet stockings with holes in them.'

'That's nothing. My kids really are aliens. You know, sometimes I think I should come home, but then I think of the children and I know I can't. They're part American, part British, part Belgian and none of the above. We're not even a family anymore, just a bunch of misplaced persons. We don't belong anywhere.'

'Oh boo-hoo. Poor Marcy, living in Europe with her cultured children who speak fluent French, love broccoli and turn their noses up at Ambrosia!'

'Why do you have to be so harsh, Mom?'

'Can I ask you a question? Why couldn't you tell me you two had separated?'

'I did.'

'You didn't.'

'I told you we hit a rough patch.'

'He'd moved out. That's not a rough patch. That's a crater.'

'I didn't want to tell you because I know you never liked Neil and I knew that if we patched things up, you'd hold it over his head forever.'

Her mother grew silent and put a hand to her chest. 'It hurts that this is what you really think of me.'

'In the end, it's always about you, Mom,' Marcy said.

'I'll tell you something,' her mother said with a laugh that was dry and joyless, 'you don't get to be my age without learning how to forgive. You're the one who can't forgive. And you didn't want to tell me because it would tarnish the image of your perfect life that you've painted.'

'You always ridicule me.'

'I do not, Marsha Louise.' And then it was her turn to sigh. 'I think you'd be a lot happier if you realised that you're no better than the rest of us.'

'I can't believe you travelled five thousand miles, spent money you don't have, for the chance to remind me of my faults.'

Marcy swung into the short-stay car park, accelerating as she drove up the circular ramp.

'Oh,' her mother gasped, grabbing hold of the dashboard. 'Such a heavy foot.'

She continued at the same speed all the way up to the top floor where spaces could usually be found.

Check-in was busy, the trail of people waiting at the bag drop-off snaked back and forth and moved at a snail's pace. Marcy watched the minute hand of her watch move around the circle. Airline personnel called for passengers for flights to Berlin, Los Angeles and Barcelona to come forward, stalling their progress. Then they waited for a wheelchair assistant to bring Marcy's mother to the gate. The minute hand of her watch was coming full circle.

'We've been waiting almost fifteen minutes,' she said to the clerk at the desk with, admittedly, a bit of edge to her voice.

'Marsha Louise, this is your mother speaking,' her mother said, giving the clerk a conspiratorial wink. 'Don't be an Ugly American.'

Marcy stared at the ceiling.

'It's getting late,' she told her mother.

She nodded. 'This is just what I was afraid would happen.'

'Late for me, I meant. You've still got loads of time before your flight.'

'So you keep telling me.'

'I only have an hour's parking.'

'Leave then,' she said.

'I'll wait,' Marcy said, checking her watch once more. 'It's just, I don't want to be late for my lesson. My student is preparing to give his first presentation in English.'

'Go on, then. I'll be fine. I can't understand a word they say to me but who cares? I'll figure it out.'

'Maybe that's him coming now,' Marcy said.

'Jeez, Louise, it's about time,' her mother remarked to the attendant, a bald black man, so large he had to stoop to hold on to the wheelchair handles.

'*Enchanté*, Louise,' the man replied in a deep baritone. 'I am Abdul.'

'We need to get a move on, Abdul,' her mother said, climbing into the chair, placing her large canvas tote on her lap. 'I want to stop at the ladies' room, if that's all right with you.'

'That is fine, Louise. Fine,' he said, smiling. The spotlights overhead reflected off the top of his head. 'No problem.'

Abdul swung the chair around and strode towards security. Marcy watched Abdul hand her mother's ticket and passport to the agent and waited for her mother to turn around for a final wave. But she was in animated conversation with Abdul and rolled out of sight without a backward glance.

Marcy hurried for the exit, walking zigzag due to the number of people with their trolleys piled high with cases, children and pets. At the exit, three young men walked abreast of one another, each pushing a trolley containing a single bag when all three could have fit on a single trolley.

Manspreading, she thought, stepping back as they rolled on past. The one nearest to her wore a Harrington-style cotton jacket and bucket hat pulled down over his head. She smiled at the sight of this young man – he couldn't be thirty – in old man clothes. He did not smile back.

Neil

8.16 a.m.

By chance, Neil's eyes glanced at the dashboard clock when the first report came on the radio. He was feeling a bit harried, a little stressed. Traffic was heavy – the peak of the school run. He was edging the car through the bottleneck of Cambre-Étoile intersection on the way to Jake's school, his mind on all the things he needed to do at work. Normally, he was at his desk by now. On the radio, Taylor Swift was just getting started with 'I Knew You Were Trouble' when the DJ broke in with a special news bulletin. In the nanosecond of silence that fell between when the music stopped and the DJ spoke, Neil felt a terrible twisting in the pit of his stomach.

No one could claim to be surprised. The police recovered detonators from the apartment in Forest, the previous week, and the risk of an attack only increased after Abdeslam's capture. The government had said as much. Neil just wished he'd thought to turn down the radio so as not to alarm Jake, but how was he supposed to know they'd hit the airport?

Why the airport? The gares de Midi and Centrale had

more people passing through them, and less security. The same was true of the main shopping districts of Rue Neuve and Avenue Louise. If symbolism was what they were after, the EU headquarters or the Grand Place would have been more powerful. Why the goddamned airport? And why today of all days?

'Mom and Nana are at the airport,' Jake said from the back seat.

'They're fine, I'm sure,' Neil replied, a reflex. He knew no such thing. In the rear-view mirror Jake's eyes were bright blue gobstoppers. 'Your mother will have left the airport long before any of this.'

He hoped. In truth, all he knew was that she couldn't take Jake to school because she was dropping Joanna at the airport.

'What about Nana?' Jake asked.

'She'll have been safe on the other side of security,' he said, to his immediate regret.

'What if the explosion happened on the other side of security?'

'It won't have,' Neil replied, kicking himself for allowing the conversation to continue but not knowing how to stop it. His mental bandwidth was shrinking. He needed space to think. He must call Marcy. Everything would be okay once he spoke to her. At the next green light he made it through the intersection, but instead of driving straight towards the school he turned right and then right again.

'This isn't the way to school,' Jake said.

'Nope,' Neil replied. 'I think we'll skive today. What do you say?'

His phone began to ring; messages and notifications, dozens of them, in the time it took to park the car and walk with Jake to the house, pinging away, each one setting off a cycle of relief followed by disappointment when they turned out not to be Marcy. Surely, she would call as soon as she heard the news.

Once inside the house, he sent Jake off to fetch his Lego while he phoned Marcy. He got voicemail, a message he'd heard a thousand times before; a friendly voice, full of optimism.

'Hey, call me back when you get this, would you?' he said. 'I'm at the house.'

A notification came through on his phone: a second attack. On the metro at Maelbeek Station, one stop from the EU. Public transport was shut down.

Memories of that night in Paris, the not knowing if this was the last of it or just the latest in a multi-pronged attack. So much easier to destroy than to build.

He tried Marcy again and got a busy signal, which filled him with hope. If only he knew when she'd left the airport, he could put his mind at ease. He considered asking Jake but quickly realised that would be a terrible idea. Joanna would know, of course, but he didn't have her phone number. Maybe Sasha or Alec had it, he thought, only to remember phones were banned at school.

8.47 a.m.

Why hadn't Marcy called? She must know how worried he'd be, she who knew him better than anyone.

He phoned her again. Once more it bounced to voice-mail. He listened to the message, just to hear her voice.

'Hello, you've come through to Marcy. I can't come to the phone right now but if you leave me a brief message, I'll get back to you as soon as I'm able.'

Those final words 'As soon as I'm able' were imbued with new meaning.

8.54 a.m.

The phone pinged with a text from Alec to say he was fine. In maths class. It was a group message to him and Marcy but the check mark next to her picture remained white, signifying she hadn't read it.

And then Sasha phoned.

'Have you talked to Mom?' she asked. Her voice, high and tight with emotion, alarmed him.

'Aren't you in class?' he asked.

'As if that matters right now. They *told* us to call our parents. Mom isn't answering.'

A stone dropped inside Neil's stomach. He could under-stand Marcy not feeling obliged to contact him, but he knew nothing would keep her from contacting the kids.

'Stay calm,' he said. 'I'm sure she'll be in touch soon.'

'I've tried like a hundred times. It goes to voicemail.' Sasha's voice trembled with panic. 'I'm scared, Dad. Like *really* scared.'

'Darling,' Neil said, hoping he sounded unperturbed and

in control. 'In situations like these, things can seem really confused for a while and then it all shakes out. We just have to be patient.'

'But Dad, what if . . .'

'I have Jake here with me,' he said with exaggerated jolliness. 'We're building a zoo out of Lego. Jake, do you want to say hi to Sasha?'

'When can we talk to Mom?' Jake asked.

'She'll be in touch soon, old chap. I'm sure,' he told him. 'Sasha, I will text you the moment I hear anything. I promise.'

That's when it dawned on him. Were he to die unexpectedly, the children's lives wouldn't change. Oh, they'd be sad for a little while, sure, but otherwise they'd carry on as before. But if Marcy were to die, it would leave a gaping hole, a chasm. The children would look to him to fill it and would find him utterly lacking. How presumptuous to think he could have handled full custody of them. Even with Sasha and Alec nearly grown, he had no idea how to be a single dad. He didn't have the skills. He had coasted along, parenting whenever it was convenient for him, doing only the parts of the job he liked best. And the children knew it. That's why they never let their guards down with him the way they would with Marcy. They trusted her to love them unconditionally, to always be there.

9.05 a.m.

His father phoned next.

'Any news from Marcy?' he asked.

'None yet.'

'You'll let your mother and I know when you hear anything, won't you? No matter what.'

'Of course. I'm sure it's all a little chaotic wherever she . . .'

'It will all turn out all right. She's a great gal,' his father said. 'Plucky.' The word caught in his father's throat.

'Plucky, indeed,' Neil said. His lungs were closing in. He couldn't breathe.

He phoned her again, picturing it ringing in a cavern full of dust and rubble and dismembered body parts, part of a cacophony of mobile phones, each one with a loved one on the other end of the line, desperately waiting for someone to answer.

This was all his fault. Marcy would not have gone to the airport this morning if not for him. Joanna would not have come if he hadn't told Marcy he was suing for custody. He had thought he was perfectly rational and prudent, doing what needed to be done to protect the children, but it was all projection, wanting to have someone else to blame for having destroyed the family. He ought to have offered to take Joanna to the airport this morning. Insisted on taking her. Instead he had groused about having to drop off Jake at school, giving the impression it was a great inconvenience and that Marcy owed him for it.

When in fact, he owed her. She would be at the top of her field right now if she hadn't always sacrificed her career for the sake of the family and his career. She never agreed to this arrangement. Neil had simply assumed his job was the one that mattered, that she would follow him, fold her life into his, even as he offered lip service to their equality.

She was the one with the talent, the one with the gift. He was a process guy, good at making sure that things got from A to B or even A to Z. He was adept at anticipating potential hiccups and roadblocks and making contingency plans. He implemented safeguards. It wasn't dramatic, wasn't sexy. It was practical. Necessary, yes, but also mundane: a fucking bean counter.

Marcy deserved a chance to shine, to go to New York, if that's what she wanted. He'd kept her away from her country long enough. Sure, she got back most summers, but it wasn't the same. She never complained. Though, now that he thought about it, every trip, she'd have a little cry, just burst into tears without warning. It always happened a couple days before they were due to leave, usually after they'd had a lovely day. Like clockwork, it was. He'd ask her what was wrong and her answer was always the same: 'I don't know.'

'Excuse me, old chap,' he said. 'I've got to spend a penny. I'll be right back.'

He needed to get a grip. He would make himself crazy otherwise. There were lots of reasons why Marcy wasn't answering her phone. The battery could be dead – she was famous for forgetting to charge it. Maybe she was concentrating so much on helping others she hadn't heard it ringing in her handbag. Or she could have lost it in the confusion of the moment, as happened to the daughter of the woman in the restaurant in Paris the night of the attacks. Or maybe she was indeed injured, lightly, or even knocked unconscious.

9.17 a.m.

News trickled in. One of the airport explosions was near the American Airlines check-in desk. There were reports of injuries, some dead.

He phoned Sasha to ask: 'Was Nana flying American Airlines?'

'I think so,' she said. 'Why?'

'Never mind.'

'Maybe not,' she said. 'Maybe it was Delta.'

Sasha started to cry. 'I can't remember, Dad. I can't remember.'

'It's okay,' Neil said, making a soft shushing sound. 'It's okay.'

He wondered if it was too soon to start calling hospitals, a thought he immediately banished. It could not be. Not Marcy, with her bottomless capacity to empathise, who always tried to find the best in everybody; Marcy, who deserved her chance to shine in her career, to see her children grow, to know her future grandchildren, and they to know her. The universe could not be that cruel.

The pressure building up behind his eyes was terrible. His throat ached with emotion. He mustn't break. For Jake's sake, and also because he had no right to cry for Marcy, no right to mourn her. He had forfeited that right, foolishly thrown away the privilege. He had forgotten how extraordinary she was. She didn't need material wealth to feel good about herself; didn't needed anyone else's validation. Her self-worth came from within.

No, he thought, wrong tense. Marcy *is* extraordinary. She *doesn't* need material wealth; *doesn't* need anyone's validation. She was alive. She was fine. Everything was going to be fine.

10.06 a.m.

Marcy's name flashed up on the screen. He grabbed the phone and then hesitated, afraid of answering and hearing a stranger's voice on the other end of the line, asking who

321

he was and what his relation was to the person who owned the phone. His heart was in his mouth. He got up and ran out into the hall to answer.

'Hello?' he said.

'Neil?' said the voice that meant home to him. 'Is Jake with you?'

'Yes. I've got him. We're at the house. Marcy!' he was crying and smiling. 'Thank God! I've been so worried. Where are you? What happened?'

'I had a two-hour session with Fabrice in that broom closet. Early start. I guess no one realised we were here.'

It didn't feel like a moment to hide inside. Sasha and Alec said people were gathering on Boulevard Anspach, in front of the Bourse. Neil and Marcy walked down with Jake to meet them. Marcy took a bag of votive candles. They stopped for flowers along the way. When the kids saw them, Sasha grabbed hold of her mother's hand and did not let go. Neil understood the impulse. He wanted nothing more than to take Marcy's other hand, but he was afraid of spoiling the moment.

Every race and colour was represented in the crowd at the Bourse. Some had brought flags from their home country to include in the makeshift memorial: Brazil, Spain, Portugal, France. The mood was solemn and dignified. People talked in whispers. A gentle breeze blowing through the square carried a promise of spring. Alec joined a group drawing in chalk on the pavement, shading and contouring, to create a three-dimensional effect, while his friend Farrah wrote *Nous aimons Bruxelles* in lovely script. Neil watched them work together, heads bent in conversation. At one point she said something and Alec looked up at her, face beaming.

From somewhere in the crowd, the song 'Give Peace a Chance' was struck up, softly and shyly. Marcy joined in, belting out the words unselfconsciously, despite her voice being only so-so. Neil chanced a tentative glance in Sasha's direction. To his surprise, his daughter was not attempting to slink away in embarrassment, but holding fast to her mother's hand, mouth open in song. As the number of singers swelled, the wobbles and defects in individual voices were smoothed over. The sound became rounder and fuller. It gave Neil chills and as the final chorus came round, he lent his own voice to the effort.

A group arrived with a banner, crudely made out of sheets stapled to sticks, and the words spray-painted in black: *Je suis Bruxelles*, and beneath it, in Flemish: *Ik ben Brussel*. The snap and whizz of shutters clicking and cameras flashing, taking the photos that would be on the front page of newspapers around the world.

'I was brought up to believe in American exceptionalism,' Marcy said, 'that we had a special mission to transform the world.'

'You mean like you did in Vietnam?' he joked.

'I'm thinking more like the War of Independence.'

'We let you go,' he said. 'You were too much trouble.'

'And being the first to get the bomb.'

'And use it, I might add.'

'Land a man on the moon.'

'Perhaps.'

She smiled. 'You Brits think you're pretty great, too.'

'Rule Britannia.'

'Belgians have no illusions of grandeur. I mean, look at them: they've been invaded and annexed by—'

'Everyone,' he said.

'They only exist because bigger, more powerful countries decided they should.'

'They're home to NATO and the EU,' he said 'I'd say that's not too bad.'

'They got NATO because France kicked the Americans out, and the EU because their country came first in the alphabet.'

'Missed your chance, Albania.'

'Yet here they are, doing their best to muddle though.'

'As are we all,' he said.

'As are we all,' she repeated. 'I feel almost Belgian.'

'Me too,' he said, wanting to take her hand more than ever. 'Maybe I'll apply for citizenship.'

'But you're already an EU citizen.'

'Only until Brexit,' he said.

'Well then, maybe I'll do it, too,' she said, smiling. 'For when Trump wins.'

They both laughed.

'This is home,' she announced. 'We should probably make it official.'

'Look,' Jake pointed across the square. 'It's Nizar!' He ran through the crowd, shouting, 'Nizar! Nizar!'

Nizar turned and smiled when he saw Jake barrelling towards him; Sasha and Marcy hurrying behind.

'Jake, my friend,' Nizar said, giving Jake's hair a ruffle.

There was a man with him, standing close.

'Where have you been, Nizar?' Jake asked.

'I live with Tahrir now, Jake.'

So that was Tahrir, Neil thought. The one who's name meant virtuous.

'Why haven't you come to see us?' Jake asked.

'I . . . I have been quite busy,' he said. 'But I will try to see you soon.'

'You'll have to come to the new apartment,' Marcy said. 'How about a week from Saturday? I'll make the lamb you liked last time, the one with aubergines.'

'I'll have to check,' Nizar said.

Marcy looked at Tahrir. 'You are both welcome.'

Nizar cast a cautious glance at Tahrir, who shrugged. Nizar's smile broadened. 'Okay, Marcy,' he said. 'That would be very nice.'

'Is Tahrir your boyfriend?' Jake asked. Sasha tried to clap a hand over her brother's mouth, but the words had already escaped.

'Anyway,' Marcy said. 'We'll look forward to seeing you both. Sasha can text you the details.'

'I need your new number,' Sasha said, phone out, at the ready.

'Well, I guess he's not a terrorist after all,' Neil said, after contact details were exchanged and Nizar and Tahrir walked off. 'Did you know?'

'I never thought about it, to be honest,' Marcy said. 'But I'm not surprised. Such a gentle soul. Can you imagine carrying that on top of everything else?'

'It would be a burden, given his situation.'

'You can come, too,' she said. 'To dinner, I mean.'

'Lamb with aubergines?' he said. 'Wouldn't miss it for the world.'

He reached for her hand. To his great relief, she let him take it.

Acknowledgements

I am immensely grateful to my agent, Caroline Wood at Felicity Bryan, who never sugar-coats things and yet still somehow manages to convey unshakable faith in me, and to my editor, Becky Walsh, whose default setting is: amazing. To Luke Brown, Charlotte Hutchinson, Emma Petfield and everyone at John Murray, thank you for your professional excellence.

I'm blessed to have the fellowship of other writers, namely Ann Pelletier, my first and most constant reader, and Mina Bancheva, who provided an essential ingredient to this book's completion: regular, manageable deadlines.

And always, thanks to Flemming, who makes all things in life hum, and to Sam, Ellio, Mitchell and Austen. Sometimes the last shall be first.

Finally, thanks to my father-in-law, Thyge Thygesen, for the gift of Bird's Day.